Also by Shirley Ann Grau

The Black Prince and Other Stories (1955)

The Hard Blue Sky (1958)

The House on Coliseum Street (1961)

The Keepers of the House (1964)

THE CONDOR PASSES

THE
CONDOR
PASSES

SHIRLEY ANN
GRAU

Alfred A. Knopf, NEW YORK

1 9  7 1

STANLEY

M E ? W H A T am I? Nothing. The legs on which dinner comes to the table, the arms by which cocktails enter the living room, the hands that drive cars. I am the eyes that see nothing, the ears that don't hear.

I'm invisible too. They look and don't see me. When they move, I have to guess their direction and get myself out the way. If they were to walk into me—all six feet of black skin and white bone—they'd never again be able to pretend that I wasn't there. And I'd be looking for another job.

I'd just as soon not do that. Because there isn't another job like this one. Not in my part of the country anyway. Right now I make more than any white man in Gulf Springs. That's the town where I was born and raised, as they say, though I don't remember my mother doing very much about us. Most times she didn't even seem to notice when we were around; sometimes I used to wonder how we got fed when we were babies. Maybe her mother's instinct was stronger then—must have been or I wouldn't be here. But anyhow, this job. And the money. Especially the money. Like I said, four thousand people in town and I make more than any of them. Except maybe the doctor but he's got to collect his bills, and that's not always the easiest thing. My money just comes to me, first of every month. Three hundred dollars a week, plus extras. How's that for a nigger's salary? For that I'll stay invisible and jump out their way.

Anyway, I'd sure hate to get out now and go to work. Real work. Hardest thing I do here is drive to New Orleans, two hundred miles. And of course every day I have to drive to Port Bella, the closest little town, an hour away, or to Collinsville, where the airport is. These people are restless, always going and coming, and I'm always driving them back and forth. But soon as they finish the landing strip on the north corner of their place, their planes will come there and I won't be doing half so much driving. It's that sort of job, if you see what I mean.

Matter of fact, Mr. Robert (he's the one hired me, standing on a street corner) looked at me the other day, chewing on his tongue, the way he does when he's thinking: "Stanley, I bet you could learn to fly a plane; you got good eyes, every damn fool is flying a plane. How do you feel about it?"

Seems I felt fine about it. So now I get two afternoons off a week for flying lessons with some clown at the Collinsville field; Mr. Robert found him. When I qualify, Mr. Robert'll get me a plane. "A small plane, like a Comanche." And I go right on nodding at him. So I'm off to the air. I can learn, I'm good at things like that. This family collects planes. Mr. Robert has two, including an Aero Commander he just got last week; Miss Margaret has her own and a pilot too, she doesn't like to fly. And the reason that strip back in the woods is so big is to accommodate the Old Man's jet; what do you call it, Jetstar or some such thing? I'd like to get my hands on that, but I won't and I know it. They got two white pilots for that.

Anyhow it looks like I'm going to do something the army wouldn't let me do when they drafted me out of high school; no black pilots in those days, boy. I'm going to get my wild blue yonder when I'm forty-four.

That's one of the things keeps me on the job. Among others. Like—I wonder if I could get Mr. Robert to let me use his helicopter. When he first got it, three years ago, he'd land just below the rose garden, on the edge of the golf course. He'd come and go four, five times a week like that. Until his wife said that the wind was destroying roses and azaleas she'd spent years cultivating. I went with him a couple of times and I liked it, felt just like an elevator. I bet he'll let me use it when I qualify. By that time he'll be bored with it; he doesn't seem to use it so much any more. He keeps it over at the airport in Collinsville to amuse his girl friends, I guess. Like Mrs. Lorimer. He used to land on the beach in front of her house. I don't know what he did about the tides. He had to figure them out someway.

I'm really looking forward to that, wonder how long it'll take. Me, the black birdman.

You see what I mean about this job. Unusual, you could call it.

It was plain luck I got here, but it's plain sense that keeps me here. Luck made Mr. Robert walk up to me when I'm standing on the corner in Collinsville watching Joe's Taxi pick up a fare from the New Orleans train. "You want a job?" he says. And luck made me say, "Yes, sir," instead of all the other things I was thinking. Like: "Man, I just got out the army with enough to live on for a couple of months and I got a nice little wife and I don't figure to work yet." But "Yes, sir," I said, just like I was still in the army. And here I am today.

It has, you might say, been worth my while.

They hired my wife, Vera, almost fifteen years ago. Assistant housekeeper it says on her tax forms. Whatever the hell that is. She comes every morning at nine and straightens out the linen closets, gives the sachets a shake to be sure they're putting out enough scent. Then she stops and talks to the Old Man's nurse; for the past five years that's been Miss Hollisher. After that Vera walks around the house looking at the walls and the woodwork, seeing if they need touching up; if they do, she calls the painter. Then she walks around the outside of the house and does the same thing, searching for paint that is chipping, boards that need replacing. The Old Man's house is always in perfect shape, not a speck of rust, not a crack, not a dent, not a heel mark on the polished floor. The Old Man is dying beautifully. At least that's what Vera says. After she's finished checking the house, she goes on home; she's always there by one o'clock. They pay her ninety a week for that.

Vera never worked before; it was Miss Margaret's idea. I didn't think she'd do it, and I said so; but Miss Margaret insisted: "Let me call her up," and she came back from the phone all grinning and smug. Vera never did repeat what she said, but these people, they could talk you into anything, when they wanted you. And they would give you anything. They bought us two houses, one in New Orleans (for when the family happened to be there) and one in Collinsville where we really live. Christmas presents, both of them. But you see, they wanted us, Vera and me. And what they want, they'll pay for.

Too bad I don't have a kid, they could hire him too. We could make it a complete family thing.

I say I'm going to leave sometimes. Twenty years on any job is long enough. But I don't go.

I can still remember how impressed I was at first; for months I just stared as I worked in their houses, the one in New Orleans and the one here in Port Bella. Could it be me, a little old colored boy from Gulf Springs, Mississippi, walking around in all this glory?

And then there's the Old Man, Mr. Oliver. He's about ninety-five, had his first heart attack nearly thirty years ago, I hear. He was in pretty good shape when I first came, then he had a stroke and he's been more or less paralyzed ever since. But don't let that fool you, there's nothing wrong inside his head. He made all this money himself, starting from nothing. Sometimes I think I can see it, like the house was built of stacks of dollar bills, or the gravel paths were made of gold pebbles. Sometimes I think I can catch a gleam or a shimmer, like when an edge sticks out. . . . But that don't matter. . . . The Old Man made it all, and he's still making it. Even when he's so weak and tired I have to hold the phone for him, he's thinking and planning and pulling in money like a magnet. A thin, dried-up man, sitting day after day in his special chair in his special greenhouse—he breathes better in the warm wet air—watching his special birds in their gigantic cage.

So there we are. I think they're crazy and they don't think about me at all.

THE SECRET THIEF

EVERY MORNING it was Stanley's job to open the greenhouse. To march formally along the corridor that led from the west corner of the entrance hall, and throw open the double doors that led into the greenhouse itself. Once inside, he was supposed to forget his formal dignity while he scurried through the welter of pots and trees, with the cool tips of climbing orchids and the furry tips of chain trees brushing his neck. Straight to the bird cage. Check the birds . . . remove any dead ones quickly. Before the Old Man comes. Next check the live birds—more quickly now, with the Old Man approaching. If any living bird looked sick or weak, Stanley was supposed to grab it at once, snapping the neck in his fingers and stuffing the carcass out of sight. The Old Man must never never in the course of a day see a bird die or flop about injured or unhealthy.

Sometimes Stanley thought that they had arranged it this way just to make his job difficult. Why, for example, didn't they let him open the greenhouse doors a little earlier? Then there wouldn't be any last-minute problem disposing of the dead birds. . . .

But it wasn't that way at all. Everything in the house had a fixed and ordered pattern. Unchangeable.

Stanley glared at the bird cage. It was a huge flattened watermelon-shaped affair made of reeds and straw, reaching from the high ceiling to the flagstone floor. It was an adaptation of a primitive Brazilian fish trap, Miss Margaret said.

Maybe it caught fish, Stanley thought, but it sure was hell on birds. They'd died by twos and threes, every day since it had been installed six years ago. That made hundreds of birds in my hands, Stanley thought.

Only instead of taking the cage down, Miss Margaret kept restocking it. A new batch of birds arrived regularly every Wednesday afternoon. If the Old Man noticed any difference in numbers according to the day of the week, he never said anything.

Finally, even Miss Margaret was convinced. She found a specialist from the state university who knew about things like that. A short bald man with thick glasses who emptied the cage, gave it a spray with some kind of powder, and put in all new birds. Of a more resistant species, he said.

Resistant to what, Stanley wondered. Except maybe the Old Man. . . .

He looked on the floor of the cage. Nothing dead. He studied the birds fluttering on their perches. Some were actually singing—he hadn't heard anything like that for quite a while. And even the silent ones looked all right. Great day, Stanley thought. He was so tired picking up those stiff bony bodies. Sometimes he didn't even have time to toss the small things out the side door; he'd have to slip them into his pocket. And once, one bad day when four or five of them had died, he'd had to tuck one up under his sleeve. A smelly swollen one at that. They swole up quick in the damp heat of the greenhouse, much quicker than outside.

This morning there was nothing, absolutely nothing.

Stanley straightened up and stood properly, hands behind back, while the Old Man came in. He was dressed for the outdoors this morning—white flannels and navy blazer, the ascot around his skinny neck tied with absolute precision. Elizabeth, the upstairs maid, was pushing him, as she did every morning.

Stanley avoided her eyes, those yellow eyes, always staring at him. He didn't intend to get mixed up with that broad. Not her. He wasn't young any more, and with a wife of his own at home . . . he just wasn't up to things like that.

Elizabeth wheeled the Old Man to his accustomed place in the very center of the greenhouse, a wall-less room completely surrounded by ceiling-high greenery, completely hidden from everything except the low whine of the ventilating fan and the nervous trickle of an occasional sprinkler.

The Old Man held up his hand, and nodded, head trembling on his thin neck. "Thank you, Elizabeth."

As she left, she deliberately and slowly crossed Stanley's vision. He kept his face straight—he'd had lots of practice—as he stood waiting in a version of what they would have called parade rest in the army. Almost, but not quite.

The Old Man sat in his wheelchair, not moving, not saying anything. Just breathing.

Which was quite an effort for him, Stanley thought. Quite an effort.

He whistled and rattled, the phlegm in the back of his throat fluttered, the sinews on the side of his thin neck, like small snarled cords, moved slightly, tightening and then loosening. His eyes were closed, those old bright eyes, hooded like a bird's—quick as a bird's too, flashing open to catch you watching.

Stanley did not look at the Old Man. He began wiggling his toes inside his black shoes to amuse himself. And thinking about Elizabeth. She had a cute ass, round and high. . . .

The Old Man gargled the steamy air through his lungs, the wet air, thick as a cloth, greasy as oil with all the flower and leaf scents on it.

Stanley no longer sweated profusely in the damp heat. Once, when the greenhouses were first built, he'd got so drenched with sweat that he'd walk around the kitchen with his coat off and his arms waving in the air like a clipped chicken. He would even stand directly in front of an air-conditioning vent, letting the cold dry air run over him until he had a fit of shivers and had to step away.

The greenhouse heat had bothered him once, and so had its heavy sweet flower smells, its dripping perfumes and musks. Reminded him of funerals. But he'd gotten used to it.

The Old Man was snoring loudly now, his square bony chin resting on the carefully knotted tie.

Soft rubber-soled steps and a faint starchy rustle—Miss Hollisher, the day nurse, had arrived; her round white cap nodded to Stanley over a low green distance. He nodded back, politely smiling. She disappeared, her reddish-blond hair fading against some reddish-blond orchids. She would wait in the hallway, reading the morning paper.

Stanley went back to wiggling his toes. Big toe, second toe, third toe, fourth, fifth. Now, big toe alone, others flat and quiet. Now the little toe alone. . . . No, no luck. Still couldn't do it.

Abruptly the Old Man woke up. His thin head lifted, his chin left the scarf which now had a small wet saliva spot on its smooth silk surface. His hand reached out.

Stanley opened the cigar box, selected a cigar, the Old Man watching. He cut, slowly so the Old Man could see, tucked it between the Old Man's thin blue-tinged lips, and lit it.

At eight-fifteen, the Old Man's limousine pulled up to the side door. Stanley heard nothing in the insulated silence of the greenhouse, but he knew that the tires had come to a smooth silent stop on the gravel under the porte-cochère— in this house everything worked on schedule.

At eight-twenty Miss Margaret swung open the door and clattered across the flagstones. "Papa, you feel like going to Port Bella? You still feel like it?"

The Old Man accepted her kiss, without seeming to notice it. "I was waiting."

She laughed. "I know, I'm five minutes late. I was changing, Papa. I put on some weight and those pants looked like hell." With a small motion of the head she started Stanley pushing the wheelchair toward the door, keeping up a running chatter. "I am absolutely going to have to go on a diet."

Stanley put the Old Man into the limousine gently, like a great bag of eggs. When he straightened up again, Miss Margaret was standing beside him. "It's nice here early in the morning." She glanced back through the wide-open door into the polished interior and then across the lawn to the neighboring houses, discreetly hidden by trees. "It's nice before the damn staff arrives and starts rattling around." She rubbed her finger automatically across the top of the car, testing for dust. There was none. The Old Man kept two shifts of chauffeurs waiting for him, and since he rarely went out any more, they polished and repolished the cars between their crap games.

The garage was hidden from view—nothing to spoil the proportions of the main house—behind a forest of blooming magnolias. You called for a car if you wanted one.

Complicated, Stanley thought: to get things the way they wanted, they made life so complicated. But they had to have it their way. . . .

"Stanley," Miss Margaret asked abruptly, "do you know what's going on at the garage? Is Michael running a nigger hotel down there?"

Why does she do that, Stanley thought; trying to see if she can annoy me? She can't. "No ma'am."

"Okay, okay, let's get going." They walked around the car, Stanley the proper two steps behind. "How does he look to you?" Miss Margaret asked. "His color isn't good."

"No trouble breathing." You had to admit, Stanley thought, the Old Man's grip on life was tight as an old crab's on bait. Nobody had thought he'd live through his last crisis. But here he was.

Stanley closed the door, and stood attentively while the black limousine moved away slowly.

He'd drive the second car, with the baggage and Miss Hollisher and her pet cat, to the airport. Miss Hollisher waited primly in the back, her pink hair shining faintly in the long slant of morning sun.

Even the motor was running. That was damned efficient of Michael. Stanley chuckled briefly: he *did* have a nigger hotel down there in the garage, all his friends and relatives came to stay with him.

As Stanley slipped into the driver's seat, he caught sight of Elizabeth. That cute round little body covered by a black uniform and a tiny starched apron—should have made her look discreet and only made her look more sexy. "I like her," the Old Man said once, "good-looking girl." And didn't the Old Man screw her with his eyes, Stanley thought, didn't he just. . . .

The Old Man traveled easily and well, napping between puffs of his cigar, until the wheels touched down gently on the Collinsville runway.

Mr. Robert's helicopter was in the hangar here, all ready to go, but the Old Man would have nothing to do with it. He wanted to go by boat. So by boat it was.

Miss Margaret disliked all boats so she went on by car, leaving the Old Man, Stanley, and Miss Hollisher at the Yacht Club. Mr. Robert was waiting; he put the Old Man aboard himself, in his special chair in a sheltered spot. The blowers were already on. Their steady dull hum floated across the little water sounds, the lapping sounds on hull and piling. On all sides boats were neatly moored along a concrete walk, long lines of parallel hulls, like pups to a nursing bitch. Nothing moved. The fishermen had gone out earlier, the pleasure sailors had not yet come. The harbor was crowded and lonely at once.

The Old Man looked about, feeling the day for the first time. He turned his head slowly and carefully as if he were afraid it might fall off, the way a seed pod leaves the stem. He stared across the silent harbor, his old eyes not even squinting in the glare. His neck relaxed and settled more squarely on his shoulders. He didn't say anything, but he nodded—barely.

The blowers stopped, the engines started. Mr. Robert climbed to the flying bridge, pulling sunglasses from his pocket as he went.

Stanley released the mooring lines; the fifty-odd feet of black hull eased out into the harbor, swung about, and headed for the passage between the stone jetties, and the open bay beyond.

The bow slipped smoothly through the still water, screws turning very gently, scarcely leaving a wake behind. Boats in their slips barely lifted and fell as they passed. The sun was beginning to penetrate the high band of heat haze to the east, and it swam in the sky, round and yolk-colored.

WITHIN TEN minutes the Old Man was dozing again.

Settled in her deck chair, Miss Hollisher whispered to Stanley: "Trip is too much for him these days."

Stanley whispered back: "But it sure is nice for us."

They left the marshy upper bay, the saw grass and the alligator reed; under the hull they felt the lift of the open Gulf. The land ended so gradually, Stanley thought, that you couldn't at any one time say: This is the boundary.

Stanley mocked himself silently: Why do I have to be so sure all the time? Like looking at a map and saying: I am right here and right now. I got no business worrying about where I am.

The Old Man dozed, hand on each side of his chair, old bony yellow hands, like birds' claws, dangling, silent and curled.

Birds, Stanley thought. Everything came out birds. . . . Take the name of the boat, now—the *Condor*. It was everywhere you looked. In gold across the wide stern, framed by heavy glistening scrolls. On the life rings by the cabin door. On the china, on the glasses, on the silverware. Even the sheets and the towels. Big black bird, flying.

Stanley yawned. And thought about Vera. She'd be rattling around their house, straightening the towels on the bathroom racks—she was very particular about towels.

Miss Hollisher said: "I hope Percy makes the trip all right."

"He will."

"He was my mother's cat."

"You told me," Stanley said patiently.

"He is such good company, Stanley. You just can't imagine."

Stanley said: "Yes, I can."

"In a way he was more company than my mother, in her last years. She was a good bit like . . ." She nodded toward the Old Man.

He'd heard all about her mother's last illness, how she'd nursed her to the end. *When she died,* Miss Hollisher always ended her story saying, *her skin was just perfect, I'd taken such good care of it.* And Stanley would wonder what the condition of a dead woman's skin had to do with anything at all. It seemed to mean something special to Miss Hollisher. At least she always talked about it, so he supposed it must. . . . Like the damn cat.

Miss Hollisher was saying: "But maybe you don't miss company the way I do."

"I got company," Stanley said.

H I S   W I F E Vera, now, she was company. From the time he stepped in the door until he left in the morning, there'd be a steady stream of talk, flowing over him like a shower. They'd been married twenty-five years and he'd long ago stopped listening. He'd known her all his life—she'd lived next door in Gulf Springs. Matter of fact, her mother still lived in that house with her brother and his wife and their six grown children. Stanley's sister, husband dead in Vietnam, lived in the other house.

Nothing seemed to change in Gulf Springs. People died and their children took their place, and it really wasn't any different.

Stanley wondered why he didn't go back more often. After all, where he lived in Collinsville wasn't more than a two-hour drive. But he didn't, and Vera never urged him to. He just didn't quite feel right there any more. He didn't quite belong back where he'd started, with his family and their children.

Maybe it was his having no children that made the difference.

Maybe a man needed children. Maybe it was his fault. He'd never found out. Now he was too old to raise a child. And Vera was too old to have one.

Maybe that was why he felt so lonely at times. Maybe that was why he was so glad to get back to Vera. Her chatter was warming, like a fire. And even more: it was what she brought to him. Somehow, someway, she remembered everything, and she could make him remember.

Like the time they were playing hookey from school, fooling around back on the old shell road that went to the Spanish fort, where you could hardly find the road for the palmettos that overgrew it, and the still unmoving air smelled musky with snakes. They'd gotten off the road somehow, and one of them—Charlie Edwards, it was—got into quicksand.

By the time they found a plank to reach him, he was down to his waist in the stuff; pulling out, he'd lost his pants and torn his shirt. When his mama found out why he'd come home half naked, stripped like a willow that's been peeled, she was too frightened to give him the beating he deserved.

That was the kind of thing they remembered. Him and Vera together. And that was fine. They wouldn't ever be alone the way the Old Man was. With just a lot of images in his mind and nobody really knowing what they were about. . . .

The Old Man. So light that the wind could lift him. Bones thin as leaves, dried as the skeletons of lizards or the shells of crabs.

Only the wind didn't blow him away. And sometimes you found him looking at you with hooded eyes that were bright and black and laughing.

Stanley squinted against the sun's glare. And wondered about Vera. Would she be thinking about him? No. She'd have found something to do. She could always wash the windows or wax the floors. She wouldn't be likely to miss him.

At least not the way he missed her. Last night, for example. He stayed in New Orleans, while she drove back to Collinsville. Without her, he hadn't slept at all, just dozed and tossed.

He was sure she hadn't done that. He could just see her settling herself in that bed, pulling the cover up just so, the same exact way every night, just to her collarbone, never any higher, never any lower. And asleep in minutes. He'd joked with her about that sometimes, the way she lay down and dropped right off. "I'm tired," she would say. "And it's *time* to go to sleep."

No, she wouldn't miss him. There was something about her, something that was so busy. And happy. She was her own group. Her own company.

Herself a crowd, he thought.

She was never lonely. Not the way he was.

He had his spells. The minute he woke up, he knew one was coming. He would lie perfectly still, eyes closed, pretending to go back to sleep: Need another forty winks, boy. Need a little more. . . . pretty soon, something, like a hand from outside, lifted his eyelids. Even though he tried rolling his eyes up under his brows, to hide a little longer, he'd pretty soon find himself looking out. And the room would be filled with that particular light, not from the window. Even with a yellow sun shining outside, his room was silver-colored, moon-colored. Fish-colored. Just exactly the color of the underbelly of a fish when you pulled it out of the water. Luminous and silvery and changing every minute you looked at it, quivering and pulsing.

Stanley thought sometimes that he was the fish. That he'd been caught—he hadn't seen the hook, but then the fish never did either; only all of a sudden he was spinning through the air—and he'd been yanked up into the funny-colored light.

He could feel it too. Right in the center of his stomach. A pressure and an ache, and he would wonder what he'd eaten the night before. He always went back in his mind, looking, even when he knew that wasn't the cause.

He'd lie there with the light seeping in behind his eyes, running around his head like quicksilver. His stomach like a bag of nails. He'd find he couldn't sit up, so he'd call Vera to come pull on his arms.

He'd find he had trouble swinging his legs to the floor. Vera would move them for him. Bang, on the floor. All the time she'd be fussing at him: If I wasn't here, what would you do? Can't get out of bed by yourself.

He did know one thing. Those mornings—if she hadn't been there—he wouldn't have gotten up at all. He'd have stayed right in bed and waited until that feeling went away.

Blues, his mother called it. Blues. She'd had them too, he

remembered. Sometimes when they came home after school, they'd find her in bed, staring at the ceiling or out the window, and her big brown eyes would slide over them as if she'd never seen them before. They got their own supper; they knew she wasn't going to move.

There was nobody to get her up. She didn't have anybody like Vera.

Vera. She was a good wife, Stanley thought. They were happy. Except maybe for the children. He missed children now and then. Especially when he lay in bed, in that fish-colored light, when he could hear old man Death laughing right behind him, saying clear as anything: When I get you, I get everything; you got nothing to cheat me with.

Well, that was true, Stanley thought. There was nothing of him to stand off time, to give old Death a pause. No child, no grandchild. Nothing like that.

Stanley wondered sometimes if Vera missed them. He didn't ask; he didn't ask Vera anything.

Those terrible mornings, she fussed steadily as she pulled and pushed at his limp body, insisting, always insisting. Until he finally stood up, leaning on the steady sound of her words as if they were a crutch.

Vera asked: "Where does it hurt?"

He had to say: "I don't know." Because there wasn't any one place. It was his skin, all of it, all the black wrapping around himself. It was his bones breaking, one by one. Even his blood. He could feel it run thick and heavy like mercury around his bones and around his muscles. Sometimes it seemed to him that his blood was about to cry out and stop. When that happened, he knew, he would die.

All the time Vera was insisting, "If you can't say where it hurts, I just got to think it don't hurt anywhere."

In a way, Stanley supposed, she understood. She might grumble and complain, but she never left him. She kept him walking up and down, first in the bedroom, and then on the back porch. He closed his eyes against the knife points of daylight, relying on her to lead him up and down, back and forth, blind man, dead man. When he felt slightly better, he'd open one eye, just a bit. Then she'd steer him back into the kitchen and set him to drinking coffee.

The silvery light faded, like a fire going out. He got dressed and went to work, only a little late. Never more than two hours. But that night he'd fall straight asleep without supper. He'd notice Vera moving around, tucking covers, fixing sheets. He'd wonder if she wasn't staying up all night to watch him. In the morning, sure enough, there'd be circles under her eyes, and little lines down her cheeks.

One day he'd ask her. He'd come right out and ask her. Wasn't it funny that after all the years they'd been married, and all the even longer years they'd known each other, he still couldn't say for sure?

He'd ask her. . . . But he knew he wouldn't.

THERE WAS the boat again. And the thump of engines. And the Old Man staring at him.

Stanley jumped up, stumbling in his hurry. The Old Man laughed. Cackled. "Stop the engines," he said. "Dinner."

"Yes sir." Stanley climbed to the flying bridge. "Mr. Robert, he's asking for his dinner now."

Mr. Robert pushed in the red-topped throttles; the boat lost way, settled back on the water like a floating cork. "If he wants dinner," Mr. Robert said, "dinner is what he'll get."

Stanley stood aside while he swung down the ladder, moving easily for a heavy man.

"I hear you got hungry, Pa." He sent Miss Hollisher away with a mock fluttering of his hairy hands. "Stanley, get us a couple Martinis, will you? Pa, you picked a great day for your trip."

As Stanley got the drinks, he could hear the Old Man begin to talk, creakily at first, like a door that hadn't been used for a long time. Then easier and easier, as he left the thick drunken sleep of old age. His frozen look was gone too. He'd come alive, this old man with his fringe of white hair transparent in the sunshine. For a little while.

Mr. Robert could do that, Stanley admitted. Mr. Robert could always get a flash out of the eyes or a smile out of the false-teeth-filled lips.

STANLEY FIXED a second Martini for Mr. Robert and then went into the galley where Miss Hollisher was getting the Old Man's lunch. A line of baby-food jars. She took two spoonfuls from each one, carefully. "There." The blobs stood in a little neat circle on the white china: two brown, one white, one bright orange, one green. They all had a shiny polished look, as if they were coated with shellac. In the center of the plate the black flying condor touched them with his glazed wings.

"Now," Miss Hollisher said, "when he calls, I'll take out the crackers."

Baby food and crackers, Stanley thought. When a man went, he went all at once.

Not me, Stanley thought. Maybe I can just die.

Whenever he talked like that to Vera, she'd say: "Lots of ways of getting out of this world, and none of them very pleasant, baby. You got to take one or the other, and it don't leave much to choose."

Funny how she always said the same thing. That wasn't like Vera. She usually had a dozen different ways of telling a story. Not this. She said this like a piece she'd learned in school.

The boat was bobbing lightly on a little swell. Stanley began to feel queasy. "I'm going up."

"Maybe you better." Miss Hollisher looked smug. She never got seasick.

His mouth got very wet, and he spun around and headed for the forward cabin. His mouth got saltier as he felt the shape of the hull close around him. Ribs like bone going up on all sides, closing over his head. And the roll . . .

He stumbled up the forward companionway to the deck, his canvas shoes making urgent sounds on the teak. Only when he was perched out on the pulpit, beyond the bow, supported by a steel cradle, water beneath him, did he feel better. He spat the nasty moisture from his mouth; he felt the breeze clean the sweat beads from his forehead. He closed his eyes and let the wind dry his lids too.

He sat on the railing, facing back toward the boat itself. The big square windows of the bridge and the empty flying bridge looked down at him.

And then Stanley's mind made one of its jumps, the kind that annoyed him so much. He found himself thinking about rowing. It was the only skill he had with boats, his quick easy rowing, and he'd learned that in the army. Well, not exactly the army. He'd been going with a girl who was crazy about rowing on park lagoons, and for her he pulled miles of water past his oars. Stanley couldn't remember her face any more, not at all. He remembered other things; like, she was a great lay. He still had his notebook, his score card. Names and phone numbers and a few little symbols after each one, their ratings, starting with a single star. If he didn't make out on the first date, he didn't go back. Those names were lined out. He rarely went back to the single stars; he preferred the fours and fives, he had a few of those listed. In those days Stanley had no time to waste. Not a single minute.

Now he was happy to sit on a boat without even a good-looking woman in sight. Just blue Gulf water, ruffled and

crinkled by very light waves, stretching off to a hairline horizon. That thin green line westward, that would be the marsh:
alligator grass and saw grass and cattail grass for maybe a
quarter of a mile before the pines and the hickories and the
solid sandy ground.

Marsh like that was a living thing: it crept out here,
receded there; those little tiny v's of the chart makers didn't
mean a thing. One day a channel would be almost closed,
silted up, six feet on the chart but no water under the keel.
The next day, or the next strong east wind, it would be clear
and wide.

Sometimes—in spite of Mr. Robert's experience—the
Condor went aground, so that it took all the force of the engines in reverse to pull them off. Times like that, you could
hear Mr. Robert cursing over the roar. He was a big man,
way over two hundred pounds, with a big voice, and he could
curse in Cajun and English.

F U N N Y   T H I N G   now, Stanley thought, a man that big
and that noisy—you should be able to remember him. He
should have made such a mark that you could look inside
your head and find him standing there. But . . . try as he
might, Stanley just couldn't bring Mr. Robert's face into his
memory. General outlines, sure. Some gestures: the way he
waved his arms; the way he walked, so quickly that he almost
lurched across the floor. That peculiar walk was the reason he
knocked over so many things. Stanley was always repairing
some piece of china, some ornament. Like those vases in the
front hall. That was during Miss Margaret's yellow phase.
Everything was done in yellow, the wallpaper in the hall and
on the staircase, the dining room, all the downstairs rugs.
And of course the flowers. "Forsythia," Miss Margaret said,

"now I want mountains of forsythia." She got it. Including the big vase in the downstairs hall. The first time, Mr. Robert came swinging in the front door, yelling hello to the Old Man, pulling his raincoat from his shoulders, spinning it into the branches. As he kicked at the puddle of water and glass on the slate floor, he said, almost quietly, *"Fi de poutain."*

The next arrangement, Stanley remembered, was tall and narrow. For two or three days it glistened in a Chinese porcelain jar on the low chest in the far corner of the hall, out of the way. Nobody ever really knew how that got broken. There was just a crash and then Mr. Robert shouting: "No more fucking flowers. I'm sick of the god damn water in my shoes."

The Old Man burst out laughing—and began to cough, so that he doubled up in the wheelchair, his chin touching his knees. The coughs themselves sounded like air rushing out a tire, Stanley thought. Not human at all, as if the Old Man had gone into a kind of mechanical life, of wheels and air pressure and creaky screws.

The Old Man coughed too long and stopped breathing. Stanley slipped an arm under his chest, lifted him from the chair; they both knelt on the floor, the Old Man dangling like vestments across an altar boy's arm. Mr. Robert ran in from the hall, leaving a trail of dirty wet footprints on the rug. The two men knelt, faces close together over the slack, whistling body of the Old Man.

It's my face I'm looking into, Stanley thought. My own face I'm seeing there. I can feel the tickle of sweat and the twitch of neck muscles. And the sick weight in the pit of my stomach—I bet he's feeling that too.

Just like me, Stanley thought, how funny, just like me.

Mr. Robert gave two hard slaps on the Old Man's back; immediately his lungs began taking in air instead of tumbling it out.

The nurse had the oxygen ready, with a squeak of valves

and hiss of gas. They stretched the Old Man on the floor, his lungs filled and emptied easily, his pulse steadied. He fell asleep. The nurse took away the mask.

"Let him there," Mr. Robert said. "It won't be the first time he slept on a floor. And it could have been the last."

He saw Stanley staring at him, and he turned abruptly and walked away.

STANLEY SHIFTED his seat on the boat's railing. Way up in the blue sky, a small puffy cloud crumbled and streaked in a kind of smile.

Laughing at me, Stanley thought. Aren't you?

He was surprised when the cloud didn't answer.

THEY WERE close to shore now, behind a chain of low sandy islands. The sweetness of titi flowers was so heavy you'd swear you could see it, streaks of it, like smoke. In these narrow passes, there were tide rips, too; the *Condor* bobbed and stamped and Mr. Robert opened the throttles to pass them. Huge smooth ribbons of wake, like roller coaster waves, rose behind the stern.

"Damn tricky tide, always tricky," the Old Man said.

He said something else, his voice lost in the roar of the engines. He lifted his good arm and pointed to the shore. Stanley and Miss Hollisher looked, but all they saw was a clump of wind-burned oaks on a tiny *chênière*. And gulls rising from the sand, circling and screaming, big white gulls and their brown young.

The Old Man's chin quivered for a minute, his eyes closed, with only a few twitches behind their wrinkled lids. They came through the passes. The water was deep and quiet, the bow settled down. They were almost home now, the Old Man's country retreat, fashioned with his money and his daughter's planning to be beautiful and remote and secure —a long green strip, reaching north as far as you could see, twenty-odd miles. A bird sanctuary, a game refuge, carefully guarded against any guns but Mr. Robert's and his friends'. Lovely gardens, measured in acres, never photographed, protected from every eye, even on a printed page. Huge gray house, protected by a fire sprinkler system and a staff of caretakers.

All for the Old Man. And his family.

"There must be a haze," Miss Hollisher said. "You can't see the house yet."

As often as they had come this way, Stanley thought, she had never learned that when Mr. Robert passed the islands, he put his bow on a straight compass course for the house.

Stanley said: "It's under the bow."

Miss Hollisher nodded. "You did tell me that last time. How'd you learn so much about boats, Stanley?"

"I just keep my eyes open," Stanley said, "and pick up things."

Like a big hawk, me. Grabbing up bits and pieces of things. And what am I stealing? Pieces of their lives. Bits of their minds. . . . Me, the secret thief, that steals what people don't miss. . . .

Stanley looked again, just to be sure. The house itself, soaring byzantine towers at each corner, was not yet visible. All he could see from this angle was the glistening white gazebo on the bluff; and on the beach beyond it, where the morning mist had burned away, the big gray rock that had been split by lightning. It happened during a September storm five or six years ago, a quick hard blow that tossed porch furniture into the lawns and twisted shutters off walls. Stanley was outside, in the rain, securing a flapping shutter, when the explosion staggered him. Flattened against the house, he spun around, found nothing. But the air was different. It was clear and light and extraordinarily clean and completely impersonal: ozone. He noticed too: absolute silence. It was days before he could hear again.

All that was permanently left was the big rock split down the middle, tossed neatly into two parts.

Abruptly Mr. Robert changed course, swung his rudder hard over, opened the throttles. The *Condor* jumped in the water, dancing uncertainly for a second before it got under way, bow high, stern down.

Caught unaware, Stanley fell across a chair, scraping his shins.

Miss Hollisher said: "Are you all right, Stanley? Stanley, did you hurt yourself?"

"Yeah," Stanley said, and then, "no." He watched little drops of blood seep down to his socks. "Look, I get a Purple Heart."

They were ninety degrees off course now; the house appeared directly on their beam. They were traveling at top speed, straight north. Stanley squinted ahead. The bay was blue-gray and empty, except for eight or ten small sails, red and white and blue and yellow. Kids from Port Bella at the head of the bay, where vacation cottages clustered back in the trees, out of sight except for their piers. They often sailed this way—to picnic at Smugglers' Cove. Though it was his land, the Old Man never objected; he even kept the big spring cleared out for them; its cold metallic water flowed down to the beach. Only, his caretakers snooped through the trees watchfully, making sure no one went farther than the beach. Some years past, when the Old Man was stronger, he'd enjoyed spending Sunday afternoon anchored off the cove, while he smoked his cigar and drank his whiskey.

"Looks like we're going to Smugglers' Cove," Stanley said. He got a pair of glasses and focused them on the boats. There were eight: three Sailfish; a small and ancient sloop, gaff-rigged; a catboat; two Snipes; and a small catamaran. The catamaran had a single boy aboard. The red-and-white Sailfish held two boys, about fifteen. The blue had two girls, and Stanley recognized them: the Foster twins. The sloop had an older boy, twenty or so, and a girl in a green bathing suit. Two more girls with flapping wet hair followed in the Snipe. The last Sailfish had one girl aboard. She had turned her face to the sun and was fluffing out her hair. She was fully dressed in a white blouse and blue shorts. And her face— Stanley studied it again—was round and pale, and black hair floated out on each side, like seaweed blown in the wind. It was a lovely face, an unusual face. A face worth going out of your way to see.

Which was exactly what they were doing.

As they neared the boats, Mr. Robert idled the engines; they bobbed there, swinging ever so slightly to the wind and tide. The small boats streamed by them, in a raggedy, irregular line, the catamaran leading. Mr. Robert passed them by with a wave to each, as he hunched over his wheel, alone on the bridge. The Old Man slept, Miss Hollisher began her knitting, Stanley watched. The girl in the Sailfish was almost the last to pass them, followed only by the catboat, its sail luffing furiously. Within ten minutes the leading catamaran had entered Smugglers' Cove and dropped its sail, the sloop close behind. Just then, one of the usual sudden gusts of summer wind came tumbling down the pine slopes and out across the water. The sailors saw it coming, saw it ruffle the surface like a million billion fingers as it raced toward them. All except the dark-haired girl. She was dangling one hand in the water, playing with the shiny lights, when the puff reached her boat. Her careless lines fouled, and slowly, before she could clear them, the Sailfish went over.

The screws turned, the *Condor* began moving. Mr. Robert yelled from the bridge, "Capsized. We'll take her aboard."

Stanley stood staring at him, thinking: A Sailfish? She'll have it up in half a minute.

By the time the *Condor* reached her, the girl *had* almost righted the boat. She looked up with astonishment, shaking her head.

"Stanley"—Mr. Robert scrambled down the ladder— "take the wheel."

Stanley couldn't quite hear what Mr. Robert said, but after a moment he laughed: "No trouble at all." He leaned over, took the girl's wrists: "Ready now," and with one heave and crisscrossing of hands lifted her to the boat.

It had been, Stanley thought critically, only a fair display of strength and dexterity. Mr. Robert could do better if he had to. He could, for example, lift a dinghy from the deck, singlehanded, and drop it into the water. He could also lift the back end of a car. Stanley had seen him do both—for women. This girl, now, she seemed impressed—she was sitting quietly, looking slightly bewildered, her slim young body hunched under the wet veil of clothes, its delicate line of spine crossed by belt and bra.

She'd be, Stanley thought, about seventeen or so. Tall. Her round pale face had bright sunburned streaks across the cheekbones. Her eyes were deep-set and dark.

Mr. Robert said: "I know your uncle. Haven't seen him in a while, but that's the way things happen."

Be seeing him now, Stanley thought, and smiled down at the coil of rope in his hand.

"I knew you weren't used to these waters or you would have known the way the wind comes down."

"I've never been here before." She had a pleasant voice, light and gentle and not too high. "But you really didn't need to pick me up, I'd have gotten the boat up with no trouble."

"You'd get chilled with those wet clothes. Next time you'd better wear a bathing suit."

Chilled in June, Stanley thought; *that was a good one.*

She had a slighter figure than Mr. Robert usually liked. Through the wet clothes you could see clearly, as she stood dripping on the deck, feet braced against the gentle roll of the boat. Narrow hips, small breasts set wide and high. A neck so thin you could see its tendons. Shoulder blades like small wings in back.

A child's body, Stanley decided. But not a child's face. Not at all. Her eyes had a very strange expression. It was— what was it now?

The Old Man woke suddenly, his eyes flew open. "Where'd the girl come from?"

"Out of the sea, Pa," Mr. Robert said. "Like Venus or somebody—who was it?—riding in a sea shell."

"It was Botticelli's Venus," the girl said primly.

Mr. Robert chuckled. "I forgot all that. You forget a lot of things, the years wear them right off you."

He had acquired a faint Southern accent. More than Southern. It was decidedly Negro. Stanley listened appreciatively. He only did that when he was coming on real strong after some woman. . . .

"I'll tell you one thing," Mr. Robert said. "Venus's sea shell was more stable than your Sailfish."

The Old Man dozed off again.

The girl asked: "Is he sick?"

"Age, that's all." Mr. Robert regarded her with paternal interest.

"Oh," the girl said, "oh, I'm sorry."

Mr. Robert patted her shoulder solemnly. "You're too young to think of such things."

Stanley met Mr. Robert's eyes across the small expanse of deck.

He knows what I'm thinking. And I know what he's thinking. He's thinking how he's going to get inside her pants. And he's pleased to have me as the audience for one of his best performances.

"Give me eight hours with a woman," Mr. Robert told Stanley once, "and I can have her. And it will be her idea, not mine."...

"Would you like some coffee," Mr. Robert was saying. "Stanley, we have some hot coffee, don't we?"

He didn't offer her a drink, Stanley noticed admiringly. Too direct. Might frighten her off.

"I'm fine," the girl said. "Really, I'll just catch up with those people," she pointed toward Smugglers' Cove.

"I'll run you over there, if you like. Or you can come have lunch with us at the house."

He stressed the last word, just slightly. The House. The fabulous house that no one sees—do you want to come?

"Well, really, I couldn't. I've heard so much, and I wish I could, but ..."

Mr. Robert carefully kept his eyes from her wet clinging shirt. "Whatever you like, my dear."

She hesitated just a moment, not because she was uncertain, but because she didn't want to seem impolite.

Well, Stanley thought; well, well, well, he's lost this one. She's leaving.

The Old Man opened his eyes and straightened his head. "Stay," he said. "It would be a pleasure to have a pretty young girl on this boat." The thin old face broke into the gentlest possible smile, so faint it was almost not there. "Sit down by me, my dear."

She did. His hand reached out, hung over her small young one. Very carefully, he did not touch her. Just let the fragile weight of age hang over her, so that she felt it, ever so gently. Let the contact between the two skins (so different, how different) flow through the air, the purifying air.

"I may fall asleep," the Old Man said, "but that doesn't mean I don't admire a pretty girl."

"Thank you," she said, and settled herself more firmly in the chair. "Thank you very much."

The Old Man smiled again. He seemed very ancient, very Chinese.

"I would like some coffee," the girl said.

As he fixed the cups, Stanley thought: Trust the Old Man to think of something. That girl was ready to leave before he popped awake. He'd come through when Mr. Robert needed him. He'd given Mr. Robert his eight hours, his opportunity.

And Stanley noticed . . . when the Old Man woke, he'd known exactly what they were talking about. . . .

Stanley poured the coffee into the white mugs that had a black bird on their sides.

I been thinking that I was the big black hawk spying on people's lives. But now it looks like there was a skinny sparrow right up under my nose, watching everything, watching me. Who's fooling who? The Old Man. It's always the Old Man.

Stanley served the coffee. "Thank you," she said.

Stanley recognized her expression now: the look of the virgin. Who knows all about it, but still doesn't know. The direct-shy look. Delicate, half eager, half afraid. Half wanting, half not . . .

And that, Stanley admitted, was attractive. It made her half the daughter he'd never had. Half the woman he'd never met, the elusive perfect woman.

Mr. Robert put on his sunglasses. "My father has gone back to sleep," he said. "When you finish that coffee, if you're not too cold, would you like to come up to the flying bridge with me? You can see better from there."

The girl swallowed her coffee and climbed the ladder to the bridge. Mr. Robert followed, staring very closely at the backs of her ankles. They were, Stanley noticed, very nice ankles, small and thin and delicate.

The Old Man was watching too. His eyes were wide open again, though he hadn't bothered to lift his head from his shoulder. His bright black eyes followed the two up the ladder, to the bridge.

Deliberately Stanley stepped into the Old Man's vision. The eyes blinked once, slowly. A light flickered in their depths.

He looked, Stanley thought, like he was laughing.

THE OLD MAN

THE OLD Man lay on his bed, covers tucked beneath his arms, linen pillow smooth behind his head. The top button of his pajamas rose and fell gently, slightly, with his breathing.

He heard the door open, he heard the creak of the chair as Miss Hollisher took up her position. He heard the rustle of cloth as she picked up her sewing. After a while there'd be the whispers of the night nurse as she crept into the room.

He could hear all these things, though he wasn't awake.

It was like being in a room with shades drawn, listening to sounds in the street. You couldn't see but you had a pretty good idea of what was passing.

Once he'd tried to talk, to cry out, to say anything, so that they would know he was still there. He hadn't even been able to move his little finger. Not so much as that.

He'd fallen into two pieces, slipping apart; mind and body, once together, separating more and more frequently.

When the parts came together, people said he was conscious and alert. They didn't know about the separation. They didn't know that the greatest alertness came during the blind time they called sleep.

Deliberately now he quieted his mind which had lately been occupied by a small nesting animal, mouse or rabbit, a shivering furry thing. He stroked its back, rubbed gently over its ears. Until it stopped racing through the empty shell of his body, hunting for a window not yet closed. Patiently, patiently caressing. Gently, gently, until it curled and snuggled in its place. There, there we are.

As for this business of having two separate pieces, well, he'd noticed that the halves came together less and less frequently. And when they didn't meet at all . . .

Then he would be dead. He knew what that meant. Endless years of lying still in a coffin. . . . And what was he doing now but that? What was he doing now but rehearsing for that time? . . .

And when the body fell apart at last—whenever that was, however long that took—then the animal inside him would find endless doors opening on echoing corridors, wind-swept walks, ultimate distances. It would be timid at first, like all animals raised in a cage. It had been sheltered by his body so long, it wouldn't go far or stay long. At first. But soon it would venture farther and farther, and return less and less frequently. And then it wouldn't come at all any more. It wouldn't come back to the dust and the bones; it would be gone running around the world, living in grasses and under hedges, cowering in the roots of trees, frightened by birds and hawks and other animals, hiding and running, free, sunlight and dark.

That was the way it would be, the Old Man thought.

HIS NAME was Thomas Henry Oliver, but nobody called him that. His mother called him Oliver, and everybody else called him the Old Man. They'd done that ever since he was thirty. He supposed it was because he'd gotten bald then, almost completely bald, just a small fringe of hair around his ears.

He was born in 1870, in Edwardsville, Ohio, and it was there he'd made his deal with God. It came of being afraid during the long nights in the tiny house with his mother. (He was her only child, his father dead the year he was born.) She always fell asleep immediately after putting out the lamp, while the smell of kerosene hung in the still air. He was left alone in a black empty world, with only the rustle of rats across the floor boards inside and the chuckle of wind and the sounds of owls and roving animals outside. Moonless nights, things walked abroad; long-legged beasties, his mother called them. "They're not something you can tell about," she said. "No words for them, no way to describe their image or shape. They're like all the things you've never seen, the inside of graves, or the center of the earth, or the dark side of the moon. If you see them, you'll know; and if you got straight hair, it will turn kinky, and if you got curly hair, it will go straight as a poker; if you got a nigger's skin, it will turn white."

He himself closed the shutters every night—making a

special check to see that the bolts were drawn securely—and his mother dropped the bar across the front door. He still sweated with fright, even in winter when water in the kitchen bucket froze solid and all night long you could hear the groan and pop of ice on the Ohio River half a mile away. Until he found the stone.

That happened in the middle of summer, on a Wednesday when his mother called for him to take her pies into town. He always delivered pies to her customers on Wednesday and bread on Saturday. This one time he hid behind the springhouse until he was sure she'd gone, then he sauntered off across the pasture, no special place to go, just moving, feeling the warmth of sun through his shirt, imagining himself a general on a white stallion, or an engineer with the rails whizzing by. He climbed the rail fence into Mr. Winslow's wood lot. He saw a squirrel and wished he'd brought his slingshot—that was supper chattering at him. He scrambled down into a dry creek bed to hunt for pools left from the spring freshening.

The pools were long gone, but on the crackled mud bottom he found the stone. Smooth and white, flat on one side, exactly the size of his foot. He tried it over and over again to be sure. A perfect fit. He laid it on the ground, stood on it, then hopped off. His stone print stayed there, frozen by the folds of the earth, memorial to his passing. He crouched down beside it, studied it carefully. Overhead blue jays screeched and squabbled and their feathers drifted through the leaves. A rabbit sat on the top of the bank and stared at him, nose twitching. After a while Oliver took out his pocketknife and cut into the tip of his thumb. He squeezed until the blood flowed freely, and then, using his thumb as a brush, he outlined the shape of his toes on the white stone. He waited while the blood turned brown and dry, and then he carried the stone up to the top of the bank—the rabbit raced away at his approach—and buried it there. He had no shovel;

he dug with his knife, with a tree limb, with his hands. When it was deep enough, he put in his white stone, stepped on it one more time to make sure, then covered it. In the loose soil, he made a small cross with his sore thumb.

When he was done, he looked at the shadowy wood lot, at the sunny smooth fields beyond, at the scattered farm-houses, fence-fringed, and he felt secure.

That night, while rats rustled across the floor and stray dogs howled in the distance, Oliver slept peacefully. He had made an arrangement.

He was no longer afraid of anything, not even the spirits of drowned men in the river. He discovered that one day as he walked home after work. (He peeled willows for old Mr. Anderson at the store and got a nickel a day for doing it. Mr. Anderson's Irish hired girl made baskets and things and sold them in Louisville.) The Ohio was past its flood, but it was still fairly high. He stopped to watch, hoping to see a log shot into the air by a hidden whirlpool. If you were patient, you were sure to see it—the heavy water-soaked log flying like an arrow. While he waited, he noticed a skiff pulling into the shallows among the sawyers and garbage. He recog-nized the two men: Charlie Healey and Tim McVay. Healey was poling; McVay hauled a line attached to a tangle of drift-wood. The brown branches broke away and a body turned slowly and lazily in the warm spring sun, one arm swinging straight up. Healey grunted and cursed as he poled. McVay, who was also the Baptist preacher, whistled cheerfully.

Oliver's bare feet squished and slipped in the yellow Ohio slime. He had never dared come this close before: drowned men's ghosts walked the banks and glided across the water at the place they came ashore. He stood and stared, his head sticking out with concentration. He saw how the shirt had split across the back, and black flesh bulged in the cloudy sun.

Healey said, leaning on his pole: "Ain't you afraid of ghosties?"

Oliver stared into the thin sunburned face. Healey, he knew, lived with his wife on a houseboat at Crawley's landing. He did all sorts of odd jobs along the river.

"Come on, Charlie," McVay said from the stern. "Let's get it ashore."

"You know who it is?" Oliver asked.

"Nope," Healey said.

McVay said, taking another hitch on his line, "Fourth one this month, we are plain getting tired burying."

"Wasn't so bad last year." Charlie spat yellow tobacco juice into the water.

"Christian thing to do, bury 'em," McVay said to the boy. "You understand that? Most times we never seen them before. They come from up beyond."

"As far as Pittsburgh?" Oliver asked.

"Maybe. Up a way, for sure, beyond where we know people."

They pulled the skiff ashore. The body slid through the shallows, turning and twisting and making a little sucking sound over the mud bottom.

McVay said: "You sure are brave, most kids been long gone by now."

"Take off," Healey said. "You too god damn curious."

"But I want to see," Oliver said, "and it's only a nigger."

"It ain't no nigger," Charlie said. "That's the way their skins look. Now get the hell out of here."

Oliver didn't move until Charlie Healey took a couple of steps toward him. Then he fled back into the willows. Charlie yelled after him: "You hang around and I'll come get you! We'll see how brave you are."

Oliver hid in the yellow-green shade and thought about that. Then he turned around and trotted over the riverbank and down the road home. He had coal to carry, and kindling to split, and the cow to bring to his mother for milking. "Ma," he said, "they just pulled a nigger out the river and they're going to bury him."

She shook her head. "Not a nigger. Now get along."

Years later he realized that if it had been a Negro, Mc-Vay and Healey would simply have towed the body out into the middle of the river, where the current ran fastest, and released it to travel farther downstream. They didn't bother burying Negroes at all.

O L I V E R S A W Charlie Healey again, months later, in November. He had delivered some of his mother's pies to Anderson's store, and he was warming by the stove, nibbling the parched crackers and corn kept in a pan on top, when Healey staggered in, blood caked and oozing from a cut on the back of his head. (Oliver immediately disappeared behind the molasses kegs.)

"Skillet did that." Healey was laughing, but his lips were bluish white and William Anderson immediately began edging him toward the door. "Bitch caught me when I wasn't looking." Healey touched the back of his head, looked at his blood-smeared fingers, smelled them carefully. "Knocked her in the river," he said and drifted out the store, forgetting what had brought him there. William Anderson stood in the doorway for a while, his breath rising straight up in the cold air, scratching under his chin where his beard always itched. "Dead drunk and mean," he said softly to Oliver. "Kill you as soon as not in that mood, boy." He walked to the back of the store and talked quietly to his son William, a big strapping sixteen-year-old. Young William put on his coat and his cap and his heavy boots, and went out, walking in his slow steady way, like his father, shoulders hunched a little against the cold.

"You going to see if he killed his old lady this time?" Oliver trotted along behind the broad muffled shape, not really expecting an answer. His feet thudded hard on the frozen ground, his ears began stinging with cold, his nose dripped down his lip and into his mouth.

The houseboat was in its usual place at the landing. There was a thin curl of smoke from the chimney, a skinny bone-like plume against the gray sky and the bare gray-brown willows. Inside, Oliver and William Anderson hesitated, surprised by the warm eye-twitching air. The odor of whiskey hung faintly in the room, mixing with the sour smell of the Ohio. Mrs. Healey sat in a kitchen chair, almost behind the stove.

William Anderson said: "My pa wondered how you were doing."

The woman was dripping wet—he had indeed knocked her in the river. Water had run all the way across the cabin, forming puddles on the uneven floor.

"That river must be mighty cold," William Anderson said politely. Mud from his heavy boots filtered into the big pool by the door, spreading yellow stain across the boards.

She was shaking all over, holding her jaw.

"You ought maybe to put on some dry clothes," William Anderson said. When she still didn't answer, he asked: "He bust your jaw?"

She kept both hands clamped to the left side of her face as she turned and looked at them—the hulking Anderson and the younger boy crouched behind him. She blinked, three, four times, focusing. "You come to see?" her voice was husky. "Bastard musta gone to town."

"Pa wanted to see if you was all right."

A tiny trickle of blood twisted from the corner of her mouth. "I shoulda killed him that first time, when I had a chance. Fish wouldn't even touch him, and he'd had to float down to New Orleans."

The boys backed out, bumping into each other, closing the door carefully behind them. The sun was almost gone and the air was colder than usual.

"I sure wouldn't like to go in that river," Oliver said.

William Anderson began his steady even walk. "Leastways he didn't break her jaw."

The boy was so surprised at being answered that he tripped over his own feet and almost fell. "You sure?"

"She's talking too good. Didn't you hear her?"

I am learning, Oliver thought, about the way things are. I am learning.

At THIRTEEN he decided he'd learned enough. He was over six feet tall, very broad and muscular. He still went to school—his mother insisted—and he was beginning to feel restless and bored with the smooth fields, with the farm animals and the endless cycle of chores, with the constant talk of the river. The river was high, the river was low, the river was near flood. People even counted time by the river: old Mr. Anderson died at low water.

Oliver knew he had to leave Edwardsville, especially after that business with Jesse Harper. For no particular reason Oliver and three other boys waited for Jesse Harper one day after school, hidden behind a little rise in Mason's apple orchard. They'd collected a small pile of stones there. When Jesse Harper walked past, as they knew he would, they waited until his back was toward them, and then they began throwing—slowly at first for accuracy, faster when he screamed. He ran and stumbled and rolled and crawled down the road away from them. They didn't follow because there were men working in the fields just the other side of the orchard. Anyway, their stones were almost gone.

After Jesse Harper disappeared around the turn of the road, and only his whimpering drifted back on the late-afternoon air, the four boys walked up and down the road, looking at the blood spots in the dust. Oliver, luckiest of all, found a tooth, dust-covered but recognizable. The boys offered to trade him a knife for it, but he refused. "I'm going to put it on my watch chain."

(And he did. He carried it in his pocket until, one day in Manila, he had it attached to a watch chain. He wore it for years, losing it finally somewhere in the German Solomon Islands. He was mate on an old sailing schooner, trading a little but mostly dealing in contract labor for the big copra plantations. And they'd had trouble. Natives, looking for heads, managed to slip on board one night. After the fight— the Portuguese trader was killed—when they were safely at sea again, Oliver realized that his watch was still in his pocket but his watch chain was gone. And what did a Solomon Islander make of an Ohio tooth set in gold? He probably hung it outside by his line of skulls. . . .)

When Oliver stood in the dusty Ohio road and listened to the fading screams, he felt a chill run through his body, all the way to the tips of his fingers. He almost stained his pants right then and there. The desire was so urgent that he barely had time to slip into the shadow of the orchard and relieve himself there. His whole stomach was burning and his hands were almost without control.

H E L E F T within the week. His mother did not argue. "Take care of yourself," she said.

"I'll send you some money, Ma." He felt bad for an instant. She'd so very much wanted him to take up farming. "Then you can hire somebody to work the place."

"You won't have extra money soon. It isn't that easy."

"I will," he said firmly. "I promise I will."

He got a job on the only showboat that passed this stretch of river, and left it at Louisville. He stayed there for a year, working first as a pickpocket and then as a burglar. He was successful because he worked alone and because he had a red farm boy's face, with shining black eyes and full cheeks. For safety, he decided to move on. He bought a train ticket to Chicago, because he was curious about that city. But he did so well on that train—an inattentive conductor, a sleeping drunk, a homosexual who paid for favors in advance, a foolish old woman with a roll of bills in her purse—Oliver jumped off the train when it slowed for an uneven stretch of track, and never got to Chicago at all. He went back to Edwardsville, to surprise his mother.

"You look thin," she said. And: "How long will you be gone next time?"

"Longer." He looked her directly in the eye, daring her to ask where the money came from. She did not. "Whenever I can, I will send you more, Ma."

He was almost fifteen then. He took only enough money for his ticket, and left the rest with her. This time he went to Pittsburgh. Within a week he was living with a prostitute: his broad fresh face had attracted her, his ability in bed held her, his changing moods frightened her. He became her pimp; he added another girl, more to his taste, with red hair and a delicate figure; then still others. He managed them dispassionately, at times marking them with his fists, other times treating them like schoolgirls. He calculated his effects coolly. Sex itself meant little or nothing to him.

Only sometimes when he was methodically beating them, he found himself stirred. And then he would immediately stop, before he lost control.

He was seventeen when he reached the West Coast. He'd decided to go to sea; he liked the vastness and the emptiness. For the next ten years he crisscrossed the Pacific, north and south, in every kind of ship, leaking old-fashioned schooners and new cargo steamers. At first he worked his way as seaman or cook; later he traveled as a passenger. He even became very selective, preferring freighters of over twenty-five hundred tons. He liked comfort. He wasn't a young man looking for adventure; he was a businessman looking for opportunities. He dealt in everything that could be smuggled: quinine, opium, women, guns. He learned a smattering of Chinese— enough for his purposes. He acquired fluent Spanish and grew a mustache to look older. His face thinned out, but its high color remained. He had four or five different fevers; in the Malay Straits he even survived the blackwater. He grew more and more successful. He sent a quarter of his profits to his mother, he himself managed the rest from San Francisco. He gave her no advice—she needed none. She had bought two farms and was negotiating for a third. Her detailed letters amused him—she ran her affairs carefully and with great profit. He wondered what the people in Edwards-ville thought of that.

When he was twenty-seven, he met Sara Chapman in San Francisco. He had handled a particularly large shipment of guns, and been paid in gold. But he had gotten careless in Mexico and was almost killed. He returned to San Francisco with a large, painful, slow-healing wound in his left side and a violent simmering anger at his own stupidity.

One morning he went into a pharmacy—he had developed a cough—saw a young woman with a starched white blouse and high-piled dark hair. He snapped out his order. She simply turned her back and began rearranging the lines of bottles. "Haven't you got it?" She still did not answer, she did not appear to hear.

He stood for a moment chewing his lower lip, staring at the little scraggly curl that twisted down the back of her neck. "Your hair is coming down," he said, hardly above a whisper.

Her left hand checked, tucked the curl back in place. Silently.

He chuckled; pain from the wound in his side made him draw breath sharply. At that sound she spun around.

He smoothed down his mustache; the beads of sweat

that had formed under it were tickling him. "I am sorry, madam. I seem to have forgotten my manners."

"You're sick?"

He leaned against the smooth wood of the counter. "Hurt," he said, "not sick."

He had tea with her that day, in the small sitting room behind the drugstore. An ancient Chinese woman brought the cups. Sara Chapman said something softly to her, and the old woman went into the front of the store.

"You speak Chinese?"

"My parents were missionaries." Her husband, a druggist, had died two years before. She ran the shop in his place. "It's very nice, really," she said, "the only thing I don't like is handling the leeches."

Oliver returned the next day, and the next, month after month. His mother wrote, asking him to come to Edwardsville. "I am very busy with work here," he wrote in precise schoolboy script. "I trust you are well." He had almost forgotten what Edwardsville looked like.

He stayed on, hating the foggy cold winter after so many years in the tropics. He found a place to live close to Sara Chapman's store. He had offers; his contacts found him completely uninterested. The rooms behind the drugstore were very comfortable, the occasional customer was hardly enough to disturb their silence. Oliver always sat in the big plush chair, the yellow-and-white cat always sat on the window sill, the coal fire always burned in the grate. He learned to smoke, and he spent hour after hour staring from his cigar's white ash to the white ash on the coal in the grate. His bottle of whiskey stood on a small Chinese tray in the corner—she did not drink. Usually he brought food for dinner; occasionally he brought the old woman opium for her pipe. At Christmas he got Sara a piano. She played quite well, he thought. He liked the sound in the small snug room, mixed with the little hissing of the grate.

They were friends. That was all. He had kissed her once; her lips tasted vaguely of cinnamon. She pushed him gently away.

"Something wrong with me?"

Her face was absolutely serious. "It is very hard to be respectable. . . ."

The way she said the word, Oliver thought, made it the highest compliment.

"A young widow, I was only married two years, did you know? And people, well, assume things that aren't true."

"I don't think anything."

"I loved and respected my first husband; I will love and respect my second, if the Lord sends one to me."

Oliver left in a very few minutes, angry and resentful. He did not go back the next day, nor the one after that. When, a week later, he walked through the shop door, between the big glass containers filled with colored water, red and green, port and starboard, she smiled at him with warmth and friendliness, as if he had never been gone.

His wound healed. He moved without pain, and he felt fine. He heard of a good deal in Singapore, but he was in no hurry to go back to work. While he waited, he put a little money into a whaling ship, one of the last to work the Arctic. It was foolish, he thought; I won't even be here when they come back. Or will I?

One April day, while he idly watched the gulls wheel and flutter over the docks, he saw his thoughts as plain as if the words were printed in the sky: *You want to marry her. You are going to marry her.*

He turned and walked rapidly back up the street.

He hardly slept that night. Two thoughts hung before his eyes: *She would be a good wife. You want her.*

Very early the next morning, he packed his two big Gladstone bags and took the ferry across the bay. He did not stop to ask the schedule. He simply took the next train. He left no messages for Sara at all.

H E S E N T the last of his money to his mother, telling her to use it for the farms. He went to sea again, as a cook on a small German freighter that plowed up and down the eastern coast of South America: Buenos Aires, Pernambuco, Bahia, Rio, Santos, Montevideo, and dozens of small ports. For three years he smuggled and prospered, joylessly. He found himself longing for the west coast—Chile and Peru— the incredible mountains, and the people, squat and immobile as rocks. He could see their flat black hats and bright wool coats, he could smell the dazzle of the bright clear air, he could hear a particular wind sound, he could see the great black condors riding thermals over the high slopes.

God, he thought, what is wrong with me? Why have I started dreaming?

He was in Bahia then—dusty streets, naked children playing in garbage-filled gutters, dogs scratching their infected scaly bodies, fly maggots crusting everything. For years he'd been seeing these things, in one town or another. Once he'd rather enjoyed the dirt and garbage smells that lifted with the morning sun. He felt powerful and clean and unbearably healthy with his tall blondness among these short dark people. By being different, he felt more alive.

Not this time. He slapped a large green-backed beetle from his shirt sleeve, heard it whirr away on metallic wings. And he thought: I have had enough.

A week later, while they were caught on a sandbar off some river, after trying to make port at low tide, he studied the little town (unnamed; he did not care enough to ask). It was so careful, so neat: the square, the church, the houses of different colors rising up the slopes. So ordered. He found himself staring at the café directly opposite the church and he found himself wishing that he were sitting at a table there, talking about the price of sugar and of coffee. . . .

This is my last trip, he promised himself. Whichever port in the United States we come to first, that will be the place I live.

He was so happy with his decision that he was not even annoyed to find that his ship would return to Bahia. He liked their rum, made from local sugar cane. There was also a whore he'd find for one last time.

She was a big woman, big as he was, black skin, black hair, black eyes, thighs thick as tree trunks, wide hips, and motions so slow it was like swimming underwater. He noticed the rash on her arms and hands and under her breasts. "What's that?"

She pulled aside her sagging breast and looked. "Flea-bites. Don't be scared, sailor boy." Because he didn't remember any disease starting like that—not one he'd be likely to get anyway, and because the house was dirty and a dog slept in a corner of the room and thumped his leg on the bare floor with his scratching—Oliver forgot about it. He was too drunk to be particular.

They were two weeks out, heading for New Orleans, plodding across the open Gulf, sprinkling the water with flecks of rust from their crumbling plates, when one of the greasers, a middle-aged Englishman, simply passed out. The second officer, who doubled as ship's doctor, looked at him, and shouted for the messboy to drag him into an empty cabin. He locked the door himself and went off quickly to tell the captain, while the messboy whispered frantically: "Smallpox."

They left the Englishman in that cabin, to live or die by himself. No one passed that way, no one went in, except for the Brazilian messboy who had had the pox when he was a child and bore the marks all over his face to prove it. Even he wrapped three or four cloths around his head, not trusting the stories that you only got it once. He brought food and water once a day, peeped in for a second before slamming the door again and stuffing wadding tightly around the edges. He brought out news too: "The pox are all over him, he's torn his clothes off." Or "He's calling for more water." But most often the messboy would just shake his scarred head and say: "The smell; Mother of God, the smell."

Oliver remembered that the greaser had been to the same whorehouse on the same night in Bahia. And he remembered the woman and the fleabites under her black breasts. He cursed in every language he knew, throwing the words across the heat-shimmering Gulf. Then he went below and found a corner to himself where he stripped and searched his own body carefully for signs. He even used his little shaving mirror to scan his back inch by inch. Because his body was covered by thick hair, it took hours. And the very next day he was nagged by new fear, and he had to find another place to make the inspection all over again.

Less than a week away from New Orleans the carpenter caught it. He'd kept it secret for days, in spite of the fever and the itch, but eventually the pox spread out on his hands and up to his face. And the delirium drove him to wander on the cool open well deck. Oliver and the bosun and the trimmer saw him and fled, shouting alarm. The carpenter, a short squat Mexican with the long almond eyes of Yucatan, called after them, his voice strangled and muffled by the pox inside his throat. The first officer, who was on the bridge, yelled at him in German but the Mexican stayed where he was, next to the center cargo hatch, swaying a little on his feet. He saw invisible things, talked to people who weren't

there, and he bent now and then to pet an invisible dog at
his knee.

The captain took the bridge, hastily, his shirt flapping
open all across his chest. The second officer disappeared. The
messboy, his head partially wrapped, scurried across the deck
to talk to the Mexican. "Get on with it," the captain shouted.
The messboy pulled at his shoulder. The Mexican knocked
him aside with a backward sweep of his arm. Still holding
the rags to his face, the messboy skidded across the deck,
relieved to be out of the whole thing. The captain shouted
again: "I'm warning you!"

The Mexican gave the dog a pat while his wobbly head
swung around, searching. His shiny eyes found the captain,
fixed, held. He straightened up, pushing the dog away with
his knee. He began walking toward the bridge, slowly, deliberately. "Stop," the captain yelled. "Stop, you god damn
fool!" He didn't. No one had expected him to. "Stop," the
captain shouted again. And then with a lift of his arm, a rigid
overhead gesture: "Fire."

The shot came from the side, near the charthouse, out
of sight of the crew. The Mexican fell against the rail, his
body hardly moving when the two other shots hit him.

The messboy got up wearily, head still covered, and
pushed and tugged and finally tumbled the body overboard.

No one went back to quarters after that. The officers
did not try to make them except for the chief engineer and
his assistant who used guns to drive each watch to the engine
room. The weather was mild, the crew slept on deck, clinging
to the edges of the ship, hardly eating, each searching the
other for small red spots.

They anchored in the Mississippi, just inside the pass,
pestilence flag flying. How long? Oliver wondered. For a last
trip, this was certainly a beauty. He stared at the green marsh
a quarter-mile away, the green he wouldn't reach for weeks.
And he decided that he'd had enough waiting. To hell with

his cook's pay, let them keep it. He'd traded quite a bit this last trip: quinine, high quality and unadulterated (people who knew him were willing to pay his price); rhinoceros horn for wealthy old men; blessed relics straight from the Pope in Rome. He'd converted most of his profits into gold—he preferred that—and fitted the gold inside his special belt. He'd made it himself, an ordinary old leather belt. He also had a few coins sewed into his coat, but they were more for luck than anything else.

That night, he slipped over the side and took his chances in the dark swift-running river.

H E K N E W the Ohio River at Edwardsville, had swum in it since he was a boy. This wasn't like it at all. For one thing the Mississippi was warmer. He thought: It's like a bath. Who would have thought it would be this easy? And then he began to see that it wasn't. That he was going to have the swim of his life. Briefly he thought of yelling for the watch. *No,* he told himself, *swim, you god damn fool.*

The water felt strange—heavy and oily—and smelled strange—sweet and decaying.

He swam with his head high, to keep the water away from his face. Like fish nibbling, the river tugged at the belt strapped to his waist, at his clothes, at the shoes tied around his neck, at the machete on his thigh. He could see very little in the dark but he kept swimming slowly toward where he knew the land must be. Occasionally he glanced over his shoulder to check his position against the freighter's lights.

The currents were strange too. There seemed to be one on the surface and another one just underneath. Very confusing—without the ship's lights he would have lost all direction. He floated for an instant and let his body rise to the surface. If he swam high, there would be less pull—but that forced his face down into the water, and he wasn't quite ready for that.

The dark river slipped past his arms, across his shoulders. Like fingers running over him. He found himself keeping his legs firmly outstretched, not letting them relax downward. He was vaguely afraid of touching something beneath him, though the river here must be very deep.

He saw a floating branch, watched while it passed him. He hadn't thought the current was that swift. He took another bearing on the ship's lights, and methodically began swinging arm over arm again. The smell of the water changed abruptly. There must be pools of different things, he thought, each carried by a current. He was puzzling over this when he swam into the whirlpool. He acted instinctively, even before he knew what it was. He flung himself violently backward, out of the water, arching his back for distance, arms spinning like frantic paddle wheels. Something grabbed his feet. He yanked them up, fetus-like. He flipped to his stomach, put his face down in the water and swam, hard. He felt himself released; he took a few more strokes for safety. Then he paused, resting. His neck hurt from the pressure of his shoes and clothes. The money belt was still around his waist. The water changed again, became quiet, so that he moved through a surface smooth as a mirror.

It occurred to him that here was the end of the journey for all those unidentified Negroes the boatmen of Edwardsville towed out into the current. This was where the drowned came. . . .

WHEN HE reached the grass, he found it wasn't solid ground at all, but a kind of soft marsh, a shifting sinking slime. He would have to go farther upriver. He worked his way along, half swimming, half wading, keeping close to the shore, out of the current. He could hear little animals splash away from his coming. Must be muskrat, he thought.

He would be out of sight of his ship before daylight, he

was sure of that. But how far would he have to slosh like this? And how long could he keep it up?

A hell of a long time, he answered himself. One hell of a long time.

The sun came up, hazy and white, and he could see all the things he'd guessed at in the dark. There was a swift current flowing some thirty feet away from him, a streak of moving yellow, while inshore the water was perfectly quiet. He looked up and saw on the horizon a clump of oaks, a *chênière*. That would be high land, oaks couldn't grow in water. He decided to push directly through the marsh. He put on his jacket, but even so the saw grass cut and tore at his exposed hands. Curiously he did not feel the cuts—his skin was wrinkled and dried from hours in the water. He looked at the blood, oozing slowly in small red drops. He licked at it and tasted only river mud.

He stared straight up into the sky. The gray hazy distance seemed to recede, the sky seemed to be running from his eyes, running into a long narrow bright tunnel, infinite tunnel.

He began testing the marsh. He found a kind of grass— reminded him of duck grass on the Ohio—a yellow-brown tangled mass of roots and leaves that could support his weight for a while. If he moved quickly from shaking crust to shaking crust, he would not sink too deeply.

Like a game of hopscotch. Hop hop hop, miss and you're out. Rest on the matted yellow reeds. If you can't find them, keep jumping. And if you got too tired to jump, and if there were no more yellow reeds to give you a resting place, what then?

Don't stop, he told himself. Just keep working toward those oak trees. He couldn't actually see them from within the tall grasses; he would have to guess his direction.

A flash of white and he leaped away, suspecting a nameless danger. After two panic hops he remembered something

familiar in the color and turned back. It was a small solid
mound, white with sun-bleached shells, rising from the marsh.
He stamped flat the few grasses—in case of snakes—and sat
down. Even this early the shells were warm. He dropped his
arms between his legs and crouched over, resting. He'd seen
people crouched like this in Bahia, on street corners, only
they wore hats. He wished he had a hat, the sun was stinging
the back of his neck. There would be shade in the oaks when
he got there.

He rocked back and forth, arms swinging between his
bent knees, chin not quite touching his chest, head dangling
comfortably from its neck.

*Like an apple, like a god damn apple. Hanging from a
stem.*

He scrambled to his feet. From the slight elevation of the
shell mound he could see across the grasses to the *chênière,*
shimmering with heat haze a half mile away. He was sure of
his direction now. Time to move on.

The *chênière,* when he reached it, was much larger than
he expected. He climbed one of the wind-burned oaks to
look: the solid ground twisted away, like an alligator's back
in the marsh, for a quarter of a mile. There was little underbrush, only some fallen leaves and a few long-dead branches.

It wasn't too bad.

He found a tree for his back and wrapped his coat
around his head against mosquitoes. If they are this bad, he
thought, in broad daylight with a little wind blowing, what
will they be like by dusk? And by night? He would need a
smudge fire. He had not brought matches, had not thought
about them. That, he told himself, could mean his bones
bleaching here on these shells. . . . But he didn't really believe it. He was barely thirty, he could feel the strength in
the band of muscles across his shoulders and back, he could
feel the thrust and steadiness of his legs, he would think of
something.

A mosquito got inside his cover and sat on the tip of his nose, drinking the salt sweat there. He moved his fingers slowly and smashed it.

HE COULDN'T rest. Mosquitoes bit through his clothes, his whole body burned and itched. He would have to see about a smudge fire at once.

First he got his tinder, crumbling old leaves in his hand until they were powdery. There were ticks in them, he stared at the little reddish forms. How had they got here? Come out with a muskrat, maybe.

Now for a trick he'd heard of years ago on the Ohio. He had to find a drop of rain, a drop of dew. He looked: the outer leaves were dusty and dry; there hadn't been any rain.

He shrugged. There had to be one somewhere.

He found it, on a reed, deep down in the cleft. A spot the sun hadn't reached.

Maybe it's clear enough. Maybe. . . .

He carried it, carefully, gently. Keep it from breaking. If it runs off, your lens is gone. The old men said this worked for them. The old men, full of Indian tales. Remembering for themselves or remembering for their grandfathers. Stories of men left for dead coming back to kill their killers and sew their own scalps back on again.

Shaking old men. Sitting out in front of Anderson's grocery, sitting in the sun. Showing small boys the tricks of skinning. *Skin a squirrel before you can turn your hand— watch me, nothing to it when you know how to start. Dress a deer, not much work when you know; you only want to keep the best parts anyway. . . . Do it the Indian way. Learned it when I was living with that squaw. . . .* Stories from themselves or their fathers, stories that came from everywhere.

Oliver hoped they were right.

He put aside his drop of dew and began collecting the other necessary things while mosquitoes swarmed his ears and rubbed their wings against his cheek. Tiny twigs, laid out in a straight line, warming on the white shells. Next the bed of tinder. Finally the puffballs. The old men said you had to have puffballs.

He searched through his shirt pockets, pulling out the lint that had lodged in their corners, shredding the matted bits with his fingernails until he had a puffball about the size of his palm.

With his pocketknife he ripped a seam and unraveled the threads, his fingers moving clumsily. He accumulated a small snarl of broken threads, took that and his puffball of lint and put them both on the small heap of crumbled-leaf tinder.

He got his drop of water, separated the leaves surrounding it, lifted it clear on a single green shaft. His lens. Hunkered down, one hand bracing the other, unmoving, steady, he held the tiny spot of white light on the lint. Perfectly still. Perfectly quiet.

The old men said it would work. The old men said they had done it.

He'd forgotten to cover his head. Mosquitoes swarmed against his face and neck. He could feel their stingers, but he couldn't move. He pretended that the back of his neck wasn't connected to him at all. To hell with it, he told himself. I'm not up there, I'm down here in my hands, and my fingers. . . . There were mosquitoes on his hands, he could see five or six, no, seven, heads down, needles sucking. . . . I'm not there either, he thought. I'm in the drop, the lens, I'm in the sun that's falling on it. . . .

It began as a little stir in the lint. He blinked rapidly to clear the mosquitoes from his eyes, willing a flame, forcing a flame. At first it was just a stir, like an insect inside, moving sluggishly. He kept staring at the white-hot spot of sunlight. A squirm. A distinct squirm.

It was working, the tiny white sun's eye.

More movement. A kind of flutter. The light lint color was beginning to darken. Now a thread of smoke and tiny red coals that ran and hid beneath the puffball, like beetles escaping. Still holding the lens steady, he began blowing. Between his teeth, ever so coaxing. As if he were blowing in a woman's ear.

He could see the shape of that ear. His eyes could trace the little curling pink channels. His breath moved along them, gentler than any touch, and more insistent.

The tiny coals became bits of flame. The leaves snapped. He began to feed his fire, little yellow live things. Babies, that he would feed. *I nurse them. Titless, I nurse them with wood.*

He built his fire bigger and bigger, ending with whole dry limbs in an arch above it. He tossed in handfuls of moss from the oaks—to make a smudge. His eyes stung, tears ran down his face, but the mosquitoes left.

He found a shady place with a slight grade so that his head was comfortably lifted. He scraped it clean with the back of his machete and stretched out, staring up at the sky which was filled with his pillar of smoke.

He woke with the feeling that somebody was watching him. His machete was under his hand, ready.

It was an old man, small and slight, with toothless fallen cheeks and a shotgun held carefully across his body. Behind him, crouched inside the rough brown shell of a pirogue, was a boy. He seemed about ten; his swollen belly pushed open his buttonless shirt; his bulging navel stuck out like a small pointing finger.

Oliver said: "You always walk up on people like that?"

The old man's eyes were a very pale blue and his face was the color of oak bark. With a jerk of his head he beckoned to the boy, who immediately stood beside him.

"Don't you talk?" Oliver asked.

The boy said, "He don't talk English."

Oliver shrugged. "What does he talk?"

"French," the boy said, "but I speak English, me."

Oliver yawned.

The boy said, "My father, he want to know why you are here?"

"That's your father?" Oliver thought: Old bastard got more life in him than shows on the surface.

"He want to know why you have a signal fire?"

"For mosquitoes . . . you close by?"

"*Là-bas.*" The old man gave a backward jerk of his head.

"That way," the boy said.

"He sure understands English," Oliver said.

"Like hell," the old man repeated. There wasn't the slightest flicker across his shrunken face.

The boy asked, "Why are you here where only my father traps?"

"I sure ain't trapping." Oliver began rubbing the mosquito welts on the backs of his hands. They seemed worse than the others. "And I'll tell you." Oliver balanced between a truth and a lie and decided for the truth. "I jumped ship."

The old man nodded. The boy said: "When?"

"Last night."

"Where is the ship?"

"How the hell do I know? In the river somewhere."

The old man spoke again, quickly, muffling the words in the back of his throat.

Oliver thought: Even if I knew the language, I couldn't understand him. Not a tooth left in his head.

The boy said, "My father, he asks two more thing."

"What?"

"What are you going?"

"You mean where. New Orleans."

"Do men come after you?"

Oliver looked at the shrunken young face that was, except for the eyes, exactly like the shrunken old one. "I don't know," he said. "I don't think so, but maybe."

The old man took one hand from the gun and pointed to the pirogue. Oliver looked at the boy.

"You can come," the boy said.

There was only one place in the pirogue—in the bow—the boy sat in the middle, the old man in the stern. Unaccustomed to the delicate balance, Oliver sent shivers all along the hull, water sloshing over the sides.

"Still," the boy said sharply. "Sit still."

Oliver held himself motionless. The water was barely an inch below the gunwales as the old man picked up a paddle. With its first bite the pirogue danced sideways, a wild sudden motion. With the second it steadied, began to make way. By the fourth stroke they were moving rapidly through the water, so rapidly that an occasional wave slapped over the bow and drained into the little stagnant pool at their feet.

They slipped through channels barely wide enough for their passage. The old man turned one way, then another.

How does he know, Oliver thought. He can't see any more than I can.

They came to a wide clear channel, like a small river, some thirty feet from side to side. Oliver thought he felt a slight current, then decided he was wrong. A water moccasin swam past; from his black head the water streamed out in a V. The old man paddled steadily.

Oliver said: "Tell your father I don't have much money but I will give it all to him if he will take me to a road or somewhere I can make my way to the city."

While the boy translated—apparently that was too long a sentence for the old man to understand—Oliver thought

of his stuffed money belt. If they knew how much he had—
he grinned out at the tassel-topped reeds—they would kill
him for it. He must look dirt poor or he would not be alive
now.

The boy behind him said: "How much you got?"

"You want it now?" He stalled, thinking. What would
they expect? How poor did he look? He had to keep them
away from his belt. "Maybe it won't be enough for you."

"How much?" the boy repeated.

Oliver decided. "I got a twenty-dollar gold piece in the
lining of my coat and four silver ones. You can have the gold."

"Now," the old man said.

Oliver turned around, deliberately clumsy. The pirogue
lurched, the boy grabbed for the sides, the old man's paddle
stabbed at the glassy water. "I start taking off my coat and
we are all going to be in the water for sure."

The old man took a moment to translate the words to
himself. Then he nodded. His paddle dug into the water
again, the bow wave folded along the wooden sides.

T H E Y   S T O P P E D   at a large *chênière*. In the oak grove,
twisted and salt-burned, was a tin-roofed house, raised high
on stilts. While Oliver rubbed the ache out of the back of
his knees—and the boy stood grinning at him—he saw that
it wasn't a solid house, just a camp with patched roof and big
gaps around the shutterless windows. But the yard was swept
clean, and four or five chickens roosted under the sagging
porch.

"Get me some water," Oliver said to the boy.

He sat down on the bottom step, dropped his machete
and his coat beside him, and waited. The boy brought a tin
bucket and a dipper.

Soon as his lips touched the water, Oliver realized how cracked they were. How swollen his tongue. (*Why didn't I notice before? Why didn't I?*) He put the dipper down and drank from the bucket.

He was sweating when he stopped, cold pouring sweat, and his head was swinging dizzily.

The boy squatted beside him, his brown shrunken face not two feet away.

Oliver told him: "You know they got gods in Mexico, little gods that look just like you."

The boy squinted, not understanding.

Oliver rubbed his neck and shoulders. He was certain that someone watched from inside the house, but he didn't turn his head.

The boy said: "Tía is coming."

"Yeah?" Oliver continued to stare away off over the marshes to the far-off glint of horizon.

"Tía," the boy repeated.

"I heard you," Oliver said. "Who's Tía? Your mama?"

The boy shook his head. "She's been dead. This is Tía."

Oliver turned his head, following the boy's finger. The first thing he saw was her legs. They were brown and thick and young. They were furred with black hair, and spattered with dirt. Her toenails were long and thick as horn, and the calloused bottom skin wrapped way up around the side of her foot. He looked at the rest of her, a young woman in a sun-bleached pink dress that still held its dark color at the seams. She had short curly black hair, pale blue eyes and a baby on her hip. While Oliver watched, the infant, who was naked except for a small short shirt, urinated. The stream shot out for a couple of feet, dripped through the porch boards. Under the house, chickens scratched and clucked.

"I come to see who was making the smoke." She had a high-pitched singsong voice that reminded him of the Chinese women in Singapore.

"You talk English too."

The old man finished at the pirogue and came toward the house, carrying a couple of ducks and a big redfish in his hand. He handed them to the girl without a word. She hung them, like the baby, from her hip.

Oliver thought: The fish eyes look just exactly like the baby's eyes.

He was still bothered by the sense of another person behind him, of another breathing just the other side of the thin house walls. But there wasn't any point in showing that he noticed. Let them think he was dense and sick with exhaustion.

But not too much. Or they might just figure it was easier to kill him.

Tía shifted the baby to the crook of her arm. The old man gave her the knife from his belt. She went to the edge of the water and began cleaning the duck. She worked very quickly.

Oliver ripped open his coat seam. Four silver dollars and a small thin twenty-dollar gold piece fell into his open palm. "Where's the nearest road?"

The old man said, "Pointe la Gauche."

"I'll go there." Oliver stood up. Behind him in the house a sudden movement echoed his own.

"Now?" The old man stared out at the marsh.

"Look," Oliver lied, "I got friends looking for me and I got to find them. I built that fire so they'd see me."

The old man thought a minute, then nodded.

As they walked away from the house, Oliver put a hand to the boy's shoulder, "I get dizzy," he said in explanation. That way he always managed to keep the boy's body between him and the house. *Whoever that is has any idea of shooting, he's going to have to risk hitting the boy.* And to make himself an even smaller target, Oliver doubled up, holding his stomach, pretending cramps. He let his eyes run over the house, carefully. He saw nothing, but then he couldn't see into the dark windows.

When they were inside the marsh again, away from the house, with the old man paddling steadily, Oliver released the boy, "I'm all right." The child scrambled into the bow. The pirogue hardly vibrated, his balance was so good.

Oliver reached into his pocket and took out the coins, very carefully. He put the four silver dollars in his left hand, and the single twenty-dollar gold piece in his right. He closed both fists firmly over them, and rested his hands on the gunwales of the pirogue, so that the coins were only slightly above water.

The boy's eyes flickered, and his face got a curious knowing look.

"You see? Anything happens to me, like that old man behind me, and plop the twenty dollars goes over the side. How deep's the water around here?"

The boy shook his head.

"Don't matter. You think you be able to find a little round piece of gold in the mud on the bottom?"

The boy shook his head again, looking over Oliver's shoulder to the old man in the stern.

"I want to see that town," Oliver said.

It took nearly four hours. Oliver smelled the town long before he saw it. Distinctly, like a long streamer over the sulphurous smell of the marshes, he recognized garbage, and the smell of people.

Pointe la Gauche had five or six houses, on stilts against storm waters, each with its own boat landing. There were a couple of oaks and a few chinaball trees and one or two oleanders, their dark green leaves shining dully in the late sun. Behind the buildings was a narrow shell road.

"That the road to New Orleans?"

The boy nodded without turning his head. He was watching a cat fishing, its black paw held motionless just under the surface of the water.

The old man drove the pirogue into the bank. The cat pulled her paw out of the water, flicking it dry.

"Every time we come here," the boy said, "she is sitting there. And I never see her catch any fish."

"Shrimp," the old man said abruptly, "she look for shrimp, her."

Oliver swung around and looked at him. "I kind of thought you spoke English, you old bastard."

"Huh . . ." His hand shot out, palm upward.

Oliver opened his own clenched fist so that the tiny gold piece dropped into the brown leather mitt.

The old man looked at it, shining in the late sun. He poked at it, clumsily turned it over. In his big hands it looked very small and very thin.

"It's worth twenty dollars," Oliver said.

The old man nodded. "*Sais ça.*"

The coin seemed brighter for the time it spent in the seam of his coat. "I got that in Vera Cruz," Oliver said. "I was matching with a big fat Mexican. When he lost, he cried and then tried to knife me."

The boy nodded and pointed to a scar on the old man's face. "A knife too."

"Some fight, huh?"

"He is too old to fight much," the boy said. "So my brother, he went back the next day."

"You got a brother?" That explained the movements in the house behind him.

The boy nodded. "And that Mexican, he had friends?"

"I don't know," Oliver said. "My ship left the next day."

The boy chuckled. "Against his coin, what did you match?"

"Me? I put up the girl I was with."

The boy looked unbelieving.

"If you'd seen her, you wouldn't think it was too much."

The old man was listening, frowning a little in his effort to understand.

Oliver said: "I used to wonder sometimes what happened after that. He got her, I guess. He owned the café and the hotel. He could afford her."

He reached into the pirogue and pulled out his coat and his machete. "Why'd your brother hide in the house?"

The child's face went blank. "I don't understand."

The pirogue swung off. Oliver watched until it disappeared into the reeds, leaving not even a trace of wake in the bayou water. He began to wonder if all his precautions had been necessary, if he hadn't just made a fool of himself. Nothing had happened, nothing had been threatened. . . . Still, he was alive, and he was going to stay that way.

He picked up his stuff and headed into the cluster of houses.

H E W A L K E D part of the way to New Orleans, methodically plodding hour after hour through the summer dust,
past orange groves and pastures, and farms, and swamps. And
part of the way he rode—in wagons and carts and even once
in a black buggy, a bouncy two-seater. The driver was a
middle-aged fat man named Pérez, who talked steadily, inter-
rupting himself occasionally to push at his lower belly.
"Busted gut," he explained each time, and went immediately
back to his talk. "Mosquitoes, they are terrible, my friend."

Oliver nodded politely. Pérez snapped his whip at a
passing dragonfly. With a little dusty rustle the insect disappeared from the air. "Mamselles like that, they eat mosquitoes all day and it don't seem to do no good. Now what a
mosquito really goes for, my friend, that is a cow. Sometimes
the poor animals, they go crazy with pain and they jump in
the river and kill themselves."

He glanced out the corner of his watery brown eye to
see how Oliver took that.

Oliver, hunched forward, arms on knees, said politely,
"That's pretty bad."

He wasn't going to argue over mosquitoes. He just
wanted to sit quiet and let his body lurch with the movement
of the buggy. "You know where I could get something to eat
and a place to sleep? That ground was plenty wet last night."

"You can pay for it?"

"I can pay for it," Oliver said.

Pérez tapped a green fly on his horse's back. "Now *alors,* I think me that the Landrys might be cooking some extra supper tonight. She's a good cook, her."

"I sure don't care." Oliver prepared to doze again. "I'd eat tortillas and Mexican peppers, and think it was fine."

H E   H A D supper on the back porch of the Landry house, chickens circling warily on the ground in front of him, cats rubbing against his ankles. He ate quickly, hardly chewing. It was greasy and hot, a heap of rice with pieces of shrimp and meat and fish. He'd wanted gin or whiskey but they didn't have any, so he settled for blackberry wine. It was very sweet and if she hadn't said it was blackberry, he would never have recognized it. But it was heavy with alcohol, and the glass was large. ("Make it usselves," Mama Landry told him, "best blackberry wine you find on the Lower Coast.") He felt the familiar warming behind his eyes, the familiar tingling at the tips of his fingers, the sting along his lips.

He propped his feet up on the railing. The last of the twilight took on a yellow glow, the chinaberry tree seemed to grow taller as he looked at it. There was a hissing and a roaring in his ears, very faint, the sound of a reef. He could see the color of the water, and the movement of it. Just as clear as if it were right in front of him.

The roaring passed, and the water became a large black-and-white cat with a torn ear and only one set of whiskers. "Fuck you," Oliver said to the cat. "I'm tired."

The chickens scattered away from his feet, the cats sat on the railing and watched him walk away. He had a blanket in the woodshed—a small room, with just enough space for him to sleep next to the big wash boilers. There were no windows. He stretched himself out, shoulder touching the door. He was safe.

H E G O T to New Orleans the next day, rode in on a brewery dray, piled with empty kegs. He surveyed the narrow dusty streets, their deep drainage ditches filled with greenish water; their small wooden houses linked one to the other by wooden fences and gates. He saw a corner sign: Music Street. Nice name. He dropped off the dray immediately. Now he was conscious of his torn muddy clothing, of his matted hair. He found a small shop and bought clothes, while the owner watched him warily and nervously. He asked his way to the baths and then to the nearest barber.

While the barber scratched away, he gossiped: there was fever in New Orleans, more than usual, even for the summertime.

Every place had its own kind of fever, Oliver thought. On the Ohio it was breakbone fever, in Panama it was yellow jack, and in Singapore—well, he'd even forgotten that name. If he was going to die of fever, he would have been dead years ago.

Oliver sat up, wiping the bits of soap out of his ears and nose. The barber pointed out a house in the next block. "Boy died there of the fever just last week," he said. "And if that wasn't bad enough . . . she used to take roomers, but they all left."

Oliver walked past the house. Like the rest of the neighborhood, it was gray-painted wood, narrow but very long—

with a brick-paved side alley and three narrow wooden steps to the front door. Oliver looked up and down the street, at the passing ice wagon, at the tufts of heavy-leafed fig trees growing over board fences, at the sky filled with heavy black cumulus clouds. He saw an old woman in a black dress tottering down the sidewalk, and a man with a great beer belly walking in the opposite direction; they both held black umbrellas against the sun, moving inside their little round shade. In the distance he heard a train's bell; close by children's voices recited together.

Oliver climbed the three wooden steps and knocked at the door. Rooms in this house would be cheaper than any other place in town. Much cheaper. And he wasn't about to waste his money.

THE NEXT day Oliver found his way to Storeyville. He'd heard about it for years, about its saloons and brothels; now he was very disappointed. It didn't look half as good as San Francisco, not one-tenth as good as Singapore. But good enough for him. . . . He tried one place after the other until he found a job. A madam named Julia Chaffee hired him because she was fond of husky blond men, and because blonds were rare in New Orleans. He helped the bartender, he ran errands, he took regular customers safely home when they'd passed out. And at Julia Chaffee's six weeks later he met Alonzo Manzini. He was a produce merchant with a fat sagging body and a thin shrewd yellow-tinged face. He came one day to talk to Julia and have a pot of coffee in the parlor. Afterward, they both stopped by the storeroom where Oliver had just finished stacking the week's supply of champagne bottles.

"I hear," Manzini said, "that Julia thinks you are a treasure."

Oliver smiled and began putting the collar back on his shirt. He had taken it off to work more easily.

"I knew Julia years ago, when she was still working; what a piece of ass that was. . . ."

Julia smiled her best professional smile. "We are both old, my friend."

The next day Manzini was back, bringing with him the police precinct captain. Instead of coffee, they had champagne in the large parlor; the bartender himself served them. After a few minutes Manzini came downstairs alone.

"Vichy," he said to Oliver, who was tending bar. "Vichy for my liver."

Oliver asked: "Why didn't one of the girls bring the champagne up?" That was the usual way.

"He don't like girls," Manzini said. "You got to know your customers, boy. He could give Julia a lot of trouble, that one, but they will come to an understanding, my friend Julia will work out something."

Oliver said, "I didn't know."

Manzini's little bright brown eyes flicked over him, gleaming, appraising. "I seen boys like you come along before; soon as you get a little money together, you'll be in business yourself."

Oliver shook his head and began polishing glasses. Julia wanted all her glasses shining.

Manzini went on, "When you get ready, you come have a talk with me; maybe I can help you."

"Maybe," Oliver said.

"My wife and my son, they can run the produce business. I can find something else to do, something profitable."

"There are problems."

"Not so many. And that gentleman upstairs, he is my cousin."

EVENTUALLY OLIVER wrote to his mother asking her to sell one of the small farms. Six months later he was in business for himself, with Manzini as his partner. Not in Storeyville where competition was stiff and protection rates high. Their house was on Conti Street; back of town, people called it. It was a quiet respectable place, and very profitable.

Oliver was the bartender and the bouncer—the bully, people said. Manzini managed the girls and the madam and the police payoffs. "You are too young," he told Oliver, "and you look too young. I will take care of all troubles that can be solved by money and a few words and maybe a laugh and a pat on the behind—the girls are like terriers, they yap all the time. I do this. You see to the bar and the staying up all night, all the things a young man can do, the ones that take muscle and a hard head and a fist. And we make ourselves fine partners."

They did. Oliver checked on him regularly, but never found him unfair in anything. Manzini watched him too, carefully, respectfully, closely. Neither could find fault in the other.

With his first profits Oliver bought two small houses in the same block of Conti Street and rented them to respectable families. "How do you have so much money?" Manzini sighed. "My wife wants to take her grandmother to Lourdes when the old lady won't live through the trip. They expect a miracle and I have to pay for it."

"I don't have any expenses," Oliver said.

He still lived in the same house on Music Street, and he paid the same rent regularly on the first of every week.

His landlady, who had six children besides the one dead of fever, called him a joy from heaven. He was so quiet and so hard-working. She'd see him come home in the early morning, she'd see him leave in the afternoon. He was always quiet and soft-spoken, with his crisp Yankee speech. He never drank, he never brought girls home, he didn't even seem to know anyone in the neighborhood. She always intended to ask him where he worked but somehow she never did. He was young enough to be one of her children, but he was not the sort of man you asked questions.

I must be putting her off, Oliver thought, I must be scaring her somehow. I don't scowl or curse, but I must be very formidable to look at.

In his small shaving mirror, he studied his square-jawed face with its blond mustache and close-set eyes. He didn't see anything there.

Still, Oliver thought, looking from his mirror and his shaving basin to the dusty narrow stretch of Music Street, it was pleasant not to be asked endless questions. Whatever he was doing, he liked the result.

In those early years in New Orleans—when for the first time in his life he wasn't traveling and seeing different sights each day—he had time to think about Thomas Henry Oliver. Every night before he fell asleep, he made plans—abstract, detailed plans for the rest of his life. He decided what he must do in each succeeding year, in his personal life, in his business. He had schedules for both, and he intended to keep them.

In the meantime he worked. He collected his money every week from his two rented houses; each time he inspected them carefully, his hulking presence keeping his tenants neat and careful. He was considering buying a small bar and restaurant. It was just around the corner, it was completely legitimate, no girls at all; he could manage it easily. Still, the price was high . . . he would think about it.

Manzini came every morning at seven and stayed until Oliver returned at five. Together they went over the day's accounts, talked briefly, and Manzini went home.

Oliver stayed the evening and the night. There was never any real trouble, only an occasional squabble among the girls or a drunken customer to be quietly removed. The nights were filled with men's drunken laughter and the metallic tinkle of girls' voices. And the steady never-ending piano playing of a tiny old Negro named Joseph.

Oliver hated that jazz piano. He could never tell one tune from another, they were all trills and banging bass. Once, early on a rainy evening when the house was empty, he asked Joseph to play something else. So Joseph played a soft gentle version of "The Rosewood Spinet" and then "Juanita." In all the years he worked in the house on Conti Street, those were the only tunes Oliver ever recognized.

Mornings he walked the two miles home. In summer it was daylight, people were out of their houses, the street vendors were yelling from their high wagons. In winter the sky overhead was still perfectly black, the houses were pulled in tight against the night, the streets were shadowed and very cold. He passed only a few old women, scuttling their way to early Mass, hunched in their black coats and shawls. Oliver took deep breaths of the peat-smelling air, felt it brush his cheeks like feathers as he strode along. He'd spent so many hours pacing back and forth in rooms and halls and parlors that he had to get the closeness out of his muscles.

A N D A L L this time, he had no women. He owned a house, but he would not sleep with whores. He'd had his fill of them; the woman in Bahia was the last. His girls teased him now and then; one, whose name was Juliette, was very pretty, but Oliver ignored her.

Finally he decided to allow his body the use of a woman. He had a particular one in mind, had marked her down in his memory weeks before. He'd seen her sweeping the front steps of a small bakery on LePage Square. She would do, he thought.

She would do very nicely. The next morning he stopped: the bread was not quite ready, would he wait? She was cleaning the shelves and the cases carefully with soapy water, head bent to her work. "I see you sweeping the steps, every morning," he said, as if that gave him a claim on her.

She looked up. "I see you pass too, every morning."

She was not pretty, he thought, her face was too pinched and thin, but she was a nice girl, in her striped blue-and-white dress and her big white apron. Yes, she would do.

Her name was Edna and she lived with her parents in the house behind the bakery. And she met Oliver in the little shadowy park across the street whenever he asked her to.

He did not see her very often; she did not really seem to expect it. Her thin buttocks and angular body seemed only vaguely female to him, and the few panting minutes standing against the dark oaks in the park inspired in him no great erotic longings. Which was exactly what he wanted. He had to humor his body occasionally so that the rest of the time it obeyed his will.

H I S S K I N lost its sea-tanned look, and turned first yellow, and then pink-white. Because he rarely slept enough, his eyes were swollen and circled with dark. He drank beer steadily while he worked, glass after glass to take the edge off his weariness. He was getting fat, a belly began to bulge through his suspenders, and his shirt collars wouldn't stay closed.

Manzini noticed. "You take a day off," he said. "Go out to the lake or take the air someplace; people are always going to Abita Springs, you want to go there?"

Oliver shook his head. "I'm not going to spend money for air."

"Take tomorrow off," Manzini insisted. "You get consumption and what happens to this place? I have to close up."

So Oliver took two days off. The first one he slept completely around the clock, only now and then taking the cover off his slop jar. He probably would have slept through the second one too, but his landlady pounded on the door. "I was afraid you'd died."

His watch had stopped. He yelled for the time. "Ten-thirty," she said. He shaved and dressed, feeling strange and aimless. He walked slowly uptown, passing the big wholesale markets, picking his way through the tangle of wagons and mules, of baskets and sacks. He stared at the mounds of fish and shrimp, decided that the day must be Friday. He stopped for a beer, his English voice startling in the chatter of Italian all around him. A short dark man shook his hand, offered him another drink: Saia—what was his first name?—sold liquor to the house on Conti Street, delivering most of it himself. Oliver had another beer with him, listened to talk of the different markets, shook more hands.

After an hour, he left and walked toward the docks, stopping only once to read a black-bordered death notice tacked to a post: thirty-seven. He hadn't had much time, Oliver thought; poor bastard.

For the first time since he'd jumped ship, he saw the river. The wide yellow expanse shimmered under the noon sun, little winds blew off it in swirling uncertain eddies. On the other side the trees were vague and indistinct behind a light fog. Two pigeons strutted along the rough wooden dock, ignoring him so completely that he almost stumbled over them. With a long fluttering hop they turned their backs to him. Oliver strolled along, heels echoing on the wood. Somewhere, not far off, someone was chipping paint. Steadily. Oliver recognized that sound. Just the way he recognized the smell that hung around the battered hulks of the ships, the wet wood of the docks.

He walked away from the river, not stopping until he reached the Canal Street business district. For a few moments he sat on the stone steps of a monument to Henry Clay, staring down the length of Canal Street, admiring the new electric streetcars. After a bit, when the blurry beer feeling was gone, he sauntered slowly along the street, on the shady side, watching the buggies and the carriages move up and down slowly. Watching ladies come in and out of the shops, parasols in hand, skirts swishing tops of ankles. He kept walking until the commercial district ended and the street was lined by big houses and tall trees and gardens with Negro nurses tending children at play. He paused in front of a Presbyterian church, figured he'd walked enough, and turned back the way he had come. The Negro nurses stared after him suspiciously and called the children closer to the houses.

He liked the strange smell of the electric cars, the faint pungent odor that filtered from their boxes. He followed their tracks up St. Charles Avenue, stopping finally for another beer and, as he drank it, staring through the open door at the steady flow of people on the sidewalk. That night, he dreamed of buildings and banks and streets of cobblestones and sidewalks of brick and ladies with hats and parasols and fine boots and uniformed doormen opening store doors.

After that, he regularly took off two days a month. Manzini beamed his approval. "It's good for you."

Oliver did exactly the same thing every time. He walked through the business district, listening to snatches of talk, marching step for step with men who were busy and hurried. He imagined the offices he passed: filled with hundreds of heavy bound account books, and bookkeepers with eyeshades and shirt-cuff clips. As he moved along the dusty streets, cleaned by an occasional afternoon thunderstorm, he thought slowly and carefully and languorously about money. Sometimes he found himself holding his breath.

He began going for lunch to a little restaurant called

Galatin's. After a few times the proprietor recognized him. Someday, he promised himself—in his rented room on Music Street—someday everybody will know who I am; they will see me walk along the street and they will say: There goes Mr. Oliver. . . .

He had a picture taken for his mother in Ohio. He looked at the man who stared out of the black-and-white print and was not too unhappy at what he saw.

On his days off, he did not seek the company of other men, the camaraderie of bars. He preferred the presence of women, the sound of their voices; he found he could think best and most clearly against their chatter. That was why his friendship with the Robichaux sisters lasted so long. They were delighted to go out; they chattered steadily to each other, ignoring Oliver as completely as if he weren't there at all. He didn't sleep with either of them, he hadn't wanted to, and neither had they.

He noticed another thing. Women never flirted with him. Never the smile, the sidewise glance that he saw turned on other men. It was always up to him to make the first move. Then they were eager to come walk with him, or have a beer with him at one of the crowded noisy German *Biergartens,* or ride with him on a smoky little excursion train to take the evening breeze at the lake. He bedded the ones he liked best, allowing himself the use of their bodies exactly twice a month, no more, no less. They were all nice girls, seamstresses, shopgirls, housekeepers, and maids. He liked to hear about their lives, he was so curious about other people. For almost a year he was especially fond of Catherine Drury, a plump black-haired Irish lady's maid. Once, riding the streetcar on her day off, she pointed out the house on St. Charles Avenue where she worked. "There, what do you think of that, mister?" A vast house of gray stone, with arched doorways and gothic windows, battlements and turrets, rising from a smooth green artificial hill.

As the streetcar passed, Oliver said, "I will have a house like that."

Catherine laughed and slipped her arm through his. "Such talk, my boy. . . . I'll tell you this. It's a bloody big place to keep clean, and Herself is always yelling to me to brush her hair: 'Not so hard, Catherine; can't you do anything gently, Catherine?'. . . You know what's happening next week?" Oliver shook his head. "A tournament, you ever hear of anything like that?"

Oliver remembered reading a novel once . . . yes, he knew what a tournament was.

"She's Lady Mathilda, and she's got a peaked hat with chiffon off the top of it. And a beautiful dress, blue and silver. Would you know the dressmaker had to throw the first one away because she didn't like the fit. And the Mister, he's going to be a knight and ride a horse."

"Where?" Oliver asked.

"In the country somewhere. Who cares where?" Catherine sighed and settled back on the straight wood seat. "You know," she said, "rich people are crazy. I've worked for one and the other since I was a little girl, and they're just not like you or me."

Like me, Oliver thought. *Like me.*

H E W A S fond of all these girls. He brought them the sort of presents he could afford: a strand of coral beads, a small cameo, an elaborately carved hatpin. If they got pregnant, and said it was by him, he never argued, never once, just gave them the money to be rid of the baby.

But he did not get married. He had calculated that he could not afford to get married until he was forty-five. By then he should be a man of property, a successful businessman, with something to offer a wife. And she, in her turn, should be a virgin of good family, accustomed to the comforts he'd be able to give her.

He had calculated it exactly and he knew he was right.

AFTER A few more years he went to Manzini and said, "I want to get out of this business."

Manzini, shocked and surprised, patted his ulcer-filled stomach, "Mother of God, what will happen now?"

"You can buy me out," Oliver said, "or I can find somebody else to buy me out."

"Why?" Manzini asked sadly. "It is so profitable."

"I'm sick of whores," Oliver said. "I'm sick of the way this place looks and smells."

"You have something else," Manzini said suspiciously. "Something else."

"Yes," Oliver said.

He had another partner, a Scotchman named McGhee, whom he'd known briefly in California when he was smuggling arms. Together they planned a gambling casino outside the city limits, at Franciscan Point. Even allowing for payoffs, Oliver thought, the money should be very good.

That same year Maurice Lamotta came to work for him. Lamotta was the errand boy at Manzini's produce office. He was small and slight with the pinched-in face and the thread-like bones of the very poor. He had no family—Oliver questioned him carefully—no, not even a cousin. He was fifteen and presently he was sleeping in the back of Manzini's office. "He's very good with figures," Manzini said casually, "sometimes I let him help with the accounts."

At that moment Manzini lost his errand boy. Quietly Oliver made a proposition to Lamotta: finish school, then come to work. In the meantime he could live in the house on Conti Street. "A two-year investment," Oliver said, "are you worth it?" "Yes," Lamotta said, and then as an afterthought, "sir."

When he graduated from Boys High School, Oliver was waiting. His ventures were now so varied that he needed a central office and a bookkeeper. With his profits he'd bought a small factory that made work shirts and overalls. With a bank loan, he acquired an unsuccessful department store, an old two-story wooden building, on Esplanade Avenue. The upstairs, now all storage, dusty and crowded and hardly used, would become his office. Oliver looked at Lamotta's thin face, which had put on only a little weight in two years of regular meals, and was satisfied with his bargain.

O L I V E R ' S   M O T H E R   sold the last farm in Edwardsville and moved to New Orleans. He'd bought a house for her, a small cottage on Kerlerec Street, a good solid house of plastered brick, with doors and floors and windows of painted cypress. The two tall front windows were kept shuttered and locked, but behind the house there was a garden, two big fig trees growing against the seven-board fence, and a wisteria vine running up the side of the wall. The river was close by—you caught a stir of breeze from it, even on hot nights, and you always heard the boats—a friendly pleasant sound, Oliver thought.

His mother arrived in June, a short sturdy woman, who looked almost the same as the last time he'd seen her twenty years before. She stepped off the train, Oliver kissed her dutifully on the cheek, and she said: "This whole town smells terrible."

"It's summer," Oliver said. "And it doesn't smell as bad as some places."

"It smells worse than any place I've ever been."

"Now, you know the Ohio on a hot day . . . it doesn't smell like violets."

She complained steadily for two weeks—about the strange name of their street; about the closeness of the other houses, an arm's reach away across a narrow brick alley; about the way the indoor walls sweated and mildewed; about the number of priests and nuns on the street; about the noisy ringing of the Angelus three times a day; about the chattered Italian of their neighbors.

But she stayed.

Oliver teased her: "Ma, you better preserve those figs if you don't want the mockingbirds to get them all." "I want some chickens," she said, "at least we will have decent eggs." "Ma," Oliver said, "I will get you a yard full of chickens." "Oliver, is there anyone who speaks decent English in this neighborhood, this whole neighborhood?" "Ma, if you are curious about what other people are saying, you should learn a little Italian; it's very easy."

"I will not," she said, "and I hope you don't either."

She preserved all the figs that summer; a line of jars filled the pantry shelves. She put red geraniums on the sunny sill of the west window and began crocheting antimacassars for the backs of the big chairs. Oliver knew then that she would stay.

She cooked dinner for him every night, refusing steadily his offer of a cook. "No black people in my kitchen."

"A white cook, then."

"No drunken Irishwoman in my kitchen."

He let her alone. She was determined.

Every Sunday they went for a walk. Though he contributed regularly to the Baptist church, they rarely went there. She did not like the minister and she did not like the sermons. She said firmly: "There's no good to it."

So every Sunday morning, they went for a long walk out Esplanade Avenue, sauntering slowly past his department store. "That building needs paint." "Ma, when I make enough profit selling the trash inside, I will paint it." Past big old-fashioned houses, all needing repairs. Along the shady sidewalks, under sharp-smelling camphor trees and musty-smelling oaks.

One bright October Sunday, when the air had an edge of cool in it, his mother wore a new dress, a deep rich green silk.

And he had a present for her that Sunday. A brooch, a straight gold bar with six diamonds. Not the finest in the world, he knew, but respectable. She would have better when he could afford it.

The diamonds sparkled nicely against the green cloth, and the soft color made her look years younger. She felt good too, she walked with chin up and a crisp bounce to her step.

"I've got the prettiest mother in town," he said quietly, expecting a sharp correction. He got a silent grateful smile.

He was still marveling at that smile when she asked, without slackening her pace or looking at him: "Oliver, when are you going to get married?"

He took care not to show his surprise. After all it was a proper question. "When I am forty-five, Mama, I can afford a wife."

"If you can afford a mother," she said sharply, "you can afford a wife."

He laughed out loud. "Have you found some girl you like?"

She shook her head. "No, but you haven't either."

"I can't afford to. I have to get you a better house first."

"I don't need a better house."

"I am looking at one on Canal Street. You know, when I first came here, I said someday I would live on that street."

She seemed to walk a little faster. "Nonsense."

"You will like the house, Mama."

"You need a wife."

He tried again. "You see how I come home, Mama, so tired I can't keep my eyes open. A new wife would want more than that."

They reached a little triangular park and sat down on the green-painted benches at the base of a brick red monument. Neither bothered to read the inscription.

His mother sat perfectly straight, protecting the new green dress. "You must find a wife who understands."

"Mama, you are the stubbornest woman I have ever met.'

"You don't know any proper girls, do you?"

"None that I would marry."

She accepted that fact more easily than he had expected. "I didn't think so."

"I have my plans, Mama. It will all work out."

H E   B O U G H T the house on Canal Street, a large house, with a wide front porch and wide red tile steps.

"Too big a house for me," his mother complained. But he could see how pleased she was.

"We will need some furniture and carpets," he said. "Will you get them?"

"That should be your wife's business."

"You'll need a maid, Mama," he said, "to clean. I'll hire her."

And he was surprised when she didn't object. "Maybe," she said slowly. "Maybe. I'm getting old."

She had put on quite a bit of weight, he noticed, but she looked all right. After they moved into the larger house, they no longer went on Sunday walks. She didn't suggest it any more; he supposed it was because she worked in the garden and got outside that way. She didn't need to take a stroll just to stretch her legs and her eyes. She'd always liked growing things and feeling mud between her fingers. He could still remember—how many years ago—the cosmos she grew by the kitchen door, the gentle colored stiff-stemmed flowers.

She could have flowers now, he thought; in this hot climate they would burst from her fingers.

After they'd lived there a year, he went to look at her garden. There was none. The grass was cut neatly, the edges trimmed—a man came every week for that—but the flower beds had gone back to grass; he could see their outlines faintly through the green.

"Mama," he said, "what happened to the flowers?"

She looked apologetic. "I haven't got to them yet, Oliver. I just can't seem to get the hang of growing things in this climate."

He didn't quite believe her, but he didn't worry. She seemed quite happy. She'd even found a minister she liked and was very busy with the Baptist Orphans Home and the South American Missions. And every six months she said: "Oliver, I have met a very nice girl."

"Ma, not now."

When he came home that January evening—early dark and the corner street light shedding a round yellow circle on the sidewalk—he felt something wrong. His heels made a louder than usual sound as he climbed the red tile steps to the front porch. The house itself, the hall behind the leaded-glass door and the rooms behind the windows on each side, the house itself was completely dark. The maid left at four, but his mother always switched on the lamp in the front window. There should be other lights also—in the kitchen where she would be keeping dinner for him, in the dining room. . . .

The skin on the back of his neck prickling, he unlocked the front door. He switched on the lights slowly, one by one, and the house opened up before him. The last place he looked was her bedroom, and by then he knew what he would find.

She was lying on the bed, she must have been napping, and she had been dead some little time. Her body was cooling. He felt her wrist, her neck, to convince himself. Then he walked out of the house to the doctor who lived four doors away. "I suppose you will have to come see," he said.

While the doctor went for his little black bag, and the doctor's children peered around the corner of the door, Oliver telephoned Maurice Lamotta. He came within ten minutes.

HIS MOTHER'S death changed Oliver's plans. Not that he grieved for her. He didn't. He knew that she would not have expected real grief from him. They'd understood each other quite well—Oliver had been a good son; she had been a loving mother. She had raised him and, in his youth, fed him in the midst of poverty. He had made her old age affluent. They had done a good job, each with the other, and both were satisfied. You did not grieve when things reached their natural end.

Only, that end had come more quickly than he had anticipated. He would have to change his plans.

He'd gotten used to living with someone, he'd gotten used to company. He now required someone waiting for him at dinner in the evenings. Someone in the living room with him after dinner, while he dozed or read the evening paper. He did not want to talk, but he did require someone within reach of his eyes, if he should lift them.

He would therefore, he reasoned, have to advance his plans a few years and marry.

In the years that his mother had lived with him, his relationships with women had changed. He no longer used them as background for his thoughts. He no longer wanted their company, but he still needed their bodies. He had a list of seven or eight women and he visited each in turn, staying no longer with them than was absolutely necessary.

None of those would do for a wife. Maybe he should have let his mother introduce him to those nice girls she had found. . . . He felt a small twinge: it would have pleased her so, but now he didn't know their names. And he wasn't about to go to the Ladies South American Missionary Guild to find out.

He said to Lamotta, "Make a list of all the men I do business with. And mark the ones that have daughters."

"Daughters?"

Oliver nodded and then remembering asked, "How did you meet your wife?"

Lamotta's face moved into a slight smile. "She was at the orphanage with me."

"I have to get married too," Oliver said impatiently. "This is the way I do it."

Oliver found people eager to help him; he was a good match, a successful man. He went to Sunday dinners, to Saturday musicales, he went on hay rides, on picnics, he learned to dance. He looked and considered carefully. In about six months he'd made his choice, a tall blond girl who played the organ at St. Matthew's Episcopal Church. "Thank you," she said, "but I don't want to get married. Not for a while."

He was surprised at first, and then he was shocked. "Why?"

"Next fall I'm going to St. Louis, to the conservatory. I'm sure I told you."

"Nobody is making you go to St. Louis," Oliver said, trying to understand. "You don't have to go."

"But I *want* to go. You don't know how important it is, to have really good teachers. I've looked forward to this ever since I was a little girl, and I've planned for it so long. . . ."

He could not quite believe that other people had plans too. "I'm too old to wait," he said.

"I don't want you to."

He went home early that evening, puzzled and hurt. For

the next few weeks he waited for her to change her mind. She did not.

He found another girl, a short slight dark-haired, dark-eyed girl whose name was Stephanie Maria D'Alfonso. She had gone to Sophie Newcomb College for one term, had not liked it, and now she stayed home embroidering enormous quantities of linens and storing them away in her marriage chest. She was seventeen, an only daughter, quiet and gentle; she did not like dancing or parties; she preferred the porch swing with a book for company. Her father was a city judge, her uncle was a successful gambler, a cousin was in the produce business and doing well, her older brother was prospering with his bag factory.

A good family, Oliver thought, he would be doing well to marry into it.

At first Stephanie D'Alfonso found him strange, and she hesitated uncertainly.

"Do you think I am too young for you?" she asked Oliver timidly. "I mean, could I be all the things you want me to be?"

Oliver was frankly puzzled. "What things could I want you to be?" He had a sudden thought. "You mean the house? Your mother would show you how to run the house."

"No, no," she said. "I think I could run your house without any trouble."

"What then?" he said. "You would have servants, as many as you want."

"No," she said, "not quite that. . . ." Something, something, unspoken, almost unthought. A shadow. I'm seventeen, there must be something except a man I didn't know two months ago. . . .

Her mother said, weeping: "You should go down on your knees to the Blessed Virgin for a fine man like that."

Her father said angrily: "He will give you everything you want, more things than you can even imagine now."

The little vague shadow in her mind dimmed and disappeared. Stephanie D'Alfonso decided she did indeed love this tall blond man. Her engagement ring was a round diamond the size of a dime.

They were married on an August Saturday noon at St. Rose's Church. (Oliver thought with a twinge that his mother probably would have refused to come.) Her great-uncle was the priest, her younger cousins the altar boys. There were eight bridesmaids, all relatives, and a ring bearer who at the last minute refused to go up the aisle and had to be carried away.

They went for a two-day honeymoon to Abita Springs. Oliver did not want to be away from his business too long.

As the first months passed, Oliver realized what an extraordinarily good deal he'd made, what a remarkable woman he'd married.

She was a fine housekeeper. He who had never liked food found that he enjoyed hers. He liked too the changes she made in the house he had bought for his mother; it was brighter and more comfortable. He grew more and more proud of her. She was only seventeen but she was as serious as a thirty-year-old. Serious, but friendly too. The house was always full of people; they never had dinner alone. He'd had no friends, but now he had come into a whole established world. About the only time the house was empty was during ten o'clock High Mass on Sunday. He himself never went to church; she never asked him to. Sometimes he stayed in the quiet house, smoking the best of his cigars. And sometimes he spent the morning at his office, his feet propped on the dusty battered desk.

He was happy. Late in the evening, when they were undressing for bed, he could feel contentment, like moisture in the air, like fog, softening the edges of things, blending them gently one into the other.

Within the year she was pregnant.

NOW THAT he was a very old man, with only the twistings and turnings of his mind to give any movement to his days, he found that he remembered very little of her, Stephanie Maria D'Alfonso, who had been his wife for eleven years and had borne him five children.

And he remembered so many other people, people he hardly knew. Their faces came floating before his eyes when he least expected them. Like that fellow—what was his name? —yes, Saia, Vincent Saia, in the liquor business, sixty years ago: thin dark face, balding head. Oliver thought: I couldn't have seen that man more than three or four times, and not more than a few minutes each time. But I remember him.

Other people too. Manzini, his first partner, dead fifty years. And the nameless people, dozens of them, people he'd seen only once. Like that boy who'd come into the casino at Franciscan Point. A tall boy who shot craps, was quiet and well behaved, came once and never came back. Why remember his face? The old woman who walked by the corner of the house on Kerlerec Street every Sunday morning on her way to seven-o'clock Mass. The shoeshine boy in the barbershop who was drafted in World War I. The Chinaman who did his shirts the first year he was in New Orleans.

He remembered all these people, but not his young wife.

He'd been so busy, just then. And so successful. A couple of years after his marriage a European war began at Sarajevo.

He thought, decided—and his shirt factory was ready to turn out American uniforms. His contracts were large, his profits enormous. . . . Maurice Lamotta nodded his admiring approval. . . . After the war, with the coming of Prohibition, Oliver gambled again. He became a bootlegger.

It began with his boatyard. He'd bought that a few years before, a small yard a couple of miles below the city. *I never made any money on that*, he thought, *but thank God I kept it.* For years that yard, called Thibodeaux's, had produced fishing skiffs and pirogues and even occasionally a big shrimp lugger. Old Thibodeaux was still there, and still a good builder. Together they worked out the design.

When the boat was finally in the water, Oliver said: "Now start on another one."

They were the perfect boats for his purpose. They were fairly large, shallow draft, open except for a small wheelhouse. They were well built, and very fast.

The yard prospered suddenly. Unknown gentlemen ordered boats—"Why do you go through so much trouble to hide the fact that you have a fleet of boats?" Thibodeaux asked. Oliver simply stared, and Thibodeaux, feeling the unspoken threat, was silent.

By the time Prohibition was six months old, Oliver was ready. His big boats left Cuba and waited outside the three-mile limit. Little boats met them, loaded with liquor, and at night raced for the marshes. With their speed they could outrun any government boat. With their shallow draft they could skim in and out of marshes almost like a pirogue. As long as they didn't foul a screw, or really ground themselves, they would be fairly safe.

At first Oliver worked a boat himself. It was, he thought, very much like the old days, liquor-running was no different from gunrunning. And in many ways it was easier. From a different rendezvous each time—by different means: in cars, in ice wagons, stowed in corners of coal barges, Oliver's cases of illegal liquor moved into the city. Slowly and carefully, Oliver hired his men, young men who were steady and cautious. He built them into a small, well-trained, well-disciplined group. "We're going to be doing this for years to come," he told them, "and we'll do it right."

After the first couple of years he no longer went out himself. His young men did all that. He also had bought enough sheriffs, and mayors and police to feel fairly secure as he sat in his office on Esplanade Avenue.

He was the best-organized, most successful bootlegger in New Orleans, and one of the best small operators in the country—at least he gathered that from the Eastern and Midwestern people who drifted by to visit him. Despite their offers, he remained an independent, and he remained small. He liked working with people he knew and trusted. "We will do better by being more modest," he told Lamotta now and then in the quiet of the office, "we will last longer."

Hidden by the maze of Lamotta's bookkeeping, his money flowed smoothly and easily into legal businesses.

He remembered that, all of that, every detail. He could even remember women he'd never met. Like the one in the Chicago railway station. She stood on the platform, very tall and elegant in a brown dress and a feathered hat, watching the train move into the station. He waved, half-hoping he knew her. She did not answer. Hurriedly, he left his compartment, found the aisle completely blocked. The porter had piled all the luggage in the vestibule and couldn't seem to unload it quickly; and there were four querulous old ladies struggling into their coats, tying scarves against the Chicago chill. . . . Oliver ran through the cars, pushing people aside, until he found an open door and jumped down to the platform. He had no clear idea of what he wanted to do; he only wanted to find her. He ran to the end of the platform where empty rails extended into the maze of the yards. He dashed back to the station door. She wasn't there. Just a steady flow

of travelers clutching bags and parcels, redcaps pushing baggage trucks—he saw nothing in their muffled shapes. He
stopped, breathless. He was beginning to be very cold; he'd
left his overcoat in the compartment. He gave a last quick
look around, then trotted back to his car. The porter had just
finished handing luggage to the redcap, and the old ladies,
scarves tied and coats buttoned, were getting down.

He could remember that woman with perfect clarity.
But he'd forgotten Stephanie Maria D'Alfonso. Not that he
hadn't been a good husband. The more he thought about it,
the surer he was: he'd been a good husband. Always been
kind and considerate, always afraid of hurting her. It had
begun that way. On their wedding night, he was appalled by
the pool of virginal blood. She hadn't made a sound, nothing
except for a stiffening of her body. He was so repelled by
what he had done that it was days before he touched her
again. And then he did so only because she asked if there
was something wrong. But he never quite got over the fear.
She seemed so delicate and vulnerable to him.

Poor little girl, the old Oliver sighed. *Poor little girl.*

Left without a mark. Unless you counted the two daughters. Two living children out of five.

Something was wrong with their children. The first one
was fine and healthy; the second, which everybody expected
to be even larger, was much smaller and weaker. The third,
a boy, was born dead; the fourth and fifth were boys also, tiny
premature things, whose chests quivered briefly and then
ceased.

T H E   F I R S T child, the healthy dark girl named Anna,
after the mother of the Virgin Mary, was born exactly four-
teen months after their wedding.

Oliver came home to find his wife in labor, his house swarming with excited people. His own cook and his mother-in-law's cook were taking a roast out the oven, giggling head to head. His two cousins-in-law and their husbands were playing mah-jongg in the living room. A white-dressed nurse he had never seen before bowed to him as she hurried past. His mother-in-law and the doctor were out of sight in the bedroom. His father-in-law poured him a whiskey just as the uncle who was a priest walked in the door. He'd brought a younger priest with him, "Cousin Umberto," he said in explanation. (Oliver did not remember him at all.) His wife's Aunt Harriet was arranging the silver service (a wedding present from his father-in-law) on the dining-room table. The big ornate urns steamed chocolate and coffee vapors across the room as she carefully arranged platters of small cakes and sandwiches.

"Why didn't somebody call me?" he asked. "Why didn't she?"

Nobody answered him.

After an hour or so, even the more distant relatives arrived. Oliver didn't know their names and didn't bother learning them. The children played outside in the yard, quietly and patiently. The women sat on the porch and watched them and drank coffee and chocolate. The men crowded into the living room and drank whiskey. Oliver went to the back porch, by himself, and waited. By ten o'clock the youngest children were fast asleep in all the corners, the women had fallen silent, and the men were pretty well drunk.

Oliver thought: They are her blood, all of them. Not one of them is mine. Except for that small thing being born in the bedroom. It is a pity that old woman my mother didn't live to see it. She would have been so busy here and so pleased.

The girl was born just before midnight. The women cried and the men had another drink. Oliver went to see his wife; she was asleep, heavily. "First labors are hard some-

times," the doctor said. Oliver shivered. He had hurt her
again, when he should have protected her. Before the nurse
bundled them away, he caught a glimpse of red-stained sheets.
He thought again of his wedding night, and he was sick with
shame. The fragile dark-eyed girl had had nothing from him
but blood and pain.

W I T H   T H E next birth, he arranged things more to his
liking. He went to a hotel and stayed for two days.

Because he knew he would never get used to birth. He
who had prided himself on getting used to anything. He who
had killed and felt nothing. He was terrified of a brown-eyed
girl. The weeks preceding the births were agony for him; he
could scarcely look at her. He found excuses to stay late at his
office; he found business to take him to Chicago or St. Louis
or Miami. As soon as he heard her labor had begun, he was
violently nauseated, and something more, something he
couldn't quite describe. Something to do with that bit of
flesh forcing its way out of her body, leaving a trail of blood.
As if he himself were destroying her.

She said nothing, but she seemed to understand. And to
sympathize. She kept the births as much apart from him as she
could. Because the last two children were premature, they
were not born at home. But neither time did he go to the
hospital with her. Once he was in Chicago. For the last one,
she didn't even wake him. She slipped out of her bed (in
which she now slept alone; weeks earlier he'd found an excuse
to sleep in another room) and telephoned her mother. Oliver
found her note in the morning.

Her monstrous thoughtfulness shocked Oliver. He felt
little beside it; he felt petty. He would have to do something;
he would buy something for her, something that was lovely

and very expensive. Women always liked jewelry, that's what he'd get. He left his office in the middle of the morning, a thing he never did, to look in the jewelry shops on Canal Street. He found nothing good enough for him. That afternoon he took the train to Chicago. He would find something there, something expensive enough to be worthy of her.

And he did. He came home feeling pleased and satisfied and at peace with himself. His wife's present was very, very expensive. Only—in later years, later decades he never could remember exactly what it was. He thought it was a long rope of pearls and a pair of diamond-crusted earrings in which two huge pearls hung like tears. He remembered his mother saying, "Pearls are tears." So that was what he got: pearls in payment for Stephanie's tears.

Or so he thought. He wasn't really sure.

It was the way everything was with her. He just couldn't remember.

YET WHEN she died, he was sick with grief. His hands and his feet turned cold, then lost all sensation. He let a match burn to his fingers, he smelled his own skin burning and felt nothing. And yet he was not sad in any recognizable way. He was—simply, suddenly—nothing. Nothing at all. She was buried with a big church funeral, choir and Mass and black cloth and stinking waves of incense and flowers. Her family wept openly, men and women together; someone shrieked, someone fainted, the air filled with sharp trails of ammonia-and-lavender salts. Her two daughters stood quietly, tearless, fingers twitching at the end of motionless arms. Oliver saw it all. Saw the sweat on the pallbearers' faces, the dust on their shoes from the white shell walk, saw the brown bruises on the edges of the white orchid coffin cover.

He himself wasn't present, not in his dry mouth, not in the dull pulsing ache at the back of his skull. The mouth wasn't really his mouth, the ache wasn't really in his head. His fingers touched none of the things his eyes saw. When he walked, he floated on air, though he could see his feet hitting solidly on the ground. Testing, he swung the tip of his shoe against the wall. He heard it and saw it but he did not feel the contact. When he dressed, his eyes told his fingers how to move. His two daughters were there, he paid no attention. His in-laws hovered around, he waved to them vaguely.

He felt like a doll or a model. A carved man. He got out of bed and put feet on a floor he couldn't reach. At breakfast he pressed wooden fingers together until little creases in the newspaper showed that he held it tightly. Then he lifted it in front of his eyes, and read. After breakfast a barber came to shave him; he did not trust his hands for that. He went to his office, tried to listen to what Lamotta was saying. "You decide." He couldn't even stay in the office, within the pressure of walls. He went for a walk, stepping hard on his nonexistent feet, walking quickly. With no place to go.

He noticed that someone always followed him. His in-laws were worried—or was it Lamotta?—they had given someone the job of trailing him about, of being sure he did not hurt himself. Oliver recognized the following figure. "Boy works for me," he said aloud and scratched his chin with a senseless finger. His name, his name? Yes, Robert Caillet.

Oliver stood, arms hanging at his side, and stared at him. Robert Caillet stopped too, making no attempt to hide. Oliver turned and walked on. He did not look back again. Just walked, until sweat streamed down his face, and his thigh muscles ached. Then he rested. Leaning against a telephone pole. Sitting on the chipped bench of a streetcar stop while he read the advertising: CCC FOR COLDS, as if he had never seen the words before. Sitting on a church's low concrete fence, watching doodlebugs work the earth under his feet. He never ate, he never seemed to get hungry. When the streets darkened, he checked the signs to see where he was, and how he could go home.

Robert Caillet was always there.

Oliver was never really sure how long this period lasted. There didn't seem to be any time to the days, or any real minutes to the hours. Only passing unmarked time. He no longer looked at his watch; he began to think that the numbers had disappeared from its face.

One dusk he did not stop. The street lights came on, yellowish and faint. It had been a cool day (A change of season? he wondered dully and without curiosity), and he was not yet exhausted. He had a plan, vaguely, vaguely. Nothing that he could put into words, nothing like that. He saw that he was walking down Carondelet Street, past the rooming houses and the shabby bars, past the sounds of aimless short-lived angers, of brawls begun and ended in a minute. He turned at Howard Avenue and walked toward the railroad station. More slowly now. This was a street of Negro whores; they lined the sidewalks, calling, gesturing at him. He stopped at one of the first. She was gangling and very black, her unstraightened hair knotted into little lumps skewered by yellow hairpins. Her green taffeta dress was torn at the seams and torn at the hem; she wore high-heeled red shoes.

She was dirty, he thought. There would be crabs on her, lurking in that kinky hair, in the folds of that black skin. There seemed to be blisters on her lips, but maybe it was just heavy lipstick. She was narrow-hipped and flat-breasted; her arms hung down in front of her body, pink palms turned outward. She was ugly and filthy and he found himself asking: "How much?"

"Seven dollars."

"Too much."

He looked down the wide street with its lines of whores

sitting on doorsteps, leaning in windows. Black skins, bright dresses.

He looked at the woman again. In the uncertain light, he couldn't see her face at all, just the whites of her eyes, dimly, and the glow of her gold-edged teeth.

"Let's go," he said.

The boy was waiting outside the door when he finished. He was much closer than usual; he had been worried.

Oliver would walk downtown now; he would get a taxi at the St. Charles Hotel.

Even in the cool night air, the smell of that room followed him. The sweaty skin, the motionless air, the bed that was musty as a snake nest, and barn-like with its reek of stale sex. He'd lain in it and rolled in it, and paid a two-fifty whore seven dollars for the privilege.

He held out his hands and looked at them. They seemed no different. He crinkled his nose, sniffing the reek of the whore, savoring it like perfume. Poverty and filth.

He began to walk more briskly. And somewhere during that walk, sensation came back into his fingers and his feet. Flooded back with a surge of real pain. When he finally reached the hotel and beckoned a taxi, he could hardly walk. His teeth were clenched and there were tears in the corners of his eyes.

"Wait," he said to the driver. He waved to the boy who still followed him, who stood not ten feet away. "We're going to the same place. You might as well come with me."

Silently, the boy got in.

Oliver leaned back against the seat, tapping his fingers together, delighting in the ripples of pain.

ROBERT

WHEN THE Old Man beckoned him into the taxi in front of the St. Charles Hotel, Robert Caillet was twenty-one years old, a tall thin Cajun from Belle River. He had no father, his mother died when he was twelve. He lived with cousins, sleeping on pallets in fishing camps, working on luggers until his hands were raw and his arms striped with welts from the man-of-war slime on the nets, working on oyster boats until his back and shoulders blazed with pain from the strain of the heavy oyster tongs. One day, on Théophile Beauchamp's boat, something hit his leg, and he looked down to see an ocean catfish wiggling against his shin, impaled by the big gig on its back. (He'd rolled up his pants to keep them dry.) The first thing he noticed was not the pain but the ridiculousness of it all. He could see himself standing there, mouth open, fish slapping against his leg.

He never went to the boats again. He hitchhiked to Baton Rouge. (Leg hurting all the way, ulcer forming, breaking, forming again. Months later it finally healed in a great flat white scar.) He worked as a shoeshine boy first, then a delivery boy. Because that drugstore was also a bootlegger's phone, he began delivering liquor. He came to Oliver's office in New Orleans on perfectly legitimate business. The bootlegger in Baton Rouge (whom Oliver supplied) sent down a bag of particularly fine crawfish—Robert walked into the office with a dripping thirty-pound sack of green crawfish and propped it in a corner. He spoke briefly with Maurice La-motta and then the two of them hauled the sack downstairs again and drove it directly to the Old Man's kitchen. Lamotta disliked crawfish, as did the Old Man, but they always received any present with extreme politeness. On the drive, trying to forget the hundreds of crawfish wriggling, fighting, eating each other in the sack, Lamotta talked to the young man. His politeness turned to real interest: did Robert Caillet want a job in New Orleans?

For who? Robert asked. Lamotta became vague: did it matter? Not so long as the money came to him, it didn't matter at all.

THE NEXT two years Robert Caillet drove bootleg liquor for the Old Man. For two years he saw him only from a distance, his business was all with Maurice Lamotta. By chance, that morning when the Old Man fled his office, Robert Caillet was waiting for a pickup. Since he was the only man there, Lamotta sent him out to follow. "Stay with him," Lamotta said, "just stay with him." Robert telephoned a couple of times that day, to say where they were. Lamotta was so impressed by his careful efficiency that he sent him back again the next day. And the next. Day after day. Robert wondered how the Old Man, in his fifties, could keep up that pace. He moved through the streets as if he were a walking doll, stiff-legged and tireless. Robert cursed and followed. He'd never known anything like this, but he wasn't going to let any old man wear him out, whatever sort of crazy energy he had. . . .

When the Old Man called him into a taxi, Robert was very tired. As much as the Old Man, he thought.

"You sleep at my house tonight," the Old Man said. "In the morning I have a job for you."

"Yes, sir." Robert was so weary that he almost forgot to telephone Lamotta with his report. It was the last one he had to do.

I N T H E years that followed, Robert did all sorts of jobs for the Old Man. He sold piece goods over the counter in the downstairs department store, sweating in the thick summer heat. He stood behind the desk in the Old Man's hotel being a proper night clerk, correct and polite because it was an expensive hotel. He made the rounds of the speakeasies and clubs that the Old Man supplied, doing nothing at all but watch, letting his presence be felt, as the Old Man had instructed him. He made small payoffs, particularly to the policemen on the beat. The Old Man always paid directly. "These precinct captains," he'd say, "you can't trust them to hand out any money." So Robert passed out the tens and twenties with a friendly smile.

And of course he still drove liquor. Once or twice a week, he took out a big touring car specially constructed to hold case after case of liquor on its extra-heavy springs. He liked driving, he liked being in the open, but he was always a little nervous. Other drivers laughed about their runs—good money for doing nothing, they said—but he never talked at all. Putting his mouth on it would have been bad luck, he thought.

One night all the Old Man's drivers had trouble; two were even arrested. Robert himself was stopped, but his car was empty. He lit a cigarette to cover his stomach's shaking and adjusted the crease of his hat to be careless and unconcerned. He had come very close—he had almost made his pickup, only some instinct had told him to circle the block.

He went directly to the Old Man.

"Money isn't worth anything any more," the Old Man

said. "That area was supposed to be taken care of, those people were supposed to be all right."

"It was the railroad tracks," Robert said.

Oliver snorted at the telephone he held in his hand.
"Any damn fool can tell a loaded car crossing a railroad
track. . . . For years I've been paying them not to see. Now
everybody gets greedy. Well, let me get those boys fixed up."

Robert knew the Old Man's reputation. None of his
boys ever stayed in jail, none of them were ever convicted.
Sometimes his information was so good—people called him
with news of an arrest, a favor that was always worth a reward
—that his lawyer would be waiting with the bondsman at
the police station by the time the arrested driver was brought
in. Sometimes a driver shook hands with the lawyer and the
bondsman and went off directly to pick up another load. The
Old Man could always fix things.

That morning, phone in hand, the Old Man said, half
in explanation to Robert, half to himself, "It gets very expensive this way and maybe I'll have to raise prices. But I still
have the only good liquor in the city and I'll still make
money."

Robert knew that was true. The imported Scotch and
gin and rum were exactly what the labels said. His unlabeled
whiskey, sold mostly to clubs, was good alcohol from small
distillers scattered all over the area. (Sometimes Robert
thought that every clump of trees in the hills and marshes
must cover a small still.) They were all permanent stills, the
Old Man knew the operators; there'd be no death or blind-
ness from their products. Robert was often sent to check on
them, and to be sure that the operators took a good stiff drink
of the stuff they were selling.

"Now I have to get the boys out of trouble." The Old
Man waved Robert away so he could telephone with only
the thin gray shadow of Lamotta standing beside him.

Robert saw the gesture and knew he should leave. But

he wanted to stretch his time, to stay in the dim brown office where dust motes swam in light streams under the dirty windows, where rusty file cases lined the walls. So he said (knowing the Old Man already would know), "I've got some more news. I know he's not one of your boys, but I heard Burt Phillips was killed around Napoleonville last night."

"Yesterday morning," the Old Man corrected him.

"Phillips had a shotgun," Lamotta snickered at the foolishness of it all. The Old Man's drivers never carried guns. They relied on nearly perfect secrecy, a constant change of routes, their own wild driving, and the Old Man's heavy bribery. If something went wrong—if they were stopped either by the police or by hijackers—they never resisted. They smiled and repeated what everybody in the business already knew: that the Old Man stood ready to buy back the carful of liquor.

The system worked well. In all his years of operation, the Old Man had had only two drivers killed, on the same night on the same road by three ambitious young men from a small town called Braithwaite. Robert remembered that— he'd just come to work for the Old Man. Within a week, these three men were thrown from a car directly in front of the Braithwaite Post Office. They had been slashed to death by razors, then neatly wrapped to lessen the bleeding. Lamotta urged the Old Man to send flowers to their funeral: "It would make the connection. It would look nice." "Sentimental," the Old Man said firmly. "People will know."

"There is no need for violence." The Old Man again waved Robert away. "When there is nothing you cannot smooth with money . . . Now, out, I am busy. . . ."

So, having nothing else to do, Robert Caillet stood at the front door of the department store under the small shabby marquee, with its row of burnt-out light bulbs like broken teeth along the edge. He looked up and down the tree-lined greenness of Esplanade Avenue and heard boats blowing on the river and smelled the slightly sour wind that came from its surface. He bowed to the few early customers, greeting them properly as he was supposed to do. An occasional young woman smiled at him warmly. This morning he was too upset to notice.

I T   W A S the Old Man who noticed Robert Caillet begin to grow. "You must be getting enough to eat, boy. Even a Cajun like you will grow if you feed him. . . ." Robert slouched and was ashamed of his added inches. He even tried to stop eating, but after a few days he got lightheaded and silly, and would burst into high-pitched giggles for no reason at all. Desperately, he went back to food. He never remembered being hungry like this before. But then there wouldn't have been as much good food in a whole week in his cousins' houses as he now ate in a single day.

Funny, he thought. All that time, when he was a child, there were people eating like this and he hadn't known about it. And because he hadn't, he hadn't believed it possible. . . .

And another thing. He noticed that he had begun to think. To puzzle about things. He hadn't done that before, but then he hadn't had anything to think about before. . . .

It was almost, he thought, as if he hadn't existed before he started to work for the Old Man. He'd just been scurrying around, like a dog, maybe, or a chicken, looking for food, scratching and grubbing for food. He hadn't really been alive in those years. He hadn't been anywhere at all.

One of the Old Man's amusements was to take Robert to lunch and then afterward to the tailor for a suit. "That sleeve's got to be an inch longer, how'd you manage that?" While the Old Man laughed, Robert comforted himself with the thought that he could probably have eaten twice as much as he actually did.

NIGHTS ROBERT did not work, he spent at his girl's house. Her name was Nella Beauchardrais; he'd met her when she came into the store with her mother six months before. Though Robert spent most of his free time at her house, he rarely saw her alone, and he never took her out alone. She was almost twenty, a respectable girl, and her family was extremely proper. Sometimes they went to the movies with her sister and her mother and a friend or two; sometimes they went on picnics; but mostly they sat on the porch or under the grape arbor in the back yard and played cards. Her mother drifted in and out, or watched from the back screen porch. Now and then her father appeared, a short bald man with a fringe of black hair over his ears and a starched white coat that rattled when he walked. He was a dentist, and his office at the side of the house was always open in the evenings. Some people, he said, liked to come after work and he had nothing better to do. He would have a few puffs of his cigar and go back to his work.

Robert was always bored. Nella was not particularly pretty, with her brown hair and brown eyes and thin figure. He did not like movies and he hated cards. He thought her mother silly and her sister stupid. He wondered why he found himself coming back and back.

This particular evening, Nella asked him: "Do you like my hair this way?"

"Yes," he said, "I do. Is it longer or shorter?"

"Oh, a lot shorter," she said. "I knew you wouldn't notice."

"I know it looks pretty."

She smiled and tapped her cards against her open palm. (He saw the Old Man tapping the phone into his open palm, annoyed at the world's stupidity.) "Robert, don't you ever think of your future?"

"No," he said. "No, I guess I don't."

"Couldn't you get a better job?"

He stared at the green grapes overhead. "The Old Man, Mr. Oliver, needs me to stay."

"You're related to him?" she asked.

He saw in her eyes that the Old Man was now known around town as a wealthy man. "No," he said firmly. "He's no kin of mine. But he's been kind to me."

"Later on," Nella said, "you can swing and pick grapes; they just hang down waiting for you. That's in the fall, when they're ripe."

"How nice," he said politely.

"But, Robert, seriously, wouldn't you feel better if you had a profession?"

"Me?" he said. "I feel fine."

"Like my cousin Noël Delachaise, he's an optometrist. Or like Daddy."

"Well," he said, "well, well, well, well."

He left early that night, he felt he was falling asleep. "Let's go to Milnebourg next Saturday."

She pouted. "You know Mama wouldn't let me go to any place like that."

"How about Spanish Fort? I'll borrow the Old Man's big car for Saturday."

She was still not happy. "Saturday is shoe clerk's night out."

He finally laughed out loud. "That's about where I belong."

They went on Saturday, her sister, her mother, and Nella. In the Old Man's big fancy new Packard they bumped along the New Basin Canal in the evening dusk. From the very moment he picked up the three women, Robert could feel boredom settling around like fog. It thickened in the jabbering vagueness of their talk until it was like a blanket wrapped around him. Dutifully he sat with them under the trees in the small lakeside park and listened to a military band pump away, tune hidden behind thumps of horn and drum. He walked with them—slowly back and forth in the cool lake breezes. He giggled with them as they stumbled over the old bricks and peered over the crumbling fort walls.

"Robert," Nella said, "let's go home. I've got a real treat for you."

"You have?" And what could that be, he thought dully, lulled by the evening.

"I made the most marvelous ice cream; do you know I spent all afternoon on the back porch turning that crank, just hours?"

"What else did you have to do?"

"Silly. The ice cream is marvelous and you'll love it. It's lemon-flavored."

They went home, obedient to her wish. While they sat on the front-porch swing—the grape arbor was infested with summer mosquitoes—he had a sudden thought. It horrified him, but he spoke it anyway.

"Nella," he said, "what do you think about getting married?"

From the smooth bland expression on her face he knew that she had been waiting and was satisfied with the words when they came.

"Well," she said, "anything as important as that, well, I will have to think about that."

"Okay," he said.

"Slang sounds terrible, doesn't it?" She made a little face. "I'll think it over for a week."

Another memorized line—she really was well prepared.

"You know how important so many things are when you are considering spending your life together."

He smiled at her formal phrase: "Like what?"

"Well," she said, "I don't want to hurt your feelings, Robert, but if we had children and they wanted to know what you did, how could I tell them you were a bootlegger?"

"Tell them I work in a department store. How about that?"

"How could I tell them you're just a clerk?"

"Then tell them I'm a bootlegger."

She sighed. "Maybe," she said, "you could get a promotion in the store."

"Okay," he said, grinning. "Where's the great ice cream?"

He stayed late that night, sitting in a corner of the screen porch with her, half hidden behind a wicker plant filled with ferns. Robert noticed that her mother seemed to have disappeared—once he had proposed. Was it because he was now admitted? Or because they felt they had trapped him and he was harmless. . . . Either way it was funny. It was the sort of story the Old Man would like too; he would tell him in the morning.

He sat rocking gently in a swing, in a soft summer night, eating lemon ice cream with his intended bride, and thinking of what the Old Man would find amusing.

He laughed out loud.

"What's funny?" Nella had snuggled very close.

"It's a kind of private joke."

"Well, I wish you'd think about me sometimes."

"You'd never guess the things I think about you."

Like: how had she and her mother communicated? How had her mother known? What was the signal, how was it done? Or was her mother hidden somewhere nearby, listening?

Yes, he thought, the Old Man was going to be very very amused at that.

T H E   N E X T two nights Robert had pickups to make. Then he took the train to Houston, his suitcase filled with neat stacks of twenty-dollar bills. The Old Man was paying off a debt. Robert delivered the suitcase to the man whose name and address he carried in his pocket, had lunch, and caught the next train back to New Orleans. Not once during the entire trip had he thought of Nella, but now, with the first swamps and shanties of the city outskirts, he could think of nothing else. Her thin figure drifted across the window shade, her face reflected in the glass.

It was still early—quite cool under the thick oak trees, acorns ripening on every twig—when he unlocked the porter's entrance and let himself in the office.

The Old Man was on the phone; he waved to Robert and went on talking. Lamotta peered out to say: "You had a letter yesterday, Robert. Messenger brought it." He took a square white envelope off the top of a filing cabinet. "Must be important. You got any big bets out?"

Robert tore open the envelope. Two lines, no signature: "I never want to see you again as long as I live."

The Old Man finished his phone call. "Everything go all right in Houston?"

"I delivered it like you said."

"No trouble?"

"No."

"Take the day off," the Old Man said. "You earned a rest."

"Okay," Robert said, and stuffed the letter in his pocket.

It was then a little before eight. He went directly to Nella's house and rang the doorbell. While he waited, he scratched his chin gently. He hadn't shaved on the train and his beard was beginning to itch in the heat.

The Negro maid opened the door, blinked at him, and slammed the door shut. He rang again, no one answered; only now and then the curtains moved.

He went home, shaved, and changed. And went back. Her mother stood directly in the door, voice shaking. "If you don't leave, I'll call my husband," she said. "My husband will throw you out."

Robert was pondering the difference in their sizes and wondering if that was possible when the door slammed again —so hard that he heard the knob fall off and go rattling along the floor inside.

"You've all gone crazy," he said to the door panels. "What the hell is going on?"

He lit a cigarette and waited. He sat in the swing behind the bank of ferns, moving gently, imagining Nella sitting next to him. Finally he went down the front walk to his car.

He finished his cigarette there, waiting for something to happen, but nothing did. The curtains didn't even move. He started the motor, noted mechanically that the gas was low, and drove off to have it filled.

It was a brand-new Studebaker; he'd had it less than a week. The Old Man liked to keep changing cars; it made identification difficult. Some were registered to him; most were in different names. This Studebaker now was in Robert's name. Not that that made any difference, Robert thought, it still isn't mine.

"Fill it," he said.

"This really is a car," the boy said. "New, huh?"

Robert nodded. "Do the windshield, kid."

"Got everything on it?"

"Yeah," Robert said, "it's got everything."

"Pretty expensive."

"Yeah," Robert said, "pretty expensive. With some people money's no object." He mocked the Old Man's remembered image. Him, he thought, him who held on to every cent that came through his fingers. Who rarely moved away from his desk or his phone. Who knew more angles and more ways to get things done . . .

Robert stopped right there, staring out through the shining clean windshield, not seeing anything, until the boy touched his shoulder. "Mister, you all right?"

"Yeah." He began to chuckle. "Kid," he said, "I have just been screwed, only I can't see why. . . ."

The boy's pimply thin face began to look worried. Robert handed him a couple of dollars for a tip, and when he drove off, the boy was still standing there, staring down at the bills.

Bet he gets rid of them quick, Robert thought, because he's got to be thinking they're counterfeit.

He drove by Nella's house once more, not stopping. Her father's car was parked in the driveway. So they'd called him after all. Was he sitting inside the door with a shotgun or was he providing a shoulder for Nella to weep on?

At the least, Robert thought, she could be crying. She could be that upset over losing him. . . .

He parked his car directly in front of the store, in the place always reserved for customers. He did not feel like waiting for the creaky elevator, so he ran the steps two at a time. Sweat poured off his body and his shirt turned sticky and wet across his chest.

At the top of the steps he paused long enough to pull off his coat.

"What's chasing you?" Evelyn Malonson said. She was the Old Man's secretary, a tall gray-haired woman with a beak nose.

"Where's the Old Man?"

"Mercy, Robert," she said, fluttering her hands vaguely across her dry flat chest.

I bet she doesn't sweat, Robert thought suddenly, and I bet she doesn't have tits, not any at all. . . . "Is he here?"

She smiled, thin gray lips sliding back across broad yellow teeth.

She'd eat her young, he thought, if she ever had any. . . .

"Come on, Molly—" he used her nickname to annoy her—"I'm in a hurry."

The yellow teeth kept on grinning. "He said he was waiting for you to come back."

The Old Man had his feet on the window sill as usual, and he was drinking a beer; the glass dripped frost in the heat.

"Help yourself." The Old Man pointed to a cooler.

"I don't want one."

"Then sit down," the Old Man said.

"Molly said you were waiting for me to come back."

"Yep," the Old Man said.

Robert took the letter from his pocket. "Did you see this?"

The Old Man looked shocked. "I do not meddle in your private affairs."

"The hell you don't," Robert said, "but look at it anyway."

The Old Man read seriously and carefully. "My sympathies," he said and handed it back.

"What happened?" Robert said.

"The course of love is never easy."

"Look," Robert said, "my girl has just walked out on me and her letter makes no sense."

"She sent back your presents too," the Old Man said; "they're out there."

"I never gave her any presents."

"A dresser set," the Old Man listed, "not too good, like the ones I sell downstairs. Three or four scarves—pretty nice ones, you must have got them at Holmes. A jewelry box."

"I'll be damned." There were half a dozen beers in the cooler. Robert helped himself to one.

"There is nothing so cooling as a beer on a hot morning."

Robert drank steadily, saying nothing. *He will tell me,* he promised himself, *and I will keep quiet.*

"She is very angry, no doubt of that," the Old Man said. "She is hurt and very angry."

Robert held his bottle up to the light and studied the yellow liquid. *Wait, wait.* . . .

"Because she feels she has been betrayed." It was surprising how softly the Old Man could speak when he wanted to. Softly and distinctly. Robert found himself straining and tensing, as if something surprising was about to happen, the walls fall down or a revolution start.

"Betrayed *and* deceived," the Old Man said, "when she found out you were already married."

Robert let the words drift through his ears and rattle around in his head. He sounded them to himself three or four times before he said: "I've never been married."

"She saw the license."

Robert put down his beer and went to sit on the corner of the Old Man's desk. "I figure you'll tell me," he said, "when you get around to it."

"She also saw the birth certificates of your two children."

Robert studied his knuckles. "How old are my children?"

"Three and four," the Old Man said. "They were born in Belle River, like you."

Robert said: "You're trying to make me lose my temper."

The Old Man nodded; his heavy bald head moved up and down against the dusty glow of the window. "I've always had a hot temper myself. Took me years to control it as well as you do right now."

"Don't put me off." Robert held out his hands and stared at them.

"You're saying the birth certificates and the marriage records are counterfeit?"

"I know god damn well they are."

"Yes," the Old Man said, "but very good ones."

Abruptly Robert found himself laughing. All of a sudden everything was funny. "How much did it cost?"

"Quite a lot," the Old Man said.

"Now tell me why."

"She believed so quickly," the Old Man said to the leaves outside the window. "She loved you as little as you loved her to get angry so easily with you."

Robert shifted his seat on the desk. "She sure didn't bother to ask me about it."

"Bootleggers." The Old Man smiled vaguely into the glare. "Everybody knows you can't trust them."

Robert leaned back on the desk and studied the corner of the ceiling. There were webs and large black spiders living up there. "You chase off my girl and I don't even get angry. I think I'm crazy."

"No," the Old Man said.

"I meant it. I was really going to marry her."

"I know that," the Old Man said.

Seated on the corner of the desk, Robert swung himself back and forth. Thinking: Nella shouldn't have given up so easily.

The Old Man was no longer looking out the window. He was staring directly at Robert, studying him carefully. Very carefully. Inch by inch.

"What's wrong with me?"

"Nothing at all." The Old Man's shoulders hunched forward a little; his intense scrutiny reached out and touched Robert's shirt, brushed over his shoulders.

"Look," Robert said, "I've never known you to do things without good reason. Now why the hell did you want to bust up my marriage?"

"Yes," the Old Man said, his shoulders still hunched, his eyes still thoughtful.

"Okay, why?"

"Because," the Old Man said softly, "I have two daughters and I want you for my son-in-law."

Robert sat perfectly still, staring at the Old Man. Finally, he said, "I think I'll go home."

The Old Man merely nodded.

TWO DAYS later, Robert left for Havana. There was a problem with the liquor people there. The shipments were not moving as smoothly as usual, and, by the time they reached the Old Man's boats in the Gulf, the cases were always short. "You see what's going on," the Old Man said. "See what you can do with it." Robert took a train to Miami and a boat from there.

Robert's business was done within two days—just a simple matter of money. That was always it. If Prohibition ever ended, Robert thought, a lot of people would be out of a lot of easy jobs. For the rest of the week he delayed, deliberately, not wanting to return to New Orleans. Most of the time he sat in Sloppy Joe's under the slow fans and drank Daiquiris. One evening he went out to the big casinos. He did not gamble; he never did. For an hour or so he watched the wheels, and the dice and the cards—all the things that flickered and danced. He sat at the quiet empty bar, admiring the women who passed slowly back and forth, all sorts of women, all elaborately dressed. He decided that he preferred the Latins because they moved much more slowly—Americans dashed by, striding like men. He also decided that sitting at this bar in the cool and fragrant tropical night was much better than Sloppy Joe's during the daytime. Finally he decided that he much preferred Scotch-and-soda to Daiquiris. Having made all these judgments, he was sitting quite contentedly, when a thin dark man in a white *guayabera* took the stool next to him. Robert turned slightly, raised his drink.

The bartender brought a glass of water, ice-filled to the brim. Robert lifted his eyebrows.

"I don't drink," the man said.

"The house never does, I guess."

The man smiled vaguely and politely. He had perfectly formed white teeth. "I hope you are not bored?"

His accent was not Spanish. Robert tried to identify it, could not. "I was enjoying myself."

"You do not play." It was more a statement than a question.

"No," Robert said, "no, I don't. I came to see the casinos because I've never been in Havana before. But I don't play."

The man sipped his ice water. "Will you accept chips from the house? We would be honored."

"No, thanks," Robert said. "I don't want to play with anybody's chips. But why me?"

"You are Señor Robert Caillet, I am right?"

Robert shrugged.

"You are here to do business for Señor Oliver, I am right?"

Robert shrugged again.

"We are happy to extend every courtesy to Señor Oliver's friend and associate."

Did the Old Man have money here too? Piece of a casino . . . outside the United States. Safe and secure. It would be like him. . . .

"I'm happy," Robert said. "I'm fine. I'm going to have two more Scotches, or maybe three, and I'm going to watch the girls go by and then I'm going home early, because tomorrow I've got to look at a sugar plantation my boss wants to buy."

The man took one more sip of his water and bowed very slightly. "If we can be of any assistance," he said, "please to let me know."

Robert saluted with his glass of Scotch.

Five minutes later, the girl joined him. She was beautiful, olive skin and blue-black hair: the house had noticed that his eye followed this type longer than any other. Fine. He'd be happy to drink and to admire her. . . .

He had his two Scotches. Then he had a third one. And then he told the girl good night and went home. Even as practiced as she was, she wasn't quite able to hide the surprise on her face.

He did not want her, a woman the house was supplying. He could find his own; he didn't need help.

"LOOK," HE told the Old Man, "no more jokes. Let my girls alone."

"When you have the right girl," the Old Man said, "I will encourage you."

"Yeah?" The Old Man seemed in high spirits and Robert was wary of that. "What was wrong with Nella?"

The Old Man sighed. "I'd hoped there'd be a girl in Cuba. . . ."

"There were lots of girls in Cuba, all whores. . . . What was wrong with Nella?"

"A silly little Cajun girl."

"I'm a Cajun," Robert said.

"Yes," the Old Man said. "Now, about Nella. She'll have a husband within three months and a child in a year. Maybe this time she will find a dentist who can go into practice with her father."

"Look," Robert said, "why do I take this from you? Will you tell me why I take this from you?"

"Because," the Old Man said, "you are young, but you have enough good sense to recognize what I am saying. Tomorrow I'll need you to drive. I'm going to the races."

At noon Robert had the Old Man's Packard waiting. It was the one he'd taken Nella driving in the evening he proposed. "This is a great car," he said.

"Expensive," the Old Man said, "so it should be. . . . We'll stop by my house first."

They'd done that often before. The Old Man wanted to change his clothes or leave some papers at home. This time, he made no move to get out. "The horn," he said to Robert.

Almost immediately a young girl came down the front steps, a black-haired girl, with large dark eyes and smooth olive skin. "My daughter Anna," the Old Man said. "Let's go now."

Robert parked the car and followed them to their box. The Old Man was listening to tips from a gambler he knew, nodding as seriously as if he were paying attention. Anna was looking about, silently. When she saw him, she smiled. Her teeth were slightly irregular and widely spaced, making her look even younger.

"Robert," the Old Man said, "show Anna the track. I'm busy here."

So Robert took her through the grandstand, the club-house, the paddock, letting her stare and be amused, keeping her carefully away from the worst of the crowd, like a child.

After that, Robert waited suspiciously. The next time they went to the track, almost a week later, Anna was not with them. Nor did the Old Man mention her again. He seemed to have gotten busy with something else.

O N E   M O R N I N G, almost a year later, Robert found the Old Man staring out the office window. "Get the car," he said shortly.

Robert asked Miss Malonson: "What's going on?"

"Warehouse," she said and went back to banging her typewriter.

The Old Man changed warehouses very often, to be safe, and he had been using this one for less than a week.

It was a shabby two-story corrugated-tin building on a weed-grown corner between a cemetery and a public park. It was actually the warehouse for a secondhand furniture store that the Old Man owned—moldy red plush sofas, iron bedsteads, platform rockers, lamps with painted shades. And in one far corner, the cases of liquor.

"Drive by," the Old Man said. "I want to see."

They saw. The sheet-metal walls had not burned but the wooden supports had, so the walls fell outward, and the roof collapsed inward. There was a truck from the furniture store parked outside, and two men poked around in the smoldering debris. As Robert and the Old Man watched, they grabbed a twisted piece of metal, pulled it, dropped it, stood shaking their hands and cursing. Their voices sounded very faint in the early morning.

"All right," the Old Man said, "I've seen enough."

On the way back Robert asked hesitantly, "Was there a lot of stuff in there?"

"Yes," the Old Man said shortly. "And I don't think this is all."

TEN DAYS later, one of the Old Man's boats exploded and burned in Chevalier Bay. It was fully loaded. The Old Man sent Robert on the seven-hour drive to Port Hébert, where the boat was usually kept.

"What do you want me to do?" Robert asked.

"Just look. And tell me."

"You don't think it was an accident?"

Lamotta, who stood holding the cash for Robert's traveling money, sighed deeply. "Like the warehouse?"

"Fools," the Old Man said. "I may have to hire help."

Lamotta sighed again.

"I don't like it any more than you do," the Old Man said sharply. "Once you get these people in, it's very hard to get rid of them again. . . . Maybe we won't need to."

"Sooner or later," Lamotta said sadly, "you will have to link up with the rest; that is the way the times are going."

The Old Man picked up his pipe and began methodically scraping the bowl. "You may be right, but we will see what Robert learns." He emptied the black ash into the wastebasket. "It was Mason and Guidry and Sylvester—maybe they added somebody at the last minute. Find out if it's widows or parents; tell them where to go, they'll be wanting their money."

For two days Robert tried to find out what happened. A dozen people had seen the flash, and the boat was gone. None of that made any sense to Robert. Boats exploded sometimes, the fuel lines or the bilge, but they didn't usually disappear completely; no matter how deep the water, there was always a piece of charred hull, or a body—the sharks weren't that bad. There had to be something left.

His first evening, Robert stood piously on the beach while the priest said a special prayer for the dead at sea, and blessed the waves and sprinkled them with holy water. The youngest children fixed candles to bits of board and set them to float off shore—their flickering course was supposed to lead to the bodies. But most of the lights went out, and the rest floated back and forth aimlessly, taking no particular direction.

Only one thing remained for Robert to do—to cruise over the bay himself, looking. Not that he expected to find anything, but he had to do a complete job for the Old Man. And that didn't mean standing on shore with the crying women and the little children and their holy candles. That meant going out to look over the place for yourself.

He hired the biggest and the newest lugger, the *Jolie*, paying triple the price of a good day's shrimping. Robert had not been on a boat since he left his cousin's house years before, but the motion of the rough wood deck was still familiar to his feet. His stomach went tight and hard and he had to keep reminding himself that this time was different, this time he had money in his pocket and the boat worked for him.

They went out early in the morning: Robert and Aristide Landry, the boat's owner, and his son Gus.

The wheelhouse reeked of fish and bait and gasoline and the tar of nets. Robert took a wood crate and set it up on the open deck.

I wouldn't have even noticed that once, Robert thought. I wouldn't have smelled it at all. But I'm not like that any more. Now I'd rather sit in a Havana casino and watch women pass by and admire the set of their ass and smell their perfume. I've forgotten the days on the boats when my back and shoulders ached and my hands always burned, and my eyes always stung with sun and wind and water.

He held out his hands and studied them.

The calluses didn't last, he thought. And they didn't leave a mark. His hands were dirty—boats were always dirty—but they were as smooth and clear as anybody's. Nails trimmed and filed, cuticles clipped; sometimes I wear polish too.

The engine vibrated beneath the deck.

Once I wouldn't have noticed that, Robert thought. And it's better not to. Once you start to notice, you're weaker. Me, for instance. I couldn't go back to the boats. I couldn't do it.

Robert was staring at his dirty smooth hands, holding them up so the sun fell on them, when he had a sudden thought. It was the Old Man who had changed him, who had made him the way he was. It was the Old Man who had blocked off his past behind him.

For a moment, the image of the Old Man danced in the sun, over the seaweed-littered bay. The Old Man sitting at his phone. The Old Man saying: "Nothing that hasn't got

a price. Nothing at all; only you've got to find it. Find it."
The Old Man who could order and arrange things, play God.

Robert began smacking his right fist into his left palm,
hard, trying to think of something to hit in the sudden anger
that ran over him. There was nothing. Nothing at all. Except
Gus coming out of the wheelhouse.

"What the hell do you want?"

Gus looked startled. "He wants to ask you something."
He jerked a thin shoulder toward the wheelhouse.

"Then let him come out; it stinks like shit in there,"
Robert said.

Gus scurried off. He was small and thin. Robert thought,
*Probably didn't have enough to eat. Like me. I didn't start
to grow until the Old Man started feeding me. . . . God damn
the Old Man. . . . They look so pathetic when they're thin
like that. Eyes too big for the faces, a kind of shrimp look,
hunched and wary. . . . I looked like that once, until the Old
Man took me over. Nothing money won't do. Fill out a boy,
turn a child into a man. Aching muscles stretched tight over
thin bones—change them into smooth muscles flexing easily
over heavy bones. Scrawny boy into powerful man. Feel the
muscles under the shirt, lift the cloth; women love to feel
muscles move like that: Oh, Robert. . . . Whole thing courtesy of the Old Man. He fed it, he grew it, and to hell with
him.*

Aristide came to the deck, leaving Gus at the wheel. "It
stinks," he said, "but what can I do about it? Where you want
to go, cap?"

"I want to find some wreckage. Or something."

"Everybody," Aristide said, "they point to a different
quarter. Some say here, some say there, and there is maybe
twenty miles between. Which way do we go looking, cap?"

Robert stood up. "Yeah, I noticed how everybody saw
something different. What about a channel out there? Any
particular course a boat'd be likely to take?"

"She drew nothing. She needed no channel," Aristide said quietly, "even loaded."

"Yeah," Robert said, "that's right. She was made that way. . . . Well, let's cruise back and forth for as much gas as you got."

"You tell me which way, cap. You paying for the time."

For a while Robert watched the water, dutifully. He saw endless bits of seaweed, loaded with bright orange berries, floating just under the water. Two sheets of newspaper. A couple of orange halves and a long ribbon of kelp, torn up from deep water. One of the candles the children had launched from the beach; the *Jolie*'s wake overturned and sank it. (Maybe, he thought, it would have better luck finding the wreck underwater; it hadn't done too well on the surface.) He saw two porpoises, arcing and splashing; they seemed to be following the boat. And that was all.

His eyes got tired. He moved his crate into the small shade of the wheelhouse and propped his back against the wood.

All morning they crisscrossed back and forth, methodically searching. Finally Robert felt the bow come about and settle on what had to be the homeward course. He went into the wheelhouse.

Aristide said, "You noticed, huh, cap?"

"I been on boats before."

"You have?" Gus said. "You have?"

"A long while ago." Robert stared out the dirty glass at the level gray water. *I did what I came for. I tried and I got nowhere.* "Too bad," he said, "nobody agrees where the explosion was. That would have been a help."

"Me, I saw nothing," Aristide said.

Too quick. . . .

He was too quick. Robert did not let a muscle change in his face. He waited, eyes following the low dipping flight of a sea gull just beyond the bow. "Even so, you'd think we'd find something."

"You hired the boat, cap," Aristide said. "You picked the spot."

"Everybody said . . . only I'm beginning to wonder."

"I didn't see nothing," Aristide said.

"I didn't say you saw anything." Robert leaned forward, rubbing his finger on the dirty glass. Smooth manicured finger moving up and down. "The boat's gone, and the men, they're dead. Those women crying back there are real enough, they got a death and they know it. I just don't think we been anywhere near the boat. Maybe she didn't get to the bay, maybe it happened outside, maybe almost anywhere. And maybe there wasn't any flash. Seems to me like too many people saw it, too many people on the beach in the middle of the night, looking out to sea."

"Me, I saw nothing," Aristide repeated. "What the others say is their business."

"Sure," Robert said, "sure, sure."

"Cap," Aristide said, "you can't come to a place four days later and find stuff lying around. We got tides, we got winds."

The boy's head jerked aside, but he said nothing.

He's brighter than his father, Robert thought. *He spotted that slip.*

Robert's finger went on rubbing the glass. *I'll get a ring when I get back to town. With a diamond. That would look good. Wear it on the right hand or the left?*

Robert said: "*Four* nights ago, when everybody was telling me three."

Aristide turned to look at him. "I meant three nights, me."

Robert shook his head. "No, you didn't," he said. "That boat was scheduled to pass here four nights ago. With every-

body saying three, we figured it was just running a day late—
that happens sometimes. But I don't reckon this one was
late. . . ." When the Old Man heard, the news was already
twenty-four hours old.

Robert whistled softly through his teeth. "Twenty-four
hours. Chance to clear the area before anybody came looking."

"You gone out of your head," Aristide said. "The sun,
my mama said, does that sometimes."

Robert said: "Everyone back there in Port Hébert, they
know. And nobody's talking, because they're scared or paid
off or both. They never would have said anything, just gone
on lighting their candles and saying their prayers, except for
one thing. They know those three families are entitled to
some money from the Old Man."

The *Jolie* slipped to the dock, rubbing against the line
of old tires; the engine idled, reversed, coughed, and stopped.
Robert stepped carefully from the toe rail to the wharf. He
didn't want to tear the seams of his pants. "Well," he said,
"you can tell everybody I'm not as stupid as they thought.
Tell them I can smell a lie too—that's what my mama said.
She was a whore." Aristide's eyes flickered; Robert laughed
again. *"Enfant garce,"* he said, "that's me. Now I got those
three women to see. They'll get their money, they earned it."

Robert walked up the wharf to the shell road where his
car was parked. There were men on the other boats; they
stared at him from behind the nets they were mending, from
engine hatches where they worked. He ignored them all.
He'd guessed the trick too late; he'd been a fool.

Now he had to see the women. There was one in particular, the only young one. Wife or sister—she had pale
yellow eyes under black brows. She'd been crying so long
that those eyes stuck out, glazed and swollen, so distended
that there seemed no lid. The whites were all red veins,

blended one into the other, into a milky pink, out of which tears formed, ran to the edge, and spilled over, steadily.

He wanted to leave Port Hébert, right now. He wanted to get away, to feel the road passing under his car. But he had to see the women. He had to go into the houses with their whitewashed fences and sit at oilcloth-covered kitchen tables and tell them how to collect their money. The Old Man paid well; that was why people worked for him.

He parked his car at the first house, walked down the narrow white shell path between the tall oleander trees, with their bright round flowers and long shiny leaves. When he was a boy, he'd heard stories of women who'd killed their husbands with the poisonous bark and leaves, mixed into a gumbo, where the heavy taste of red pepper covered everything.

Those three men lived in a poison grove and died on a boat.

That was the house. Behind its rusted porch screen, he saw many vague shapes moving; when he reached the steps, all talk stopped. There was only somebody crying deep inside the house. Oh God, he thought, how can she still be crying?

Smells from the house drifted out to him. Sweat and dirt and oil, and bad teeth rotting in their heads, the smell of beans and rice and fish and shrimp and poverty. . . . That had been familiar to him once but not any more. For a moment he hesitated, his hand on the screen door, his face properly solemn. Good God, he thought; good God, they stink.

Now the smell of tallow, of candles burning inside. On that little altar. He'd seen it the last time he was here—a six-inch shelf stuck up in a corner. In the center a small figure of the Star of the Sea. All around her, candles flickered in their red glasses, wicks swaying in their puddles of oil, shifting and uncertain.

He'd probably have to see the damn altar again. These people seemed to think there was something special about it. What good was the Star of the Sea when you were running liquor?

And they'd lied, every one of them. But it didn't matter. He only had to tell the Old Man that it did look like somebody was moving in. Somebody who wouldn't be bought off—the Old Man would have to send for the professionals now. And that meant a lot of trouble. . . .

He opened the screen door and stepped inside the porch. Jesus God, he thought, it's her. He found himself staring into the tear-ruined yellow eyes.

R O B E R T F I N I S H E D as quickly as he could, hurrying through his expressions of sorrow. To each woman he gave the same address, the same explanation. "You understand," he repeated over and over again. "You come to New Orleans, to this address, and the money will be there for you. I don't carry any money with me. You come to the address right there on the paper."

It was a butcher shop on Frenchmen Street. When they came, the butcher would telephone Miss Malonson: "The veal leg you ordered is ready and waiting." Malonson would tell Lamotta, and Lamotta would send the cash by one of the boys in the office. The whole thing took less than half an hour, and the messenger always brought back a veal leg for the Old Man. He liked it roasted with garlic and rosemary.

The Old Man never went near the shop. He kept himself far away from the operation of his business.

Robert left Port Hébert in the early afternoon. The narrow shell road was rough and very dusty. He began sneezing, quick spasms. He wiped his nose on the back of his hand

and glared at the sky. And in that stretch of sky he saw a huge eye. *That woman's eye, Jesus God I see it everywhere.* It was big enough to fill the whole north, it was yellow and swollen. God damn woman crying like that. Sitting by her altar, crying like that. Because her man got killed running liquor. What did she think he got paid for? . . . Just that big eye. Grieving.

A flock of chickens in the road. He braked and slammed his hand on the horn. The flock scattered, screeching. A woman poked her head out the house window. He grinned at the frizzled gray head and toothless jaw. *"Comment ça va?"* he yelled.

She'd been washing dishes, she tipped the pan of water over the window sill into the yard. The chickens rushed over to peck for specks of food on the wet ground. The last skinny body flicked into the yard; Robert waved and drove off.

Looked like my cousin, the old bitch. If she knew I had a job, I'd be hearing from her soon enough. "Oh, *cher,* you got to give us a little something. We took you in when you *maman* die and we shelter you and we raise you like one of our own. . . ."

Now that, Robert admitted, staring down the white shell road, was absolutely true. They'd treated him no different from their own kids. Only he'd resented it. Maybe because of that nameless man who'd sired him.

The sharp sweet smell of a chinaball tree blew in the window. There it was, thick trunk and small round top. Almost every dooryard had one. They trimmed the limbs back sharply every year, for firewood. It wasn't the best fuel, but it was cheaper than the charcoal they burned in the small grate at his cousin's house, on winter nights when the mist came off the slick slimy glassy surface of the bayou.

He shivered and hunched his shoulders under his shirt. That was years past, why think of it now? He drove faster, deliberately closing his mind to everything but the stretch of white ahead of him and the dust rushing up behind his wheels. After an hour or so, he reached the state highway. The driving was easier now.

His wheel pulled strongly to the left. A flat. He stopped and got out. The cement of the road burned through the soles of his shoes. Son of a bitch, he thought slowly, son of a bitch. . . .

He took off his tie, tossed it on the seat. He rolled up his sleeves and he got the tire from the back. He kicked at it; it seemed firm enough, so he got out the jack, fitted it together.

He worked furiously. *I never did change a tire that fast; what the hell's got into me?*

Take a leak while I'm stopped anyway. . . . He climbed down the steep slope of the road and stood, waiting. Nothing. *Why am I so edgy I can't even piss?*

He went back to the car. It wasn't until he had shifted to second that he saw what he had instinctively felt—why he had been so nervous. A car behind him, quite far behind him, had stopped when he stopped.

He shifted to high, watching the rear-view mirror. They started with him. They were coming up very fast. He chewed the inside of his cheek, and wished he had a gun. He had nothing, except the speed in the Ford's special engine. You can outrun anything, the Old Man insisted. But open up slowly. It's a light car, you've got to remember that. Don't race it off the road. . . .

Robert blew through his teeth in a soundless whistle.

He accelerated, fast as he dared, still watching behind him. The pursuing car swerved and stopped. Two men jumped out and ran to the side of the road. They stared at the hyacinth-littered water; one man edged his way down the slope.

Abruptly Robert understood. Around town, the Old Man had a reputation for dealing in drugs. *Son of a bitch, I am a lucky son of a bitch. They thought I left something*

*there. They thought it was a drop, when I went to piss. They
thought I had it hidden in my tire. . . .*

The Ford skittered on the road. Too fast. He released
the accelerator. The other car was out of sight in the dusty
heat haze. They were hunting very carefully. Again he accelerated, again the car shivered. Too much engine. The Old
Man was wrong. Without a full load of liquor, this Ford
didn't have enough weight to hold it on the road.

He wanted to urinate, badly, the whole bottom of his
belly was burning. He took one hand off the wheel and
rubbed his stomach. That only made the pressure worse.

He concentrated on his driving, trying to see exactly how
high he could push the speedometer needle before the car
seemed ready to leave the road.

"Fly, man," he said aloud. The sound of his own voice
comforted him. "Fly right in a tree." No trees here to land in:
just saw grass and cattails and now and then a small low bush,
killed by the brackish water, its dead twiggy arms stuck
straight up. He said aloud: "Never find a dead man back in
there, if they sank him. Not this time. And not me."

He was nearing the city. A couple of cars appeared ahead
of him. He passed them both with a blast of his horn. The
third car was a big tan Studebaker; he swung around it carelessly. He didn't notice the approaching car until it passed,
missing him by an inch or so. Then all he saw was a mass
that flashed by and all he heard was a puff of a scream. A puff
like a bit of smoke passing, here and gone.

"Sainte Vierge," he whispered aloud, "Mother of
God . . ."

Down the inner side of his pants he felt a running
spreading warmth. With the sudden release of pressure, he
shivered all over. The car jumped to the left, two wheels
went off the pavement. It tipped and bounced, springs bot-
toming, something dragging, metal screaming. He slowed,
eased the car back on the pavement. A few more minutes

and he realized there was a puddle under his feet and a spreading wet stain on the seat beside him.

By nine o'clock he was in New Orleans. For some reason, he began to count the churches he passed, Episcopal, two Baptist, Christian Scientist. *That makes four churches in three blocks on Claiborne Avenue. Isn't that interesting? Must have more churches on this street than any other. Except maybe that stretch of Canal where the Old Man lives. To hell with the Old Man.* He turned into his street, saw the garage where he kept his car, gates sagging open, just the way he had left them. How long ago?

He lived in the upper apartment of a small duplex. As he climbed the back stairs, his landlady, standing on her little screen porch, yelled up to him: "You sick or something, Mr. Caillet?"

He took a deep breath before he answered. "I'm just tired. I been working and I'm just tired."

"You want something?" Her voice was all interest. She loved to mother things, from her plants to her sick cats. "You want me to bring you some ice?"

It was a point of great pride with her. She had an electric refrigerator. His apartment had only an icebox. "There's ice up here," he said. "Thank you."

He went inside before she could race up the steps after him.

He loosened his pants and let them drop to the kitchen floor. He stripped off his shirt and his underwear.

A white enamel coffeepot stood on the stove. He'd used it, when? Last week. He lifted the top: only dry brown grounds. There were a couple of dirty cups in the sink, and a yellowish stain on the drainboard tile. What would that be? He didn't remember anything yellow. He opened the icebox door. Quick sour odor, sharp and nasty. Green-and-black mold climbing up the white porcelain sides.

Got to get this place cleaned up.

In the dining room the bare wood floors were hazy with dust. Three chairs circled the table. Shouldn't there be four? . . .

The whole place was hot and stuffy. He began opening windows. Why are all the shades drawn? That woman downstairs, she must sneak in and pull them, to save her precious furniture. This room now, all wicker, loose ends to spear you if you leaned back in any chair. The lamp table had a cracked glass top, twisty line like a hair curling across the corner—when would it break? And that vase full of pink feathers . . .

He picked it up, feathers bobbing gently, sifting out little trails of dust, and put it in the living-room closet which was completely empty except for spider webs. He studied them for a minute, counting the white egg cases. Never saw so many in my life. When they hatch out, they'll fill the house.

Carried out by spiders . . . he could see himself borne along on their hairy backs, like a football coach in triumph. Maybe I could train them. . . .

With all the windows open, there was a sudden quickening of air, a cross-draft ran over his naked skin. He'd really got sunburned—he touched his face gently—he wasn't used to that much exposure any more. He looked at his arm. Covered by a shirt sleeve, he had not burned there. I've got pretty white skin, he thought, peeping through the maze of black hair; my old man must have been white after all.

(He'd had one big fight with his mother, and him a little boy still: "I betcha my father was some old nigger. Betcha anything." His mother fetched him a slap on the side of the head that cut his lip and sent him spinning into the wall. She walked away while he howled at the sight of his own blood. At the horror of what he had said. At the fear of everything that glared at him from all the corners everywhere.)

Robert looked at himself in the bathroom mirror. How

can you shave over that sunburn? There's the fancy shaving bowl the Old Man gave you.

He lifted the bathroom screen and dropped the bowl into the yard. To hell with the Old Man.

He looked at his watch. It was now ten o'clock.

"I quit," he told his watch's second hand as it stuttered around the dial. "I'm going to find another job."

He kept his liquor in the clothes closet. The bottle of bourbon was missing. His landlady had got it again.

And what was left? Not much except an unopened bottle of Chivas Regal. He put that carefully in the middle of his bed, reached for the telephone, and dialed the Old Man's house. A girl's voice answered—he'd almost forgotten the Old Man's daughters.

"This is Robert Caillet." He spoke slowly to be sure she understood. "I want you to give your father a message for me."

"He's right here," she said. "I'll call—"

"No, honey." That slipped out; it wasn't proper, he wanted to be so correct. "Tell him I'm coming over. That's all."

He hung up. Dialed another number. "Betty, please." He waited again, eying the Chivas Regal bottle.

"Hi di doodie . . ." A sharp, metallic voice.

"Baby doll, I've got a bottle of Chivas Regal sitting right next to me."

"Oh, Robert," she said, "how cute of you to call."

From the tone he guessed her mother was close by. "What about tonight?"

"I think I'll go to bed early, Robert," she said. "Mother and I are both tired."

"About an hour?"

"Yes, I suppose so."

He lay back on the bed; he had plenty of time. She lived not five minutes away, on Claiborne Avenue. It was handy having a girl in the neighborhood. The past two days were slipping far back in his memory; the pounding blood was washing them away.

He parked his car, as he always did, in front of a vacant lot on Jena Street. Carrying the bottle in a paper bag, he walked to the big white raised house at the corner. There was a gate, always open, into a yard full of hibiscus and paper plants and ginger lilies with drooping pink flowers. A wet elephant-ear slapped his cheek. Damn things dripped no matter how dry the weather. . . . He stood next to a crêpe-myrtle tree, his fingers absent-mindedly fingering its smooth trunk, waiting for the basement door to open.

HE'D COME here first, a year ago, with a guy he'd met at the track, Al Stevens. Al hung around the stables, a short dark-eyed young man, who worked at City Hall and was a fourth cousin of the mayor. "You really want something, my friend, I have got it for you. You never had anything like this."

That was how he met Betty.

ROBERT WONDERED why he stood so patiently in the darkness. You could always find a girl: at a speakeasy, at the movies, waiting for a streetcar, even walking down the street. He'd done that once—on Girod Street; he went there to a bookie once in a while. He passed a woman, green dress, black hair in the new short cut. There was something . . . he circled the block, so that he could approach facing her. He walked by casually. He was sure. He spun on his heel and followed her. She stopped to look in a window, and he stopped beside her. "That's a Greek restaurant," he said. "Maybe you like Greek places?" She smiled slowly. She was the woman, he remembered, who said she was forty-five and a grandmother. He didn't believe her—she was more like twenty-five. Women had funny kinks sometimes, and that was one of them.

But why, when there were so many women in the world, was he standing in a wet garden, waiting for a door to open? What was so special about her that he brought a very expensive bottle of real Scotch? Chivas Regal, people would pay a lot for that. More than a musty basement and a lumpy couch, a couple of grimy glasses, and maybe, only maybe, some ice, if she'd been able to smuggle it from the kitchen.

There was something with that couch; they rode it together like a live thing. His loins throbbed and ached, excruciatingly, demandingly. "It hurts so good, honey," he whispered, "hurts so good." He saw that his body was glowing, like waves at night, blue bright and shining on all its surfaces. The glow shivered and flickered until it exploded and poured off, surf-like, and he spun and shook and balanced and came to the end of his breath. And in the quiet there for a moment he was the only man in the world, perfect and alone.

You horny bastard, he told himself, shifting his weight from foot to foot. He felt his way to the side of the house, leaned back against the clapboards. When the door finally opened, he did not move. Let her wonder. She hesitated, then stepped into the dark. Left foot, right foot, on tiptoe against the mud, robe pale blue in the light. Uncertain, never had to wait before. The hundreds always pounded eagerly forward: Open your door the least crack, we'll rush in. . . . Let her wait, stand there, little toes sinking deep in the mold. Nobody ever raked up the leaves. Season after season gathered soft and yielding underfoot. Sexy leaves. Full of worms. Male and female worms undulating up and down together.

Another step, long robe hitched up now. Never saw her venture so far out in the garden. Ruin those slippers and how will she explain that? I got muddy slippers chasing the cat, Mama. . . . Did she have a cat? No dog, no barking. She whispered "Robert?" Too low, too soft. Wait a bit. "Robert, Robert are you here?" Looking toward the place he'd always stood, never thought to turn around. "Robert!" That was nice and loud. Good for her. Talk to her now, watch her jump: "Boo, you pretty creature!"

LATER, AS he got into his car, he remembered: the Old Man expected him. He sat in the dusty Ford and squinted along the dark street. All the overhead lights had little colored halos, and his head sang with the receding tides of alcohol. He felt light and floating and very thirsty. The car's engine sputtered in the night damp, hesitated, and settled down to a shivering rattle. The clutch didn't engage, the gears grated, stuck. He jammed his leg down, silencing them. The back of his head twitched. One of his ears was moving; it was dancing and wiggling on the side of his head. Maybe, he thought, the Old Man's given me up. If the house is dark, I'll go on home.

Every light in the Old Man's house was burning. Robert looked up the terraced steps into the blazing glass-paneled front door. All that, he giggled, for me. I'll leave in a burst of glory.

He began to climb the stairs. *Never knew there were so many of them; my ears are popping like I'm swimming under water. . . .*

The moment his foot touched the tiled surface of the porch, the front door swung open.

"We were waiting for you," Maurice Lamotta said.

Robert stopped, in mid-step, his hands dangling in front of him. "I didn't expect you'd be here."

"We've been waiting for almost four hours."

Robert squinted at the thin narrow head, the expressionless face, the fragile body in its striped seersucker suit. "I've had a hard day," he said slowly. "I am just plain not used to getting killed."

Something focused at the back of Lamotta's brown eyes. Mockery. Surprise. Maybe only interest. "It does make a difference," the thin lips said. "As a matter of fact, it can be quite annoying."

"To hell with you," Robert said.

The Old Man sat in the big blue armchair by the imitation fireplace, filled now with dried flowers. There was a highball on the table next to him, sweating away in the heat, almost untouched.

"I know I'm late," Robert said. "And I quit."

The Old Man's eyebrows went up a fraction of an inch. Silently he pointed to a chair.

Robert ignored him. "I don't like being chased by people. It makes me nervous. And I didn't find out anything except that everybody's lying: I don't even know where your god damn boat went down. So I'm going to find another job, me."

He stopped, startled for a moment at the Cajun in his speech. Thought I was farther away from that. . . . Thought I had some courage too, but I don't. "I'm alive, and I quit. Jesus, not even a gun. You know what that's like?"

"A gun would do no good," the Old Man insisted. "They are much better at that than you are. A gun would only make you feel that you could fight."

"I been in it without a gun," Robert said, "and me, next time I want one." There was the damn Cajun again.

The Old Man pointed again to the chair. "How can I guess what happened?"

He was so tired. Maybe if he sat down for a minute. "Just so you stop pointing your finger," he told the Old Man. His back hurt, and his eyes felt like they were jutting out. *Damn woman. Should never have gone there.*

His fingernails were dirty. How could he get dirty hands in bed with Betty? "I'll tell you what happened."

When he finished, the Old Man said nothing. He drank his highball slowly and the condensation fell on his lapel. Lamotta sat motionless, too.

"So I quit," Robert repeated.

The Old Man did not seem to hear. He stared into his empty glass, now and then shaking the ice, listening carefully to the little crisp rattle. Robert faded from anger to annoyance to boredom to, finally, a fitful drunken sleep.

After a while, through his doze, he was conscious of the Old Man and Lamotta talking, arguing. Of Lamotta saying, "You are wrong." Of the Old Man saying, "I'll call right now—what time is it in New Jersey? Louis won't mind waking up for a deal like this."

Robert heard the Old Man walk heavily through the hall to the telephone and begin jiggling the receiver impatiently. Robert shifted, opened one eye. Maurice Lamotta was staring at him, his face twisted with anger. "You've just cost the Old Man a very great deal of money, do you know that? He is getting out of the liquor business."

"Me? I just quit."

"He won't let you quit."

"Look," Robert said, "he don't tell me what to do. I can always go back to fishing."

"And I hired you." Lamotta went to look out the night-blinded window.

Robert yawned loudly. *Fish, fish, see all the pretty fish.* He was dozing again when the Old Man came back.

"That's done," the Old Man said. "I was sure Louis would be interested."

"Do you know how much that will cost you?" Lamotta said.

The Old Man fixed himself another drink. "Bootlegging will not be with us forever, my friend. I see the end of it and so do you."

Lamotta sniffed. "One day I will figure out exactly what you have lost by quitting because of a fight."

The Old Man chuckled, a dry humorless sound. "My friend, you know better."

"These people are amateurs." Lamotta was actually pleading. "You could take care of them."

"Mossy," the Old Man said, and for a minute Robert did not recognize Maurice Lamotta in that name, "it would not be easy, and there would be," he hesitated, looking for the word, "some trouble."

"And Louis," Lamotta was still arguing, "what do you think Louis will do?"

"He will probably kill every one of them."

"Right now Louis is thinking you've turned coward."

"Why do I care what Louis thinks? I'm not in the liquor business, I don't need a reputation. Let Louis have the profits and the troubles. Let him have the last few years. . . ."

"You sold too cheap." Lamotta almost choked on the words.

"Mossy, my friend, you forget there's money in legitimate business. I am now respectable."

Lamotta sighed, almost a sob.

The Old Man said: "I would not risk the boy, you understand that. No amount of money would make me risk his life again."

ROBERT WOKE up with a lurch, almost jumping out of his chair. The Old Man sat in the same spot, but there was breakfast on a tray beside him, and the room smelled of coffee. At the window, daylight was beginning—the faint green flush of the east, beyond the puffy crest of a palm tree.

"Why didn't you wake me up? You let me sleep all night."

"It's more peaceful with you asleep."

He looked vaguely sad, Robert thought, or was he just tired? "I'm going home."

"Sit down," the Old Man said.

"I quit."

"You did not quit," the Old Man said. "This afternoon you will be on a train to Chicago; tomorrow you will be on a train to Denver."

"I'm tired traveling."

"You stay here," the Old Man said, "and you will get killed."

Robert just stared at him, facts slowly sinking into his consciousness.

"I've paid a lot for your safety," the Old Man said, "and I do not propose to waste my money." He got up slowly. "You heard us last night, and contrary to what Lamotta believes I do not like to lose money. . . . Now, shave if you want to, but don't leave the house. I'll wake my daughters and have them pack."

Robert blinked at him. "Daughters?"

"We're all going on a vacation," the Old Man said. "The school year is almost over, the sisters at the convent will not mind if my girls miss the last month."

"I've got a hangover and I don't feel good," Robert said. "Where are we going?"

"Next time don't drink so much because you're scared," the Old Man said. "We're going to see the West. The whole West; maybe I'll buy a ranch."

THEY SAW the whole West, as the Old Man promised. From Montana (where he did buy a ranch: "I'd like to go hunting sometimes") to Arizona where they dutifully surveyed the Rio Grande. For months they toured methodically, jarring on horseback over rock-littered ground, on muleback over trails so narrow Robert closed his eyes against dizziness, on narrow-gauge railways to abandoned mine shafts, on sleek fast trains that raced hour after hour through empty stretches of nothing at all. Robert remembered endless look-alike mountains and on their slopes flowers called columbines whose skinny ugliness appealed to him strongly. (I am going queer, he told himself, when flowers begin to mean something to me.) Moonlit desert flats that gleamed like snow. Piles of stones commemorating births and deaths and battles. And winds, hard dry winds. The Old Man loved mountains; the sound of the wind made him smile gently to himself, as if he were remembering something.

The winds made Robert nervous. So did the Pacific. They went to Seattle and then Portland ("I've never seen them," the Old Man said), and somewhere between them they made a special trip to see the Pacific. They stood on a bare crumbling cliff and looked down over the brown beach to the ocean. The surface rose and fell, waves like breathing. After that day, Robert never looked at the Pacific again—he felt somehow that it would not have been safe.

They were gone almost four months. The Old Man never mentioned business to Robert. Maurice Lamotta came several times, stayed overnight and left. Otherwise nothing. The Old Man did not even seem to be on the phone very much. It was, as he said, a complete vacation.

By the time they returned to New Orleans, Robert was engaged to the Old Man's daughter Anna.

H E W A S never sure how that happened. He did remember thinking: She's seventeen and she has a blouseful and
she's ready for a man. He did not remember mentioning
marriage, but he must have. He was positive she hadn't suggested it. She was too gentle and too polite. Even her voice
was soft and hushed and lingered in the air after she had
stopped talking.

Robert wondered. She wasn't vague, she wasn't silent.
She spoke well and intelligently. She, like her father, loved
the mountains—Robert could feel the excitement shaking
her body. She was young and beautiful, and he had the feeling that at any moment she might turn into smoke and disappear.

Maybe that's why, Robert thought, restless already with
his unusual introspection, *I have to try. . . .*

He would marry this beautiful girl. No more muddy
gardens and standing in the dark.

He tried to imagine what it would be like, a wife waiting for you at home. A place of your own. He'd never had
that—even when his mother was alive they'd lived with relatives. A series of cousins' houses, all strange, all smelling of
other people. His place now would smell of him alone. It
would be his and nobody else's.

The Old Man seemed neither happy nor unhappy. "It's
time for Anna to think of getting married," he said, and that
was all.

And Anna herself, she seemed no different, except that
her color was higher, her smooth olive cheeks had a tiny spot
of pale pink. Now and then, when she put her hand on Robert's arm, a gentle soft gesture, he felt a twinge straight
through his body, all the way back to his stomach. And he
decided, after a couple of jolts like that, he was very much in
love with her.

Back in New Orleans one evening, he sat in his stuffy
bedroom where moths beat against the lamp, and considered

the whole thing, carefully. When his vague wordless thoughts receded and only the slap of moth wings and the buzz of an occasional mosquito disturbed the quiet, he decided that everything he'd ever wanted was within his reach, and waiting for him. *For the first time, it's enough. It feels like it's enough.*

ANNA

E VER S I N C E she could remember, Anna had planned her wedding day. Even her dolls were brides. She had hundreds of dolls in those days; her aunts and uncles and cousins brought them regularly. They were all sorts and sizes, large and small, fair and dark, soft-bodied babies and hoop-skirted ladies. Anna did the same thing with all of them. She stripped off their clothes (throwing those into the kitchen garbage) and put the naked dolls carefully on shelves and in corners. When she was six, she told her father: "My dolls need new clothes." The very next day her dressmaker, Miss Evelyn Boissac, arrived and settled into the big sewing room. Little lady, what would you like? I have scraps from your dresses; would you like your dolls to wear dresses just like yours? "I want them to be brides," the child Anna said, decisively. All of them? "Yes." When Miss Boissac hesitated, Anna gave a bellow of rage. Her Aunt Cecilia (who acted as housekeeper, because Anna's own mother was always pregnant and worried about the health of the baby, and everybody knew she needed quiet and rest so the little unborn thing might go to its natural term) flew in the door scolding with rage: Miss Boissac, you know what the doctors said. . . . Miss Boissac nodded and her thin lips grew thinner. For the next week she sewed nothing but wedding dresses for the dolls, all of them, even the baby dolls. They were made of every kind of white material, shiny soft satin to stiff organdy. There must be a hundred dolls, Miss Boissac complained. "I have never counted," Anna answered calmly.

One by one, in their long white dresses, with their veils thrown back to reveal their painted faces, the brides lined the shelves and filled the corners. Anna never left the room—it was summer vacation—day after day, while Miss Boissac drank glass after glass of iced tea, she stayed right beside her and watched the darting needle of the sewing machine, or rummaged through stacks of materials selecting the next dress. They were sewing the morning when, in spite of the quiet and rest, Anna's mother went into premature labor. The house filled with weeping, bustling relatives and black-skirted priests praying in rows in her empty bedroom. Anna looked at them once and returned to Miss Boissac. "It won't work," she said, flatly. What won't work? "The baby won't live, it's got bad blood." What a terrible thing to say. "I was healthiest because I was first; my sister was smaller, you see that. By the time the others came, the blood was so bad they couldn't live." Who told you that? Who ever gave a child ideas like that? "Who?" It had been the Negro cook, but Anna, suddenly secretive, said calmly, "God told me."

Anna kept those dolls for seven or eight years, then packed them all into many boxes and sent them to St. Vincent's Orphanage. She was no longer interested in them. By that time she was filling sketchbooks with ideas for her wedding.

She was a clever artist, a good draftsman. She studied fashion magazines, books of design; she gathered details from all of them, combining them to suit herself. She even went to the public library to copy the wedding dresses of ancient Rome. Her shelves, emptied of dolls, filled with sketchbooks, all neatly arranged and organized. One book for flowers, this done in watercolor. One book of dresses for the maid of honor—all selected to minimize her sister Margaret's stockiness. One for the bridesmaids. Another for the ring bearer, a slender small boy—Anna was sure that among her many cousins she could find one to approximate the appearance of her sketch. Another book for the cake, sketches adapted from the *Larousse Gastronomique*, for the endless buffets. Another for the wedding celebration itself, the entertainments, the pavilions, the gardens, the ballrooms. And finally book after book of brides' dresses, of every possible style.

She began, with infinite care and precision, to acquire her household goods. At fifteen she had an entire convent of Guatemalan Carmelite nuns doing her needlework. They embroidered, they monogrammed, they did draw work, they tatted. They worked steadily for years to her order and design. When the finished things arrived, she smoothed them inch by inch, and put them away in boxes lined with blue paper. . . . A Belgian convent stopped everything but prayers to make her lace tablecloths. Slowly, steadily, her closets and chests began to fill.

Anna felt a great sense of happiness, of readiness, at the accumulation of these things. She felt part of the endless line of women who had gathered dowries in chests and boxes, sealed away against the coming of the unknown bridegroom.

At sixteen she ordered her china, her own design, executed by Minton. It took two years and arrived barely in time for her wedding.

At sixteen too, she bought her house. She found it one afternoon, while on a pious outing with her convent class. They visited the site of a small miracle by St. Jude—some flashing lights and a weeping holy picture—in a small dark house that smelled of urine and mold and cabbage. The woman around whom these remarkable things happened, a cripple with a stiff hip and a fingerless hand, lay in her bed, snuffling with a cold. The uniformed convent girls filed by her bedroom door, staring, but she did not open her eyes. On the way back to school, as Anna looked idly out her window, she saw the house, half hidden behind its iron-fenced garden. That one glance was enough. Her father bought it the next day, paying triple its value. She planned the remodeling with her usual thoroughness—more sketches, more books. Two years later, when she was engaged to Robert, the plans were complete, but no actual work had been done. She had to hurry. She hired two crews, who worked well into the night while the neighbors complained. Every day, after school, she tossed aside her books and went to check their work. The men grumbled at her demands; some quit, but others stayed and the house took shape as Anna intended.

ANNA COULD never remember a time when she had not planned her wedding—and she couldn't remember a time when she had not gone to the Ursuline convent. She knew every one of the nuns, from the ancient dying ones in the infirmary, to the novices with their young round faces. She knew every inch of the dark building: the huge echoing attics and the narrow between-wall climbways; the time-suspended stillness of chapels and vestibules, the cold formality of the parlors. For twelve years she had been contented and happy, a good student, quiet, well-behaved. (Her sister Margaret set off firecrackers in the library, lit all the vigil lights in the chapel at once, poured ink in lunchboxes, played truant, blew spitballs filled with BB's in class.) Now, in her last year, Anna was restless and anxious. During her Latin class she decided among the dress designs that crowded her sketchbooks, during rhetoric class she rejected her decisions, during French she almost cried with frustration.

The dress she finally selected was ivory white, without a train, high-necked, long-sleeved, seed pearls worked over its entire surface. She adapted that design from an illustration in *Ivanhoe*. She would wear no jewelry except earrings of her own design, a long cascade of pearls, made by Tiffany.

Once she'd decided, she felt much better, but she still had no time to study.

At midterm she was called to the Mother Superior's office. The crackling wimple, shiny with starch, the dusty folds of black wool skirt—Anna thought: *When I first came here, I was so scared of them. The rustle of that coif would make my neck prickle, and the clack of their big wood rosaries would send me scurrying around a corner out of their way. I used to think they were a mixture of God and a black ghost and I'd have nightmares about them. . . . Everything in the convent is black; the halls have no windows and the floors are black linoleum. The chapel is dark wood with only a vigil light or two (makes it seem darker, those shivery single points of light) and the red sanctuary light hanging and swaying in the drafts. All darkness for God's presence. Except twice a year. Midnight on Christmas, red and green. And Easter, white and gold. . . .* She half-heard the lecture on improving her grades. Then she said quietly: "I suppose it doesn't really matter whether I graduate or not. I'll be married in June, and Robert and my father don't care."

She saw astonishment on the nun's face, then stony concern. She went on demurely, "I've had my schooling, and whether I sit on a stage and carry some flowers doesn't really matter."

She kept on smiling vaguely, deferentially. And went her own way. "I have to get a house ready," she explained. "Robert and I need a place to live. It's so very important to have it nice, don't you know?"

In February she stayed after school every day for two weeks for tutoring in math and Latin. Then she stopped. "I'm very grateful," she said politely, "but there is so much I have to do every day after school."

The tutor, a round red-faced nun, nodded silently.

"I've been wondering, why don't I drop school altogether; it would be easier for you, don't you think?"

The nun's calm red face said: "I think it would be a great pity, my dear, not to finish something you've started."

Anna smiled her great new bland smile. "But I'm not quitting. I've started something else."

Wrapped by its starched bands, the flushed face smiled very slightly. "I think tutoring has helped you quite a bit. I suspect you will manage to pass."

"I do hope so," Anna said. For that one moment she meant it.

Then she forgot all about it. She was so busy with her house and Robert. She thought about both constantly during that last semester of high school: Robert's face floated among the rugs and curtains and sofas and chairs. She read her Shakespeare without seeing, scanned her Virgil with random squiggles, while she contemplated the shape of Robert's ears, the way his hands were shaped: short square nails, little tufts of hair on the fingers. . . . Sometimes he met her after school. When she saw him waiting, there were prickles along her scalp and a little singing in her ears. It was all she could do to keep from throwing down her books and running. Of course she did not; she behaved with propriety and dignity.

"I believe my fiancé is meeting me this afternoon," she said to the nuns; "yes, I see him there."

They crowded the windows behind her as she walked slowly out to meet him. She could feel their eyes running over her, passing over her like tiny fingers.

The next day they told her: "A fine-looking young man; you make a lovely couple." She nodded, smiling shyly, not minding in the least that they said the same to every girl. Because it was pleasant to feel their disinterested admiration, their far-off window-limited glances.

S H E G R A D U A T E D in May with the rest of her class, white dresses and bouquets of red roses. Her father sat in the audience, Robert next to him. How lucky I am, she thought. My father is so distinguished-looking, nobody in the auditorium is as tall as he is. And Robert is so handsome, with shiny black hair, shiny black eyes. . . . They are both wearing the same beige silk suit. Different ties. My father's is darker. . . . They look like the same family already. . . .

Anna looked at her cousins and her aunts and uncles sitting row after row on all sides of her father—and she decided that there was not a single person in her mother's family she really liked. I will be honest, Anna promised herself, after I am married; I will stop seeing them, gradually but firmly.

There were times when you put things behind you. Like giving away the dolls you'd kept all your life. Like opening doors to closed rooms. . . . After her mother's death—of a broken heart for the last dead baby, the family said—her bedroom door was kept closed. Anna and Margaret always tiptoed by it, hurriedly, just as they had done when she was alive. That door stayed locked, year after year. Once Anna's grandmother took her inside. (Margaret, the younger, was not invited.) Her mother's clothes still hung in the closets, already slightly out of style to Anna's quick eye, protected by little bundles of vetiver against the nonpresent moth. On the bed, under the spread, the slightly wrinkled pillow on which she died. Her book permanently face down on the table. Her shawl folded and waiting on the chair. . . . "You see," Anna's grandmother said. "Just the way your mother left it." And a single tear ran down her cheek. Anna, with a child's calmness, watched the tear leave a shiny trail across the broad cheek and wondered how long you grieved, how long there was pain. She herself felt nothing. She had scarcely known her mother

alive, how could she miss her dead? She had no memory of
the woman whose ghost inhabited this room, whose clothes
hung in the closet, whose shoes lined the polished wood floor.
Like paper from which dolls are cut, these were the marks
her mother left behind. The silver brushes on the dressing
table: "The last thing your father gave her, she almost never
used them, but look, here in the bristles, the long hair, see,
that's hers. You see how long her hair was, see how black.
No, don't touch it. We never do; we dust and put it back,
that's all."

Anna looked carefully around the room, wrapped within
its always drawn shades. The spicy smell of vetiver in the still
air made her pant for breath. In the closets dresses hung
limply, the hems sagged unevenly. The shoes tipped a bit on
their heels, leaning on each other.

"Mama is happy in heaven," Anna said. She had been
taught that, by whom? "Everybody is happy in heaven."

And when another tear wriggled its way in the path of
the first, Anna stared, not understanding.

O N E   D A Y   that special shrine was gone. Simply, completely. One day after school she found the door open, and
the gray fall sky shining beyond the curtainless windows.
She went inside, curiously. A new spread was on the bed,
she peeped beneath: all fresh linen. The dresser was cleared
of perfume bottles and brushes and vases. She opened the
closet: empty. Her father said nothing; her grandmother did
not come to the house for a very long time. Anna did not
question the change.

She learned that it was part of life, this putting things
behind you. Her father had taught her that.

A N N A   F E L T   a vague fondness—tinged with pity—for her grandmother. That poor old woman who dried her tears only to have them creep back.

She died in April of a sudden attack of jaundice. She suffered patiently and silently in her hospital room, with flowers and holy lights. She was eased toward immortality by the massed chanting of six priests, all her relatives. Her gasping yellow body was surrounded by her entire family—latecomers were left in the hall, unable to crowd into the small room. They carried chairs and boxes from all over the building, stood on them to peer through the door. When the Archbishop came, he too had to climb on a chair and send his blessing to her over the massed backs of her family. Perhaps if he had been wearing his full ceremonial robes and his mitered hat—perhaps then they would have made room for him. But perhaps not, for death was a family business and they had their own priests.

Anna, trapped inside the room, felt her skin creep with horror at the presence of the unconscious woman. Her sister Margaret said, "I'm going to throw up," and dropping down on her hands and knees she crawled out of the room, pushing through the forest of legs. Anna stared at her engagement ring (a square sapphire: "Diamonds are so common, Robert"), and saw Robert and her future in its blue depths. She hardly heard the shrieks and cries when the old woman's breathing finally struggled to a stop.

The funeral was barely two months before her wedding. The D'Alfonsos assumed a postponement—a wedding so soon would be disrespectful. Anna cried bitter tears on her father's neck.

"What on earth are you crying about, Anna? She was an old woman."

Anna said, angrily: "Not her, not her. I wanted a June wedding."

A pause while her father understood her. "Anna, if you

want a June wedding, and you've got the man, I don't see a reason in God's earth why you shouldn't have one."

"They say . . ."

"They say all sorts of things."

"They say they won't come."

"They'll come," the Old Man said. "There's nothing they love more than a big wedding. Better even than a big funeral. Have it the way you want it, Anna, and to hell with the rest."

THE D'ALFONSOS grumbled a bit, but soon stopped. The Old Man was right about his in-laws: they loved a big wedding. And, as they learned bit by bit of the plans, they realized that Anna's wedding, supported by great amounts of the Old Man's money, was going to be the biggest event in the family's history. More glorious, even, than the old women's tales of long-vanished Sicilian opulence.

There was to be a week of festivities, some not mentioned above a whisper. Like the two-day drinking party on the Old Man's farm at Abita Springs—men only, with special whores from Chicago. While their men were gone, the ladies went on a quiet cruise through the lakes to an elaborate picnic on the Gulf Coast. There were gambling parties with the Old Man's entire casino reserved for them. There were dances and concerts and occasional quick visits to church to remind everyone that matrimony was a sacrament. The Old Man was rarely seen, but nobody missed him. Robert went to one dance, got drunk, and left early. Anna seemed hardly to notice the crowds: without apology she avoided most of the gatherings. She was following her own schedule, her own plan.

T H E   D A Y before her wedding, Anna took out the pictures of her mother, that ghost of the empty room, in her wedding dress. The photographer had placed his lights to catch the gleam of her finery, the sheen of the satin, the glitter of the tiny glass beads around her neck. Too brightly lit, the bride's face appeared as vague as shadows. Patiently Anna studied the glazed indistinct features, the cloud of black hair, trying to find some link between her mother and herself. A resemblance—there, around the eyes, the angle of the cheekbones. It was so little, so very little. For almost an hour, Anna looked at the pictures, trying to see if the dead had any message for her. Nothing. It might have been a stranger. But then, she thought slowly, it was a stranger. Her mother was dead, nothing of her left any more, except maybe some blood. Anna closed the album slowly. That was all. Her mother was gone, she was floating in heaven, propelled by the everlasting Masses of her family. . . .

Anna put the pictures away. She felt vaguely annoyed, as if a promise to her had been broken. You're being childish, she told herself severely; you are nervous and silly and childish. You're behaving just like every other bride. How foolish you are.

After she'd lectured herself, she felt better. She always did. Because she knew that she was not like anybody else. Not like anybody else at all.

T O   C L E A R away the feeling of disappointment the pictures left with her, Anna decided to drive to her house, her own house, the one she had remodeled according to her exact wish.

Why, she thought, do I always get angry at my mother?

For not leaving me a memory, for being so vague and gentle and so busy with her job of procreating that she hardly noticed her children once they left her womb. . . . She would ask her father about this obsession to breed; had he wanted a son that much? He had one now, she thought smugly, in Robert. . . .

The lush green June shade washed over her house, softening the crisp white lines, blurring the sparkling paint. Even the harsh smell of turpentine disappeared in the heavy scent of Sweet Olive and Cashmere Bouquet bushes. The entire block was wrapped in layers of different fragrances—such a wonderful neighborhood, she thought. It seemed to hang in time; all the houses were nearly a century old, the street itself was cobblestoned. A circle of time, she thought, a perfect circle of time.

Her mother's family disapproved of the house. For weeks the cobblestones echoed as they streamed by, clucking their displeasure. Her second cousin Bernadette, who was building a new house in a suburb called Metairie, said: "Anna, there is a marvelous lot across the street, it would be a lovely place to build." Her husband Andrew, who was a state senator and in the slot-machine business, flashed his professional smile. "We'd be proud to have you for a neighbor. I hear Mike's coming out our way too, all the young families are."

Anna smiled right back at him, conscious suddenly of her own will, her own ability to decide. I can say no, she thought, I can control what happens to me now. I'm no longer a child. I control myself. . . .

"How sweet of you, Andrew."

"Tell your father to build you a fine house. He can afford it. . . ."

Anna went on smiling, the soft vague smile that masked a definite and final refusal. "I've found a house I like very much."

"But a new house . . ." Baffled by her smile, his voice trailed away.

The day before her wedding, Anna looked at her house and thought: It's what I wanted, and I have it. I will live there with my husband and we will be happy. It is mine, it is like me, and I love it.

How many times will I do this, how many times will I open this gate, this old-fashioned iron gate? Along the walk, slippery and mossy underfoot; old bricks always are. Up the wood steps punctured by drainage holes, black eyes staring up from the ground. Open the door, key heavy and cool in my hand. Lovely door, oval leaded glass, cut facets to catch the light. I like the door most of all about the house.

She stood in her front hall, so clean and crisp and waiting. *This is me; I make things belong to me.*

Not like my mother. If I died, people could see my reflection in these things. My mother left no reflection. Nothing but some clothes hanging in the closet. And me. And Margaret.

She crossed the hall, dragging her fingers across the polished surface of the small mahogany table. Peeped into the living room, pale green walls and green curtains and heavy dark furniture. Waiting. Even the cigarette boxes were filled. She opened one to be sure. Yes. Would she learn to smoke? Perhaps. She pictured herself sitting at the fireplace, looking out the window at the bushy spread of Sweet Olive, gold holder between her fingers, gold case open on the table before her. . . .

She put a cigarette to her lips, testing. The sour tobacco taste seeped into her mouth, she savored its sting carefully. That was the taste of the adult world.

Dangling the unlit cigarette from the corner of her mouth, she walked through the house. Not a speck of dust on the polished floors, not a smear on the shining windows.

In the kitchen she dropped the cigarette, unlit, into the brand-new trash can. The kitchen smelled of wax and new paint and crisp linoleum underfoot. The stove was untouched, the refrigerator held only ice. No soot or food smoke had brushed along these walls. No smell of sweat. It was perfect and unused. Soon the stove would be speckled with grease, the pots would lose the first of their sparkle, there'd be food on the refrigerator shelves, footsteps would begin to wear the shine from this waxed floor. There'd be smells of cooking and echoes of movements even late at night, when everyone was gone. Kitchens were places where a house's echoes concentrated. . . .

She glanced into the small back yard. Against the wood fence ginger lilies drooped their pink waxy flowers. If I opened the door I would smell them, she thought. But she did not. Dust might blow in.

The house was perfect, except for the second bedroom, which she had furnished as a kind of study. The big Scott radio was in there, and a couple of bookcases with glass fronts. She'd done that room hurriedly, with no special plan. It would eventually be the nursery. Then she would have organdy curtains and mounds of ruffles, and in the corner, an old-fashioned cherry-wood cradle. She could see the baby asleep there, near the window where the crib would catch the sun, where the curtains would swing lightly in the breeze. She could see the slate-blue eyes strain to focus. . . . She'd considered leaving the room completely empty with its door closed, but that reminded her too much of her dead mother's room. She'd also considered doing it right away as a nursery. That would have been most practical, she thought, because when she was actually pregnant, she could devote all her attention to her swelling womb. . . . But you couldn't furnish a nursery before you were married. . . .

She hesitated at the bedroom door: all pale coral—curtains, walls, rugs—the room glowed at her, it smoothed her skin, it flattered her. Even the lampshades were tinted. *This is better for a wedding night, better than a hotel, a strange place I'd never see again.*

She had planned that too; they would come here after their wedding reception, and begin their honeymoon the following day.

"Does that seem silly?" she asked Robert.

"Whatever you want, honey."

She rubbed her lips together nervously. "Robert, do you remember in *Little Women,* when Meg is married to John Brooke, they walk across the common to their cottage and that's the beginning of their life together? Simple and, well, dignified."

(Her sister Margaret said sourly, "That was just because they couldn't afford anything else.")

"I never read *Little Women,*" Robert said.

"So many things are cheap, don't you see, Robert?" Her voice shook just a little.

"Honey, any kind of wedding and any kind of honeymoon is fine with me."

"I'm nervous, Robert." She half-smiled. "I'm just nervous."

But it was something else. She had tried to talk about something that was very important to her; she had tried to put her thoughts into words. And whenever she tried to express herself, she felt a loss.

Her invisible arms reached out, scooping up her words, carrying them back inside. It was quite a while before she was certain that she had found all of them, collected them from the floor of air where they scattered like broken beads, and put them back inside herself where they belonged. It was quite a while before she felt secure.

(More than anything else now she wanted to be left alone, without advice or help. If she could not exactly imagine the marriage act—she turned that phrase over and over in her mind: the marriage act—it was nobody's business but her own. She resented Aunt Cecilia's nervous little talk: "It's something all women go through, my dear. Put an extra pad under the sheet, don't forget." Aunt Cecilia, such a good housekeeper; her own house shone and glistened, her sons left their shoes in the front hall and changed to slippers. . . .

Anna gave a final shake to the potpourri hidden in little china jars around the bedroom. She had made that herself, a lemon-rose mixture. Half tiptoeing, she left the room.

When she got home, at least a dozen of her family were waiting. As she parked the car in the driveway, her Uncle Joseph called: "Hi, little bride!" And she thought again: I must do something about my family after I am married. I must be rid of them, so there is just Robert and me. And Papa, she added. She felt sad for having forgotten him for even a minute.

She waved vaguely at her uncle and his sister-in-law, who was rocking on the porch. She grinned at her two young cousins crouched on the steps. She pushed past the others and went inside.

"Where were you?" Aunt Cecilia's forehead, ordinarily smooth as paper, was crinkled.

Anna smiled, deliberately not answering. "I didn't know you'd be looking for me."

"When not even your father knows where you are . . ."

The Old Man was sitting in his chair, the one he always preferred, next to the window. His face was perfectly serious; only a slight change in the color of his eyes showed his amusement. "I admitted to your aunt I didn't have the slightest idea where you were."

"Oh my," Anna said.

"We even called your new house," Aunt Cecilia said, "and when you weren't there, I could just see you lying in a hospital somewhere."

The phone had not rung, Anna was sure. "Do you suppose that phone is out of order?" Everything had to be perfect.

"Well," her father said slowly, "I wouldn't really worry about it. It's just possible I dialed the wrong number."

"Oh," Anna said, "oh." She kissed him briefly on the cheek. "I wish I were as patient as you, Papa," she said softly.

He rubbed his finger across her cheek. "It comes of practice, child."

Perversely, tears gathered in the corners of her eyes. She refused to let them fall.

A N D W H A T did you expect of a wedding? The bluest skies. The most transparent sunlight. A rainbow reaching from one horizon to the other in full prismatic simplicity. Crowds to line the streets, smiling, bowing: "The beloved couple, how beautiful they are." Castles and turrets and knights on horseback. Silent cheering, effortless movement, pageants, kings and popes and emperors, pomp and glory. And even more. A sign. A sign of favor . . . the essence, the memory. Dear God, let me remember. The most wonderful day, the loveliest day, let me remember it all. Holy Virgin, let me remember from the moment I wake up. I've been to confession and I'm free of sin, state of grace. Does that help? Total recall, that's what I want. I want to keep one day with me totally until the day I die. . . .

What did you find at a wedding? Clouds of sounds and blurs of faces. Breaths full of alcohol and coffee and sugared cakes. Fetid smell of sherry and paregoric smell of anisette. A dress surprisingly heavy with the weight of its satin, the weight of its pearls. (And somebody whispering: "Pearls are tears, how terrible for her, such bad luck.") Back that ached and shoulders that had to be braced against sagging, legs that had to be kept from shaking and staggering. And over everything, a mist, a fog of exhaustion. At times her drooping eyelids turned everything hazy, gold-dusted.

Those moments she thought: How exquisite it all is.

T H E   D A Y started early. Precisely at five o'clock, with a discreet knock and cough, the fitter and the hairdresser arrived. Behind them her sister Margaret came whistling, drawing curtains, rattling windows.

"Oh my," Anna opened her eyes. Against the shimmering square of blue-white window, Margaret's face appeared—round dark head, eyes too close together, mouth too wide, too curved at the corners, a comedian's face, a puppy's face.

"Up, oh lovely one," Margaret said. "The day breaketh, the birds singeth, the bridegroom cometh."

"Oh my," Anna said again.

"Come on." Margaret pulled at the covers. "They're going to do my hair after yours. My hair, imagine." She yanked one of her short crisp black curls derisively.

"The hat is very becoming."

"Bet anything my kinks push it right off the top of my head."

She drifted away. When Anna next saw her, she was quietly standing on her head. Her sturdy dark legs, shadowed by black hair, stuck thin toes toward the ceiling; her pink pajamas tumbled around her hips. Her wide bright smile was upside down. That grubby little upside-down figure haunted Anna all the long morning. It followed her into church, hung grinning in the clouds of organ music. It dangled over the altar, shiny and gold; swam among the musty incense and the stiff vestments.

(All through her life whenever Anna thought of her sister she thought first of her grin: the wide melon slice, the square harsh teeth.)

Anna was relieved when the shadow finally disappeared. She wanted nothing to cloud her wedding day. She wanted only the ritual, the Mass, and her husband. Together forever, one flesh, death do us part. Death—other Masses all black, other music, other sounds. The soul goes to face its judgment, drums and fire and thunderings. Dear God, not soon, not for Robert and not for me. . . . Such stupid images. First, Margaret standing on her head. Then, death. Why think of dying? Because I'm tired. My bones hurt like an old woman. Aching. Feeling the pull down toward the earth. . . . Not today. Think about Robert.

I want to touch him I want to kiss him I want to feel the way the hairs on the back of his neck grow down into his collar. Today he'll have a haircut and be all smooth. I'll have to wait a couple of days to feel the crispy new hairs. . . . And the way his hair smells, the lotion he uses to keep his hair straight; Cajuns always have curly hair. . . . Was it true that his mother never knew who his father was? Terrible. No, he said, it wasn't terrible; she was good to me, she didn't have anything herself to be giving to me. . . . Robert little, Robert poor and hungry.

She was ready now. Bathed and combed, wrapped all around by luxury and expense. The choir sang, the organ roared its waves of sound for her. As she walked carefully up the church steps, hand lightly on her father's arm, she felt serene and glowing.

FOLLOWING CONVENT tradition, Anna went immediately after her wedding Mass to pay a formal call on the nuns. Her dress gleamed and sparkled in the dim parlors of damp furniture polish and unmoving air. Robert waited patiently beside her, black-habited nuns crowded around her, admiring. With a tiny flash of fear, Anna thought: I am the only white thing here. All these figures are black and even Robert is wearing black. Even he.

The Mother Superior kissed her cheek, the harsh starched wimple crackled against her shoulder. "The very first of this year's girls." Two real tears ran down the nun's cheeks. "The very first of our girls to get married this year."

The first of this year—Anna stiffened. She did not quite like that, though it was true. She didn't like the vaguely sour smell that rose from the folds of the Mother Superior's robe either.

Robert said: "Are you ready?"

"Oh, yes, yes." The black veils around her fluttered again, this time to open the huge oak doors.

Anna handed her heavy bouquet to the Mother Superior. "Will you? For me."

The nun nodded and with a swirl of white Anna moved out the door and down the steps, blinking a little in the sunshine and the bright blue sky.

Robert asked: "Why did you leave the flowers?"

"They put them on the altar in their private chapel."

Robert grinned. "That's really the bride of Christ for you."

"It's just a custom," Anna said, "all the girls do it." She waved back to the convent's door. In answer, one of the black shapes lifted the white bouquet, holding it high, triumphantly.

The little finger on her right hand began to ache, fiercely. It did that only when she was upset.

"Look," Robert said, "did I say something wrong?"

She turned deliberately away from the group of nuns. He was her husband, and she was off to her wedding reception. She stared into his eyes and she felt her irritation slip away. It was the same feeling she got sometimes during chapel when the Gregorian was particularly well done. A sensation like softly flowing water up and down the spine, over the bump of each vertebra, all the way into the skull, to circulate in small neat waves there.

"You're adorable," he said, holding her hand with the new rings on it.

She went on studying the color of his eyes. She was, she told herself, fulfilling her life. She was completely happy.

B Y   T H E   middle of the afternoon, she floated with happiness. At the country club (the decorations were perfect, she noted, exactly right) she drank two glasses of champagne, stood in the reception line for hours, danced with Robert, then with her father.

The day, according to her plan, proceeded smoothly, like a well-oiled machine. To the orchestra's gentle violins, she danced with her uncles and her cousins, the ones who were eighty and shaky on their feet, the ones who were twelve and so short that she stared down into their brilliantined hair. She had more champagne; her head began to sing lightly, gaily. A pink powder mark appeared on her white satin shoulder. She brushed at it briefly. "I know who that was," she said to Robert. "Cousin Loretta. Nobody else wears that shade of powder. She's that gaga old lady, with the purple flowers on her hat. Over there. See, that color powder makes her skin look green."

Robert said: "Are all these people related to you?"

"Well, some are Papa's business. . . ."

"I know those," Robert interrupted, waving his arm to include the crowded room, the endless reception line, "but what about the rest?"

"Relatives, I suppose, one way or the other." She felt a sudden surge of concern for him. He had no family at the wedding; he'd wanted none. Not for me, he said; ones I've got I don't want. . . . So he stood alone.

He would have a family and a home now. She would make it for him.

She was feeling something—what was it?—and the intensity of the emotion was upsetting. Almost as if there were something she should be explaining to him, some words, some phrases inside her that would not come to life.

"Robert," she said seriously, "I love you."

He winked back his answer.

H A L F   A N   hour later little Peter Gondolfo stumbled
into the fishpond. His head hit the tiled side, his skin split,
melon-like, and blood poured down the side of his face. The
other children stood in perfect silence, openmouthed and
watching. He climbed from the pool, too dazed to cry; he
walked into the largest pavilion, dripping blood across the
polished dance floor. His mother screamed, somebody else
shouted, the orchestra stopped.

"What's that?" Robert jumped.

"One of the children," Anna said calmly. "I was sure
one of them would get hurt, but it's all taken care of."

The screams got fainter and then stopped entirely. The
orchestra began again.

"Sounds like they died."

"Papa's car was waiting at the side drive. Just in case.
I arranged with Aunt Cecilia to go along to the doctor's. To
take care of things, if the mother's too upset."

"You've thought of everything," Robert said. "You really
have."

"You haven't even seen the circus we put together for
the children."

The golf course directly behind the country club was
filled with striped tents, and the ammonia stench of animals
was thick in the June heat.

"Where," Robert said, "did you get this?"

"I told you. A circus." She added, "Just the harmless
animals, Robert."

Two elephants, in procession, lurched across the space
beyond the tents. They were painted gold and white, and
their trappings flashed with rhinestones; mahouts in gold
satin rode their heads, and from the palanquins on their backs
children laughed and waved wildly.

"Elephants?"

"For the children now. Later, when it's dark, I thought

they would be fun for a romantic ride. We can have the first."

"If we stay. . . . What else is out there?"

"Well, the usual clowns and trapeze acts. And there's a juggler to show them how to juggle."

"A sword swallower too?"

"You're teasing."

"Yes, ma'am. . . . It's quite a wedding."

"Robert, I wanted everybody to remember this. It's easy with grownups—mounds of caviar and flowers and music. But I wanted the children to remember too."

Robert threw out his hands in that gesture he disliked and couldn't help making. "They'll remember."

In the soft late afternoon, the party became drunken and noisy. Margaret and some of her friends ("Who are they?" Anna asked) dragged a piano out on the veranda and a black-haired boy began banging on it. His knuckle-edged jazz clashed with the smooth strings from the pavilion ballroom. Margaret was dancing, all by herself, her face flushed, her pink gown wilting in the heat.

"Robert," Anna said, "look at that child. She was in my room at five o'clock this morning."

"Child? She's not two years younger than you."

He wouldn't have the memory of the grinning upsidedown face, and she couldn't explain. "Well," she said, "I'm a married woman."

"Not quite," he said, "not quite."

She thought it more proper not to hear him.

WITH THE first dark they quietly left the celebration. Their car was a new Studebaker. Anna had selected it— Packard or Buick was not suitable for them.

Margaret caught them at the door. "Best wedding you'll ever have," she said, her grin a little lopsided. "Did you know the Bishop's drunk?"

"Oh, really," Anna said.

"Don't be condescending with me." Margaret did a quick Charleston step. "I'm a good Catholic. . . . You going to float that veil out the window as you drive away into the sunset?"

"Have another drink, little sister-in-law," Robert said. "You're in pretty good shape now."

"Just champagne." Margaret's grin widened, flickered. "And it's a good holy Catholic drunk. Just look at all the priests. The bar back there looks like High Mass."

Robert helped Anna into the car, folded her veil and train after her.

"Hey," Margaret yelled. She twirled around and around, arms stuck straight out. "I'm a whirling crucifix. Look at me."

In a way she did look like that, Anna thought.

ANNA CAME to her first house a bride in white satin, just as she had planned. There was pain where she had expected it, and pleasure where she looked for it, and there was blood to prove her worth to her husband. She fell asleep, completely content. Robert was restless; he turned and tossed all night, jabbing her with elbows and outflung arms. He's not used to sleeping in a double bed, she thought reasonably, but he will learn.

She was wrong, she decided years later, wrong about so many things. For all her piety, the Lord did not correct her ignorance.

MARGARET

MARGARET STOPPED whirling to watch the car drive away. No veil fluttered from the window; only a faint trail of summer dust hung for an instant, then disappeared. She pulled a handkerchief from her belt, scrubbed at her perspiring face. It was hot, and the tight-fitting dress was very uncomfortable. It shrank on me, she thought, it feels like it shrank on me. *Innocent young girl found strangled to death in mysterious crime. The poor victim was strangled to death over her entire body. The police are at a loss to explain. . . .*

Maybe I should just take off my clothes. *Naked bridesmaid runs amuck.* My father would laugh, Anna would never speak to me again. . . . I guess I should get married pretty soon. If there was anybody I wanted to marry. I'm waiting for Prince Charming to ride out of the sunset. I could do what Anna did: mountains of linen, warehouses of furniture. Poor guy in whose honor it's all done. He ought to die of fright or suffocation. . . . I won't do that. Not me. I'll just be my sweet little old self. Prince Charming will have to go for that. . . .

Margaret smoothed out her heat-rumpled skirts. Why did she feel like crying? She never cried; the nuns taught their girls that. Blink quickly, they said, and think about the goodness of Jesus.

The nuns . . . I've gone to their school for eleven years

and what did I learn? The Greek alphabet. Caesar's wars in Latin. To crochet lacy shawls for the Little Sisters of the Poor. To chant the daily Office. To read the novels of Dickens and Scott, but never Hardy. That's what I learned. To add a column of figures. To write an English letter. . . . That's eleven years of school. . . . That and learning to curse in Spanish. . . .

She'd learned during Spring Retreat, sitting in the chapel with her small black copy of *The Imitation of Christ*. Margaret managed to read the chapter headings: "Of Resisting Temptations," "Of Prudence in Our Undertakings," "Of the Love of Solitude and Silence.". . . She gave up. Thérèse García, sitting next to her, offered to teach her Spanish. In proper convent manner they sat looking straight ahead, abstracted expressions on their faces, talking almost without moving their lips, almost inaudibly. The first words Margaret learned were *"Tu puta madre."*

Those words, Margaret thought, were likely to come in handier than all the prayers she'd learned. Her class once made four separate simultaneous novenas: St. Jude, St. Joseph, Sacred Heart, and Our Lady of Prompt Succor. . . . Only one trouble with prayers and prayer books, she thought. They never gave you any foolproof tricks; they never really said: Now, this one will *work*. You had to try them all, and hope. Like a lottery: pick a number, lose, try again. Too bad, your luck, have another go. . . . And like a lottery, it wasn't fair.

Nothing was fair, she thought. Like that girl in school, in the third grade. Her name was—it was a long time ago—Rosalie; yes, Rosalie. She was crippled; infantile paralysis had fused her spine and given her a hump on one shoulder. The other girls always followed her to the bathroom and teased her, poking their small fingers into her bony excrescence, laughing. They had her in tears every day, though she never complained to the nuns. She just stopped going to the bathroom entirely. One day there was a puddle of urine under her desk and the following day she did not come to school. She never did again.

We probably would have killed her, Margaret thought. If we'd had enough time. Like we were going to do with Matthew.

He was her fourth or fifth cousin, and her age exactly. He was always at the children's parties and picnics, a large fat effeminate boy with breasts like a woman's. They—Margaret and six or eight other children—tried to drown him in the pond in Aunt Cecilia's rose garden. He had almost stopped struggling when Aunt Cecilia happened to come out. . . . Margaret still remembered her scream. . . .

All kids were mean, Margaret thought. Like that crazy big girl in school who'd yanked her hair so hard, one day while she sat on the toilet, that there was a bare patch left at the nape of her neck. After that, Margaret carried a spring knife with a four-inch blade that shot out at the push of a button. "I will cut you up wop-fashion," she threatened, "so that your own mother wouldn't recognize you."

And the nuns went their way, not knowing what their girls were doing. That wasn't fair either.

And Anna getting all the family's looks. . . . That really wasn't fair. . . . I'm short and square and I've got kinky hair and stupid brown eyes. While Anna is slender with straight black hair like an Indian, and soft melting eyes like a cocker spaniel.

She'd complained once to her father. He answered seriously: "Margaret, you are attractive in your way. Unlike Anna, you can also think.". . . "Gee, thanks," Margaret muttered. "I'm dying to be Jean Harlow, and you tell me I can think. Thanks a lot."

T H E   C A R   with Robert and Anna had vanished. Margaret stared at an empty street. My sister is married and gone; so much for my sister. Pity. Pity.

Her father stood beside her; he put one arm around her sweat-soaked shoulders. "Did they manage to sneak away, honey?"

She nodded, thinking that her father had special names for each of his daughters. He called her "honey," but never Anna. Anna was always "sweetie" or "child."

"Pa, these shoes are killing me."

The vague sadness of his face changed to a smile. "You've been standing for hours."

"Satin never does fit right, but Anna had to have it."

"Anna knew exactly how she wanted things."

Margaret kicked her pink satin shoes into a potted gardenia bush. "Marvelous!" She picked a single white flower, sniffed it dramatically, then tossed it away. "Incredible."

Behind them the sound of glass breaking and then shouts of laughter—her father lifted an eyebrow. "The real party seems to have begun."

"You remember Uncle Harry's birthday when A. J. and Joseph started to fight and everybody threw things?"

"You expect another one of those? I suppose so. Honey, liquor has a very bad effect on your mother's family."

They walked slowly inside. In the ballroom the sedate orchestra had disappeared; in its place, a dance band sweated away under blue lights. Her father said, wearily, "Honey, I'm having a whiskey. Do you want one?"

Her close-set brown eyes snapped. "First time you ever asked me that. I've been drinking champagne."

"You are now grown up. You can change from wine to whiskey."

"What if I got drunk, real drunk?"

"In the bosom of your mother's family?"

"Something like that."

"You could all lie down together." He pointed to a black-clothed man stretched on a pale green couch. "There's Ambrose. The lion and the lamb lie down together."

"Where's that come from?"

"Damned if I know," he said. "I read it somewhere years ago."

He'd never said damn with her before.

He handed her a highball. "For the bridesmaid."

She sipped warily. "I am so damn thirsty in this heat." She hesitated a little over the word, uncertain of his reaction, but he seemed to hear nothing. He lifted his glass in a mocking toast to her. Then in a formal toast and a bow to Aunt Harriet, who had appeared at his elbow.

She saw her father once more during the evening. He was sitting alone in the corner of one of the smaller pavilions. (They all had names according to their decorations: "Kismet," "Ivanhoe," "The Sultan's Tent," "The Ice Palace." Margaret didn't remember which it was.) He was almost completely hidden behind a mass of palms with white peonies wired to their branches. There was a highball on the small table beside him, and he was smoking a cigar while staring up at the ceiling.

"You look just the way you do at home." Margaret dropped into a second chair. She crossed her legs; the dust-streaked hem of her pink skirt flipped up, showing a pair of dirty white tennis shoes. Her father stared. She followed his eyes. "Oh, them. . . . I sent home for them, Papa. I kept stubbing my toe when I walked barefoot."

He took another puff and went back to staring at the ceiling.

"You tired, Papa?"

He arched back in the chair, stretching. "Your mother's family has always tired me, but no more than usual today."

"Did you know that Tootsie's new father-in-law went to the hospital? He said it was his heart."

"Tootsie's father-in-law . . ." He paused, trying to remember. Tootsie was a third cousin who had just married a girl from Houston. "Which one was he? The dress business or the night-club business?"

"I forget. You know, Anna's ambulance service wasn't so silly."

Her father smiled. "Anna is never silly."

"Can I have a cigarette?"

He shook his head. "Tonight you are drinking, and that's enough."

She giggled. "I don't feel a thing."

He shook his head. "You do."

"How can you tell?"

"You look older."

She leaned toward him and deliberately crossed her eyes over her shiny nose. "I want to grow up to look like Greta Garbo and have men go mad over me."

Just outside the silk walls of the pavilion an argument started—three or four voices shouting unintelligible words.

"You know," her father said, "with this one party, I have married a daughter and paid my social obligations for the last ten years."

Margaret said: "Papa, do you miss not having any family?"

He shook his head.

"You never talk about yours."

"There isn't anything to talk about. I never saw my father and my mother was like any other old lady when she came to live with me."

"That isn't what I wanted to know." She teased the ice around in her glass with her tongue.

He shrugged and went back to his drink and his cigar. Margaret wandered away, leaving her drink unfinished. She did not really like the taste, even if it was real Scotch and very expensive and completely illegal.

THE GARDENS bloomed with soft colored lights. A pale moon hung over the golf course, stuck in the sky like a bit of paper. She stared into the fishpond looking for a flick of tail among the lily pads, but all she saw was the moon—shivering and swinging back and forth between the circles of green.

"What are you looking at?"

She jumped aside so suddenly she almost fell into the water. "Don't do that!"

"Do what?" It was Andrew Stefano, her second cousin Bernadette's husband.

"You scared me." He was very handsome, Margaret thought, dark and sleek like a seal. Like Robert.

"Margaret, you've been drinking." A sudden change in Andrew's tone.

"I am seventeen years old," she said, "almost. And I can drink if I want to." She blew through her lips, fluttering them derisively.

"Young lady, I'm going to feed you. I think you need it."

One arm firmly around her waist, he urged her toward a buffet. Canopied in blue silk, guarded by a multitude of gilt cupids, a huge ice swan melted slowly in the exact center of endless dishes.

"Hey, listen," Margaret said. A steady metallic ping. The swan was dying into a metal bucket concealed beneath the lace tablecloth. "Swan's bleeding to death."

"Well," Andrew said, "the food looks very good."

Margaret waved off a waiter. "Let's go outside, Andrew."

Andrew filled two plates, tucked silverware and napkins into his pocket, and they went looking for an empty garden table. There were none.

"We may have to go inside," Andrew said.

"Just keep going, Cousin Andrew, there has to be somewhere."

They wandered through the gardens, peering into the

seated crowds at the candlelit tables. Finally they stood on the edge of the golf course. "What now?" Andrew asked.

The night was perfectly still, as summer nights always were, and the air was heavy with moisture. Beyond the thick heavy trees, across the open grass, heavy cumulus clouds were piled at the edges of the sky. Every now and then, bred by the slope of the golf course, by the warmth of the sun-baked open ground and the cool of the trees, small half-breaths of air stirred, vaguely. Like a night moth brushing past.

Margaret licked one finger and held it up in the air. "Feel it? They say it's not a wind really. It's the ground breathing."

Andrew was still looking for a table in the shadows. "Can you see anything?"

Margaret swirled on her heel, tennis shoes squeaking on the brick walk. "We'll use the grass." She flopped down, back against a tree. "I'm starving."

He sat beside her, gingerly. "I hope you like it, you didn't tell me what you wanted."

"I'm so hungry I could eat nails."

She wolfed down her food with quick gulping swallows and pushed the plate into an azalea bush. "We'll see if they can find that in the morning. . . . Cousin Andrew, where's the wine?"

"You've had enough to drink, young lady."

"Don't use that tone with me." She jerked upright. "I'll go steal a bottle from somebody's table." She scrambled up.

She was back quickly, on silent tennis shoes. "Is this red or white?" she giggled. "They were real busy necking. . . . I couldn't get any glasses, but I got this."

He sneezed with the sharp smell of powdered sugar. "Cakes?"

"What's wrong with that?"

"Give me the wine," he said.

"You're missing it, Andrew. These cakes are great, whatever they are."

"Can't you taste?"

"Nope."

"Young lady, you *are* drunk."

"I hear singing, do you?"

"No," he said.

"Well, listen. . . ." All the party sounds: the band playing "Valencia"; laughing and loud talking; and closer, all around them, soft whispers in the dark.

"I don't hear any singing."

"Maybe it'll start again," Margaret said. "I think I'll wait for it." She threw herself back, flat on the ground. "I feel so *good*." She crossed her legs; her foot very nearly hit Andrew in the face. He caught it, and held it, feeling the rubber sole, canvas, laces. "Margaret, did you wear tennis shoes to a wedding?"

"Of course not," Margaret hiccuped. "I wore Anna's satin slippers, and I behaved very well."

"You were grinning coming down the aisle."

"Glad you noticed me."

"You are crazy."

From the path, a waiter asked politely, "Serve you something, sir?"

Andrew jumped. There was just a white coat and a glinting silver tray. "You look like a ghost."

"Scotch-and-soda," Margaret said.

"Miss Margaret, your father wants to know if you're ready to leave."

"Tell my father that Cousin Andrew will drive me home."

The tray rose, floated away, leaving behind a smell of whiskey and the crisp odor of starch.

"And that's why they call them darkies," Margaret

giggled. "Can't see 'em at all. Cheers and Happy New Year and all that sort of thing."

"Take it easy," Andrew said.

"You know," Margaret said, "before today I only sneaked drinks, when nobody was home, or nobody was looking."

"I don't mind driving you home, but I don't want to have to carry you up those stairs."

"You know what I want to be? An old lady with white hair who tells dirty jokes to young boys."

Andrew took a final sip from his glass. "You're going home right now."

When she didn't move, he pulled her to her feet, and held her steady. She leaned against him for a minute, then tossed her glass away into the dark. "Okay, cousin." She could still feel his fingers at her waist.

Andrew's car was a Packard, almost new. "Nice car," Margaret said. "Business must be better than I thought."

He backed carefully, inching his way out of the parking lot. "Still plenty of people here," he said. "Looks like an all-night party."

She leaned her head back.

"You sick?" he asked immediately. "I don't want any mess in the car."

She said, "I'm thinking." And then: "Don't you ever go faster than this?"

"I'm not the soberest person in the world, and I don't want an accident."

The street lights sailed slowly overhead. They were winking at her, she winked back. "Let's go for a drive in the park," she said.

"You go straight home."

"I want to go to the park, by Magazine Street, that pool with the naked ladies."

"Really, now . . ."

"You are so damn handsome to be so damned dull."

"Just for a minute."

Almost before he stopped the car, she opened the door, flashed through the beams of his headlights, and disappeared.

"Where are you going?" he yelled.

She raced through the dark, sure-footed in her tennis shoes.

She stood at the pool, hugging the naked body of one of the three bronze nymphs whose urns poured water endlessly into the marble basin. The cold metal felt green to her hands—and she knew it was. As a child, she'd often come here on sunny afternoons with her nurse. There was always a crowd of white children wading in the pool, and lines of black nurses sitting on the surrounding benches. Once a little boy pulled down his pants and peed on the starched skirt of her dress.

Andrew found her. "So this is your pool."

"Cousin Andrew, you are right."

Picking up her bridesmaid's dress, she stepped down into the knee-deep water. The folds of pink billowed over her arms as she waded back and forth, splashing water into the dark. Andrew sat on a bronze lap, waiting.

She tired of the game. Her tennis shoes squishing water at each step, she walked toward Andrew. Sitting down, he was exactly her height. His features were so blurred she hardly recognized him. It could be anybody, she thought. It could be just any man at all.

"The water's nice," she said. She did not see his hands reach out for her shoulders, but the world gave a spin, the tops of the trees shifted, left to right and back again. "I'm drunk."

"You are." He held her shoulders firmly. "And you don't know what you're doing."

"Yes, I do," she giggled and the trees lurched again. "That's what Anna said: I do." And she lifted her mouth to be kissed.

Funny, she thought, my first kiss with a boy, years ago, was wet and slimy and cold, and I didn't like it. I still don't like it. I'd rather he'd kiss my breast than my mouth.

She squeezed her shoulders together so that her breasts were more prominent. Maybe that would do it. He followed the movement and his lips ran down her neck.

That's all there is to it. That and something else, a burning and a twitching. The tips of the trees jittered and she winked at them.

"JESUS CHRIST," he said, "why didn't you tell me?"

"What?" The trees had stopped moving. Too bad.

"The seat, god damn it, the seat."

She squinted, then scrubbed at it with her skirt. "It is kind of messy. I didn't know there'd be so much blood, Andrew, I always heard it was a symbolic drop and you hung the sheet over the balcony and everybody in the street cheered. In Sicily."

"How the hell am I going to explain that seat to Bernadette?"

"You could pull it out and say you lost it."

"Very funny," he said.

She could see him quite clearly—she must be getting used to the dark. He looked terrible; he had dark circles and bags under his half-shut eyes.

"Look," she said. "How about my problem? I've got to get in the house without anybody seeing me. And that is pretty difficult in my house."

"Tell them you were kicked by a horse. In Sicily."

She reached up and flicked the end of his nose. He

jumped back as if she had slapped him, banging his arm on the car door, doubling with pain.

"Dogs don't like to have their noses tapped either." She got out the back seat and climbed in the front, carefully.

"Watch it," he said, still holding his arm, "watch it, for God's sake."

"I *am*. Let's go."

He drove silently, and very fast. "I've got a great idea," she said, as they stopped at her house. "It just came to me."

"Spare me."

"Put some gas on the seat and set it afire. No evidence."

"No car either." He leaned across her, opening the door.

Holding her dress carefully and precisely, wet shoes squeaking, she got out. He left at once. "Have fun," she said to the two red dots of taillights. They promptly disappeared.

The back door was locked. She considered ringing the bell, decided against it. She would manage by herself.

On the porch post there was a large hook that had once held an awning. With a toe on that hook she could grab the roof and hoist herself over the gutter. From the sloping roof, a couple of steps along a trellis, flip up the screen, and tumble into her room. Home free.

Her dress was in the way. She tucked it under her waist, where it was so bulky that it made breathing difficult. *Forget it, kid,* she told herself shortly.

She had no trouble getting to the roof. Now the small back yard was below her: neat flower beds, spots of color— roses or something like that—and by the back fence, the tall fan-like shadows of paper plants. Beyond that, the blind windows of the house next door, curtains drawn, properly sleeping.

Margaret stood up slowly. *One more, old girl.* She put her toe into the trellis, giggling at the tiny squash of wet shoe. She shifted her weight, moved again, hung on the wall, lifted the screen. As her shoe slipped. She heard it even before she felt the change of balance. She swung her left arm wildly, hooked the sill, then almost lost it in the sudden pain of impact. She kicked wildly, propelling herself forward. *If I stop, I'll be too tired to start again. . . . Push.* The upper part of her body was across the sill. Now only the dress wrapped around her waist was in the way. *Feels like I'm climbing a mountain. Anna and her flowing dresses.*

She rolled slightly to one side, ribs grating on the wood, shifting her weight crosswise. And tumbled inside.

Her breath scratched through her throat, fast and dry. She sat on the rug, legs doubled under her, and panted. *I'm a puppy dog, with a long red coat and a shiny black nose.*

There was also a very funny feeling behind her eyes. Like wires crossed. . . . She bent forward until her head rested on her knees. Collapsed. Like a puppet with tangled strings.

She stripped off her dress—her fingers seemed swollen and stiff—put on a robe, and padded down the hall toward the kitchen. Every light was on, but the house was empty. She found a Coke and drank it standing by the open refrigerator. It was the only cool place on a summer night. There seemed to be a party downstairs. Because her father liked to play, the entire first floor, a single large room, held three pool tables and endless racks of cues and balls. Nicest place in the house, she thought, with its leather chairs and faint wood smell from the paneled walls. Who'd be down there now? Was it still part of the wedding party? Her bare feet felt a regular beat: music. She opened another Coke. *I couldn't care less.*

Downstairs, a muffled shout, then breaking glass and more shouts. A fight. You had to admit, she thought, that when her father gave a party, he gave a good one.

On the hall table there was a mass of white flowers in

a tall brass vase. She thought: I'll get married without flow-ers, and I'll never have a single cut flower in my house. Only things in pots, slowly strangling to death.

She herself seemed to carry a musty odor. Of course. She'd been wading. . . . *Water must be full of algae and cater-pillars and God knows what.*

She held out her arm and studied it. The dark hairs seemed to twitch. *Microbes pushing them around. Pretty soon they'll turn green. Dull green like the bronze ladies at the pool. And what would it be like to sit season after season watching generations of children pass in front of your eyes? Eat the little monsters, serve them for breakfast, catch one here after midnight and we'll have him for sure, eat a child and release the bronze curse, we'll be free, free, free, free.*

She tucked a single peony behind her ear, and went to take a shower, singing over and over again: "Goodbye, algae; goodbye, bugs, goodbye, goodbye. . . ." She tried to sing it to "Good Night, Irene," but kept losing the tune.

She went to bed. And thought.

About Anna, white gown and floating veil, properly mar-ried in her perfect little house. About bronze ladies sitting with naked breasts and discreetly folded legs. About moons that skipped around in the sky, about trees that tipped and swayed.

And that perfume, so much like the patchouli that her aunts used, who had worn it? Cousin Andrew. Yes, indeed.

As she relaxed, her fingers began twitching by them-selves, and a muscle on the outside of her thigh squirmed.

She scowled into the dark. She'd expected so much; she got nothing. Maybe that was the wages of sin, maybe Anna had done better with her first man. . . .

Disappointment like a nasty little worm crawled across her, leaving slimy spoiling trails. . . .

She cried a few hot tears that hurt to shed and burned the flesh of her cheeks as they fell.

I T   W A S   the afternoon of the following day before she felt herself again.

"You want to hear the news?" her father asked. "It seems to have been quite a party. Philip Wilson drove into Bayou St. John on his way home, missed the bridge by thirty feet. Sally Mitchell had a fight with her husband and left him that same night, so he called Tess Christina and she moved in half an hour later. Andrew Stephano's car caught on fire. Robert Lemoine's son went over to Norma's and got in a fight at the bar instead of going straight for the girls, so his ear's almost bit off. Tootsie's father-in-law said he had a heart attack and he did. What else—I can't remember now."

Margaret heard only one thing: "What happened to Cousin Andrew?"

"He dropped a cigarette or something. The whole back seat was afire when the milkman saw it."

Margaret giggled; she drew up her knees, put her head down on them and giggled. How funny, funny, funny.

"What's the joke?"

"He's such a stuffy ass, and he was mad for that car."

"Was he?"

She stopped giggling. He might suspect, but he would never ask. "It was a great wedding, Papa, did you hear them downstairs last night?"

"I wasn't home," her father said. "Margaret, no more big affairs. You elope. Go across the river to Gretna and get a justice of the peace."

"Papa, if you weren't home last night, where were you?"

He did not look up from his restless twitching of the newspaper. "That, little lady, is none of your business."

OLIVER

HER NAME was Helen Augustine Ware, and she was a widow. Her husband had been an accountant with Southern Railway, a hard-working man who'd been promoted to vice-president six months before he died.

Helen Ware was short, and slender, and very proper. She was terrified that her married son would discover her affair with Oliver.

"What can he object to?" Oliver asked reasonably. "You're a widow, I'm a widower, why can't I take you to dinner? Or pay a call?"

"Not so often, don't you see? People are suspicious and I couldn't stand to have any gossip about us."

"Who notices," Oliver said, "who cares?"

Helen Ware shook her head, "My dear, you are so naïve. People do watch. So we have to be careful."

They played a hide-and-seek game. To visit her, he had first to wait for her call, then take a taxi and get off two blocks from her house. "You must never get the same driver," she said, "and you must get off at a different spot every time."

"Sure," he lied. And then took the same cab every time and had him wait just around the corner. He liked having the same driver. He liked getting used to faces and seeing them over and over again.

Maybe, he thought, part of Helen Ware's charm was the games he played to see her.

When she came to his house, her arrangements were even more elaborate. She drove her car to a different spot each time—she favored crowded streets near hospitals: "I can always say I'm visiting if somebody recognizes my car." "How can anybody tell your car from all the others?" "Well, they might." He drove himself; she would not have his chauffeur see her. He had to find her, stop close by, while she waited for the proper moment to dart into his car, and huddle far down in her seat

His teasing had no effect. She insisted. Then, on the day of Anna's wedding, his patience ran out. He was standing next to one of the buffet tables; the waiters were arranging it with great precision—he looked at the cold meats and the indistinguishable covered dishes with sudden repulsion. He'd been eating; now he put down his plate, hastily. He'd been drinking; now the smell of alcohol made him sick. He found himself standing on the front steps, the parking lot in front of him, lines of white-jacketed Negro boys waiting to bring cars. The lot was crowded. These people were never going home, he thought. At daylight they would still be drinking and eating and rubbing around in the shadowy shrubbery.

He went down the steps to the white gravel of the parking lot. The party sure wouldn't miss him. Now who would he miss? Who was there that he would ever want to see again, if he had the choice? His dead wife's family and their in-laws, by the hundreds? It seemed to him that he had always been surounded by her family. Drowning in them, jammed to death by them.

Their pressure was like a weight on the back of his neck. "Where's my car?" The big Packard limousine, flashy badge of success, stopped in front of him. He waved his chauffeur away. "I'll drive." Where? Where did he want to go? He hesitated, one hand on the door. And then he knew. "Wait," he said, and hurried inside. To call Helen Ware. She'd come to the wedding and to the reception, but she had not stayed

long. She was always so very correct. He kept ringing, humming cheerfully to himself. Until she answered.

"I'm coming over," he said. "Put a light in the window
for me."

"Now?"

"No, in about five minutes."

A pause. "You've been drinking, that's what it is."

"Comb your hair, or whatever you have to do."

"You just can't come walking in at this hour of the night
—do you know what time it is?"

"No," he admitted, "but I don't care either. Answer the
door."

"I will not," she said. "I've told you so often how careful I have to be."

"You've told me," he said, "but I'm tired of sneaking
around corners. I'm going to park a big black Packard limousine right in front of your house, and I'm going to kick in
the door if I have to."

"I will not allow any such thing."

"Helen," he said, weary of talk, "you'll open the door."

The streets were empty; he wondered vaguely what time
it could be. There seemed to be a lightening over there, would
it be near morning. Or was it just his eyes?

Though he'd often been to Helen Ware's house in the
two years he'd known her, he had trouble finding it now.
The quiet uptown streets, with their heavy greasy canopies
of camphor trees, all looked alike. He peered at the street
signs: Hampson, Perrier, Coliseum. What was the name of
her street? He turned a corner, stared. No, not this one. Go
the other way. Where the hell was it, that white house with
a magnolia tree directly in front, that low white house with
a fringe of wood gingerbreadwork over the screened front
porch. Where'd it got to? Must have disappeared. He peered
down another street, and then another. Maybe I'm in the
wrong part of town.

He actually drove past the house before he noticed. There. He backed up, hastily. Sure enough. That was it. Have I been passing it all this time, going round and round in front of it?

The door opened at once, she must have been sitting right behind it, waiting.

"Good morning," he said cheerfully, "did you see me drive by a few times before?"

"I wasn't looking out," she said.

She was in terrible humor, that was clear. He grinned, knowing that in his lined, weathered face, his grin was still boyish. "I had some trouble finding your place."

"How much have you had to drink?"

"Haven't any idea. Would you care to offer something to a gentleman caller?"

"I would not."

"You keep it in the dining-room cabinet, right?"

"You can't come here any hour of the night and expect me . . ."

He poured himself a neat Scotch. "To your health."

She was still sulking. Her underlip was definitely pouting. He decided to ignore it. "You like the wedding?"

"It went beautifully."

"What did you think of the reception?"

"Everyone seemed to be having a marvelous time."

"They still are," he said to the yellow Scotch.

"You don't mind."

"The liquor will last longer than they will."

"You're very patient."

"I'm not there." He pulled a chair away from the table with his foot and sat down. Deliberately, because he knew it annoyed her, he put his glass on the polished mahogany surface.

She slipped a coaster under it, wordlessly.

"What about a whiskey, Helen?"

"No, thank you."

"Take one," Oliver said. "It'll make an old drunk like me look better to you."

"You must stop thinking of yourself as ancient."

He shook his head, grinning. She refused to think of him as old. She also refused to think of herself as old. "Have a drink with the Old Man," he said. "Everybody's called me that for more than thirty years. And by God, they're finally right."

"We are both middle-aged," she said. "Middle-aged."

She would never change. Oliver himself rather liked the idea of getting old; if he managed it right he'd be venerable, like the pope, and people would think him very wise. . . .

Helen Ware said "middle-aged," as if it were a charm that held back time. How foolish women were, how silly. *Middle-aged.* Not any more. And not for a long time past. You could see age in her body, could see every one of her years clearly marked on her skin. Hollows on the inside of her thighs, little caves where the flesh had fallen away. That wasn't middle-aged, he thought with a silent laugh. That was old. Like those bulges along her jaw that she smoothed and pressed and treated with creams each day. And the way her skin felt thin and dry and brittle and scorched. . . . Sometimes it seemed to him that time was like fire, burning as it passed. The heat of the blood dried and withered the flesh it supported.

Now, lying in her bed, he held one of his arms straight up into the air and looked at it. Sometimes it seemed to him that he wasn't really connected to himself. The memories of the person he'd been didn't seem possible. This arm now. He had a hard time believing that it belonged to him as a boy. The arm that had been with him forty years ago in the alleys of Singapore and the streets of Manila was sunburned and thick with light hair. This arm now—the one he held over his head—had white skin and dark hair. Like a photograph

negative. . . . Feelings went that way too. Things important
to the boy, the man never thought about.

He turned his arm about, staring at the corded veins
along the inner side, trying to see the blood running inside
them. When a man was cut, the blood pumped out in squirts,
just like a pump emptying a boat. He'd seen that when he was
little, back in the Ohio Valley; a saw slashed his thigh, his
blood pumped red into the snow, steaming. Oliver remembered thinking that it was like hogs' blood at slaughtering
time.

Now, here was his arm, again, stuck up in the air. He
whistled through his teeth at it. Old man's arm, old man's
body.

"What are you doing?" Helen Ware asked.

"Thinking."

"About what."

"When I was young."

"For heaven's sake." She thought all memories were bad.
She snuggled closer to him, her fingers tapping at his ribs,
the insistent demanding call on his body. For two years he'd
had answers for her. This time there was no response.

"I'm sorry, Helen," he said.

Funny, he thought, it doesn't bother me; it ought to,
but it doesn't.

"You've had too much to drink."

She was annoyed, he thought calmly. Very annoyed.

And what happened to his desire? Into what strange
corner had his lust drained?

It had troubled him for so long, this lust, as it raged and
burned sporadically. Times when clouds looked like breasts
and mountains like buttocks. Times when the entire air
quivered with the smell of musk. When any woman was
beautiful, because she was necessary. When he could not sit
down, could not keep still. He jammed two-bit whores, with-

out noticing their scars and filth. He ordered expensive women, and had not noticed the details of their superb bodies. Even when he changed whores for decent women, nothing was different. It was still the same blind urge.

He was driven to their flesh, impelled, as if it weren't his doing at all. As if he weren't really present. As if there were just a naked joyless male drive and a nameless woman to satisfy it. When it was over, he'd come back to join his body again—in the emptiness of satisfaction there was room for him.

With this woman now, Helen Ware, he felt comfortable. Her house was familiar to him, he recognized even the smallest objects. Just as he knew the rooms around him, he knew the body next to him. He knew the feel of the thin skin, the little perpendicular wrinkles of the neck, the dry thighs. . . . There'd been a whore once, so long ago; she'd been oily all over, inside and out, slippery skin, slippery hair. Juicy was her word for it, but it reminded him of ice-skating. . . .

It was pleasant to lie in Helen Ware's bed in the semi-darkness, and study the shape and form of his arm, and feel his daughter's wedding liquor sing in his brain. And know for a fact: the end of lust. He had expected to be afraid and horrified. He wasn't either. He was only, vaguely, surprised. That was all. The first death. So quiet. A tide you didn't see go out until it was gone.

She shook him and asked: "Are you sick?"

"Just old age." The first death; yes, that was right. When was the next?

"I don't know what's the matter with you tonight."

He lowered his arm and looked at her. "It's rough on you," he said. "I'm sorry."

She had a lot to say, but he didn't listen. He was still considering himself, with surprise. So this was the way it went, gentle. He'd never even considered the possibility of that. Nature fixed it for you: desire and ability went together. Neat and proper. He felt lighter now. A burden, a requirement, was gone.

She was crying. He turned to her but she pushed him away, angrily.

"I know I don't have the body of a young girl."

He frowned. What was she talking about? What had she taken it all for?

"I know perfectly well that no woman fifty-five can be beautiful. Not like a young girl."

"What?" he said. "What?"

She didn't listen. "You don't have to do it like this. . . ."

"What are you talking about?" he asked. "What am I doing?"

"How can you be so insulting, so cruel. . . ."

Well. Like that. She thought it was her fault. Which of course was the way a woman would think. Too bad. If she'd only understood, they could have lain in bed and had a drink together. And she might even have felt some of the gentle softness he was feeling. The great release. My dear, what you've missed. But maybe it never comes to women. My dear, what a pity and a shame.

He thought he knew what to say, and he said it to the ceiling. "Would you like to get married?"

In the silence that followed he waited patiently.

"Are you serious?" she asked.

And then there was a great weariness that ran around the hollow spaces inside his body, filling them like smoke. "No," he said. "No."

He drove home in the red light of the early-June sun. This isn't so bad, he thought; this isn't so bad at all. At least he felt free.

ROBERT

Robert STOOD in the corner of his new bed-room, the inside of his skull shaking and shivering. Like jello. Or an earthquake. One or the other. He couldn't decide which.

The whole room was full of pink roses. He squeezed the nearest bud between his fingers until it burst.

"Robert," Anna called from the dressing room. "Why don't you open the champagne?"

There it was, single bottle in a silver stand. Two crystal goblets next to it.

He expected Anna to be shy. Or afraid. But it was he who was nervous. She held his hand, and opened the iron gate and led him along the path to their house while her long satin skirts made little crisp noises against the bricks. He managed to unlock the door, but it was she who slipped the night latch across behind them.

The champagne opened with a loud plop. He poured it gently and carefully into the two glasses. It was pink. Or was it just the room reflecting? He found himself staring at the pink silk curtains. Was there really a window behind all that? . . .

The room seemed foggy; hazy. It was the soft lighting, the wall sconces with their tiny flickering fingers of light, the pink-shaded lamps.

He was married now. His life was organized and planned.

A steady series of successes. Work bringing its rewards. Esteem and love. Increasing happiness. Bask in the approval of your wife's brown eyes. . . . Me, the man of property, the successful businessman, growing distinguished gray hairs, the soft cushions of money all around. . . . And what the hell was bothering him?

The house hadn't looked familiar. . . . He'd been here a hundred times. He knew the studs, and the laths, and the plaster; he knew the brick foundations and the underfloor. He knew the clapboards; he had looked into the buckets of paint. And now that he had moved here, nothing in the house seemed familiar.

"Is the champagne ready?" Anna wore a long white robe that billowed around her, fluttering and lifting and sending out waves of perfume.

"I never noticed that your hair was straight," he said.

"I've always had straight hair," she said.

"I don't know why I never noticed."

He picked up a glass, his hand shook. The frothy liquid ran along the finished surface of the table. Hastily, he reached for his handkerchief.

Anna put a hand on his arm, "Robert, everything in the house was made to be used, don't worry about it."

She was right. It was all his to be used. He handed her the glass. "Happy wedding, Mrs. Caillet."

He'd expected a blush or a giggle. He got only a quiet smile. "I'm very happy, Robert."

He said: "I like that, it looks lovely on you." He reached out to touch the floating panels and his fingers were appalled by the dry scratchy feel. Like feeling dead leaves, he thought.

"I would like some more champagne, please."

He filled her glass, without spilling this time. "I'm getting the hang of it."

Learn all sorts of things. Learn to get used to this: me a married man. Wife all in fluffy white. That scratches like starch. Why would she wear that? Me with a house of my own. Floors so polished the rugs skid on them. It's a long way from the oyster boats. With Ti Chou yelling: "Quick quick, you work to fill your empty mouth! You sit at my table to eat, you got to work." . . .

Anna held out her glass again. "I must be nervous."

He kissed her lightly. Her lips were very smooth and tasted vaguely sweet. Clouds of perfume hung around her face.

"I'll wait for you," she said.

Wait for me. Yes. I'm her husband. Take what's mine. Can't leave things untouched, cause for divorce. To say nothing of her thinking I'm a queer.

"I'll be right back."

He found pajamas and robe behind the door. Everything arranged. He stepped into the shower, letting the water pour over his face and hair. What the hell was wrong? Usually he couldn't get to a woman fast enough. Like Betty. Sometimes they didn't have time to get to the creaky couch in her dusty basement, and he actually felt the floor through her body. Even before the door opened, he was straining at his pants, wanting to jam into her. And that basement. He had never really seen it. Just smelled it: musky and close with the faint sweet odor of rats hanging in the air. Just thinking about it now and the movement in his loins began. Damn fool, you can only make it in a dirty basement. . . .

The bedroom was darker, just a single lamp burning. Pink light in a pool on the floor. The white wings of her robe hung motionless on a chair. Clouds settling on the mountains.

He climbed into bed, slowly. Methodically, he held her, letting his hands smooth and pet, while his panic grew. What the hell is wrong? . . . She had smooth skin, cool even in June. Marble would be the word for it. Betty had sharp prickly hair growing under her armpits; her skin was rough, pitted with occasional pimples and old craters of chicken-pox scars. She was always warm, too, even on winter nights. Sweat popped out of her pores in little beads that formed quick streams. She smelled of sweat, faintly sour.

Anna sighed contentedly. He was doing all right. If he could just keep it up.

Her nipple lengthened and hardened in his mouth. His hand reached her crotch. She was ready. He wasn't. My God, he thought, why did I have anything to drink?

"Do you like to kiss," she asked very softly.

"You just wait," he said, "and you'll see."

He'd never had a woman like that. For him it had to be a virgin.

He thought: Every woman moved alike with her spasm. Every one. The same shift, the same lift upward. Same pleasure, virgin and whore. Anna and Betty.

He had never really seen Betty; she was always a shape in the dark, speaking in whispers. But he remembered her, God, he remembered her and he could feel her now. The snake-like movements. The desire, not so much for him as for any man. But while he was there, he *was* all men. For that one moment the force and power of the future drove through his loins. He would break and destroy, he would remake in his own way.

He mounted Anna blindly. But it was Betty he entered, whose receptive body waited for him. It was on Betty's body he consummated his marriage and from Betty Anna's blood flowed.

"Jesus God," he said aloud. "Jesus God."

WHEN THE image of Betty had faded, and the small circle of blood soaked into the padded sheet, he rolled off her body, and reached, without thinking, for a cigarette. (There were some right by the bed. How did Anna know that about him?) He lay on his back, watching the smoke rise and lose itself in the pink shadows. He was trying to think of something to say, something that wouldn't sound foolish. Something tender. Something profound.

By the time he finished the cigarette and snubbed it out in the pink leaf-shaped ashtray, he found that she had turned slightly on her side, slightly away from him, and fallen asleep.

IN THE morning, even before he opened his eyes, he knew that she was awake. He could feel her steady stare begin to pry him open.

"Hi," he said vaguely and was surprised at the weariness in his voice. One little time and he felt like he'd been grinding all night.

Her brown eyes were almost round this morning. There were shadows under them, blue shadows, but the eyes glowed as if lights burned behind them. "Robert," she said, "we are going to be the happiest couple that there ever was in the world."

He frowned, blinked, and found the brown glow still there. Only a cat looked like that, that gleaming look, when it located the prey it was going to eat.

"Robert," she said, "I love you so very much, and I will love you all my life."

"You know I love you," he said. He had an earache. He hadn't had one of those since he was a child.

She didn't even seem to be listening. "I like to think of us getting old together, and having grandchildren."

"You do?"

"Two loves put together, the way God intended them to be. I wouldn't want to live without you."

Before her blazing certainty, he felt himself shrivel and die.

ANNA SLIPPED out of bed. He noticed that her long white gown was spotted with blood. Would she fold that away to keep, he wondered, like a certificate, a testimonial?

For a moment he thought she'd come back to bed. He felt a faint stir of desire, a twitch, a familiar burning. (Either that, he thought bitterly, or he had to piss.) But she walked silently out the door, and in a few minutes the smell of coffee reached him.

At noon they left New Orleans. At ten o'clock they drove through Collinsville's Main Street; at eleven o'clock they passed the single grocery-and-post-office that was Port Bella. They missed the turn on the unmarked road and didn't find their hotel until shortly after midnight.

There was no moon, but they saw clearly by starlight. The Gulf, a couple of hundred yards away, white, sand-fringed, reflected the night dully, like a sheet of unpolished metal. The lawns, treeless and smooth, rose from the beach to the hotel itself, gables and turrets and high peaked roofs, a wooden castle guarding the crab-filled waters.

At the front door Anna said: "There's got to be a bell."

Robert struck a match. "No bell, no pull, no knocker." Overhead, disturbed by the faint yellow light, a couple of birds fluttered. Farther off an owl gave its soft descending cry.

Anna laughed: "Wouldn't it be silly if we drove all that way and couldn't get past the front door?"

Robert pounded the wood with his fist. It gave a kind of muted thump, stifled and faint.

"That's the littlest sound I ever heard."

"That's oak," Robert said, "and the door must be a foot thick."

"We could camp on the lawn. Or down on the beach. That might be fun."

"Well, not for me." In annoyance he leaned against the door, hip pushing against the brass latch. The latch clicked; the hinges moved smoothly in well-oiled silence. The door opened.

"It wasn't locked." Anna giggled. "We never thought of that."

The hall was wood-paneled and very dark, its high ceiling invisible. At the foot of a wide stairway, a life-sized turbaned Negro figure held a feeble torch.

Under the arch of the stairs hung a small discreet sign. Robert pointed. "Let's see if that's the office."

They found a small desk placed across the alcove, and behind that the vague outlines of a room. There was no light at all.

"Oh, for God's sake!" Robert shouted: "Anybody here? Anybody here?"

The sounds didn't echo, they flattened and died under the arch of the stair.

"I'm coming," a quiet voice said. "I've been waiting for you. I'm coming."

The desk clerk appeared from somewhere close behind the desk. He wiped the sleep from his eyes with one hand. With the other he pushed the registration form toward Robert.

He's naked, Robert thought. And then: I'm seeing things.

The clerk switched on a small lamp bent almost double on its thin gooseneck. Robert filled in the form, hardly knowing what he wrote, staring intently at the man's navel and the hair that radiated from it.

"Thank you," the clerk said, slipping the forms into his

drawer. "I'll find the boy to take your bags. These niggers are never around when you want them."

He turned and marched through the door, lamplight sliding off the thin planes of his buttocks. His bare feet slapped the floor briefly, then a screen door slammed.

Anna held the counter and shook with silent laughter. "It's a hot night and I suppose he wanted to be comfortable."

Robert said: "I want to see what this place is like in the morning."

BY DAYLIGHT it was just a large gray old-fashioned hotel. There were four elderly couples—printed voile dresses and white linen suits. One fat widow who carried her canary with her. Two spinster sisters who sat in rocking chairs on the porch and did crossword puzzles all day long, never speaking a word to each other, never looking at the sky or the water, only now and then consulting a large dictionary on the table between them. There was also a redheaded man who left every morning at four to fish and was brought back, staggering drunk, in midafternoon by the charter-boat captain.

No one ever seemed to use them, but there was a croquet lawn on the east side of the hotel and a shuffleboard court on the west. There was a tennis court splotchy with Johnson grass. There was also a long pier out into the Gulf, at its end a square platform roofed with palm thatch.

That first afternoon Anna and Robert stood in the shade of the dry leaves. "Nothing here," Robert said. "Let's go back to bed."

Anna smiled her sleepy contented smile. "What would people think?"

"They'll think we're madly in love."

Their windows opened on the Gulf, flat and waveless and heat-smeared at its horizon. Starched white curtains hung straight down, motionless in the air. Glare poured through them, hot as sunlight.

Later he said: "It's blazing hot."

Lines of sweat glistened over her eyebrows and across her upper lip. His chest hair matted and clung in streaks to his skin.

"Just feel the bed," she said, "it's like a stove."

"I'll pull the shade." He stood at the window for a moment, looking down the slope of brown grass. Two children, wearing identical blue sunsuits and wide straw hats, walked down the beach. Had they just arrived? Or were there other houses around the point? They had a toy boat, shiny white, and they squatted down to float it in the shallows.

He watched the bit of white wood riding on its string. Maybe the hotel had a skiff, and tonight, when it got cool, he could take Anna for a row. Not far. Just enough to feel the lift of the water. Floating apart from shore, they could look back to where they had been and where they would be again.

He'd always liked that. Even when he was very little, he'd liked to take a pirogue or an old skiff and paddle out into the bayou, just to float there. He was doing that when the *Bozo,* a big shrimp lugger that the five Cheramie brothers owned, came plowing up the bayou. He was daydreaming and hadn't noticed in time, though you could hear that engine— one piston missing, everybody knew it—for half a mile. He couldn't get clear. He knew enough to put the pirogue's bow directly into the wake and hold it there. He was too young, and the pirogue too sluggish. She swung broadside, flipped over, and he found himself swimming for the first time. The water felt heavy and thick; he was so terrified that he saw colored sparkles in front of his eyes. His legs began running frantically, his fingers clamped around the paddle, and he whimpered through tight-shut lips. He stepped on something and slowly realized what it was—the pirogue had not completely lost its buoyancy. It was hovering slightly under the surface. Like a little island, he stood on it. The *Bozo* had gone on; the waves were subsiding and he had no trouble balancing, the water reaching only to his shoulders. He screamed until somebody pulled him out. He got beaten with a razor strop the moment they dragged him ashore, but his cousins did not bother going after the old pirogue. It was a Saturday evening, they had boiled shrimp and beer, and they were tired. In the currentless bayou the pirogue would wait for them. The next morning they had a few more beers while thinking what had to be done. Then the *Bozo*, going down to trawl on Sunday because the weather was good, smashed into the pirogue, hidden in the muddy water. There was a lot of shouting and cursing but no harm done beyond the loss of a few hours' fishing. After that, when the welts from his beating healed, Robert taught himself to swim. He'd gotten sick several times from the filthy bayou water, but he managed to learn.

"Anna," he said, "do you know how to swim?"

She didn't hear. She was lying, naked, face down, her long smooth back and buttocks gleaming with sweat.

Funny, he thought, all the things I don't know about her. He touched her shoulder. "Can you swim?"

She opened one eye. "Are we having a flood?"

"Go back to sleep," he said. Under his hand he could feel her muscles relax, her flesh turn soft and heavy.

He put one hand on the bed. All the heat of the long afternoon seemed concentrated there. When Anna got up, there'd be a sweat shadow left on the sheet, a dark clear imprint. The perfect outline. The shadow without the flesh.

He tossed a pillow to the floor directly under the window, off the rug, and stretched out.

The boards were slick and cool and comfortable. He

put his hands under his head and stretched slowly. He'd spent all his childhood sleeping on the floor. On the porch in summer, if the mosquitoes weren't too bad: sun-bleached boards, with the grain standing out high and hard, like a washboard. When the mosquito plagues came—when the air was thick with them and people plastered their milk cows with a thick layer of mud twice a day to protect them—he had to sleep in the house, again on the floor, but inside the mosquito barre. He hated the nights spent huddling within the dust-laden net folds, listening to the insects buzzing outside, to the creaking of the bed ropes, to the deep heavy breathing of the other children. Their breaths ruffled his hair, stifled him so that he pulled up a tiny corner of the net and stuck his nose outside. . . . But winters were worst, when a cold gray rain fell steadily and all the children slept wrapped in their pallets, jammed body against body around the dying warmth of the stove, eyes squeezed shut to keep out the creeping cold.

He did not like people sleeping close to him. He could not stand being touched; he always woke up with a jolt of alarm in his stomach. That was the hardest thing about being married—the double bed. Every time he jerked awake, it was hours before he fell asleep. But how could he tell Anna that? She hadn't even asked him about the double bed. She'd asked about everything else: the color of the living-room rug; of the outside shutters. Did he like a garden or did he want the tiny yard bricked over, patio-fashion? Did he think Queen Anne would look silly with a Sheraton sideboard? . . . But not the bed.

There was nothing to do. If his flesh cringed every night and shrank from contact when he was asleep, well, he would just have to get over it. Right now it looked like he was going to lose quite a lot of sleep.

He rubbed the bare boards with his finger tips and smiled grimly at the ceiling. Nice. Nothing close by. Not even a wall. When he was little, he'd never put his pallet against a wall, the way he was supposed to. He slept in the middle of the floor, so that people getting up to use the out-house or to urinate from the edge of the porch, scattering the chickens roosting there, those people would stumble over him, and stagger cursing through the room. He always man-aged to be in his proper place, pretending sleep, before they lit the lamp. They saw only a line of children, him no dif-ferent from the rest. Soon as they were back in bed, he'd sneak again into the center of the floor. It was the only way he could sleep.

Robert yawned. . . . Even if Anna should ask him about the bed, he thought, his mind refusing to leave that problem, he would never tell her. You weren't a man unless you slept in the same bed with your wife. You were something else. A stud, or a lover. But you weren't a husband, not a proper husband. Anna expected a husband. And he was going to be one.

He woke, Anna kneeling next to him. The light was different, yellower. It was getting toward evening.

"I couldn't imagine where you'd gone."

"It really *is* cooler here." He was apologizing. Like he'd been caught doing something wrong.

"Doesn't your back hurt?"

"I've slept on floors before." He saw her face freeze.

"Would you like a drink?" She was changing the subject. She was being kind; she did not want to remind him of any-thing unpleasant.

Suddenly he was angry. At her. She didn't understand. He'd been a dirt-poor kid, who didn't even know his father's name; his family had too many children, but they all worked, and there was almost always enough to eat. And his mother had been wonderful to him. He remembered her hugging and kissing him, holding his face between her hands. Later he wondered if she wasn't trying to guess his father's identity.

But then he hadn't thought like that. Then she'd just been his mother, pretty like all mothers. He didn't really think much about her, until she died. For weeks then he'd shivered with fear and horror until, just exactly the way he hadn't thought of his mother when she was alive, he learned not to think of her when she was dead. . . . His days were dirt and sweat and being tired all the time. But none of that bothered him then.

Anna was wrong. He didn't want to think back to all those different houses on different bayous, yards full of scrawny chickens, everywhere the smell of outhouse, shrimp, and bait. He didn't want to remember all that, and he didn't think about it unless he had to. But he wasn't ashamed of it.

"I never slept in a real bed until I got to Baton Rouge. And I had a hell of a time getting used to it."

A shadow flickered across her face. "You told me."

He insisted. "All sorts of people jammed into one little house. I never did figure out why I didn't catch consumption from my mother."

"Robert, you told me all about that. Do you want to tell me again?"

The way she said it. He curled with silent anger. *Do you want to confess your sins to me?* What the hell did she know?

"What do you know?" he said.

"Just what you've told me, Robert."

Something in the smooth patient contours of her face. Something unchanged, and unchanging. His anger washed up over her insistent love. Crested and retreated. And disappeared. He wondered why he'd ever got angry; it wasn't her fault. She didn't have to understand. And he didn't have to care what she thought.

He got up, his back stiff and aching. So he wasn't used to sleeping on boards after all. He felt vaguely sad about that. As if he'd lost something of great value.

For two days he was patient. By the third day he was acutely restless. Because he didn't sleep well at night, he dozed all the long afternoon and woke time-confused and groggy. He was exhausted and bored by the endless progression of empty sunny days.

HE WAS asleep that afternoon when Anna answered the phone. She did not call him; he woke from his sweaty sleep to find her sitting by the window.

One look at her face—he sucked in his breath, the fogs of sleep and monotony disappeared.

"What's the matter, Anna?"

"Papa was hurt."

The more upset she was, the less showed in her face. Robert wondered if she could also control her feelings that completely. Could she stop her stomach churning and her viscera contracting? Could she quiet fear by will? They'd taught her self-control at the convent, but had they also taught her a deeper control?

"Was there a call?" He spoke carefully: that quiet china face might crack.

"Aunt Cecilia telephoned about an hour ago." No emphasis, no color; only gray sounds.

"How was he hurt?"

The hands in her lap didn't move. They lay motionless, palms down. "You can't be sure Aunt Cecilia gets things right." She was staring out the window at the white-blue summer sky. "She says there was a holdup at the store."

"That doesn't make sense."

"I don't know, Robert." The hands lifted for an instant, in apology. "Papa wouldn't let anyone tell us. She had to sneak her call."

"Anna, do you want to go back?"

She went on staring out the window. He thought again how strong the mark of the convent was. Her head, balanced delicately on its thin neck, seemed to have a coif around it. And if he slanted his eyes slightly he could see her starched wimple and black veil. It was in the way she held herself. Patient and secure—hopelessly arrogant.

Those thoughts left an unpleasant aftertaste. Like an odor, it clung to the curtains and hung in the rug and lingered on.

"We'll go back, Anna."

"Not for my sake."

"No," he said, "but we'll go back."

She packed in half an hour, not even forgetting her collection of sea shells.

The afternoon air was thick and dusty and hot; the thunderheads over the Gulf seemed heavier than usual. Robert could see flickerings of chain lightning in their black bases. It was, he thought, going to be a rough drive.

It was past midnight when they got to their house. Two of the street lights were out, and in the darkened block the small white cottage was almost invisible under its heavy shrubbery. Roaches scurried across the porch boards and paint-tinged heat poured out when they opened the door.

"Oh my," Anna said.

Methodically Robert began opening windows. The outside air seemed fresh and soft, leaf-cooled. . . . He could hear Anna at the phone, jiggling the receiver impatiently for the operator. He hadn't eaten since lunch, but he wasn't hungry. He was thirsty. On the shelves the glasses looked faintly dusty. He rinsed one and filled it. The water tasted like putty. He opened the liquor closet and took out the first bottle: Irish. He poured, stirred with his fingers, and drank it down. You didn't even miss ice that way.

Anna called: "Papa's home, Robert. He says we are not to come over."

To show them that nothing mattered to him. That he did what he wanted; circumstances or bad luck had no effect on him. . . .

Anna was saying, "Papa, I just want to convince myself you're all right. You know I won't sleep until I do." And she hung up.

Robert whistled under his breath.

She fiddled with the phone, running her finger around and around in the mouthpiece. "Don't be angry with me, Robert."

"Who's angry?"

"There's nothing wrong in being worried about your father."

"Look, Anna," he said, "if you want to see him, we'll go over. That's all there is to it."

ROBERT RECOGNIZED   the stocky man who opened the door for them—Jasper Lucas. He'd worked for the Old Man for years, one place or the other. He'd started tending bar at the Old Man's first casino, the one out at Franciscan Point. When the Old Man got a larger club at Southport, Lucas worked there as a dealer. When the Old Man bought the St. John Hotel, Lucas became a detective. For a while he was the Old Man's bootleg distributor in East Texas. When the Old Man quit the liquor business, Lucas became a department-store detective.

Robert nodded to him as they passed. . . . With Lucas here, the Old Man was taking no chances.

He was in bed, waiting for them. He was wearing bright

blue pajamas and his left arm was bandaged heavily all the way to the shoulder.

"Oh, Papa," Anna said.

"Now that you've seen," the Old Man said sarcastically, "can we all go to sleep?"

"Aunt Cecilia was terrified," Anna said.

"She is an ass. I sent her home hours ago."

Robert said: "We could drink to your good luck if Jasper would fix us a whiskey."

From the doorway Jasper nodded.

"I've been drinking Irish," Robert said. "What about you?"

"Fine," the Old Man said. The skin was drawn tightly over his forehead and his cheeks. It wrinkled sidewise like carelessly stretched fabric.

Jasper brought the drinks. Robert drank half, then rubbed the icy surface against his sunburned face and heard the little crackle of whiskers.

"At least," the Old Man said, "you have no curiosity."

"I'll hear about it tomorrow," Robert said. "Did they intend to hit you—is that why Jasper's here?"

"No," the Old Man said. "It was an accident." He reached for his glass, twisted his lips with pain. Robert handed it to him. "I was in the wrong place. I just feel better with him here."

Jasper's square face smiled, briefly, then collapsed into its usual dull mask.

Robert said, "How'd you get the doctor to let you out of the hospital?"

"He would not have been my doctor very long otherwise."

With a rustle of starched cotton, a nurse appeared in the doorway. "Mr. Oliver," she said, "do you want your shot? The doctor said you could."

"To hell with the doctor." The Old Man let himself slip back on the pillows.

"Okay," Robert said. "Anna and I will stay here tonight." In the hall, he asked Jasper: "What happened?"

Jasper hesitated. Robert had the feeling that Jasper spoke more carefully with him, as if he were translating from another language. "It was in the garage."

"The garage?" With delivery trucks and pushcarts and old display counters and leftover advertising signs.

"I know it don't make much sense. Except they figured it was a big drop there. They damn near tore the building apart."

"Yeah," Robert rubbed his unshaven cheeks, "I had something like that last year. Funny, the Old Man never did handle narcotics, but people sure seem to think he does."

Again Jasper searched for the right words. "When you bootleg, pretty often you got other things going for you. Like meat. There's lots of meat around. Even the Old Man, he had meat too, years ago, when I first come to work. So people figure like this: he had meat, he had bootleg, he's got something else. See?"

Meat? Robert thought, What the hell was meat? Sure, sure, whores. The Old Man had started that way. . . .

"Yeah, I see. What's the rest?"

Explaining left him out of breath. Jasper settled down in the living room, shifting his shoulder holster so that he could lean back comfortably. "That early, there wasn't but one kid in the garage, and a couple of niggers. When them four come in, there wasn't no argument; the kid shit in his pants, you shoulda seen that. . . ."

Jasper paused, silently laughing. "You shoulda seen him when it was all over. Wouldn't move. Tears running down his face."

Could have been me, Robert thought. I remember. . . .

"They been there an hour and they got the place pretty well torn apart and they ain't found nothing and they're getting real nervous. When the Old Man drives in. Now you know he don't ever go in there, only this one time he tells Macaluso to turn in the garage, and when they see that big black limousine, they start shooting."

"Who's they?"

"Shit come from Biloxi," Jasper said shortly. "You know Rizzo, the bookie? His cousin was one."

There was a .38 kept under the back seat. Robert could see the Old Man reaching for it.

"The Old Man rolls out one side and ducks down. Me, I'm just coming to work, so I get over there quick." His shoulders shook again; Robert wondered if he ever laughed out loud. "And Macaluso nearly runs me down, backing out forty miles an hour."

"There was a gun up front too," Robert said.

"He didn't look for it." Jasper bent forward to untie his shoelaces and massage his swollen ankles. They had puffed and ballooned over the tops of his shoes. "Moving the car like that, he leaves the Old Man in the open."

"Sure," Robert said, "sure."

"And right after Macaluso those three bastards come roaring out. They're burning rubber and the trunk lid is flapping up and down. And they are gone." Jasper loosened his shoelaces again, and rubbed his legs violently. "I got high blood pressure," he said, "and I just can't stay on my feet no more."

"Hey, wait," Robert noticed suddenly. "I thought there were four, not three."

Jasper looked up from his aching feet. "Was. I told you. Rizzo's cousin. The Old Man killed him." He pulled off his shoes. "Jesus Christ. . . ." He took off his socks too. "I'm going barefoot for a while, nobody here to see me but the nurse."

O N   H I S way to bed, Robert thought: Me, I'm a coward. I know I'm a coward. I belong with the kid and the shitty pants in the back garage. Only luck that I wasn't there.

There were twin beds in Anna's bedroom. "I'm so sorry, Robert," she said. "I'm so sorry."

"It's all right, honey." Keep a straight face, boy. Don't grin. You can sleep tonight.

"And I'm sorry that we didn't have a honeymoon."

"We had a fine honeymoon." A couple more days of nothing to do and you'd have run out, over the hills and far away.

W H E N   T H E Y woke, the Old Man was already up. They heard his steady hacking morning cough. The rasping, frog-like sound drifted through the house.

In Anna's room, even in the security of his single bed, Robert squirmed uncomfortably. He dressed quickly and left.

Away from her, he began walking up and down the hall from front door to dining room. Back and forth. He could feel his heels striking hard, as if he were trying to drive the carpet through the floor. He fancied that he was walking in his own tracks, that each step blurred a clear print going the other way.

He stopped at the front door, tapping the screen with his fingers. Beyond the porch with its white-painted chairs, its cement planters filled with maidenhair fern, a few cars passed, and a man walked by. Robert could see his gray pants and big black umbrella held against the sun.

It must not have rained for days; the street looked very dusty, and even the palms sounded dry—he could hear their hollow fronds rattle together. And invisible tree frogs were calling for rain. He'd always intended to catch one of those alive. He never had, though one had fallen on him once, and he felt the tickle of its little suction-cupped feet.

H E C O U L D N ' T stand at the front door all day long, staring into the street. He was supposed to be doing something; he was supposed to be busy. Anyway, he wanted a cup of coffee.

In the dining room Anna said, "Robert, I have the most marvelous idea."

"Fine." The coffee was very hot and black. He added more milk.

"Don't you think the hotel in Port Bella would make a marvelous house for us?"

"The hotel?"

"If you cut off a lot of those wings and that terrible kitchen."

"I never thought about it."

"I know it sounds silly and sentimental but I'd like to own the place I spent my honeymoon."

"Well," he said. (*No. Not live there. I don't like it there. Too quiet and far away. I don't like the pinewoods, rustling all the time, even without a breeze.*) "I suppose so."

"We could use it for a summer place. That point is really lovely. I'll go ask Papa right now."

"You think he feels like talking business?"

"Papa's not going to let an accident upset him. Lamotta came in a few minutes ago."

"Fine," Robert said. Could he say anything else? And began another cup of coffee.

"Brother-in-law, how are you!"

Margaret. He'd forgotten about Margaret. She twirled

across the room and settled herself at the table. "You look sick, Robert." She was wearing a light green slack suit that made her look like a child in her mother's clothes. It was great for Carole Lombard, Robert thought, but it sure looked funny on a fat Italian girl. Anna would never have made that mistake, but then Anna could have worn the slacks and looked beautiful.

"Look," he said, "yesterday I was on my honeymoon, with nothing more to think about than whether we wanted to play croquet or tennis."

She grinned. "Aren't you just a little glad?"

"Of course not."

"Bet you were bored silly." She pulled a lock of curly hair, stretched it out full length, and let it pop back into place.

He said stiffly, "We liked it so much, we are trying to buy it."

She giggled her choking laugh. "You're a kick, brother-in-law. So that's why Anna went rushing to Papa."

"Lamotta was there earlier."

She raised her eyebrows. They were thick and bushy and almost met across her nose. "I might have known. You'd think they were a couple of fairies."

Robert looked disapproving.

"Bothers you?"

"No, damn it. Say anything you like."

"Lamotta is devoted." She pursed her lips. "That's for sure. The devoted lord marshal—see, I went to school. I got lots of references in my conversation."

"Try not talking."

"Robert," she said, "let's go sit on the front porch."

"Why?"

"Because we're both so stupid we haven't got anything else to do."

They sat on the porch, and he decided that she looked a lot like Betty. He'd never noticed before, but it was in the shape of their faces.

That hot June morning, rocking among the ferns, Robert found himself wondering about Betty. What *did* she do during the day? He'd never known. He'd only seen her at night.

T H E Y   D I D not resume their honeymoon. After weeks of negotiation, the Old Man managed to buy the hotel at Port Bella and Anna was satisfied. She began methodically planning the rebuilding with notebooks and sketches.

Robert went back to work. He now had lunch every day with the Old Man at Galatin's. Overhead brass ceiling fans stirred the thick air lazily.

"You getting gumbo again today?"

"Yes," Robert said.

"I never learned to like Cajun food."

"I guess I'm a Cajun," Robert said.

"You sure look like a Cajun," the Old Man agreed. "Fact is I don't like poor people's food. I don't like gumbo and I don't like red beans and I don't like jambalaya."

Why had the word "Cajun" brought with it the smell of oily bayous and decaying shrimp shells? Robert said: "It tastes good when you're hungry."

"Catfish used to taste pretty good to me once. Full of Ohio mud and I was damn glad to eat them."

"You get so you like it," Robert insisted. "And then you keep on liking it all your life."

"*You* keep on liking it," the Old Man said. "That's your taste. . . . What time is it?" The Old Man carried a pocket watch—he had a dozen or so jumbled loosely in his dresser drawer. This one was new; on its cover was a blazing sun, done in rubies and diamonds.

"You really like watches," Robert said, "don't you?"

"That's *my* taste," the Old Man said. "Let's go back to work."

ROBERT'S DAYS were neat and ordered. Every morning the Old Man's limousine picked him up at seven o'clock, at 7:15 they picked up the Old Man, at 7:30 they walked into the office. Every day. Except Sundays, when he went to Mass with Anna. They were dusty sweaty summer days in the dense heat of a breathless river town. Electric fans buzzed from all corners. Anna's white poodle puppy got caught in the big floor fan and bled bright red blood all over the blue Chinese rug. And the Old Man began a reorganization of his affairs, and formed Esplanade Enterprises, Inc., just to give Robert something to do.

ROBERT WAS tired all the time, and feverish; his head ached, faintly and steadily. He felt strangely detached, as if he were really living next to himself, like an invisible shadow. Mornings when he walked to the car, there were two Roberts, step for step, coming down the brick walk. When he opened the door, two hands pulled at the handle. He even found himself keeping a little to one side, to make room for his shadow.

Every morning he woke very early, burning with the heat of the double bed. He moved to the living room and fell back to sleep on the sofa. In July he developed huge red blotches of rash. Anna immediately installed two more ventilating fans—the whole house shook with their buzzing. Robert said, as he was supposed to, that he was much more comfortable. The blotches turned crusty white and scaled small flakes. And did not heal.

One August morning, as he stood outside the Old Man's store, delaying the start of his day, he caught sight of Betty. She was passing in a car; he was sure he recognized her. The next few mornings he waited at that same spot to see if she'd come again. She did not. Now and then, he'd dream about her, the same dream over and over again. She was standing in the basement doorway, in the shadow of a paper plant with leaves big as umbrellas.

Maybe that was a memory and not a dream at all. He found it harder and harder to tell the difference.

It often seemed to him that somebody else lived in his perfect little house. Somebody else went to work every morning and came home every night. Somebody else smoothed his wife's body and felt the twisting spasm of love.

But it was Robert who telephoned Betty, who said: "I'll be there at ten tonight." Who stood in the dark and watched the shape of the giant paper-plant leaves against the lighter night sky. And waited until the door opened.

Later, driving home, he thought: I have been married three months.

Anna said: "You're scowling."

"I'm just tired," he said. "I'll take a bath and get over it." So he sat in the hot water, body emptied by Betty's grasping, sucking muscles, and thought: I've been married three months. Imagine that. I've got a doll house and a doll wife. Look at her white robe, all embroidered with something or other.

He stood and shook himself all over like a dog. Carefully, without bending, he wiped his feet on the bath mat. Then he shook himself again and walked out of the bathroom.

"You do look cool," Anna said.

"I'm on my way to the kitchen, I think I'm hungry."

The drops of water were drying on his skin, tingling slightly as they cooled. Great. He found a salami in the icebox and sliced it, the smell of garlic spreading smoothly across the room. Anna came into the kitchen. Abruptly he dropped salami and knife and reached for her crisp white robe. He found himself laughing: maybe there was a charge in garlic after all, like the old women said. The muscles along his back and thighs tightened. Going home, baby, baby-o.

H E W E N T to the Old Man's tailor now, and the Old Man's shirtmaker. "Silk shirts," the Old Man ordered. "Makes my skin creep," Robert argued. "Silk shirts," the Old Man repeated flatly.

So here he was, being measured for shirts he didn't like. Look at me, he thought as he left; look at me.

It had begun to rain, the usual sudden September storm, sheets of rain and slashes of lightning. A taxi was passing slowly; Robert grabbed the door handle and swung inside, getting only a few sprinkles on the shoulders of his white linen suit. "I want to go to Esplanade—no, wait." He opened the door quickly. A woman stood there, her hand still half raised, her lips forming into a disappointed O.

Robert called: "Sorry if I grabbed. Which way are you going?"

"To Canal and Burgundy." Her voice had a faint accent.

"I'll drop you off, if you like."

She hesitated a moment, looking up and down the street.

"Look," he said, "I'm not going to get soaking wet to be a gentleman."

She held her packages tighter and ran for the open door. "Thank you very much."

She straightened her hat, wiped the splashes from her

cheeks with a handkerchief. The cab filled with her faint musky perfume.

She was very well dressed, he decided, in a conservative way. She wore almost no make-up, almost no jewelry. Just small gold earrings, and a large gold watch. The best quiet taste. But still, there was something. . . .

The rain-slicked streets were jammed with traffic. The taxi moved slowly. He kept perfectly still, not even moving his feet. Perfectly still and perfectly silent. Waiting.

"I hope I'm not taking you out of your way," she said.

"No," he said. "And I wouldn't mind being late for work."

"There's my corner, the next one." She turned and looked straight at him, large eyes under thick black brows. "My father will be ready to leave, I hope. If all the old ladies with rheumatism have finished complaining to him."

She opened the door and dashed for the entrance. Overhead a painted sign said: "Marine Life Building."

It was a long dull rainy afternoon for Robert. First the books with Lamotta. Then with the Old Man to an appointment at the Roosevelt Hotel. He was buying some Long Island real estate.

She'll be home by now. What was the name of that perfume? He could remember every single word she'd said in the car. He even counted them: thirty-seven.

The Old Man was chewing his underlip slowly. Robert thought that he might be just a bit nervous—no, not nervous, anxious. Whatever this was, he wanted it very much.

Well, Robert thought, he always got what he wanted. . . .

This time Robert would wait for the Old Man in the lobby. That was all. Just wait.

The long arched space was almost empty—late afternoon. Through the glass doors at either end he could see the rain still falling. A cruising prostitute, small, discreet, saw him; he shook his head. God, no. He really wanted to go to the Turkish bath—but the Old Man hadn't said how long he'd be. . . . Robert sauntered past the florist's counter. Look at the colors, he thought, look at them. Just because women liked flowers, and there was always some guy buying them. . . .

He took a twenty-dollar bill from his wallet, and signaled a bellboy. "That's for a two-block walk," Robert said. "Find me a name. I think he's a doctor. I know he's got an office in the Marine Life Building. He took the afternoon off today, and he's got a good-looking daughter with a Spanish accent."

The bellboy nodded.

"And another twenty for hurrying."

Robert felt the familiar tight clutch of excitement at his chest. You are beginning to be an operator, he told himself. He settled next to a potted palm where he could see the entire lobby, and lit a cigarette. The Old Man did not come for two hours. His message came in fifteen minutes. He glanced at the slip of paper, handed over the second twenty. Not one word; everything was done, the bellboy disappeared. There was only the slight rustle of paper in his pocket.

He walked back to the florist's counter. "I want one rose a day delivered here for the next four weeks. No card."

Riding home with the Old Man on that rainy September evening, Robert felt proud of himself for thinking of the flowers. It was a nice touch.

That night, last thing, with Anna next to him already fast asleep, breathing her deep regular contented swells, he thought: Maybe tomorrow I'll call Betty again.

A M O N T H later he telephoned the dark-haired girl at home. "Did you like the flowers?"

A very small pause. "Are you always so extravagant?"

"Only when the situation requires."

"What else does it require?"

"I'll leave that to your imagination."

She laughed and this time he heard her nervousness. He felt a familiar tug in his throat and twitch in his stomach. She would. His hunter's instinct had been right.

H E R N A M E was Aline Gonzales and he met her almost every week for the next year. She had a perfect olive body and large, high, widely separated breasts. They stare in opposite directions, he thought.

It was a fine year with Aline Gonzales. A wonderful year. . . . Because of her he built a two-room fishing camp on Bayou Courville. He needed a place to meet her—a safe place because she was a respectable woman who would go to none of the usual boardinghouses. His camp was an hour's drive from town—when the roads were dry. Even she felt safe there.

He liked that high sandy hardwood country. He'd seen bear signs and deer, but he'd never shot anything. He'd seen fish in his bayou but he didn't own a rod. He made sure that the bed was new and very comfortable, and that was all.

It was there, one sun-spotted afternoon, that Aline said: "I'm getting married."

"That's great." He was relieved. God, how he was relieved. "I'm very happy for you."

"You might be a little sad to hear it."

"Honey, I know any woman wants to get married. Is he nice?"

"I hope so."

Still the note of hesitation in her voice. Got to stop that, he thought. "A house, and kids, you'll be great at that. Sorry I can't meet the lucky guy."

"I'll send you an invitation."

The hesitation was gone. Good. Voice was firm and determined. She'd settled.

"You know I can't come."

She twisted her mouth and made no answer.

Well, he thought, that was that. Found her in a taxicab and left her in a fishing camp. Started in the rain and ended at the altar. . . . He'd remember those funny-shaped breasts and have no regrets. It was time to end it. He'd gotten out of it pretty well, he thought. Took as much skill to get rid of a girl as to get one. He was learning how to do both.

OF ALL his women, Robert thought, he only remembered two vividly—Aline Gonzales and Betty. He never heard from Aline after her marriage. And he'd lost track of Betty after a few more years. He supposed that he'd gotten too busy to call her, that their meetings were less and less frequent, until she dropped from his schedule altogether. But he could close his eyes and see her. And Aline. But not the others. Occasionally, very occasionally, he remembered silly things they did. Like the one who'd brought two pots of pink geraniums to his camp. For months they flourished; and he saw the bayou between stiff flower spikes. Eventually the geraniums disappeared and the clay pots filled with air-borne grasses and small wild flowers. They thrived and died, seeded themselves and returned in their seasons.

He began selecting girls who were free to spend weekends with him, discarding the ones who could not. Keeping only a few of the most exceptionally beautiful for afternoon turns in boardinghouse bedrooms.

And he had trouble with none of them. I got this down to a science, he thought; pick them carefully and they behave right. . . .

Even if they hadn't, he thought, Anna would not have noticed. She was too busy remodeling the old hotel at Port Bella. She was doing the whole thing herself, without architects. "It has to be perfect," she explained eagerly. "I've got lots of time and I can do it right."

"It's going to take years," Robert said.

"I know. But we've got our whole life to live there, so it doesn't matter."

Robert thought, now and then, plunging in and out of slimy red membranes, drowning in flesh, dreaming of breasts hanging in their perfect beauty from clouds, fingering sea shells: I am alive, I am here, I leave tracks on the sheets. Do I wear channels into the membranes? Do I break myself where I fall?

THEN MARGARET. Two days after she finished high school, she eloped with Harold Edwards to a justice of the peace in Gretna. The Old Man took the bridal suite in the Roosevelt Hotel for them. "Flowers," Margaret said afterward, "the whole place was full of lilies. I kept waking up wondering who'd died."

Harold Norton Edwards had a round smooth face and round smooth blue eyes. His family were shocked by his hasty marriage and intrigued by rumors of her wealth. At their ritual once-a-week dinners, Margaret deliberately horrified them with tales of Sicilian vengeance and the Black Hand. Actually, she did not even like Harold Edwards. She married him simply because he loved her. It was marvelous, she discovered, to have someone in love with you. . . . Their marriage lasted eight months. One cold February morning Margaret moved back to her father's house. For two days Harold Edwards sat in their small honeymoon apartment (waiting to hear from her, answering all phone calls on the first ring, just in case); then he took a handful of sleeping pills and five minutes later called his sister-in-law Anna. He was completely unconscious by the time she and Robert half-dragged, half-carried him into the hospital.

"Well," Anna said, sniffing the cold soggy winter morning, "well, well." It was seven o'clock and the passing cars still had their headlights on. "We were at the wedding, and we were almost at the funeral."

Robert had never liked Harold Edwards and hadn't been in the least worried about him. He yawned.

"I called Margaret to tell her he was going to be all right and do you know what she said?"

"I can't imagine."

"Being a widow is easier than getting a divorce."

Robert stared down the oak-lined street. "That was pretty cold-blooded."

"She says things like that, Robert." Anna tugged him along to their car. "Let's go home."

"Is she going back to him? After all this display of love?"

"Ask her," Anna said. "I've done my bit. I'm going over to Port Bella soon as I've had a little nap. The roofers were supposed to begin yesterday."

"The *roofers?* Haven't you got beyond that?"

"We had to wait for the slate," Anna said. "There is one kind of English slate that is perfect—"

"And nothing else will do." Robert interrupted her. "I don't think that house will ever be finished."

"It takes time," Anna said. "Oh, by the way, I'm not pregnant after all."

"Well," Robert said quietly, "we haven't been married that long. . . ." Anna wanted a child so badly. Perhaps it was his fault. Perhaps he was spending his seed too prodigally to fertilize his wife. He would wait another year, and then, he promised himself, he would sleep with no other woman until his wife conceived. . . . (Sometimes he dreamed about a baby, no bigger than his hand, looking exactly like him, wearing a diaper and a mustache.)

Robert left work early. He was too sleepy to do anything. "Go home," the Old Man said. "I'll see you at dinner."

Well, now he had all afternoon, and nothing to do. He found a bowl of tangerines, took one into the living room, and peeled it slowly, sniffing the sharp pleasant oil that spurted into the air. He dropped the peel into the ashtray, put his feet on the coffee table, and ate the sections one by one.

Until Margaret walked in. "Why are you here?" she said. "Where's Anna?"

"Anna's at Port Bella. I came home early because I was kind of sleepy."

"Who isn't." She slumped down in a chair, not bothering to take off her camel's-hair coat. "Sorry my ex-husband kept you up all night."

"Well," Robert said, "well."

"He wanted to be saved."

"He damn near wasn't."

"Oh, Anna always does things right. That's why he called her, instead of his own family."

He went back to his tangerine sections. "Lucky for him."

"Robert, look, will you come over to the apartment with me? I want to pack a few dresses while they're pumping Harold out."

"I don't think they're doing that any more."

"Well, whatever. Come help me for a few hours now; then we can go on to Papa's for dinner."

He got to his feet slowly, started to pick up the tangerine skin, then decided to leave it where it was.

T H E   S U N never really came out. Now and then the light got stronger, sometimes even bright enough to make metal objects give off a feeble reflection. And sometimes the shape of the sun hung like a yellow moon in the sky for a few minutes before it disappeared. But fog clung everywhere, wrapped around houses as if it were growing out of them, hung among tree branches like moss. The wet air smelled strongly of burning peat, a sharp, ageless smell.

"I bet the world smelled like that right after the creation." Margaret wrinkled her nose and sneezed.

"February is always like this," Robert said reasonably.

"Fine weather for killing yourself. I can see what Harold had in mind."

"Stop being funny," Robert said. "Anyway, you're *not* being funny."

She turned sidewise on the car's seat. "Robert," she said so quietly that he almost didn't hear, "I don't know any other way to do it."

He wanted to stop and hug her, but he kept looking straight ahead. "It's all right, cutie," he was surprised how tender his voice was; "it's rough on you and everybody knows it."

"You know what Papa said? When I moved back with him?"

"I can't imagine."

"He laughed. You figure that. Not a lecture. Not: Your duty is to your husband or anything like that. Not even: I'm disappointed in you."

"Maybe he didn't think there was anything to say."

"When he got through chuckling—with me feeling stupider and stupider where I'd felt dramatic and heroic before—you know what he said? 'You don't like him; I'm not going to tell you to live with him.' "

"What's wrong with that?"

They pulled up in front of the small yellow stucco apartment building.

"I can't think of anything wrong with it," Margaret said.

They hurried through the smoky fog, up the blue tile steps, wet and very slippery underfoot, and into the apartment.

It was as cold there as it was outside. Harold had left three or four windows wide open.

"Do you suppose he was planning to jump out?" Margaret turned on all the heat and then lit the kitchen oven too, leaving the door ajar.

"It will warm pretty fast," Robert said. "The rooms are small."

He got down her suitcases and she began folding clothes into them. After half an hour, there were three filled suitcases and the apartment was passably warm. They both took off their overcoats.

"Any more?"

"I'll send somebody over tomorrow." Margaret walked up and down the apartment, trailing her fingers over the dusty surfaces of the furniture. "When I was thinking of leaving, those last days, I marked everything." She held up a silver lamp. On the bottom was a clear red nail-polish mark. "See."

"I don't get it."

"I sorted everything, all day long. I put the presents from his side of the family into the dining room. All of mine went in the living room and the bedroom. If I couldn't move it, I marked it with nail polish or chalk." Abruptly she flipped a chair upside down: a large chalk M. "And do you know something, Robert? I don't care a damn about any of this stuff. It just gave me something to do."

Robert said: "You are as methodical as Anna. And just as foolish."

They both laughed over that, laughed far more than they needed to; the kitchen oven was blowing heat into their faces, and the windows were covered with frost. Then they were in bed—a big double bed that had not been made, whose pillows still held the imprint of Harold's head, whose covers were still on the floor where he had left them.

My God, he thought, it's Harold's skin I'm smelling. With a sweep of his arm he knocked all pillows to the floor.

They were both silent, hardly breathing. Then the body-twisting spasm, in silence too. He distinctly heard a joint crack, some cartilage rub raspingly together. Whose, he thought, mine or hers? He couldn't tell. There seemed to be only one. The familiar lights were in his eyes, and the familiar colors—he knew them all, and knew them very well. He thought: I've gone deaf, it can't be like this; I'd hear a heartbeat, or the air going through my own trachea.

His body arched and twisted, pulling away, to hide, to run. Her body twisted too, following him. Fastened, eternally demanding. He twisted all the way to his back, arms flying wide. She lay on top of him, riding successfully. Present. And requiring.

A roaring. She was breathing directly into his ear. It tickled. He pulled his head away, and she lay stretched on top of him. Still in place.

THEY WENT to the Old Man's for dinner. Margaret looked no different, and Robert hoped he looked only as upset as a man who has rescued his brother-in-law from suicide.

They played poker after dinner—the Old Man hated bridge—and the time slipped away pleasantly enough. Anna called from Port Bella to say that the weather slowed the roofing work considerably. Robert went home very early. The mist was worse now; street lights had yellow strips of fog wrapped tightly around them, and his headlights seemed to bend and turn back toward him.

He sighed and settled back against the seat. Jesus, he thought. My balls hurt.

THE DEPRESSION deepened, 1933 became 1934. Robert could smell poverty all around him in the streets; he turned away from beggars, holding his wallet tightly.

What do you want? Don't look at me.

Afraid all the time. Hiding it carefully. From Anna. From the Old Man. *The world's coming apart, the Communists are taking over behind machine guns. There's Huey Long, Share the Wealth. . . . Take from the rich, give to the poor. There're so many poor; soup lines, and WPA leaning on shovels and staring into the sky.*

Don't take mine; you can't have it. I'd kill you for it.

Day after day, he followed the Old Man around, trying to learn his confidence, his skill. "Lower things go," the Old Man said, "the better for me."

Robert was amazed at the complexity of the Old Man's affairs, bewildered by Lamotta's never-ending reports. All the different businesses, the different companies. Now there seemed to be a lot of oil—land and leases. The Old Man said: "Would you believe I bought some of that land as a dairy farm for my mother?"

Maurice Lamotta smiled discreetly. "She wouldn't even look at it."

Robert also noticed that the Old Man used the Depression to buy out all partners. There were no longer any business connections with his wife's family. There were fewer social connections too. With Anna at work on one side, and the Old Man on the other, the D'Alfonsos were disappearing rapidly.

"I've gotten honest in my old age, Robert."

Lamotta laughed out loud.

"Now take the D'Alfonso family. They were ruined by Prohibition, completely ruined. They can't imagine any way to make money except illegally. Cousin Andrew, I hear, is in trouble with the tax people. If they can prove one-tenth of what I know, he's off to prison in Atlanta."

"He will have an uncle for company," Lamotta said.

"It's hardly worth it," the Old Man said.

M A R G A R E T G O T a divorce and moved to Paris to study at the Sorbonne. She never wrote letters but she dutifully sent a single postcard every Sunday.

"Here's another," the Old Man said one morning in the office.

Robert looked. "Same picture again. She's been sending that one for the past year."

It was a Notre Dame gargoyle. The Old Man flicked it into the wastebasket.

"I imagine she thinks it's very funny."

"Oh," said Robert, "I never thought of that."

The Old Man swung around and put his feet on the desk. The same battered oak desk, the same gray dingy office. The same windows, streaked with dirt, overlooking the dusty trees on Esplanade Avenue. The same river sounds coming through the open windows.

"You still go out to your camp?" the Old Man asked the dusty window. "You still like it?"

Robert felt his throat tighten, his chest grow smaller. Aware. Alert. "Sure. I was down a few days ago."

"Fishing good?"

"I don't know. I sat on the porch and looked around."

The Old Man swung his legs to the other side of the desk. "You handle your women very well."

"What?" Not believing what he heard, knowing he'd been caught.

"Even so," the Old Man said, "Anna knows. . . ."

"Anna does not know."

"Anna guesses," the Old Man interrupted. "She wants a child. It hurts her not having a child."

"She has never said a word."

The Old Man smiled slowly. "She knows that you are like my own son. She is very fond of her father and could never take his son away from him."

"That's stupid." Robert smacked his hand on the desk.

"Because others know what you thought was a secret—" the Old Man went on smiling—"don't rage. She is not stupid. She is doing just what I hoped she would."

Robert sat down and put his feet on the opposite corner of the desk. The Old Man immediately took his feet down.

"If I have a woman now and then," Robert said, "what's wrong with that?"

"Did I say there was?"

"You said—" Robert stopped, remembering the Old Man's words exactly, finding nothing accusing in them.

"Maybe," the Old Man said, "it is the only way to live with Anna?"

Robert shook his head.

Frightened, for the next six months he had no other woman. Until he was absolutely positive that his wife was far along in her pregnancy. Then he went on a hunting trip that lasted three days, with a night-club dancer named Willie Mae, a stenographer named Corinne, and a nurse named Tanya. And two cases of whiskey.

FIVE MONTHS later Anna bore a son named Anthony, a chubby dark-haired baby who looked very much like her.

MARGARET CABLED from Paris: "Coming home at once to see baby." She did not actually arrive for almost a year.

MARGARET

THE TRAIN left Mobile for the last slow two-hour crawl into New Orleans. Margaret sat at the window of her compartment and stared at the unbroken line of green marsh. Pure monotony, she thought.

She tried walking the length of the train, but after her second trip, she was bored by the endless car doors. So she opened her very elaborate alligator case and began redoing her make-up. She worked slowly and carefully and she finished not more than ten minutes before the train pulled into the Canal Street Station.

She checked herself in the full-length mirror behind the door. She was much thinner; her eyes, always dark and slanted, were accented by light make-up. Her curly hair was cut very short; it shadowed her head like a cap or the painted top of a china doll.

She was not beautiful, but men's eyes often followed her. "Only men with taste watch you," Georges Légier said. They'd met one afternoon at the Rotonde, three or four tables filled with students, laughing and drinking. James Joyce was supposed to be there, but he wasn't. Hemingway was supposed to be in town, but he didn't appear either. Margaret was disappointed and impatient, until Georges Légier spoke to her. He was very tall, very thin, with dark deep-set eyes and a beaked nose; he was training to be a cook, and eventually, he said, he would go back to his father's restaurant in Lyon.

They spoke French for two weeks before she discovered he was from New York. And even that was an accident. One night, in his apartment, groggy and sweaty with sex, he reached to turn off the light and touched the frayed wire instead. "Jesus Christ," he said, "Jesus Christ."

Margaret stared at him—burned finger stuck in his mouth, scowling—and she burst into laughter. "You son of a bitch."

He insisted that except for one mistake, she would never have known. "After all, my father was born in Lyon. I could have been French. And he does have a restaurant."

"That doesn't make you French," Margaret said. "That makes you a liar."

Margaret remembered: his naked chest, almost completely hairless, his scowl of concentration, his thin arms and shoulders, muscles showing through the pale skin like tangled knots of small rope. She remembered every inch of his body. "Bag of bones," she told him scornfully.

"You seem to like it."

"Don't be so conceited. I'm just humoring you."

"Humor me some more. I'm beginning to like it."

Then one day, suddenly, he had to leave. It was a winter afternoon; the streets were foggy and misty and shiny as Margaret climbed the damp urine-smelling stairs to his apartment and pushed open his door. He was waiting for her, sitting at the table directly in front of the single window. Behind him the hazy gray sky was filled with twisted chimney pots. "I have to go home," he said. "I've got my ticket."

An empty falling in her stomach. "Why?"

"No more money. I didn't think I'd last this long."

"You're going to New York?"

"Sure. And go to work for my father. Be a bus boy. Or the sauce cook, if I can talk him into it."

Margaret made a face. "I could lend you the money to stay."

"No, thanks." He kissed her neck. "Anyway, the restaurant business in a depression isn't really so great, and maybe I can help out."

"Why don't we get married?"

"No," Georges said, "I'm not the marrying type."

"I'll go back with you. I like New York."

"No."

She was on his ship when it sailed. "What the hell are you doing here?"

With her wide bright childish grin she produced the cable from Anna. "My sister had a baby, I'm going to see. Isn't that a coincidence?"

He fingered the telegram as if it would explode. "Real? Or phony?"

"You could say you're happy to see me."

"You know," he said, "I really am. I'm afraid I really am."

SHE LIVED with him for the next eight months in New York. She found a small apartment on Twelfth Street, close to the restaurant. Because his family lived so far uptown, he fell into the habit of spending most nights with her. "It's just practical," Margaret said. "You work so hard."

Within hours of her arrival, she had secretly telephoned her father. "I've got to fill up a restaurant, Papa. Don't you know people in New York? This has to work."

"We will see," her father said.

Immediately, the restaurant began to prosper. Margaret wrote her only letter: "Thanks, Papa. The best hoodlums in town now eat with us."

She asked again: "Georges, why don't we get married?"

"No," he said.

"Then I'm going home."

"Why?"

"Because I don't like this."

"You're being foolish."

"No," she said. "You have your key. And the rent is paid for this month."

When he came that night after work, she was gone. The apartment was dark, and her father's telephone number lay in the middle of the dining-room table.

W E L L ,   M A R G A R E T   said to the junk heaps and filthy back yards of New Orleans; well, well, well. What if this doesn't work? . . .

She missed him already. She had been on the train for a little over twenty-four hours and she was aching with loneliness.

Why?

Georges Légier wasn't handsome and he wasn't rich. He wasn't funny, he wasn't serious. He didn't talk much. He worked until he was yellow with exhaustion. He liked to go to baseball games.

None of that was any explanation, really. When she thought about him like that, he seemed dull. But when she was with him, she felt excited and alive.

It was, Margaret thought, simply sex. Whenever he touched her, even a hand on her elbow to cross a street, his fingers left their invisible prints, fiery prints. Her whole body twitched for him, throbbed. Her blood raced, stopped entirely, then raced again. And yet he was not extraordinary in his love-making. Though he thought he was. . . . Margaret smiled. He wasn't the biggest, or the thickest, or the slowest. But there was a quality in him, an intensity. . . .

Love, she said to the night-blackened mirror. It's god damn love. How did I get mixed up with love? . . .

HER FATHER was waiting. When she saw him, she felt the usual shift in her feelings. A lift, a jump, a tug. Pleasure, but not totally. Love, but not completely. Dependence. Fear, familiarity, identification. That's part of me there, walking along. Tree from which I sprang. His spasm produced me. Shake of his body and here I am. . . .

THAT NIGHT—familiar peat-smelling winter night— before she fell asleep, she thought: Papa won't like what I have to do. But I have to just the same.

All those months in New York, while she fitted herself into Georges Légier's life, she was bothered by one fact: I am over twenty-one years old and I still get an allowance from my father. . . . I want my own money. . . .

She stared at the cracks of her bedroom ceiling. There should be seventeen, she thought. When I had measles and lay here in the dark, I counted the cracks in the ceiling, and played that they were roads, and highways and rivers. . . . She counted again. There were still seventeen. Things didn't change at all.

She delayed speaking to her father. I've got time, she thought, lots of time, more than I want here in New Orleans.

In the morning, first thing, she sent a telegram to Georges Légier: "Do you want me to come back." Then she drove out for a weekend with Anna at Port Bella. She spent the entire time surveying the unfinished rooms, pacing off the measurements of the gardens, following a maze of sticks that marked the future walks.

"Well," she said finally, "you didn't ask me, but if you want to know exactly what this place is going to look like, I'll tell you—Ivanhoe's castle, but a lot more expensive."

Anna, who sat in the shade of the half-finished porch, baby on her lap, playing with the fragile pink feet, smiled at her gently. "I suppose so."

"You like that?"

Anna tickled the small face. "Yes."

"I saw you do this with your doll house in town." Margaret spun around surveying the piles of raw lumber, the carpenters moving slowly up and down their ladders. "It took years."

"Don't take it out on me," Anna said. "It's Georges you're angry with."

"I don't know what's the matter," Margaret said. "Even his family's crazy about me. Everybody but him."

"Well," Anna said soothingly, "wait awhile."

"I look good, I'm rich, I'm in love with him—what does the bastard want? You know, I heard his father ask him that same thing one day when they thought I couldn't hear."

Anna said, "I think he will. I think he'll have to."

T O   H E L L with love, Margaret thought. It's an ache in my stomach, it's a terrible feeling in my head, it's a skin-crawling fear that I've done something wrong. I've forgotten the password. And the frog isn't going to change into Prince Charming, the secret door isn't going to open. And the world is going to end any minute.

W H E N   S H E   got back to her father's house in New
Orleans, there was a telegram propped against the bisque
figures on the living-room mantel.

"Papa, why didn't you tell me!"

The Old Man stretched his legs. "You were gone."

"Here." Her eyes shining so brightly that they were two-
colored, she handed the paper to her father.

" 'No. Quit. Georges,' " the Old Man read. "What's to be
happy in that?"

"He answered," Margaret said. "Don't you see, he
answered."

She wired back immediately: "Do you miss me." There
was no answer.

She refused to listen to the silence. Twice a week, on
Mondays and Fridays, she wired Georges Légier: "I am
waiting." Some telegrams she sent to the restaurant and some
to his family's house. She wanted them to know.

She insisted on going to Robert's fishing camp. "I've
seen Anna's great construction, now I want to see yours."

They went one cloudy afternoon. All the way Margaret
hummed and sang "Valencia." "Georges is crazy about that
song."

"Not if you sing it like that."

"You sound just like Papa." She stuck her nose out the
window and sang loudly into the wind, "In my dreams it
always seems. . . ."

Robert drove steadily. "There it is, lady."

She shook back her hair, stopped singing, stared. "It
looks like nothing to me."

"I didn't say it was anything." Robert got out the car.
"You wanted to come."

"Well, let's see inside." She raced across the tall frost-
burned grass and up the steep stairs.

He followed, deliberately unhurried, brushing away the
sticktights from his trousers.

"Smells terrible in here," Margaret said. "Half mildew and half new paint."

"I've never heard any complaints."

"I bet not." She sauntered through the two rooms, looking. "What a big bed you have. And what was in the flower-pots?"

The ones on the front porch. "Some pink flower."

"You buy them?"

"Look," he said with a flash of annoyance, "stop trying to start an argument."

"God forbid."

He slammed down the window he had just opened. "Okay, lady, do we go back? Or do we try the bed?"

"We go back." She'd dropped her purse on the table next to the oil lamp. She picked it up again. "I told you exactly; you just didn't believe me. I wanted to see."

They drove in silence. Margaret amused herself by counting trees and passing cars and then she put her head back and closed her eyes. I wonder, she thought, if today there will be an answer for me.

The small fearful voice that haunted her constantly replied: He has someone else. He will marry someone else and he will send you a wedding announcement. . . .

She jerked herself upright to silence that voice. "You mad at me, Robert?"

"Why should I be mad at you?"

"Look, I'd have hopped into bed with you—why not? Georges won't even answer, so how does that make me feel? But you shouldn't take things for granted."

Robert ignored her.

She stared at his heavy dark profile. "If you just hadn't been so *sure*."

"Typical female reasoning."

"I want to choose too. . . ." To have what men have. To

initiate, to choose. Not to wait, not always to wait. For the sleek, preening male. Because I need him. I don't want to need him.

Her father now, look at him. Two daughters and he couldn't care less. No penis, no use. He had to have a son, one way or the other. Even marry off his daughter to get what he wanted. . . . What was it the Chinese did, leave their girls out to die? All those squalling female ghosts wailing around the mountain. Did a baby stay a baby after it was dead, or were all ghosts the same? Maybe those girls even turned into boys, got in death what they missed in life. . . . And her mother who went on a procreative race to produce a male . . . while a blood disease frustrated her at every birth, and all she got was two insignificant girls. . . .

"She killed herself breeding," Margaret said.

"What?" Robert turned.

"My mother killed herself breeding."

"I know that," Robert said.

"All around the house it was: 'Shush, Mother is resting, Mother is expecting another baby.' I used to tiptoe around, scared out of my wits, forgetting that I didn't even know what the hell she looked like."

Margaret crossed her legs and began a cigarette. She did not really like to smoke but it helped that uncomfortable angry fluttering in the tips of her fingers.

(Aunt Cecilia at the funeral: "Sad, sad, that poor man left with just two daughters." The child Margaret—in a black dress quickly made for the occasion—wondered what was so wrong with the nakedness of girls that the pronged belly of a boy could solve. . . .)

She inhaled and coughed. "Robert, all this last year in New York I've been wondering. Do you think my father would let me come in business with him?"

"No," Robert said.

"I just can't sit around laughing at my own jokes."

"You asked me and I'm telling you, I don't think he will."

"Would you mind?"

"Why ask me?" Robert said, "I don't run things around here either."

"NO," HER father said.

"Why not, Papa? All you do is shake your head and never say why."

"You know nothing of my business."

"You taught Robert, you could teach me."

"It's no place for a woman."

"Papa, I don't feel like a woman."

He snorted, loudly.

"I don't feel like anything. This last year, I've been watching and listening and I have some ideas of my own."

"Like buying a restaurant for your boy friend?"

Margaret felt the warm bleeding sensation of anger begin in her stomach. "No," she said. "Not my boy friend. I'll never see him again unless we're married." The flooding blood of anger was almost choking her. "Don't talk to me about buying, Papa." He gestured in annoyance; she raised her voice. "Not as long as Robert's around here. That poor slob's so crazy about money he'd do anything for it. Even Anna. He wouldn't look at her if you weren't paying for it."

"That is enough," the Old Man said.

"Matter of fact, Georges would probably have married me a long time ago if I hadn't been a damn fool about money."

Stupid, how stupid can you be? I can still see the expression on that thin hatchet face. "This is a cold apartment,

Georges, and climbing the stairs up here is just terrible.
There's a place right around the corner from me, why don't
I take it for you?" . . . I knew I'd ruined everything. The
bed, the only warm place in that freezing room, became the
same temperature as the air outside the blankets. I could feel
the surface of his skin turn cold, and that useful male twig
fell down just as if it had been cut off. . . .

"If you don't like money, why do you take it?" The Old
Man picked up his paper.

"Why should I give up anything that belongs to me?"
How had she gotten this angry? She was going to have a
stroke, all the blood boiling inside her was going to burst out
her mouth and she was going to die. . . . "Papa, will you
listen?"

He did not answer.

Georges didn't answer her telegrams either, she thought.
Georges didn't like the feeling he got around her. And she
didn't like the feeling she got around her father.

She stared at the knobs of her knuckles, their fingers
tucked neatly out of sight in her lap. A proper convent
gesture.

Instantly she unfolded her hands, put an elbow on each
chair arm, a clenched fist on each knee.

"Quit reading a minute, Papa."

"There is nothing to talk about."

"Yes, there is. I've got something to tell you."

He went on reading. Her jaw began to tremble. Am I
scared of him, she thought, or am I just mad?

"I want what's mine, Papa," she said slowly, distinctly.
"I'm not going to sit around any more and be grateful for my
living."

"You have never asked for anything you didn't get."

"I want what's mine."

He lifted his eyebrows. "What's that?"

"What comes from my mother."

"You have gone crazy."

"You listen, Papa, and I'll tell you. Community-property state, you know that. Half of whatever you had was my mother's when she died. Her estate goes to me and Anna. I want mine, and I'm willing to go to court to get it."

His face was bright red. "What the hell are you saying?"

"I tried asking you politely and you said no. You want what's yours, Papa, and I want what's mine."

He began to chuckle, very softly. "Take it and good luck to you," he said.

MARGARET WAS in New Orleans for six weeks. The cool peat-flavored winter days drifted into the warm rainy weeks of spring before Georges called: "I want you to come to New York—are you coming?"

Margaret caught the Crescent Limited that same evening, with a single suitcase. When she walked into the apartment on Twelfth Street, he was just getting up. He'd finished shaving but was still wearing his pajamas.

"I have to go to work early," he explained. "I do the books today."

"Oh." Margaret put down her suitcase. The room looked exactly the same, quite clean and neat. No greeting for her, no kiss. As if she'd just come back from putting out the garbage. His fresh clothes were spread on the bed, as they always were. He began dressing, his thin angular body moving rapidly. "Your train was due almost an hour ago."

"It was late," she said.

"Look," he said, "do you still want to get married?"

The collar button popped out of the back of his shirt. Automatically she picked up the round bit of ivory and handed it to him.

"Do you?" He was doing his tie now, his mouth twisted with the effort.

"Yes," she said.

"It will make us both miserable."

"I want to."

He finished his tie and faced her directly. "There was somebody else, did you know? Within two days of the time you left, I had somebody else living here."

"That's why it looks so neat. Nothing like the woman's touch." She walked slowly into the small kitchen. "I was just about sure you'd found somebody you liked better."

"I did; don't flatter yourself about that."

"Why didn't you marry her?"

"I don't know." He reached for his coat and swung it around his shoulders. "I kept thinking about it and putting it off. And I didn't." He buttoned his coat carefully, settling it over his shoulders with a shrug. "I don't want to marry you, I never have, but I will. That's the difference, you see."

There had to be more, it couldn't all be like this. She said: "That's all right with me."

"Okay. I'll take next Wednesday off."

FOR FIVE years Margaret was happy.

She had the man she wanted. (He for his part was surprisingly contented, surprisingly domestic.) She had her own money as her mother's estate came into her hands. (Far more than she expected; her father was being generous.) She bought a brownstone on East Fiftieth; the restaurant moved there and prospered. She had her office upstairs, and her apartment on the top two floors. Neither she nor Georges need ever leave the building—she felt protected and enclosed by the thought. Each morning she opened her eyes with a feeling of excitement; each night she closed them smugly delighted with the progress of the day. She began collecting celebrities, methodically, by categories (the idea had come to her one morning)—first the Algonquin group.

Pictures of large drunken literary parties appeared on her office walls. When she tired of their practical jokes, she moved to politics, then to Hollywood, collecting any name that sounded familiar to her. She redid the apartment three times, keeping not a single piece of furniture, ending finally with dark red walls and heavy opulent baroque.

"Will you let the place alone now?" Georges asked.

"I like it now. I'll have to find something else to do."

"Children," Georges said flatly. "Ever think of that?"

She shook her head. "Not just yet."

She met Edward Matthews. He was a baseball player and she was collecting famous athletes at that time. For three months he commuted every week on the Twentieth Century Limited from Chicago to see her; then, as suddenly as it started, their affair cooled off. Too much time on the train, Margaret thought with a silent smile. She already had another lover, a small chunky *New York Times* reporter; she was fascinated by his circumcision, the first she had ever seen. She left him for a tall Irish coffee importer who lived in the same block on Fiftieth Street. And then Georges Légier got a letter, unsigned and typewritten, in a *New York Times* envelope. He checked and found the information quite correct.

He did not interrupt his schedule. At midnight he finished with the restaurant, kissed his father good night, saw him to the waiting car. Then he unlocked his apartment door, crossed the black-and-white foyer, and turned in to the living room.

Margaret was waiting. She noticed nothing—he was often pale when he was tired; he often entered a room silently. She stood up, showing the new lamé pajamas she'd bought. "What do you think?" She turned slowly; as she completed her circle, he slapped her with his right hand, then with his left, slamming her finally into the red damask-covered wall, splitting open the back of her scalp. She slid to the floor and sat there like a dazed doll, legs sticking out stiffly. *What,* she thought, *what, what?* She felt something trickle down her neck; she touched it, found her fingers bright red. They'll be ruined, she thought, two-hundred-dollar pajamas and they'll be ruined. From her position on the floor she watched while he swung chairs into walls, smashed tables, threw lamps through windows. Methodically he crossed the room, destroying inch by inch. The big sofas and armchairs were too heavy. He kicked at them, upending them; then, pulling a pistol from his belt, he began methodically firing into them, sometimes hitting them, sometimes sending wild shots into the wall. He seemed to have forgotten about her, at least for the moment. The gun emptied, the cylinder turned smoothly with only small clicks. He threw the gun at the chandelier, missed. She put both hands to the back of her head, holding on. He picked up a small chair, swung it at a huge gilt-framed mirror. It cracked, sunburst lines ran across it, but the glass did not shatter. He swung the chair again, this time holding it by one leg. The splintered back caught behind the mirror's edge, caught and held. He yanked, hard; the mirror tipped, rolled off its hooks, fell forward. He was so blind with rage—Margaret wondered later if he'd had his eyes open at all—he did not see the mirror until it fell on him.

Margaret thought: Feel it trickle down my neck. How much blood do you have to lose before it's serious? He's half under the mirror. The cornice got knocked off, after all the trouble I had getting it here; not a chip or a scratch on it, great Empire piece, perfect shape. And Georges broke it. Must look for those pieces, maybe glue them back together. Put the gilt on thick to cover the cracks. It was a gorgeous mirror. . . . Why doesn't he move? Do I call the police or do I call a doctor? I call a doctor. What was his number? It's gone, disappeared. Right out of my head. God, what a headache.

She was standing by the phone, one hand holding the receiver, still trying to remember the number, when the police kicked in the front door. She hadn't heard their knocking or their shouts.

WITH HER scalp neatly stitched and a new hat covering the shaved portion of her head—while Georges was still in the hospital with a fractured skull and a broken arm—Margaret went to Reno. Georges sent no message. Her father-in-law argued against her leaving. "You are in love with him, and I know my son, he is in love with you. . . ."

"Look," Margaret said, "I'm not going to get killed by your son."

"He lost his temper; a man loses his temper sometimes."

Margaret stared at the small round red-faced man who bounced up and down like a ball in his anxiety. He looks like a headwaiter, she thought, a very nervous anxious headwaiter. . . . And then she thought wearily: I know why he's so worried. . . . "Look, you don't have to worry. You can keep your restaurant. I'm not going to insist on taking my money out."

Her father-in-law stopped moving abruptly.

He was listening, Margaret thought, to what he wanted to hear. . . . "You can buy me out over a period. Or something; I don't care, whatever you want. But you don't have to worry about it."

Six weeks later, divorce proceedings completed, Margaret sent her last telegram to Georges: "A broken mirror is seven years' bad luck. Be careful." Then she went back to her hotel. Thinking: What do I do now? Where do I want to go? I can go anywhere, but I have to have a place name.

Just inside the broad palm-lined hotel lobby, she saw

them—the tall heavy man, the tall slender woman. "For God's sake." She walked on steadily, letting a polite smile crease her face.

She had to think of something to say. Something short and direct. Something that would put everything in its proper order. "Fancy meeting you here, Papa," she said. "Which one of you is getting a divorce?"

That wasn't too good, she thought. She could have done better if she'd had more time. But still it wasn't bad. It put a funny look on both their faces. And it let them know that they were not coming to rescue her.

MARGARET WENT back to New Orleans. I guess it really is my home, she thought; it's where I go when I can't think of any other place.

At her father's house, she thought: I was born here and I lived here and I never noticed how shabby it is. How the red tile steps have cracks in them, and the stucco is cracking because the house has settled. How the passing streetcars rattle and clang, and the ground shakes with them. How miserable the rooms are; nobody's looked at them for twenty years. Like this living room—fake tapestry on the wall, fat china angels on the mantel, and a fireplace so small it looks like a black hole. No wonder fires don't burn well. . . . She squinted into the grate. Only a few tiny red coals winked at her.

"Papa," she said, "this place is terrible; you've got to move."

"If the house bothers you, find another."

Margaret considered this tall old man with the ruddy wrinkled face, the shiny bald head. *Because of a couple of convulsive movements with my mother, here I am. Related to him forever. How do you shed a father? Snakes shed their skins, leave them lying on the ground. How do you get rid of your beginnings, your genes?*

"I'll find you a proper house, Papa, and I'll run it for you. I'll live with you like a dutiful daughter."

"Settled," the Old Man said.

"But I run my own affairs." She poked at the smoldering fire; the gray coals fell open, flamed for a moment, went out. "I had a good house in New York, but I'll have a better one here."

"And your next husband?"

"I wonder." She blew at the coals, waited to see if her breath would reach to them. It didn't. "I'm still in love with Georges."

The Old Man folded his hands meekly. "Then why the others?"

"I don't know, Papa, I never did figure that out."

The hall clock struck the half hour. She looked up. "That's the first thing to go, that damn clock."

"Agreed," the Old Man said.

"Now for the rest." She picked up a bottle of Scotch, shook it to check its contents, took a second unopened bottle. "I'm going to bed. I'll see you tomorrow evening, or maybe the next day."

"Agreed," the Old Man repeated.

SHE DRANK directly from the bottle, singing with each small sip, "Over the river and through the woods to grandmother's house we go." Why that? Have a sip, m'lady. Hail and farewell, Georges. Go join Harold. Growing list of ex-husbands. Get a few more and we'll have a club. Well. There it goes, the first lurch. Merry-go-round starting. The gears slip at first. Listen to it creak, sounds like metal rubbing. Have another sip. And wait. The room will start to move pretty soon. Round and round. The perfectly circular spin flattens out and the circle becomes an ellipse. From shallow and flat, it gets deep and deeper. Way down at the bottom, it's perfectly black. That's where I'm going. Hooray for me.

She lay back and sang *Veni, Creator Spiritus.*

Wouldn't the nuns be proud of me? All those four-note Gregorian chants. Little black boxes of notes, marching up and down across the sheets. Droning, fragile women's voices. Sounding dry as locusts, in the arches of the chapel. Sheltered within her uniform, white blouse and blue skirt, she sat in the furniture-polish dusk. The eternal dusk within stained-glass windows. . . . Little round hat, little round face, look at me, God, look at me, Margaret Mary Oliver. The fourth hat from the end of the pew; count it and find me among all the others. Lined up like bees in our hive, sipping the honey sound, the thin ancient sound. Not even an organ fluttering its reeds. Pass a miracle, God, do something. If you care whether I believe. Give me a hundred in my math test to-morrow. Translate my Virgil for me. Make me beautiful so that men stare at me on the street. But do something. . . . God lurking in that locked little oven on the altar. Why would God live in the dark there when he could run around, sail with the winds, and bounce with the sunbeams? Why would he wait for a priest to unlock him and release his presence into a damp chapel full of women who are thinking of everything else? Except maybe the nuns. Do nuns think? Faces look empty. Look like they even stop breathing. Maybe they're waiting to levitate, like St. What's-Her-Name, go flying around, stretched out stiff as an ironing board, sailing like a paper glider, black robes fluttering, starched wimple rattling and crackling. . . . She'd prayed for that once, prayed hard, lit candles every day—red vigil lights too—and even made a novena. I don't have to fly, God, and I don't have to have any thunder and lightning. But move me just a little bit. Lift me just an inch over my chair. Raise my feet from the floor. Or shake me side to side, just one shake would do. Just once.

Margaret smiled at the ceiling. Only motion I ever had came from a bottle of Scotch.

The circle flattened into wider swings. Lovely, lovely. This is the way we go. She'll be coming round the mountain when she comes, she'll be coming round the mountain. . . .

Was she singing out loud? She wasn't sure; there was too much noise for her to tell. The old gears were really creaking, protesting. Need oiling. Listen to the racket. Great. Singing of the spheres. Here we go round the mulberry bush. . . .

That deep point of perfect black wasn't so easy to reach. You had to go slowly and if you made a mistake you fell off the sides and tumbled back to where you had begun.

She looked at her wrist watch, couldn't seem to make out the hands. Foggy in here. How'd a fog get inside? There was a crack in the wall; the crack wiggled and made a little hand, a little black-and-white hand, and waved to her. She waved back, politely. Always be polite to cracks. She reached for the bottle again. Gently, old girl, gently. . . . This time I've got it. There's the stretching circle, there's the bottom. I've got it.

A perfectly shaped, perfectly patterned shower of yellow fleur-de-lis exploded in the dark.

''W E L L,'' T H E Old Man said, "I thought we'd lost you."

"What day is it?"

"Thursday."

"And what time is it?"

"Two-twenty-two." The Old Man held out his watch.

She set hers carefully. "Back on schedule. . . . Papa, what are you doing home in the middle of the afternoon?"

"Wondering whether I should call a doctor for you or an undertaker."

"You stayed home because you were worried?"

"Is that stupid?"

"It was sweet, Papa. I'm just not used to people being sweet any more."

"More used to hitting them on the head with mirrors."

"All those years with Georges, all those good times when everything was fine, and I only remember that last day."

"Happens," the Old Man said.

"I'm going to have three cups of coffee and then I'm going to find a hairdresser." Margaret pushed her fingers through her wiry hair.

"Then you will find me a new house?" He was mocking now.

"Sure," she said. "And run it too. Just like my mother." For a moment she stared at the glass-faced oak bookcase on the far wall. There were only four books in it, their bindings faded and unreadable. What would they be—her father didn't read—where had they come from? Four books, and six—no, seven—china figures. Elephants, all in a row. Pink lady with a parasol. Good God. A poodle with a ball on his nose. Did they date back to her mother's day?

"Papa, what was my mother like?"

He looked startled.

"What was she *like?*"

"I don't know," he said.

SHE WAS so sleepy, so tired. I've got hepatitis, she thought. Or an infected mosquito bit me and I've got encephalitis. Or I've got a brain tumor and after the operation I'll have a great wad of bandages wrapped around my head so that I look like a zeppelin.

Anna asked: "Margaret, are you pregnant?"

"Why?"

"Something about the shape of your face, the expression."

Margaret frowned, trying to remember. "Seems to me I used a diaphragm for everybody."

"You'll have to get married now," Anna said. "Is there anyone you like? I mean, anyone who would do to marry?"

Margaret shook her head, slightly.

Way down inside her, around her backbone, she could feel a stirring. A twisting, like a fish. Minuscule baby curled and swimming in its shell. Dragon in an egg. Swishing its tail, stirring up the primeval waters.

Margaret looked into her sister's face, so gentle, and so clear. Like a china cup, she thought. You could break it to bits, but you couldn't penetrate it. Not that shiny beautiful surface, that security of purpose.

"Anna," she said, "I'm not going to get married."

Anna's lovely discreetly rouged mouth closed firmly. "What name will the child have?"

"Well," Margaret considered. Flash of tail, sudden twitch, tiny speck of flesh to be making all this confusion. "I could give it Papa's name. He'd like that."

"Would he?"

Margaret laughed out loud. "Anna, why don't you stop being the perfect housewife and the great mother and the Holy Virgin and all those other things?" Maybe, Margaret thought, she's played at them so long, she's really become them. "Haven't you ever noticed? Papa thinks I'm a scream."

THE PREGNANCY moved her into violent action. She was racing the baby, she was struggling against the steady thickening of her belly. Determinedly, she hunted for houses and lots and contractors and architects. And found nothing.

Until one morning, on the front page of the paper: "Papa, John Maroney killed himself."

He nodded. "Seems he used a shotgun in the bathroom."

She made a face.

"I imagine he thought the bathroom would be easier to clean."

Suicide amused him, Margaret thought. It was odd, it was unusual, it was funny.

"We'll just have to tear out that room," Margaret said.

"You planning to buy the place?"

"It's a good house. Who's going to handle the estate?"

"The man is hardly at the embalmers yet."

"Make an offer."

"Before the funeral?"

"They'll want to get rid of that place. What with Daddy smeared all over the walls."

"Margaret Mary," the Old Man said, "you have a terrible sense of humor."

"It's exactly like yours."

"You do want the house?"

"I thought that was settled." She slapped down the newspaper. "We're not going to have another fight about money."

The Old Man was surprised. "What a thing to say to your aging father."

She looked at him appraisingly. "You know, Papa, if you killed yourself," she said, "I'd feel terrible."

"That fact will stay my hand on the trigger."

"Oh, for God's sake." She got up, restlessly. "Just get the house for me."

H E B O U G H T the house within the month. Margaret, belly swelling steadily, hounded architect and contractors. "I want it finished before the baby," she demanded.

"Really," Anna said. They had gone together to the half-finished house. "That just isn't possible."

"Put on some more men."

Anna's gentle smile appeared. "There are more men here now than can work. You see? They're stumbling over each other."

Margaret grinned. "It does look like a WPA project. Poor baby, he'll have to be born without a roof over his head."

"His?"

"Sure," Margaret said, "it's a boy and his name is Joshua. I wouldn't have a girl, not me. I wouldn't make a mistake like that."

IT WAS a boy. He was born in a rush of green-flecked ammonia-smelling water on her bedroom floor and he lay on the rug with slimy coils of cord twisted beside him. Anna hastily wiped his mouth and nose. "Where is the damn doctor?"

Margaret, still crouching between bedpost and chair, said, "I never heard you cuss before."

"Margaret, do you know whether you cut the cord now or wait for the afterbirth?"

Margaret closed her eyes, feeling another smaller spasm. "It looks horrible."

With a slamming of doors, the doctor arrived. "Oh my goodness," he said. "Oh my goodness."

Margaret wiped the sweat from her forehead. "You came too late for all the fun."

"My dear lady, sometimes there are rapid labors."

"It wasn't rapid. It's been going on for the last six hours or so."

"Oh, Margaret," Anna said. "Oh, Margaret, why didn't you say something?"

"I wanted to see if I was a coward."

"My dear lady," the doctor took her pulse, hastily. Then turned to the baby.

Margaret stood up. My God, my insides are falling; I've been pulled inside out like a sock.

Leaving a slimy trail behind her, she got into bed. She was very tired and she was sleepy. She could hear people rushing by, and the baby chirping, bird-like. Wearily, she turned over, pressing the flabby distention of her stomach into the bed.

That was September, 1941.

YEARS LATER, Margaret thought that everything happened between 1941 and 1945. All the wars, public and personal. All the casualties, visible and invisible. . . .

Robert Caillet, with a new Navy commission, went to England. The Old Man had his first coronary and his first stroke. And there was the business with Anna's son Anthony.

Yes, Margaret thought grimly, they were terrible years.

ANTHONY

W H E N H E was very small, he thought his mother was the Virgin Mary. She looked quite a lot like the pictures: the same dark hair pulled straight back, the same smile, the same blue dress. He was even quite sure that once or twice he'd seen her halo.

But when he said so, his father laughed, with a rasping angry edge to his voice: "You started his religious training too soon, Anna. Take him off that steady diet of priests' books, before the boy starts thinking he's Jesus Christ."

"It's hard for a child," his mother said, quietly as always. "It's very confusing."

But it wasn't, Anthony thought. Not any more. His father had made it perfectly clear.

It seemed to Anthony that there were two worlds: when his father was home and when he was not. When he wasn't home, there seemed to be a cover of silence, an invisible shape that slipped over the house. Everyone smiled steadily, moved slowly, was kind and thoughtful and serious. And of course they all loved him. His mother, his nurses, they all loved him very much. But it was so quiet, so motionless. Even his Aunt Margaret, when she came, spoke slowly and her baby seemed to cry more softly than usual.

When his father was home, there was shouting and arguing. The servants rushed about, the house buzzed and hummed. Anthony felt himself vibrate with sympathetic excitement. "Hey, Anthony," his father would shout every Sunday morning, "you coming sailing with me?"

They went out on the lake, just the two of them, and when his father thought they'd come far enough, he'd drop the sails and they would float there, motionless for the rest of the day.

They sailed every Sunday, in all kinds of weather. Sometimes Anthony trembled with chill inside his heavy clothes. Sometimes he shivered with fear while lightning smacked into the water all around them and the roar of thunder shook the boat. Sometimes he burned with reflected glare.

After one of those white-hot Sundays, while he sat straight and correct at the dinner table, he began to feel dizzy and sick and left his food untouched on his plate. His mother said, "I hope you haven't had too much sun, Anthony."

"He's fine," his father said.

"He looks scalded, Robert."

"Well, after dinner, put some of your cold cream on him." His father winked at him between the twin flickers of candles. "It'll make you feel better, and it'll make him smell better."

Slowly, deliberately, conscious that his mother was looking at him, Anthony winked back. He saw his father's face disappear and then appear again. He saw the answering grin, and he felt happier.

But when he went to bed he turned and twisted, skin burning, head aching. His mother brought an aspirin, though he hadn't asked for one. She must have been standing outside his door, listening to the small sounds the bedsprings made.

"You're terribly hot." She glanced around the room. Anthony knew that look very well: it ran over him every morning before school, to see if his clothes were correct. It ran over every room in the house to see that the housework was done. It ran over his father every day when he came home from work. It was smooth, light, impersonal.

"Mother," almost before he realized what he wanted to say, the words came out. "When you leave, would you put out the candle, please?"

She turned to him, questioning.

"There." He pointed to the dark heavily carved Mexican altar on which a red vigil light flickered. "I don't want it any more."

"It's a lovely old thing."

"Put it in your room, if you like it." His father would never stand for that.

"Go to sleep now," his mother said, and left.

He dragged a chair noisily across the floor and blew out the candle himself.

At dinner again, a week later, he asked, "Mother, would you take the altar off my wall?"

"Take it down?"

"That's what the boy said." His father chuckled. "I guess he got tired looking at the ugly thing."

His mother's face expressed only calm interest and pleasant attention, so Anthony knew she was very upset and very angry. "Are you really, Anthony?"

"Yes, ma'am," he said, politely.

"Anna," his father said, "the boy is getting a mind of his own."

"I don't think that's very funny, Robert."

Anthony leaned back in his chair, hopefully. Are you going to fight? I've never really seen you fight. Will you say all the words? Will you yell?

"Anna, there had to be a time when the boy got enough of your telling him what to think and what to do."

Almost whispering, his mother said, "I have tried to show the child the way to do things decently."

Now, thought Anthony; oh boy, now. . . .

But his father's tone was gentle and conciliatory. "You've done wonderfully well with him. Just look at him, brightest boy in his class, and a perfect gentleman."

So, Anthony thought, his father didn't want to argue today. But maybe . . . "I don't like my school," Anthony said aloud, pouting a little to show that he meant it. "Nothing but nuns. Can't I go somewhere else next year, Father?"

Maybe that would do it, appeal directly, see what happens. Out of the corner of his eye—though he was careful not to look directly—he saw his mother move slightly against her chair. Here it comes, he thought with a silent giggle; that did it.

"No," his mother said, "it's a fine school."

"We'll see," his father said. "We can probably find one you like better."

His mother stood up. "Please finish your dinner, Anthony." And she walked out of the room.

No words, no shouting—too bad.

His father rang for more wine. "And a glass for the boy."

Anthony watched with great seriousness while his father half-filled a glass with water and then poured in the wine. The thick red thinned to a pale pink.

His father said: "Never let a woman upset you. Your mother's mad, but she'll get over it by tomorrow. And there's no reason to let her temper spoil tonight."

Anthony lifted his glass carefully, trying to imitate Ronald Colman. He even tried Ronald Colman's half smile but he didn't get it right. He'd have to practice.

"Look," his father said, "I'm going to your grandfather's. Why don't you come along?"

"I've got homework."

"Forget it. If I leave you here, your mother will probably eat you alive."

"I'm not afraid of her," Anthony said.

"We won't even tell her we're going. Save a lot of trouble that way."

HIS FATHER said: "Anna ran us out, so we came over here."

It wasn't funny, Anthony thought, and it wasn't especially true, but his grandfather's eyes crinkled with amusement.

"You're teaching the boy about women," the Old Man said. He didn't look right, Anthony thought. His color was strange, like a sunburn that is fading.

Anthony found a new copy of *Redbook*: there was a Nero Wolfe novel he wanted to read, all about smuggled jewels and the Spanish Civil War.

He had almost finished it when his father said, "What do you think about spending the night at the camp?"

"Sure," Anthony said, "fine."

His grandfather walked with them to the door. He must be very tired, Anthony thought. His feet didn't seem firmly fixed to the ground, and when he walked he put them down extra hard, as if he weren't quite sure where the surface was. And his hands didn't swing alongside, but dangled straight down. Like they were tied on at his shoulders.

That was what it was like to be old—Anthony tried to imagine it for himself, tried to imagine his arms hanging that way, his heels hitting down that hard.

How did it feel being old? Was it like being tired all the time? Or was it a special kind of feeling, like swimming was a special feeling, and holding your breath was a special feeling. When you were old, were you different? Like—did a baby feel different, because it was a baby? He ought to know that but he couldn't remember. So many things like that, answers he should know, but had somehow forgotten.

His grandfather said, "I'm about ready for bed."

"Me too," Anthony said.

His father snorted. "How do you expect to chase girls if you get tired so early?"

AFTER A few minutes Anthony climbed into the back of the car. Before he slipped into a heavy sleep, he began wondering how he was ever going to find out about girls. His school had nothing but boys and he knew all about them. In the toilet, where they urinated into a line of porcelain bowls, the boys always measured each other with their eyes and their fingers. Until Jerry Hanneman brought a ruler. "Here, you bastards, measure your thing against this, man." So they had, and Jerry Hanneman was the winner, until— just this morning—they discovered that he was jamming the end deep into his belly. They stayed in the toilet so long and giggled so much that the nuns sent the janitor to get them. When he saw what they were doing, he showed his toothless gums in the dim light. "Used to spend hours doing that in the army, whole barracks, all measuring and bragging. . . . Now you kids get outa here, before the good sisters chew off my ass."

His father was shaking him, and it was jet-black night all around, with only little pieces of stars stuck up in the sky. "We're here." He followed his father's flashlight into the camp, and while his father lit the lamps and opened the windows, Anthony crawled into the nearest bed. At daylight he smelled coffee and staggered out, eyes half closed.

His father sat on the porch. It was still early—there was a flat haze rising from the bayou, and the cypresses on the other side were wrapped in strings of gray cloud. Nothing moved; only a ricebird called monotonously in the foggy distance.

"You sleep good?"

"Fine," Anthony said. "I'll be late for school."

"And I'll be late for work." His father wore yesterday's dark suit and white shirt, his tie tucked into the coat pocket. Those clothes looked funny, Anthony thought, against the bayou and the swamp.

"You want some coffee?"

"No," Anthony said. "Yes."

His father laughed. "Good answer."

The coffee smelled of his grandfather's house. The wide entrance hall, the curving stair, the fireplace with its flanking green velvet chairs—they swam before his eyes, blotted out by the cypress trees and the smeary windows and the maple furniture of the camp. That was homesickness, he thought. Only it wasn't for his own home. "The coffee smells just like his house."

His father understood. "Places have smells. I remember some myself." He shrugged. "We'll drive back, soon as you comb your hair."

Anthony washed his face in the strange-smelling cistern water, dried it on the tail of his shirt. He looked for a comb, but found a brush—ebony-backed with long soft bristles— on the bedroom dresser. He picked it up, hesitated, holding it in the bright spring light. Tangled in the bristles was a long blond hair. He looked again. There were shorter snarled ones wound down into the base. He rolled them between his fingers, testing them. . . . He felt tremendously relieved. He'd known all the time. Of course he had. Women came here with his father. . . . And now he, Anthony, was here. His father had brought him to this special place, this secret place. . . . He stood smiling down at the brush, wondering what she'd looked like. . . . His father called: "Ready,

Anthony?" He kept on smiling at the brush; then very slowly, very deliberately, he lifted the brush to his head, mixing his own hair with the blond strands. He felt pleased and proud to be doing it.

H E   S P E N T   that summer with his mother at Port Bella. His father did not appear at all. Not once. His Aunt Margaret came now and then, and her son Joshua and his nurses spent a few weeks. And of course, his grandfather came every weekend.

O N E   L A T E   August afternoon when the days were long and dry and dazzling hot, he and his mother played cards in the trellised gazebo overlooking the Gulf. "Father isn't coming at all this year," he said.

She shuffled steadily. "He will when he has time."

"Grandfather does."

She began dealing. "There we go."

Anthony picked up his cards. "Mother, do you ever wonder why Father married you?"

She answered him levelly, without hesitating. "No."

"Did he love you?"

She went on solemnly. "I loved him, Anthony, and that is nearly the same thing."

He nodded. He seemed to understand. Not the words, but the message behind them.

"Do you think he married you because there was a lot of money?"

"Your father would have found money with or without me, anywhere in this world."

Suddenly he didn't want to talk about it any more. He was angry with her for not changing the subject. Why was she always so serious with him, why did she always treat him like a grown man? Why was she always so honest? Invincibly honest. . . . He liked that phrase; he repeated it to himself: invincibly honest.

"Your hand's shaking, Anthony."

The cards in his left hand were quivering. He slapped them down immediately. His body was always betraying him.

He flicked his cards into the middle of the table. "I am just sick of being in this house out in the country. I wish school would start." He stalked down the sun-bleached lawn toward the water. He could feel her brown eyes following him, understanding, sympathetic. He picked up a small beach rock and hurled it with all his strength at a boulder. It splintered into fragments and sprayed away.

He remembered suddenly that he had never been in a fight, had never punched or been hit, had never really wrestled. Supervision at home and school allowed only a little shoving and pushing. He had never felt his fist hit tissue-covered bone. . . . He tested it into his palm. It felt nice. He did it again, with more force, repeating until his hands hurt. He wished there was somebody on the beach. Win or lose, he would have fought with him. He would have felt his muscles push against something. Something instead of air.

The beach was empty, as it always was. Just green water and a small skirt of yellow sand. Not even a shell, not even a sea-wrack line; two yard boys picked it clean after high tide every day. He squatted down and, scooping up a handful of sand, he began to blow the grains from his open palm toward the Gulf. Squinting, he tried to see if they reached it. None ever did. But then, he really couldn't expect to distinguish a grain of sand falling into the water.

There would hardly, he told himself, be any splash.

IN 1942 his father went to war. He telephoned Anthony twice a week until he was ordered to England. Then he sent only an occasional letter; he'd never liked to write.

That year Anthony grew three inches. His clothes were all too small; his ankles stuck out sharply, his wrists dangled from the cuffs of his shirts.

"Anthony," his mother complained, "you look like a scarecrow."

"I can't help growing."

"Oh, well," she said, "we'll manage. You look pale."

"I'm tired," he said.

He'd been tired for months, and he hurt all over—no specific pain, just a cloud that filtered through his body and ran from place to place, touching, fluttering. It was his dreams, he thought; they were nothing but war and blood and explosions. His father was never there—just Anthony and some other faceless people, and noise and confusion, and falling. Every night, every night. He could sleep only in the afternoons. As if the shapes that haunted him waited for dark. . . . He'd seen pictures of the brain with its cracks and crevices. Lots of hiding places in there. . . . After a few months he came to expect those dreams. To look for them, even. Once, when he had a cold, he'd taken a codeine cough syrup, and hadn't dreamed a single image. He felt irritated and disappointed; he had actually missed them.

In 1943 his mother closed her house in New Orleans and lived entirely in the big house at Port Bella. Anthony spent weekends with her; during the week he lived with his grandfather. He was there that April afternoon—just come from basketball practice, still sweating so that his pants stuck to his skin and pulled at his legs when he walked. He came up the drive, in the side door—as he always did—and through the hall toward the stairs. He passed the living room, glanced inside. He stopped and looked again, blinking against the duskiness of the drawn curtains. In the middle of the room his grandfather was on hands and knees, crawling slowly toward the door. Very slowly, one arm moved; it dragged across the carpet for a couple of inches, stopped. The other arm began moving in exactly the same way. His head hung down, swinging from side to side, like a hound's on a scent. His bald head rotated like a searchlight sweeping the ground.

Where did the shine come from, Anthony found himself thinking. What light fell on that bare skin? . . .

His grandfather crept another few inches. His back sagged until his belly touched the floor. His shoulders stayed up; though his arms trembled visibly with the strain, they held firm. After a couple of minutes, he lifted his back and inched forward again.

For all of that effort, Anthony thought, he had moved about a foot. . . . He went into the room, calling "Grandfather! Grandfather!" He stopped, right at his side, so close that the tips of his brown oxfords actually touched his left hand. His grandfather was breathing heavily. Each breath came out so slowly, rattled so loudly, that Anthony thought it would never stop. Then, when it did, the strangling gurgling struggle to inhale began. "What's the matter?" Anthony shouted. "Tell me what to do!" His grandfather's left hand moved forward again, brushing past the brown oxfords, settled on the rug, stiffened and bore the weight of the body as it crawled another couple of inches toward the door.

Anthony backed out of the room. He meant to shout, but somehow the shout turned into a scream. And once he had started screaming he couldn't seem to stop.

H E   S T O O D   on the column-lined porch, one step away from the big mahogany front doors, while people rushed past him, and cars wheeled down the drive, spattering gravel like water. His Aunt Margaret pushed him aside angrily. "Can't you even keep out the way, for God's sake?" Anthony stared through the open door, first at the smooth stretch of parquetry flooring, following the squares over and over again, then eventually allowing his eyes to rise to the broad stairs and the curving dark banister. He reached out to touch the wood of the doorframe. His fingers fell away from it as if it were hot and burning.

There's something wrong with me. There must be something wrong with me.

A couple of blocks away a car horn blew sharply. In the oak tree a big blue jay rasped, and a mockingbird imitated him. A cloud passed across a corner of sky, hazy and thin as a veil. A yellow cat sauntered across the lawn while mockingbirds twitched bits of fur from its back. Once the cat crouched and spun. And missed.

Inside the empty house a phone began ringing.

I should answer it. Hello. This is Anthony. Everybody's gone to the hospital. I'm the only one here. . . .

The phone stopped ringing. He gasped. He'd been holding his breath, and not even aware of it.

The cat rubbed against his legs, complaining.

"Shut up." Anthony kicked. The cat dodged away, yowling. Then slowly, tail high and fluffy, it crossed the porch and went in the front door.

The cat could answer the phone.

But the phone had stopped. . . . Anthony listened carefully. There was no sound at all in the afternoon, except a far-off hum.

I'm listening to my own skull sing like a sea shell's echo. The sound from inside my head, full of spongy white and spongy red.

The house walls moved, exactly one inch, one inch closer to him. Carefully, stalking him. It was the cat inside.

How stupid, he told himself. But he backed away. When he felt gravel under his shoes, he turned and ran. After a while he stopped running, and only walked very fast, and after that he just walked.

He saw a streetcar coming, swaying on its narrow track. He fumbled in his pocket, came up with a quarter and a couple of pennies, and trotted over to the car stop. He only needed seven cents. . . . After half an hour's ride, the slow steady rocking of the car made him feel much better.

HIS PARENTS' house was closed and locked. He climbed the fence, broke a window on the back porch, let himself in. He remembered it was dinnertime and found a can of vegetable soup and ate it, unheated. He went to his own room, and lay on his bed, a book in his hands. *Tom Sawyer;* he'd read it a dozen times, until his mother objected: "Aren't you ever going to read anything else?"

His mother . . . she would be at Port Bella, combing the grass in her gardens. Had anyone told her? The phone didn't always work. . . .

He read the familiar words of *Tom Sawyer* until he fell asleep.

HIS AUNT Margaret was shaking him. "Wake up."

He scrubbed at his eyes until he was able to see her. "Yes, ma'am."

"I figured we should look here before we called the police."

Her curly hair was uncombed; it stood up all around her face in little ragged stabs and wisps. She kept smoothing it down, but as soon as her coaxing fingers passed, the curls rose up jagged again.

"I assume you're all right?"

"Yes, ma'am."

He rubbed his leg where he had a bruise from last week's basketball. He winced.

"What's the matter?"

"A bruise."

"You get a lot of bruises. You ought to be more careful."

"Yes, ma'am."

She patted his sock-covered foot. "I shouldn't have yelled at you, Anthony, I forget you're still a kid. But you were being damn stupid. . . . You going to ask how your grandfather is?"

And he told her the absolute truth. "I thought he'd be dead."

"You get that directness from your mother. He's still with us."

"Is he going to live?"

"Well," she stood up, "I don't know, Anthony, he just blew out one whole side of his heart, or something like that. But he's not dead yet, and somehow I don't really think this is the time."

TWO MONTHS later—another summer vacation— Anthony and his grandfather were at Port Bella. His Aunt

Margaret drove over with them in their slow-moving convoy of ambulance and four cars, stayed the weekend, and hurried back to New Orleans. ("With Robert in England and Papa flat on his back, there's nobody but me to keep things going.")

The road dust settled over the flurry of her tires, and the weight and length of the summer remained. Like all the summers, Anthony thought. With a few changes because of the war. Most of the gardeners had been drafted; only Philip, the redbone, and his young sons still worked the gardens, hiding their daily supply of whiskey under the thick trunk of the wisteria vine. But evenings, Anthony decided, evenings were the worst. The house sweltered airlessly behind its heavy drawn curtains. (All coast houses were blacked out with the first rumor of German submarines offshore.) The hot light-proofed rooms did not seem to bother his mother or his grandfather, but Anthony found them unbearable. After dinner, while they listened to the radio and plotted the progress of both war theaters on the huge wall maps in the living room, Anthony slipped outside to sit on the porch, to let his eyes run around in the night. There were clouds of mosquitoes; he could see them thick as hair on his bare arm. He could imagine their mouths buried in his skin, sucking his blood. It was still better than being inside.

ONE AFTERNOON when a rain had left the air cooler and fresher with the sharp smell of lightning-produced ozone, Anthony sat with his grandfather on the damp pillows of the ornate gazebo. "What are you writing?" Anthony asked.

His grandfather put the notebook away. "Things to do, when I go back to town next week."

"Oh." Anthony looked out at the rain-spotted Gulf.

His grandfather grinned. "I know what your mother will say. But I've spent over two months on my heart attack and that's enough."

A small green lizard ran across the window sill and watched them, fluttering his red air bladder nervously.

"People used to think those things were poison," his grandfather said.

"It was nice with you out here all the time."

"Thank you, Anthony," his grandfather said formally.

Anthony flicked the lizard away. "When you had your heart attack," he asked, "were you afraid?"

His grandfather scowled into the vine-covered lattice walls. "You know, Anthony, I remember sitting down in that chair, not feeling too good, and then the next thing I knew I was on the floor feeling like a hole had been blown through me by a shotgun."

"But"—Anthony studied his own browned hands, their nails edged with dirt—"were you ever scared?"

"Of dying?" He smiled wryly. "With all the people staring at you, well, you get a little self-conscious and you start watching what they're watching."

"But you weren't scared?"

"No."

"Well"—Anthony pulled a moonflower and tossed it away—"why do you suppose that is?"

"I suppose," his grandfather said, "when you're that close to dying, you see it for what it is; it doesn't look that bad."

HIS GRANDFATHER left for New Orleans. Because the trip was tiring, he did not come every weekend any more. His Aunt Margaret did not come either—she had married suddenly, and three weeks later started divorce proceedings. Her husband waited in the big azalea hedge, shot at her, missed, turned the gun on himself, missed again, shooting off a piece of his ear lobe. By the time the police came, he was in tears.

Anthony heard all these things from a great distance. Nothing happened in the house at Port Bella. He sat in the corner of the porch and watched his mother in the garden; when the glare was not too strong, he watched the empty blue-gray stretch of water. At times he felt that it took all his energy to breathe. I used to play basketball, he thought, and I used to be on the baseball team, but now if I bump into a chair I have a black-and-blue mark. And if I punch my thigh I have a bruise. . . .

Day after day he sat on the shaded porch. "You can't just sit still all day," his mother said, "you should move a little."

"I'm not just sitting, Mother," he said, "I'm reading." To prove it, he brought a different book each day, and flipped its pages. That wasn't too bad.

What was bad was the sudden pain in his wrists. One morning it was not there, the next it was. His wrists hurt so badly that he could no longer carry the book to the porch; he could not even manage to pick it up. Each morning he forced himself to dress; the pain was so intense that tears ran down his cheeks. He could leave his shirt unbuttoned, saying he wanted to be cool, but he had to fasten his pants. And that was almost more than he could do. He could not even rest his hands on a table. The pain was only bearable when his arms hung straight down from his shoulders, unmoving.

It took his mother two days to notice. He was surprised; he'd thought she watched him more closely.

"Anthony, we will have to see about that."

They went first to the doctor in Collinsville, a red-haired

old man, who'd practiced there since finishing school in Georgia forty-five years before. He was exaggeratedly polite, and his courteous drawl lengthened so that Anthony had trouble understanding him.

"Madam, I am dumfounded. I have delivered women by the hundreds, I have stitched cuts by the mile, I have set bones, I have pronounced the dead. But not this. I could hunt through my books, but I wouldn't be sure."

Anthony's mother said impatiently, "I suppose we'll go back to New Orleans."

"There is a young man in Pensacola—a diabetic, so the army did not take him—he would be closer and just as competent."

"Fine," his mother said. "Call him and we'll go there right now."

Anthony caught one glance from the pale blue eyes. Quick, sharp in the round freckled face. Why that, he wondered; why that?

They stayed two days at Pensacola, at a tourist court in a grove of mulberry trees. At night Anthony listened to the ripe berries falling on the tin roof, and the boards of the porch were stained red by their juice. Shiny green-and-blue flies swarmed on the rotting fruit, and thick-bodied jays followed the flies. In the early morning he watched them from his window, until his mother's alarm clock rang and she woke up too.

He didn't remember too much about the days, except that again the doctor was red-haired. The second afternoon he fell asleep on the examining table. He woke feeling much better, sat up, and collapsed whimpering with the sudden pain in his wrist.

"We'll go," his mother said. "We'll go home now."

They drove home at once; for all those hours he lay on the back seat and cried silent pain tears, shielded by the dark.

He stayed in bed for the next few days. She did not try

to coax him, or rouse him. When he felt well enough, he got up; she kissed him at breakfast without the least sign of surprise—as if he had been there every morning. He went to the same shady porch corner. She went back to her gardening. She did not mention the doctor; he did not ask. It was as if it had never happened.

He seemed to doze with his eyes open, to rest himself against the moisture-filled air. Everything was soft and vague and far away.

Once he wrote a letter to his father, a short letter because writing hurt. "I am sick," he wrote; "can you get a leave? I would feel better if you came home."

Bit by bit the pain in his wrists subsided, the September days turned sharp blue, and he woke from his doze and looked around. He saw changes.

His mother had gotten more religious. Much more. She went to Mass every morning—a forty-mile drive—and the house was full of saints and flickering candles and the funny smell of incense. One day as she sat reading the newspaper, her skirt slipped aside and Anthony saw that her knees were covered with calluses and lacerations. As he watched, a trickle of blood ran down the front of her leg, bright red blood twisting among the little black hairs. She felt it, thought it a mosquito, slapped at it. The blood splattered, wet and oily; she jumped up and hurried away. And Anthony remembered a sound he heard whenever he wakened at night, the jingle of rosary beads. . . . He sometimes sneaked up to her door at night, but it was always firmly closed with the key in the lock. There was only the dry rattle of the heavy Ursuline nun's rosary.

He noticed that now his mother often seemed to have a fever, her eyes glittered, the skin across her cheeks was dry and crinkly like paper. Now too she wore only loose dresses that hung straight from the shoulders, and she walked as if she were in pain. Routinely rummaging through her room, he found the bottle of red ants. And peering through her half-closed bathroom door, he saw that her breasts and stomach were covered by the large suppurating blotches of their bites.

"SCHOOL'S STARTING," Anthony said, "I've got to go back."

"I thought you would stay here," she said. "It won't hurt you to lose a term. After all, you're a year ahead of your age."

That was true. "I wish you'd told me, Mother."

"You didn't seem interested, Anthony."

And that also was true. He'd hardly spoken to her for the last month.

"Grandfather doesn't come at all."

"I asked him to wait until you felt better. You didn't seem to care."

"Maybe I would have cared if he'd come." He was furious at her total devotion, her selfless care.

"Anthony, you have to tell me those things if you want me to know them."

"Well, I want him."

"Anthony," his mother said levelly, "you're forgetting. Your grandfather had a heart attack, and now your aunt is having a terrible divorce. They are both busy."

That was true too. His mother had a lot of single truths but when they were all put together they were no longer true. "I wrote my father a letter, asking him to come home. Why didn't he answer me?"

"Your father writes whenever he has time, Anthony."

"But he never has said anything about coming. Not even

about not being able to get a leave. He would have, if he got the letter."

"I threw that letter away," his mother said quietly. "It was foolish and it would have worried him very much."

"You didn't mail it." His anger disappeared in the face of such simplicity. He went back to his shady porch and stared out at the Gulf, a rain-freshened blue stretch where no ship ever sailed, no boat ever moved. Only a sea gull now and then.

Later when she sat beside him, pulling off her gardening gloves and brushing her hands against her dress, he asked: "Why are you always praying?"

She too stared out at the Gulf. "Because God is the author of our life and the hope of our salvation."

And then Anthony stopped asking questions.

N O W E A C H morning when he stepped from the blackout shrouded house into the bright September day, he saw how horribly empty the Gulf was, how bare and still. He would not look at it any more, he would move to the other side of the house. There were the gardens, and beyond the gardens were the fields and pastures, where cattle fattened on the soft thick grass, where wild birds came to feed on specially planted fields of buckwheat. Beyond the fields were the woods, the soft yellow-green pinewoods, their smooth sand covered by dry needles, clear of brush except for an occasional clump of palmettos. He'd never gone exploring in there; his mother was afraid of snakes. He had seen the big rattlers men killed; they brought them to the kitchen door and the maids and the cooks gathered to stare at them, and giggle. They skinned the biggest ones and tacked them to the side of the tool house, to cure in the sun. He'd never seen a live rattler. So many things he hadn't done. . . .

"You've moved your seat," his mother said.

"I like the trees," he said.

They didn't seem quite so empty, as they shimmered in the clear air.

A couple of days later he telephoned his grandfather —his mother was in the garden. "Are you coming this weekend?"

His grandfather answered: "Your mother doesn't seem to want company just now."

"I want you to come."

His grandfather hesitated but only for a moment. "When your mother says she wants to be left alone, Anthony, I can't do anything about it."

"Then I want to come to New Orleans."

"Your mother says you have an infection to get over."

"Is that what the doctor said?"

"That's what she told me." His voice was mildly annoyed.

"I think I'm sick," Anthony said slowly. "I think I'm very sick and I want to leave here."

"I'll speak to your mother."

Anthony hung up.

She said: "Your grandfather called me."

"Can I go?"

"When you are stronger, Anthony."

"What have I got?" he asked.

"You're tired from growing so fast."

"You won't let me out. You won't let me go."

"Anthony, don't be silly."

"You won't even tell my father."

That night he wrote a letter to his father, and starting just before daylight, he began walking to the post office at

Port Bella. He thought he could make it before his mother came after him. He almost did. Some Negro children craw-fishing on the outskirts of town found him by the road in a ditch, buried to his waist in slime and water. He had fallen there when he fainted.

AFTERWARD, WHEN he was quite sure where he was—back in his own room with his mother sitting at his bed—when he was quite sure that he had failed, he did not feel angry any more, or trapped.

"Mama," he said, "what did the doctor say is wrong with me?"

"Nothing at all."

"Mama," he said, "you are lying."

"Anthony, really," she touched his forehead, "you have a fever and you're overtired."

"He said I was going to die."

He watched while the color drained from her sun-tanned skin. It turns yellow, he thought, not white but yellow. Now isn't that funny?

He went on staring at her, at the frozen set of her face, at the blotchy movement of color under her skin, and he wasn't afraid, he wasn't even upset. He was simply rather pleased at having guessed. And he was very pleased at having hurt her.

"Anthony, you mustn't say that."

He began to laugh. Way down inside himself. It started as a little tickle behind his spine and it spread over his body until he was shaking all over. But there wasn't a sound on the surface, not a single sound to disturb the silent air. He just went on laughing and laughing all by himself.

H E   F E L T   lighter now, and happier. There seemed always to be laughter bubbling inside him. "You prayed a lot last night," he said, smiling, to his mother, "maybe you should pray harder." She was standing between him and the light, just a tall thin shape against the dazzle; he couldn't see her face. She turned away without answering.

Again he spoke: "Where are the priests, Mama?"

"Anthony, you're getting better."

"No, I'm not," he said.

A N T H O N Y   S T O P P E D   eating; he drank pitcher after pitcher of iced tea. "Anthony, you've got to eat," his mother said.

"I want to go back to New Orleans. I want my father to know."

"There is nothing for us in town, Anthony; you know that."

He nodded, smiling his secret little smile. "You know the name but you won't tell me. And I know how it feels but I don't know the name."

"The Lord is the source of many miracles," his mother said abruptly. "He does what he wills."

"He does," Anthony said, and that time his hidden laughter broke to the surface.

B U T   T H E N   the nights became a burden to him. After a couple of hours, he had had enough sleep. He would turn on his light and sit up and try to find an all-night station on his radio. His mother—she didn't seem to sleep any more either—would come in to see why he was awake, and he would deliberately not talk to her, would lie with his back toward her until she went away.

(You would think she would cry; he wondered why she did not cry. Her eyes, even in the middle of the night, were round and dry. Only, there was a certain light to them. Another light, wherever it came from, whatever it was. They were the brightest eyes he had ever seen. Like a car's head-lights. Artificial beams shining to light the road. She could see at night with them. . . . She could make a miracle happen with them. . . .)

He learned to creep down the back stairs—they were farthest from his mother's room—and out the kitchen door. Sometimes he sat on the porch, listening to the raccoons and skunks rattle the garbage cans. Sometimes he walked in the gardens, studying the shapes and patterns of leaves. And sometimes he went to the beach, to the end of the long wooden pier, and pretended he was crabbing by moonlight and that the crabs he caught were gold and covered with rubies, with pearls for their eyes.

It got more and more difficult for him to walk that far, even when he stopped to rest two or three times. Pretty soon, he thought, I won't be able to get out, my mother will have caught me inside that house forever.

He thought about that, sitting on the rough wooden edge of the pier. The moon hung upside down and low on the horizon, reflecting shiny bright in the motionless mirror water. He stared out at a star-spotted gulf, endlessly empty, flawlessly still. He glanced down, saw the pirogue; it was moored under the pier, suspended on the glassy surface, gleaming with moonlight. The gardener's boys had forgotten to return it to the boat house.

Tipping his head, he watched the moon with his right eye and the pirogue with his left. *Moon's cup turned over, water spills out.* . . . but there wasn't a sign of rain in the night sky. The rough half-finished wood (it was an old-fashioned pirogue cut from a single log) looked smooth and velvety against the moon-polished water.

Soft, he thought, how very soft. Like an upholstered chair. So comfortable.

He knew it wasn't. He'd been in too many pirogues—they were rough uncomfortable little shells that danced on the surface of the water.

All the money my grandfather's made—he squinted straight up at the moon, as if expecting an answer—and we only have a pirogue, like any dirt-poor Cajun. War took the other boats, gone to the Coast Guard. At least we should have a new pirogue, or a skiff. With all that money . . .

And what was money like? When he was little, he'd thought of it as piles and piles of dollar bills locked in a closet somewhere. My father married my mother to get the key to the closet, and my grandfather likes my father better than my mother. . . . I wonder what he thinks of me. Not much. Not enough to come see.

A school of minnows broke water directly beneath him, flashing silver specks that fled the invisible pursuer, and vanished with hardly a shadow of ripples left behind.

He counted stars: four, five, and three more over there, where the Dipper was so low—it must be late. Light comes slow this time of year. Past the middle of October. Now comes Thanksgiving and Christmas and days that are shorter still. I haven't seen dawn once, not this summer. I'll wait for it this morning. . . .

He looked back at the house. Wide and tall and gray against a blue night sky. His mother's light was on. And the one in the hall. She'd missed him already.

He let himself down the ladder and into the pirogue. It shuddered and bounced on the water, but he steadied it, sat down carefully in the proper spot, and released the mooring line.

His mother would look for him in the gardens first, then along the road to town. She wouldn't think about the beach until the very last. He had plenty of time.

He dug the paddle in the water, uncertainly. After a few tries he remembered how to do it, remembered all the things he had been taught.

He paddled straight out on the smooth windless Gulf. He rested frequently, the pain in his wrists was beginning again, but he kept on, he had a plan. When he had gone far enough to be safe, when he could no longer be seen easily from shore, then he would turn toward the west: the current, he remembered, went that way, and he would drift to that little town—what was it called? Longport, or some such name—and when he got there he would see what to do.

But his wrists hurt too much. He had to stop. He dropped his paddle into the bottom, into the pool of water there. He rested his aching wrists on both gunwales as he lowered himself to the bottom of the pirogue. The water that sloshed along his back felt warm and comfortable. He floated secure, contained in his shallow cradle. When, lifting his head unsteadily, he peered over the side, there was still no sign of lightening in the sky. The moon had set, leaving only star-flecked black overhead. On all sides the Gulf gleamed dully, turning back the starlight in an even glowing sheen. He lay back, carrying with him the image of what he had seen. A smooth clean satin expanse, soft and white and inviting. Like a bed, like an endless bed. He tried to lift his head again to look but found he lacked the strength for that. Without thinking, he turned on his side and spreading his pain-torn arms he rolled softly and gently into the endless spread.

AT THE memorial service in Metairie Cemetery there were three priests and the Archbishop and a dozen altar boys. Incense hung like fog at the new red marble tomb, wrapped its white fingers around the crouching grieving angels at each of the four corners. But only Anthony's name was there, chiseled in foot-high letters. For, in spite of their searching, in spite of the rewards his grandfather offered, Anthony eluded them all. He stayed in the bed he had chosen.

ANNA

ANTHONY WAS gone, he'd walked away. He'd slipped from his room, he'd crept down the stairs, he'd fled across the gardens to the barrier ocean. His highway.

He'd even kept the pirogue hidden from them, those hundreds of searchers who prodded among the marsh grasses, who searched the Gulf from low-flying planes and fishing boats. Why did Anthony keep the boat; where was he going that he would need an old pirogue? Where was he going?

She'd run screaming all over the house, up and down the hills and gardens, across the pastures. She'd sent her servants in every car to look along all the roads. While she herself stood on the porch, huddled in the shadow, hands clasping her face as if it would shatter, and watched the sun rise. . . .

She'd never thought to look at the beach. . . . She'd known him that little. She'd been that wrong.

Time and process were reversed. Anthony dwindled, curling into a fetus, slipped back into her womb; retreated into initial parts of ovum and sperm; and still further, into the nothing that he was before their mating. His ultimate concealment.

He was gone.

She accepted that hurt with the dumb stoicism of exhaustion. She did not pray for the recovery of his body. Her father did, her sister did: they set whole convents of nuns praying for Anthony's return.

Anna saw only a poster tacked on the gates of heaven: "Wanted, Dead or Alive."

Endless prayers, prayers rolling out like an enormous carpet, to lead Anthony to heaven.

And where was he? Slipped away.

The prayers would find him, the prayers would bring him back. Like filings to a magnet. He would be drawn from his hiding place, to the bosom of his family, to the right hand of God. . . .

Only Anthony was even trickier, more devious, more cunning in his concealment.

WITH THE infected ant bites, her fever shot to dizzy heights. She plastered herself with wet soda, and then poultices made of seven greens, the way Negroes did.

Anthony, come back.

Now, even now, a week later, walk out of the Gulf, walk on the water, hair shining blue black, my face surrounding your eyes, my skin across your bones. . . .

Anthony, come out of hiding, back in the reeds, among the white underwater stems, bubbles and drift and bright fish eyes, all the soft shell-less things like you. Hide-and-seek, catch me if you can. But the game's over. It's time to come in now; it's time to come home.

SHE SAW masses of candles, banks of candles, rising like hills in thin air, where she knew no candles were. Triangles of lights, floating. She shook her head to dispel the sight, to shake it to pieces, to send it away. Secure in their own unhurried order, one by one, relentlessly, the candles went out,

leaving behind the blank black-red glass cups that had held
them.

She heard a bell where no bell could possibly be. Four
or five times a day, sunlight and dark, she saw it outside the
window, swaying back and forth, suspended by nothing,
swinging free in the air. Not the peal of a wedding. Not the
ordered threes of the Angelus. Not the flat funeral clang.
A rhythm all its own, broken, hesitant, sometimes a single
stroke as if the clapper were hitting one side of the bell
only. . . .

She found that she could see through people, through
skin to skeleton. The tracing of their bones was as clear to
her eyes as to an X-ray. She counted their ribs; she watched
their stomachs churn food, the coiled intestines contracting
and pulsing, like worms through the ground; she studied the
flow of blood through veins and arteries like small canals.
Faces lost their features and sockets their eyes; skulls looked
back at her. She lifted her own arm and a skeleton hand
appeared, purified of skin and muscle, only the enduring
bone.

There were signs too. Of the Virgin, the Immaculate
Conception, blue gown and naked foot on the curled serpent.
Bare foot that moved, drew back. Half smile that flickered
for an instant on the pink-and-white face. Crown of stars
that shone a little brighter and then dimmed. The serpent
that solemnly and sleepily winked.

Other signs. The shadows. Sometimes she thought they
were people she recognized—she'd known them a long time
ago; she couldn't quite bring back their faces hidden there
in the dark. . . . And sometimes the shadows were animals—
no, they were almost animals. But not really. They weren't
anything but they were there. . . .

Robert's letter: "You killed him. You let him die." She
tore it into small pieces; she put it in the fireplace, burned
it, and stirred the ashes.

We are all guilty, she thought; all the two-legged people tottering and strutting on the crust of the earth. We never know what we do, never know what sin. All of us. Even Anthony. The lovely lost boy. All the forked creatures, stripped and naked. What did we do? The round white skull, skin and hair over it, camouflage. Circle of white bone, bottle of bone. Inside, the nameless horrors. That no prayer or incense dispels. Thoughts like worms before the grave.

She was dead, she was dying, she was alive. The shapes faded, the bells ceased, the flickering invisible candles turned back to air.

THE WAR ended with a telegram from Robert in New York. "Shall I come back." Instantly she sent a one-word answer: "Yes." She would be glad to see him, because she did not love him. Precisely that. (A pity I can't put this in a telegram, she thought; it would explain so much.) Because she would have no more children, she no longer needed him as a stud. He was merely a business associate of her father's, an old friend. He would come—in sexless friendship, no pulse stirred her body any more—and she would be very glad to have him back. Gently, quietly. Like two animals trotting wearily in the same direction, untouching.

Yes, she thought; yes, indeed. . . .

She had loved God and she had loved her son. And that was enough. Love was a burden she was glad to be rid of.

ROBERT, 1942–1955

ANNA DID not write him of Anthony's death. The letter came from the Old Man. Robert in his London office stared at the paper and thought: What? Over and over again: What? Even when he knew he should have gotten beyond that, even when he knew he should have understood, he found himself still saying and thinking: What?

The Old Man's letter was perfectly clear, perfectly direct. Almost formal. Almost business-like. As if he had a routine for telling a man his son was dead.

But what? Robert found himself staring out the curtainless window across the bombed-out rubble. His building, converted into American staff offices, showed hardly a dent. But across a small square (treeless now), block after block was totally destroyed—heaps of brick and blackened wood and isolated walls that crumbled with the freezes and thaws of winter. One of the men from the Provost Marshal's office upstairs, a cocky little red-headed fellow, said: "You better hope we don't get any hot weather. It's a lousy cemetery over there."

Like Germany. He'd spent almost six weeks in Germany, never knowing why he was there, a lieutenant commander from Navy Supply, in the middle of the army's war. He lived through a series of unnamed towns and villages, all one-dimensional, standing single walls, not a four-walled building left, matchsticks sticking up into skies that stank with the dead. And through it all, twisting and turning, miles of white tape. The engineers used it to mark areas not yet cleared of mines. You followed the white tape, like a child's party game. . . .

He watched civilians come out of those ruins, pushing the stones aside, Christs from the tomb. Funny round eyes. Cringing, obsequious. Hail to the new conqueror; have you something to eat? "Jesus Christ," he heard a sergeant say, "even the women ain't worth fucking."

What did you expect of a corpse, he thought. They just rose up. It's Resurrection Day without the glory. Just the stench, the pervasive constant stench.

H E S A T at his desk and read the Old Man's letter over and over again. Anthony. The tall thin boy. His son.

Someone asked: "Is this ready to go, sir?"

"Yes," he said.

How could the boy drown? That wasn't possible. He'd seen him summer after summer, first hardly more than a baby, splashing in the warm shallow Gulf water. The baby changed into a lanky sinewy boy; the splash changed into a deliberate stroke, steady, relaxed. . . . Robert watched him by the hour, as if he'd never seen a child before. Watched him in the water, watched him at parties in the garden, following streamers round and round the flowers. Follow the tape and get the prize. . . . That same streamer ran through the ruins. Follow the tape, live until tomorrow. . . . Anthony playing. Anthony running on green grass in the rose garden, among the flaming-red roses. Anthony laughing as he ran along the length of white tape, reeling it in.

Robert's helmet was on the side of the desk. He picked it up and swinging it like a hatchet he broke every glass in the window, and then methodically pulverized the wood frames. When he was done, all he had was a better view of the cemetery rubble below. He threw the helmet toward it.

THE GLASS cuts healed. The doctors provided him with seconal and dexedrine. He found that if he took them both, followed by a stiff drink of whiskey, he could survive. He wrote one letter to Anna, then only to the Old Man.

Day after day he stared out at the ruins as they changed with the seasons, glistened under the rain, gleamed softly under the snow.

The war was so nearly over that the English began clearing the rubble. Sometimes Robert watched the crews at work, noticing without emotion that the bodies they found were always headless. He thought about that seriously, ponderously. The head was so delicately attached. He'd noticed in Germany that it blew off first in an explosion, leaving behind a jangle of arms and legs. Now, in these fallen buildings, they found flattened bodies, heads missing. They must have popped, he thought, like oranges, been squeezed dry and evaporated. That was very funny, he thought. Very funny.

The English carried the bodies away, to bury them decently. It bothered Robert that they should at last be taken from the rubble; they seemed to have snuggled there so comfortably—like the waves that rocked Anthony eternally. The living pulled the dead out like potatoes to replant them in a green stretch somewhere. Would they grow underground, like potatoes, multiplying out of sight? He could see a hazy green slope and under it lines and lines of skeletons standing at parade rest: little ones, and big ones, and some tiny ones that must have been infants, all in proper rows, all headless. . . .

Every night he could manage, Robert walked to his girl's apartment, stumbling, dodging cars that raced out of the black. There always seemed to be an American voice shouting, "Taxi!" His girl said that you could hear them yelling even over the air-raid sirens, even during the lull between the bombs. . . .

Her name was Norah; she worked in the Transport Office next to his building and lived in a small apartment that belonged to her mother. ("The old lady took off at the first explosion.") He'd met her not two weeks after he arrived, went to bed with her that same night. She was his regular girl, and he was even faithful to her.

Because she'd been born in India, she cooked him curries with her mother's hoarded spices and the food he got from military supplies. After a while he began to think all England smelled of curry. The scent got in his uniforms and into his hair and nose. It walked around with him like an invisible shield.

He was very happy with her. At times he knew he loved her, but he never mentioned Anthony's death. Not a word, not a hint. Nothing, except on some nights he fled to the bathroom, retching until he bled.

"You're sick," she said.

"No."

"It's me?"

"Don't be stupid."

"It's me," she said, "I know it's me."

He should have told her about Anthony. But he couldn't. Any more than he could tell her about those party ribbons he saw twisting around bombed-out ruins every time he closed his eyes.

"It's nothing," he said.

He knew she did not believe him; there was a shadow across her broad face that hadn't been there before.

In April she told him she was pregnant. "It will be November, I think."

He blew into his teacup, watching ripples form on the yellow surface. It was the pattern waves made as they crossed the Gulf sands. Sheltered shallow sands where Anthony had kicked and crawled.

"I'm glad," she said. "I want a child."

"I can't marry you."

She smiled her pale small-mouth smile. "I didn't expect you to, Commander."

"I don't think it's so god damn funny."

"Anyway," she said quietly, "all those years we lived in India, my parents would talk about home. Isn't that queer? I got used to thinking of London as home too. And I still do. I'll stay here." She scratched at a nick on the rim of her glass. "I've wanted a child for years, Robert. During the worst of the war, I couldn't. I was too afraid of getting killed."

"You can get killed anywhere," he said. "You remember when we went down in the country?"

THAT WAS a year ago, or even more, when he and Norah managed a few days' leave together. Going to the country was Norah's idea; the air is good for you, she insisted. It was late fall, gray sky, gray land. They slept in cold wet beds, with strange-smelling sheets. They pedaled bicycles for miles along empty gray lanes, through deep ruts filled with the opaque gray cloudiness of freezing water. Norah loved it. Robert, his hands and feet numb, his nose running, knew that he had never seen such animation in her face, such beauty. Her cheeks were flaming red and her eyes an extraordinary blue. All because of some frost-burned fields and dark dripping hedges. . . .

Nobody expected the raid; everybody said that German planes would never be in the skies again. "Oh, no," Norah said when the siren went off. "Oh, no!" Robert rolled over: "Forget it, maybe it's a false alarm." They dozed until the all-clear; then Robert said, "I'm hungry. Let's eat." "There was one," she said, "one explosion." "Forget it, I'm hungry," he said.

They bicycled later, both of them a little drunk from three beers at breakfast. "Look," Norah said. It had been a big farmhouse, impressive, with a wide scattering of outbuildings. Robert whistled softly: "They took a direct hit." "Robert," Norah said, "why would they bomb that?" Robert took a flask from his pocket, passed it to her; in the cold it was difficult keeping an alcoholic glow. "I can guess," Robert squinted into the gray sky. "They sure as hell didn't start out to hit a farmhouse. They were turned back someplace else and had to get rid of their bombs before they went home. The book says you've got to find a secondary target, and when they saw a good big building, all by itself, they made a run. You know, I bet that was the only time they ever hit a target. . . ."

"THAT'S WHAT I mean," Robert said, "the poor bastards in that house, thinking they were safe way out in the country. . . . It doesn't matter where you are."

I had a son once, killed in his own front yard, with his mother in the house. I've been shot at and I'm alive. He was safe, and he's dead. . . .

But he said nothing of that to Norah, that April day in London.

"You'll be going home in a few months," Norah said,

"and you weren't going to ask me to come with you, now were you?"

"No," he said.

"There, you see."

He was getting a headache. He wondered if he had any aspirin in his coat pocket, maybe even some codeine. He got up to feel through his pockets. "Just one thing," he said. "You're so sure that I won't care a damn about the baby."

He found a small box of codeine and swallowed one of the tiny white pills with a beer. Realizing she hadn't answered, he said again: "Norah, how do you think I'd feel leaving a child of mine?"

"It isn't your child."

For a moment he did not believe it; he did not think he had heard it. "Well," he said. The single sound hung in the air, so nakedly that he did not say another word.

He stared at the wall, thinking that it needed paint. And there was a very small noise: the beer in his hand was rattling. He lifted it closer to his ear. Yes, that was it. Bubbles popping from the surface, disappearing into air. He drank from the glass, slowly, letting the foam accumulate on his upper lip. He stopped and listened again; he could hear the tiny pops of bubbles leaving the surface of his skin.

He finished the beer, wiped his mouth on his open palm. He put on his overcoat, buttoning it methodically. He left Norah without saying a single word.

He went to the Officers Club, and sat quietly at one end of the bar, looking up only when somebody slapped his shoulder. "Come on, Rob, old pal," they said, "have a drink with us." He shook his head. The stool was too comfortable, his legs wrapped exactly around it, his elbows fitted so nicely into the shelf of the bar.

They carried him to his quarters that night, his friends, though he remembered nothing of it. They woke him the next morning and got him to work on time. They gave him oxygen from the special tank they kept for problem hangovers; they fed him dexedrine and coffee until he was able to sit at his desk, with his head straight against the straight line of his shoulders. They even did his work for him. He seemed to drag a huge body around slowly, a hermit crab in an outsized shell. Hour by hour the shell shrank until—at night— it turned into his own fitting skin. And, with his skin settled over his bones again, he began wondering: Was Norah telling the truth?

I've one son dead, he thought. Do I lose this other one too?

A month later Norah married a man named Edward Harris, and they lived in the same apartment, her mother's apartment. Once or twice Robert walked by, half intending to knock on their door. With the child due in November, Norah would be visibly pregnant now. Would the lump of her body help him identify the child?

He wondered if she ever saw him passing, if she ever looked through the curtains. If she ever stood in the window, as the months rolled by toward November, with her belly swelling bigger and bigger, watching the street below.

He knew the child was his; he was certain.

In August he was ordered to New York. In October he was in New Orleans, a civilian again. I wish I could see the child, he thought. But he never went back to England, and he never heard from Norah again.

H E F L E W to Pensacola on a Navy plane, got a jeep from the transportation pool; he was going home to Port Bella. It was a long drive, he was tired, and in the dark he kept running off the road. He stopped and, rolling up his useless heavy overcoat for a pillow, stretched out on the grass. He woke in the hazy first light, a stray dog sniffing at his feet, his face and hair dripping with dew.

Great beginning, he thought: flat out in the dirt while some woolhat's dog stares at me.

He got up, staggering with cramp, tossed the coat into the back seat, noticing with satisfaction the dust smears on its clean Navy surface.

The gates were closed and locked; he had no key. The phone to the caretaker's house was at the side, but Robert didn't bother. He simply drove the jeep straight into the gate, three, four times, until the wood splintered away from the hinges, and the jeep slipped through.

Underbrush crowded the winding sandy road, the drooping faces of palmetto brushed the car's fenders, fallen pines littered the woods. In the open sunny spaces blackberry bushes ran unhindered into tangles of thorn. The buckwheat field was waist-high in Johnson grass, with a dozen scraggly ailanthus trees.

Even the lawns looked raggedy. The grass was mowed neatly enough, but not edged. Most of the flower beds were gone. Only the rose garden still blazed with color. Trust Anna, he thought; she would always have a rose garden.

He swung the jeep toward the beach. Beyond the narrow sand the empty Gulf was the same flat calm winter blue as the sky.

Anthony had come this way. He had walked slowly across this grass, across this yielding sand, out on the sun-bleached pier.

The boards shook with Robert's weight; sea gulls fled from their perches.

Anthony had walked along these boards.

Robert stared into the shallow water. A big blue crab scuttled by, then a school of minnows nibbled the weeds on the pilings.

Anthony stood here once; and saw this. Anthony got into a boat here.

Robert sat on the end of the pier, legs dangling, shoes almost touching the water, and stared out toward the hazy bright horizon.

Anthony went that way. The last place he'd been was on the pier. Robert put out both hands and patted the rough boards. Here.

The sun was high now, and beginning to get hot. Robert could feel sweat running down the back of his neck, soaking into his wool coat. For a minute he saw himself as clearly as in a mirror: a gray-haired man, grown too heavy, cheeks smeared with beard, dark uniform striped with braid and spattered with ribbons. . . . He'd put on his dress blues. To come home.

He had a picture of Anthony in his wallet. He'd never showed it, never looked at it himself. He took it out now, studied it slowly and carefully; then, stretching out his arm, he dropped it into the water. It would float there until the tide carried it away, carried it along the twists and turns and curves like highways, all the invisible well-defined patterns of the water. As Anthony had been carried.

Robert got to his feet very slowly. "Anthony!" he called.

For a moment he heard—his body tensed and tightened, but there was only the slap of water against piling and the far-off chatter of a blue jay.

There *was* something. Yes. Anthony stayed here, diffuse as mist over the water.

For a second Robert saw his unborn English child, saw him floating in the dark womb waters. Then it was Anthony's thin dark face, floating too.

He had never been found. He had escaped them all; the grave had not caught him and he drifted free. . . .

Robert lifted his right hand in an Indian salute, silently.

H E   S L I P P E D   smoothly back into his prewar life.

When he walked into the house that October morning, Anna was arranging a great flat bowl of anemones and ranunculus, flaming-red heap. She did not even look surprised to see him. "I didn't know you were coming, Robert." And she kissed him gently on the cheek.

He was home.

A T   F I R S T   nothing looked different. Only Maurice Lamotta was gone—dead of a coronary at Sunday Mass. And the Old Man, half healed from his last stroke, walked with two nurses.

After the first weeks, Robert began to see that everything was different. His exclusive relationship with the Old Man was gone; Margaret was always there. The Old Man now had two sons. . . .

Robert moved into furious activity. I've forgotten so much, he thought, all those years, almost four years. I'll have to catch up.

His concentration was physical; it left him completely exhausted. He was in bed by ten every night, and fell asleep instantly. In the morning his eyes flew open, as if they were strung like a puppet's, and he bounded wide-eyed into the day. His head spun with figures; he thought he must rattle or whir like a computer.

"Are you trying to kill yourself?" Margaret asked. "Take it easy."

"I feel fine."

He did. His body moved smoothly and obediently like a well-oiled machine. He could almost hear the humming of his joints.

He forgot it was December until he saw a Christmas tree.

December. The child would be born by now. He moved his thoughts carefully along their paths, and he found that they did not hurt too much. He found himself willing to believe that he had no children. Norah had taken this one. God had taken the first.

After December things were much easier . . . when he knew that the live child moved and breathed air and no longer floated in dark womb waters like Anthony.

DAYS AND months followed each other in their steady procession. Robert's life was as neat and precise as the pens he kept in perfectly parallel lines on his desk. That worried him: keeping those pens in line. He checked them first thing in the morning—the cleaning woman might have knocked them aside with her cloth—the first thing after lunch, and the very last thing in the evening.

Though he often had dinner with the Old Man, he still lived in his own house, his wife's honeymoon house, so small, so perfect. (Anna stayed at Port Bella.) It had not changed at all: the same furniture, the same decoration. He did not remember if the walls had ever been painted; probably, he thought, they had, but they were exactly the same color. It was as if fifteen years and one child left no mark; everything still looked as fresh and unlived-in as a house in a glossy magazine. Its emptiness comforted him. Its silent efficient functioning fascinated him. He saw no one, but his breakfast dishes were washed, his bed made. Sometimes to amuse himself he hid his dirty laundry—a shirt stuffed behind the bed, socks tucked away down into the dark toes of his shoes, suits hanging in the wrong closet. The invisible people always found them. And restored the house to its perfect order.

All through that year, the first after the war, his life

worked as perfectly as his house. Powered by the invisible force of the Old Man's planning, their businesses prospered, their holdings grew. Even Anna now had her interest—the Pine Tree Foundation. Almost all (Robert shuddered at the amount) of her father's wartime profits had gone into that. Anna was redoing the town of Collinsville—she was building a hospital, she would soon begin the first day nursery. She was planning an economic revival. And God knew what else, Robert thought, but it was going to be very expensive. . . .

It seemed to him sometimes that money was a set of invisible wheels on which he glided through his days. That the Old Man was a magician flicking his cloth and making objects appear and disappear. Always the Old Man. The family's force and drive and shrewdness came from him. Robert knew and he did not really mind. He even suspected that those successes which he called his own had been suggested to him by the Old Man, deftly, cleverly, invisibly, so that he was not aware of the hint.

(Once he asked Margaret: "Do you think we'll be able to manage without him?"

She rubbed his cheek, very gently, with one finger. "Well, Robert, I will. How about you?")

He began going to Margaret's parties, found them quite pleasant, though a week later he could not remember who had been there.

It started with a telephone call. Margaret said: "Phil's sick, Robert, and I've got to have a man tonight."

"Who's Phil?" Robert asked. "And why?"

"For God's sake, because the table will be uneven and I can't get anybody else this late. It's *tonight* I'm talking about."

"I understand that much."

"Can you stay awake during dinner?"

He felt a twinge of annoyance. "If there's anything to stay awake for."

It was strange, seeing a crowd of people he did not know in the Old Man's dining room, (the Old Man himself retreated to his upstairs apartment; he disliked company), hearing the laughter and the small clinks of china, seeing Margaret's dark face across the table, split into three by candle flickers. At ten o'clock he was very sleepy. Almost at once, Margaret joggled his arm: "Wake up." He grinned sheepishly. "Look," she said, "go sing with them over there." She pointed to a gray-haired man who was banging the piano.

"I can't tell what he's playing."

"Clyde only knows one song. Don't you, Clyde, boy?"

Clyde peered through his glasses, nodded. "Good old college song, only thing I learned." He bent over the keys, concentrating, then threw back his head and sang: "Bulldog, bulldog, bow-wow-wow . . ."

A tall thin woman in a yellow dress slipped her arm through Robert's. "You're nice, let's sing."

He let her pull him to the piano and lean against him. Once upon a time, he thought, the pressure of a female body would have made the tips of his fingers tingle and his loins ache, and he would have felt a great urge to push and tear and explode. But he didn't feel a thing now. The yellow dress was very pretty, she was very attractive, her perfume was heavy and deep and woodsy. And it made no difference to him at all.

He was nauseated with tiredness by the time he got to bed. He felt dreadful all the next day. Never again, he thought, never again. . . . A few days later, Margaret said: "Robert, I haven't got a date tonight, and the Blue Room has Frankie Laine; let's have dinner, I don't feel like sitting home alone."

It was, he thought later, the implied insult in her tone that made him accept.

After that it was easier. She took him to parties—a haze of faces—one later than another. Always on the way home, in the early morning, with just a streak of light showing in the east, he would fall fast asleep, leaving her to chatter with the Old Man's chauffeur.

ABRUPTLY AS it started, his social life ended. His new boat—the fifty-five-foot cruiser he'd ordered the previous year—arrived. He'd had sailboats before, but always with Anthony, that dark-haired boy who'd been the indistinct reflection of his own face—he would never have a sailboat again. Anthony would always be waiting for him there.

This now, this was fine, this was handsome with its teak decks (first of that material since the war), its sleek hull, its comfortable cabin. Every afternoon Robert drove to the yacht club, hurried along the maze of concrete slips to his boat. Through the long soft summer twilight, he sat alone in the cockpit, whiskey in hand, watching shadows slowly darken the harbor. When it was completely black, he went home, stopping for dinner at a white-columned grill called Magnolia House. It was always filled with students; they lined the counters, giggling, head to head. In spite of the noisy air conditioning, the place reeked with onions and frying fat and heavy perfume. Robert ate two hamburgers, ordered a chocolate frappe, stared at the huge pictures of white magnolias—feeling all around him the bustle of young lives. There was one seat he particularly liked, the last one against the wall. From there he could see the entire length of the counters; he could see the door, and the cash register. He could feel the vibrations of the girls with their swinging hair and summer shiny faces. He could sniff the metallic sweat of the boys.

As he walked to his car in the dense summer night, heavy with sweet olive, spotted with crêpe myrtle, he thought how healthy they looked, how young. . . . He'd never looked like that. He'd never been young. He'd only been small. Once, a long time ago.

Just for a flash he saw the small old man he'd been as a child. . . .

Now he was old. He'd lived through a war. He'd seen his own son's grave. And his own dead manhood: In the absence of lust there was only a great emptiness, a windy lightness, a giddiness.

I see and I think but I don't really feel. I have a life and a business and a good wife to take care of me; people stand up to shake my hand. I am respected. I watch my money grow, I can feel it grow like grass under my care. Even the Old Man nods now and then. I am his son, the one he looked for and found.

When he was little, people tripped over him, pushed him aside. *"Tais toi!"* Shut up. Not now. They made room for him now. He'd wanted it when he was young; he got it when he was old. . . . And he was old. He could see it, all different ways. . . . His body still functioned, his joints still moved without pain, but his skin had lost its shiny elasticity. However strong he was, however powerful his arms and his shoulders, it was the heavy bunched muscle of middle age, not the ribbon smoothness of youth. His body was square and heavy, like a crate. Its sleekness was gone. . . . He found himself wanting to finger that smooth young skin, to rub it between his thumb and forefinger, to test its shiny surface. Either skin, male or female. . . .

THE OLD Man got his own plane and pilot so that he and Robert could both go regularly to Anna's house at Port Bella. The Old Man left on Thursday afternoon, returned Monday evening. He'd taken these long weekends ever since his second stroke, a mild one, left his mouth slightly twisted, his hand slightly stiffened. And he enjoyed the time at Port Bella, enjoyed it very much. Robert, on the other hand, came only for Saturday and Sunday and only because the Old Man expected him to. He was always bored and restless, impatient for Monday morning.

"Why don't you bring your boat over?" Anna asked. "Wouldn't it be more fun here than in that lake?"

"I will," he said. "As soon as I'm ready."

"I bet he hasn't even started the engine." Margaret grinned at her father. "He just pets it."

"It is a very handsome boat," the Old Man said.

"Papa, you always take up for him." Margaret flicked the side of his cheek, gently, grinned into his eyes. "If he's going to spend all his time with that boat—and there are times I absolutely must have an escort—he's going to make me get married again."

The Old Man said dryly, "That prospect can't be so frightening to you."

"Oh, stop insulting your baby girl."

Anna said: "Robert, you don't have a name for the boat."

"You pick one," Robert said to the Old Man.

He thought a minute: "Condor."

"For God's sake," Margaret said.

Anna asked: "What's a condor?"

"A big bird," the Old Man said. "In the old days people used to carry gold dust in the feathers."

"A golden bird," Anna said slowly. "How nice."

The Old Man shook his head. "A black bird. They used to fill the feathers with gold after he was dead."

THE NAME went on the stern the next week. Margaret drove out one afternoon to see. "It looks nice, Robert."

"Why do you suppose he wanted it?"

"Hell, Robert," Margaret said, "my father always has a lot of complicated reasons, even to name a stupid boat. . . ." She pushed her sunglasses to the top of her head. "Wish me a happy vacation."

"I didn't know you were leaving."

"I didn't tell you? New Orleans in the summer gets me, Robert. And life with Anna in that gothic mansion is pretty bad too. I'm taking three weeks off for a look at Mexico. I've never seen it."

"Nice," Robert said, "nice."

H E M I S S E D her. In the morning at the office he found himself asking for news of her. He lifted his phone, eagerly, expecting to hear her demanding that he take her to lunch; saying that she needed an extra man for dinner. He missed her strident laugh in the corridors. Even evenings on the boat were different. The quiet harbor, the slap of the halyards, the nibbling sucking of water on the pilings, the slight gentle movement of the deck under his feet—they only made him vaguely uneasy. One evening he fell fast asleep, highball in hand. The club's watchman shook him shortly after midnight, and he drove directly home, forgetting dinner, hurrying along with a vague feeling of disquiet, as if he'd misplaced something.

H E B E G A N taking the *Condor* out of the harbor and into Lake Pontchartrain. He went alone, and cruised methodically up and down the shore.

Now when he stopped for a sandwich late in the evening,

he was conscious that his sun-tanned wind-burned face looked healthy and alive, and less out of place among the students. When his hands rested on the counter or reached for the shaker of sugar, they were tanned too, and marked by occasional rope burns from his lines. He could even smell a faint salt air from his clothes, a freshness rising from him. He knew it was all veneer, that the tan covered aging skin, that the salt tang came from brackish water. But still he felt protected by it. He felt he looked a little better.

ONE THURSDAY evening he stayed quite late on the boat—even the summer-lengthened light was completely gone. He was in the galley, putting back the ice tray, wiping up the splashes of water. He had turned on only a single small light.

"Well, sail ho, or ahoy or something!" Margaret shouted.

He heard the clack of her heels on the deck.

"Take off your shoes," he called automatically.

"What sort of a way is that to greet me?" She popped over the edge of his circle of light, her curly hair fuzzier than usual, her face thinner, her eyes larger.

"You've lost weight," he said immediately.

"Aztec's revenge."

"What?"

"You could at least look happy to see me. I came straight from the airport, cab's waiting out there now with my bags."

"I'm glad you're back," he said. "I missed you."

"You did?"

She was standing very close; he could feel the warmth of her body penetrate the cloth of his shirt.

"It's very quiet without you," he said.

"My father and Anna think that's a very good thing."

"Would you like a drink?"

She stood perfectly still, without moving, directly in front of him. She stood without blinking, her brown eyes more like holes than anything else. . . . He took her arms to move her aside politely so that he could reach the highball glasses. Her arms were so thin under his fingers, his hands went around them, fingers touched. His own body was so big, so thick, it bulged like a balloon; she was miles away, at the edge of himself. Her shiny curly black hair was wet; there must be a fog tonight. He thought of curling pubic hair, and little red lips. He remembered driving her home once, a long time ago; she had just left her first husband, she seemed small and frail that night too.

She stepped back, pulling away from him. She turned and walked into the forward cabin and sat down on the bunk. He could see her slowly begin to undress, tossing her clothes across to the other bunk.

I can do nothing with a woman, he thought, and went to stand and watch.

She had taken off everything but her bra; she was just twisting to release the snaps. "The last time it was freezing, Robert, and the whole place smelled of mildew."

"I didn't think you'd remember."

Naked now, she waited on the edge of the bunk. He sat across from her. "Look, I'm trying to tell you. It isn't like it was."

"It isn't?"

"No." The loss of weight made her breasts seem enormous. And the nipples were twisted up. Like squinched-up eyes, almost. He began to laugh. "You sitting there bare-assed, and me with my tie on." He giggled again.

She waited, not smiling, not angry. Just patient. When his giggles ended in little catches of breath, she reached across the cabin, half rising, took his hand and pulled him across to her. He sat on the floor between her legs and her murky odor flowed out and around him.

I wish I could, he thought. She knows. I've told her. So plainly. You'd think she'd let me alone. After that.

It was a fine soft odor, like quince flowers. Where had he, years ago, smelled a whole branch of these pale pink flowers?

His pants were too tight. They must have gotten twisted. He squirmed. She was holding him firmly on the floor. Damn strong woman.

She slipped to the floor beside him. It was almost completely dark there; the small galley lamp sent its dim rays above their heads.

"Jesus," he said, "I told you I can't." The pants hurt now. He squirmed: "Damn balls got twisted."

She bit him, hard, through the cloth of his shirt. "Quit, god damn it." She bit him again. Then caught the tip of his ear in her teeth, dodging his backhand slap.

She held on, pain ran down his neck. And a quick warmth flooded his body, a twitch, a burn. Familiar. Blind in the dark and rooting.

''N E X T   T I M E , '' she said, "take your pants off. The zipper hurts and I'm sure I've got a bruise from your belt."

He almost couldn't hear her.

"Look," she said, "I've got a cab out there waiting for me."

"I'll go pay him off." He spoke with difficulty. "We'll put your bags in my car."

She was dressing quickly. "I'll come with you."

All the long walk along the concrete pier, he held her hand. On the drive home, he held even tighter.

"Aren't you glad to find out you can?"

"Maybe I only can with you."

Time was, two and three women a night didn't bother him. And a little something in the afternoon. God, he'd loved women, the shape of their asses under their skirts, the way their legs angled out. Most beautiful thing he'd ever seen. He remembered years ago, when he was still small enough to be taken to church, he'd seen written on the white-washed walls in big black letters: CUNT IS GOD. He read those words every time he went to Mass; nobody hurried to paint them over. He finally decided that the priest himself had put them there, for he was great at womanizing. Robert was a little surprised to see how "cunt" was spelled. It should have been a longer more impressive word.

He played with Margaret's fingers, pulling them back and forth.

"You hurt," she said.

"Maybe I want to."

"And maybe I don't."

She tried to pull her hand away; he held on. "Look," he said, "why don't you spend the night in my house, with me?"

"No," she shook her head, smiling gently at him.

In the glow from the dash, he could see clearly the little crinkles at the edge of her eyes. "I'd like you to."

"Just think how the neighbors would talk."

"To hell with the neighbors."

She managed to pull her hand free. "I bet in all your years of chasing tail you never had a girl in that house. Right?"

He said slowly: "I would think you'd find that flattering."

"I do," she said. "But I'm a respectable divorcee and I'm going back to my father's house."

They drove silently along the New Basin Canal, its
waters slack and littered. Finally, he said: "I'll spend the
night with you. In that big barn, who'd ever notice? Anyway the Old Man's gone to Port Bella. It's Thursday, remember?"

She crinkled her nose at him; even in the dark he could
see that gesture. "What's all this spending the night business? Don't be foolish."

I've done that all wrong, he thought. You approached
a woman lightly, touch and go, flick aside. Bear down heavily
and they started thinking about the consequences. Push them
and they started thinking something was wrong. You had to
brush gently with the old magic wand. That was all there
was to it.

In the morning, before he was fully awake, when there
was just a crack of light behind the drawn curtains to tell
him the time, he telephoned her.

"What's the matter?" He could hear the rattle of china;
she was having breakfast.

Another mistake; what was the matter with him? "I
wanted to see if you were all right."

"Of course I'm all right."

"I know that now."

Margaret swallowed noisily. "All through Mexico I
didn't have a decent cup of coffee. Lousy country. Look,
Robert, I always thought it was the woman who called up
next morning and said things like 'Wasn't it marvelous?' Or,
'When am I going to see you again?' "

He flushed with anger and hurt. "It usually is," he said.
"But I know where I'm going to see you again."

She laughed again. "No, buddy boy, you won't see me
in the office today. I'm going to Port Bella."

"What's there?"

"My sister," she said and hung up.

Everything was wrong that morning. He couldn't manage to get out of bed. Only the thought that Anna's invisible housekeepers would soon be arriving got him dressed.

He was late, but he wasn't going directly to his office. He drove to the yacht club, snaking impatiently through the morning traffic. He hurried along the concrete piers in the white midmorning sunlight. (He was walking on them with Margaret in the moonless night, last night, and he could feel the warmth of her hand, the softness of her skin, the delicate bones lying in his fingers.) He unlocked his boat and went into the cabin. He could smell her there; the stale unmoving air was heavy with her musk. Her glass was on the table; he picked it up, noticed a trace of lipstick, rubbed it against his cheek and then his own lips. He put the glass carefully into the proper cabinet, not washing it. He went to look at the bunk, its linen covers still bearing the faint rumples of her body. He stared at it for quite a long time, not touching it; then he fixed himself a drink and sat down on the opposite bunk and drank it slowly. He fixed a second and came back to the exact same spot. When he finished, he washed the glass and put it away.

Driving into town, he slumped against the door, wearily watching the familiar streets. He rubbed his cheek, found a rough patch by the jaw. He'd shaved too quickly. Well, he sure couldn't walk into the office like that. He kept fingering the little tuft of whiskers. By the time he slipped into the barber's chair, he could have sworn that it was five inches long.

It was nearly noon before he reached his office. His secretary looked up, hesitated, and said nothing.

"I slept late," he said.

"Yes, sir."

He still smelled of barber's cologne. He disliked that odor intensely. Like an undertaker, he thought. Nasty sweet. Abruptly he laughed out loud.

His secretary did not even look up this time. With studied care she arranged the papers on his desk.

Automatically Robert began signing letters, marveling as he always did at the Old Man's empire.

Esplanade Enterprises was a holding company of great complexity. Robert sighed—the strangest sort of things. Like that drugstore chain in Chicago, the toymaker in Atlanta. Apple orchards in New Jersey and Virginia, a couple of thousand acres of Mississippi cotton land, three small banks discreetly placed around the country, half that big jewelry store in St. Louis. And through various other corporations— a small newspaper, oil lands and leases, a brand-new television franchise, blocks of Long Island apartments. . . . The Old Man kept track of it all, flawlessly playing one against the other, the total against the outside world.

I feel like I'm drowning, Robert thought.

His secretary was staring at him. "Battle fatigue," he said.

She was probably the only totally unattractive woman he'd ever met. With her pinched face, small body, she resembled those inmates of concentration camps he'd seen in Germany. Did she bother to eat, he wondered. She was perfect, she was marvelous, she was nothing at all. Miss Jones. Female, so marked by the title. Human species, so marked by the last name. Good old generic name, fits her perfectly. Great name for a shadow. A walking efficient intelligent shadow that talks and types and answers phones and sorts through miles of papers. You wonderful Miss Jones. Child's drawing of a woman, flat and colorless.

"Miss Jones," he said, "you are a magnificent secretary."

"Thank you, sir."

She didn't even sound pleased.

How could the Old Man keep up with all these independent operations? How was he ever going to do it himself?

Times like this he was just plain scared by his job—how could he follow the Old Man? He, who could hardly remember the pieces—but Margaret would be there. Margaret would help.

He stared out the dirty window, chewing the skin on the back of his hand, reflectively. Thinking suddenly: Anthony, my son. My lost son.

A cluster of convent girls waited at the bus stop. A saint's day, a half-holiday, they were going home at noon, pleated navy skirts swirling back and forth impatiently. . . . Anthony would be in high school now, Anthony would be dating girls like that. Breathing into their mouths, wanting to wrap their skins around him, their beautiful shiny skins, their secret dark wetness, their tight virginal passages. . . .

His own loins ached. Hard asses, firm thighs. What you missed, Anthony, what we both missed. . . .

Behind him Miss Jones said, "You haven't forgotten the conference with Snyder?"

"No."

"The file's on your desk."

"Good old Miss Jones." He flipped the pages too quickly; they slid under the desk.

Miss Jones got them, silently, quickly. "There is also some background on the Eastdown group. And, by the way, the title to the old Morgenthau tract is apparently all right."

"Thank you," he said.

What was the Morgenthau tract anyway? He couldn't remember a thing about it. He'd known once; he'd forgotten.

He went back to the window and looked down the dusty tree-lined street. The girls were gone, all the pretty little walking bits of skin.

He glanced over his shoulder. Miss Jones was still there, still waiting.

"Miss Jones," he said, "will you call the proper people and tell them I can't make today's meeting? If they want to reschedule it—if they do—I would suggest that they choose a day when either Miss Margaret or Mr. Oliver is in town. Not me."

And then and there he resigned from the world he had so laboriously entered years before.

"Miss Jones," he said, "I'm going out."

He had finally, he thought triumphantly, gotten an expression on her face. Surprise and horror.

He walked rapidly, feeling the beginnings of sweat on his skin, out Esplanade, almost to the river, then up Royal. It was slightly cooler in these streets; more wind stirred in their narrow corridors. Streetcars rattled past him, their open windows jammed with students. It had to be a big holiday, he thought, so many schools were out early. Three girls, books fluttering carelessly from their hands, crossed directly in front of him, laughing. Their shiny curly hair glistened, their thick hips moved in unison; they were practicing some sort of dance. He found himself staring through their clothes. His eyes ran along the crease of the buttocks, along the circles of smooth tight skin. . . . They would be a little too old for Anthony; they were about eighteen. He would never approve Anthony going out with a girl that old. . . .

Robert kept walking, the girls turned away, glancing over their shoulders with a giggle. A couple of blocks later he passed an A. & P., saw the telephone in the front window. Yes, he thought, that's what I want. I need to call Connie. . . .

She'd been a whore years ago, become a madam, and then, feeling the pressure of postwar puritanism, she'd retired to a successful restaurant. From there she ran a discreet and expensive call-girl operation. The Old Man had bankrolled her first house and later financed her restaurant, keeping only a small percentage for himself. It had been an old, pleasant, and profitable association for both. And now, Robert thought, another bit of business.

"Oh, Mr. Robert," she said, "how nice to hear from you

again. Would you have a drink with me and we can talk business in comfort?"

He chuckled; she was so careful on the phone. Outside the grocery window another group of girls walked past. These were younger, about fifteen, the right age. . . . "Connie, I can't come by. I only wanted to talk to you about your stables." She actually did keep a stable with a few animals— she was that careful.

She said: "Mr. Robert, all of my animals are real thoroughbreds, every one."

"I'm looking for a filly, young, completely untried. Do you have one?"

"No," she hesitated momentarily. "I don't have a single colt."

"A favor for an old friend—can you locate one for me?"

"Of course I can."

"Today."

"No, no . . ."

"Any price you want. No tricks; I can tell the difference. I'll be home after five, come there."

That was good enough for an emergency, when you were in a hurry. After this he would provide his own. . . . He could taste the young flesh on his tongue—Tonight he would use Anthony's room.

MARGARET, 1955–1965

TROUBLE, MARGARET thought; who'd have thought Robert would be so much trouble?

He no longer seemed interested in business. He did his work casually, carelessly, foolishly. He had done nothing right, Margaret thought, since his abrupt refusal to meet with Snyder. A damn stupid stunt, but no worse than the one that followed.

The next morning, a Saturday, he appeared at Port Bella, on schedule, with a hangover so bad that his skin smelled of sugar, and insisted on a game of tennis with her son Joshua. Margaret did not go to the courts, but she did look out the window in time to see the butler stagger up the slope with Robert slung limply over his shoulder, and then stretch him out on the porch floor.

She thought: I was a fool to have anything to do with him. Why am I always such a fool with men?

Anna said: "He played a wild game with Joshua, then collapsed."

"I've got a great way to bring him around," Margaret said. "Watch."

She unrolled the garden hose, turned it full force on Robert, up and down his sweat-stained clothes.

"Stop it," Anna said, and grabbed for the hose. "Stop it."

Margaret skipped away, squirted her sister directly in the face, then as she sputtered, turned the hose on Robert again.

He caught the stream in his mouth, choked, rolled over, hunched up his shoulders.

Margaret hopped lightly across Robert's body, lowering the hose directly onto his neck as she did.

"Margaret, you've lost your mind," Anna said quietly.

Robert moved again, pulling his legs up under him, hugging his body until he looked like a turtle. Margaret waved the hose, making lazy eights of water across his back. "Watch"—Margaret giggled—"water in the ear. Look at him jump."

Then, in the midst of her laugh, something moved in her body, something completely unexpected. A roar, a jolt. Unpleasant and unfortunately familiar feelings: pity and, right behind it, love.

A mistake, Margaret thought again and again, as the years passed. A real mistake. . . . Why had stopping by his boat seemed like such an amusing idea? Why had she started anything at all? He could only be a problem for her. He was foolish, he was ridiculous, he was completely impossible. About the only thing he did well was get on with Joshua. As a matter of fact, they got on so very well, Margaret thought dryly, they must have a great deal in common.

Joshua said: "Money, always money. That's all anyone talks about here."

Margaret looked at her tall lanky son. "You not only look like your father, you sometimes even sound like him. That's what he'd say: 'Money, money, always talk money.' "

Robert said quietly, "I suppose it is dull, if you're not interested, Joshua."

"Well, I'm not."

Robert went on in the same even tone: "We've been hearing lots of complaints. What do you really want to do?"

The boy hesitated. Margaret chuckled. "He wouldn't know."

"Wait a minute," Robert said, "while he thinks."

The boy gave him a quick grateful look. Like his father, Margaret thought. Just the way his father used to look after making love: soft warm eyes. Damn fool, Georges Légier. Damn fool me too. Messed up that marriage. Never should have. . . . But there was no reason to spend your time regretting. It was finished. If she still had twinges, well, there was nobody to blame but herself.

Joshua ignored his mother and spoke directly to Robert: "I know exactly what I want to do."

"Shoot."

"Well, first I want to live with Aunt Anna."

Margaret's eyebrows shot up, but Robert's attention did not waver.

"I can finish school there."

Robert nodded. "I'm sure she'd be glad to have you, Josh."

"Yes, sir," Joshua said quietly. "I admire her for the things she's doing. And the spirit she's doing them in."

"You mean her interest in Dr. Schweitzer?"

"Yes, sir," Joshua answered respectfully. "She gave me some of his books."

Made a convert, Margaret thought. Out of my own son.

"Well," Robert said, half to Joshua and half to Margaret, "I don't see why he shouldn't try it, do you?"

"Fine with me," Margaret said.

Joshua gave her one quick grateful glance. My God, she thought, the thing that makes him happiest is getting away from me.

"Mama," he said suddenly, "I don't want you to think that I disapprove of your life. . . ."

"Oh for God's sake," all the anger at him and at Robert showed in her voice, "I don't care about your approval."

"You don't understand." Joshua rolled his eyes toward Robert. "You just don't understand."

I understand, Margaret told herself. I understand perfectly well that my son will never be a help to me. Like Robert, he will always be a burden. An annoying ever-present fact of life.

ROBERT. SHE WAS busy; she hardly had time to think of him. She noticed his increasingly obvious pursuit of women. (Anna seemed to see nothing.) But she had her own loves, she could not bother with his.

She was truly surprised when he called, early one morning.

"Hi," she said cautiously, "where are you?"

A high-pitched embarrassed laugh. "I'm at a pay phone on Rampart Street."

"That is a damn-fool place to be."

"I want to see you tonight."

"You run out of girls?"

"It's your turn."

She held the phone a little away from her and stared at it. Trouble. Always trouble.

"I am busy, Robert."

"Break the engagement."

"I haven't the slightest intention of doing that." She heard a roar as traffic passed close by—at least he was telling the truth about the outside phone.

"I said break it."

She hung up.

He rang back within a minute. "No," she said. And hung up again.

Within a minute it was ringing again. This time she pulled the pillow over her head and did not answer.

There was a note on her breakfast tray: "Mr. Robert called to say he will pick you up tonight as he planned."

She crumpled the paper and threw it away.

She played golf that afternoon, as she always did on Tuesdays, and came home late. She bathed and changed, dressing slowly and carefully. She checked her watch. How strange. When Edward Briscoe said seven o'clock, he usually meant exactly that. Maybe he'd left a message with Ellen. She rang, but Ellen failed to answer. Where had she got to; she was supposed to be on duty tonight.

The bedroom light blazed out the open door across the hall carpet, but the hall itself seemed unusually dark. Margaret hurried downstairs. Only the night lights were burning —the house looked exactly the way it did at three in the morning. She checked her watch again, just to be sure. It was quarter past seven. She looked in the kitchen and the pantry. Empty. All the servants were off this evening, except her maid. "Ellen!" Lord knew where she had gotten to. Give her hell when she gets back. She's supposed to stay available until the mistress gets herself launched. . . . She turned on the pantry lights and reached for the phone. And could not remember Briscoe's number. It was unlisted; she kept it in her address book by the library phone.

She hurried through the hall again, shouting, "Where the hell is everybody?"

She turned in to the library, angrily switching on more lights. Why were they all off this time of evening? Was that Ellen's idea? She pressed the call button twice with a sharp rap of her fingers—maybe Ellen will hear—found Briscoe's phone number, and began dialing.

"Put it up," Robert said.

He was standing directly behind her, almost touching her.

She held the phone in her hand, the first two numbers dialed, the line blank. "Where in God's name did you come from?"

"I was sitting in the chair over there. You walked right by me."

"Look, Robert, I'm busy."

He shrugged. "Put down the phone."

"I'm calling just now." She dialed the third number; he flicked his finger down, cutting the connection. "Robert, stop it."

He pulled the phone from her tightening fingers, twisting the plastic handle free. "I told you to put it up."

"I've got a date."

"I canceled it."

"You don't know who it was."

He pointed to the desk. "Your appointment book. And I got the phone number from your address book."

Anger ran prickles over her scalp. She tried to keep her voice from shaking and only half-succeeded. "What did you tell him?"

"Had a nice talk. Told him it was family business and your presence was required."

She put both palms on the desk top and hunched over it, swinging her weight on her arms, staring at the careful array of crystal obelisks that lined the polished leather. Stupid thing, crystal. Why put them here? "How long have you been sitting in the dark?"

"Oh, quite a while." He put one hand on her left shoulder, she tensed her muscles against it, and he lifted it again. "I came just after you started dressing. At least that's what Ellen said."

"Ellen." She fingered one obelisk, noticing her own prints on the spotless crystal. "What happened to Ellen?"

"I gave her the evening off. Told her we had unexpected business."

She still held the ornament. She wanted to smash something, she wanted to jam her fist through something, she wanted to scream. And she wanted her thoughts to line up properly the way they always did, the way they weren't doing now.

"Ellen was delighted. Said she had a date."

With a quick jerk of her hand she knocked all the pieces of crystal to the rug. She had not intended to do that. Her thoughts weren't working right and her hands weren't working right. What did that leave?

"Get out the way." She pushed him aside and picked up the obelisks. There were three, there should be four. She crawled on hands and knees under the desk, felt her stocking snag. She straightened up, twisted to look, saw a run half an inch wide. Just one more thing.

She put the obelisks back into position; they didn't even seem chipped. She felt a little calmer now. Robert was standing not two feet away, arms folded, watching.

"You're so clever," she said. "Because you've got a pair of balls, you think you run things. Well, you can take your precious balls and shove them up your ass."

"Quit yelling," Robert said.

"You're here because my father decided to buy a husband for Anna. I never did figure out why he picked you, but you were a lousy bargain. Chasing every piece of tail that goes by. I bet Anna wishes she were out of the whole thing."

"Shut up and get on the sofa," he said.

"To hell with you."

She did not think a heavy man could move that quickly. He caught both arms, twirled her around and back on the sofa. "You god damn fool!"

He held her firmly with one hand planted in the center of her chest. She tore at it, but the clenched fist would not move. The pressure against her breasts made breathing difficult. "Stop it."

Holding her with one hand, he slowly dropped his pants. "Like I told Briscoe, family business won't wait."

His face was much darker than usual. The skin around his lips seemed almost blue. A flicker of fear left her limp and dizzy. "I can't breathe," she said.

He lifted his hand, a flow of pain followed it. Her breasts hurt all over, tips tingling and flesh aching. Every breath, against no weight now, was an effort, a burning.

He was laughing, a soundless assured laugh. "You're wet," he said between his teeth, "you're god damn dripping wet."

I N T H E morning she woke to find only the empty sheets. He'd left without her hearing. She hurt all over, particularly her hip—she'd stumbled coming upstairs. Or had he shoved her into the railing? She fingered the spreading blue mark on her skin. Old people used to put leeches on bruises like that.

She got out of bed and staggered into a blistering-hot tub. She emptied two different bath oils into the water and found that the heavy odors canceled each other, leaving only a faintly chlorine smell. She rubbed her lip; it was swollen and puffy. Well, she thought, I suppose I'm lucky my teeth are still there. Damn-fool performance at my age. . . . He'd have a clear set of teeth marks on his shoulder. . . . She smiled, then shuddered as the swollen tissue flamed and twitched.

When the water cooled, she went back to the bedroom. First she drew up the bedcovers to cover the spots and smears of blood. Then she took two dexedrines and looked at the clock. Almost nine, time to get to the office. She dressed quickly, a severely plain beige linen suit; did her face carefully. The hot bath had made her hair curlier than ever; she brushed it, sprayed it, brushed it again.

She stopped at Robert's office, nodded to his receptionist: "He in?"

"No, ma'am." She was a pretty young woman. Margaret caught herself wondering if she too were Robert's girl. "He just called to say he'd be staying home today."

"Thanks, hon." Margaret waved amiably. "Tell him I asked."

At five o'clock, on her way home, she stopped at a florist shop. She bought all the violets they had—half a dozen little blue bouquets ringed with white lace—and sent them to Robert. She wrote the card in her own spiky handwriting: *For a delicate soul. I missed you at work.*

THIS IS what age is, Margaret thought, with the steady passing of years. A slow diminution in feelings, in activities. . . . While the self makes fewer demands. (After a lifetime of screaming, Margaret thought, that silence was pretty ominous.) Her interest in men lessened. She admitted them to her bed more from habit than from raging desire. She still enjoyed the conjunction of bodies, but she no longer looked for any special value in their union. No longer did any shirt stretched over sweat-stained shoulders make her restless with desire. No longer did every square of thigh, every set of jaw look supremely good to her. She no longer stared at pants to see the charming shadow. But, curiously, her pleasure was greater than ever before. With precision, with experience, without passion, she arranged her orgasms into wide undulating bright-colored explosions. Proficiency and lack of real interest came together. She inspected each new male body carefully, detachedly, comparing it to others. No longer even seeing the individual. Her smooth appraising glance no longer saw a man, but a composite of all men, of male bodies. . . .

And she herself, the casing of skin and the frame of bone that supported her, showed signs of age and wear. The increasing heaviness of her thighs. The sagging flesh of her forearms. The steady graying of her hair.

She began getting regular tints. And going to gyms

where batteries of rollers knocked off the accumulating fat. Where massages comforted her aching back. She could feel herself settling down into her life, pulling it up around her, like covers. The excitement, the hysterical amusement had disappeared—they'd seeped away so slowly she did not miss them. In their place was a calm competence: I am eternal, nothing can ever happen to me. Wherever I am, everything looks familiar to me. . . .

She sent her son to college and dutifully attended his graduation ceremonies in the rain. She kissed him off to divinity school and made no comment.

She saw her father through two more coronaries and a series of minor strokes. She noticed too that he breathed more comfortably in warm wet air. And it was she who devised the huge greenhouse—a way to give him comfort without being therapeutic. She designed it herself to run the entire length of the New Orleans house. (She hired two men to wash the windows, day after day, inside and out.) And then because the silence of so many plants—from the creeping bougainvillaea on the roof to the ficus and the orchids at eye level—seemed oppressive, she added the bird cage. It was made of bamboo, a copy of a primitive Brazilian fish trap she had once seen. It was a huge almost perfect teardrop; its tip reached the top of the two-story glass roof. Within it, dozens of birds fluttered and sang on the branches of a changing array of large potted trees—orange, lemon, gardenia.

"What the hell is that?" her father asked.

But he was amused and interested. You could find him there almost any time of the day, resting easily in the thick heavy sweet-smelling air.

(Immediately afterward, Anna constructed an almost identical greenhouse at Port Bella; the only difference was a floor of polished slate rather than one of white marble.)

Margaret had redone her father's house a dozen times— she began to tire of decorators and color swatches and finding the right furniture. As a last swaggering gesture, she imported a New York decorator and did over every one of the bathrooms—sea shells of onyx and swans of gold, fluted columns of alabaster and marble, and mounds of white fur underfoot. When she'd finished, and looked at it carefully, the pale blue veining in the marble struck her as quite obscene. *I have reached the end of this, the sobbing end.*

"Papa, do you know how foolish this whole house is?"

"What do you do now?" he asked. "Do we move out and start another?"

"Good God, no. This is the best house in New Orleans; it's taken me years to get it to this gorgeous point. . . ." She stopped and giggled. "There isn't a single thing in it that's not overdone."

He insisted. "What do you spend money on now?"

"Do I have to?"

"You like to."

"I know I do." She thought for a minute. "And I know you don't, Papa. It's enough for you to know that you have it. Would you believe that sometimes I dream that money's like the yeast bread we learned to make in the convent, growing big and fat and swelling all out of the pans and bowls? Like it was alive, growing and creeping and walking. Like it was taking over the earth."

The Old Man laughed. "It does, and it is."

"Well, I make money and I like to spend it on me. Anna can do the good works."

"Try jewelry. You have no great jewelry."

"With my face?" Margaret leaned over and kissed his dry, papery cheek. "Papa, nothing would make my face look worse than jewelry hung around it. Like a lamb chop with a frill." She sat back in mock resignation. "No, Papa, I've got to find something else."

"Well," the Old Man said, "how about art?"

Margaret shook her head, but his words lingered. A

week later, after an especially late party, she put on her galoshes and her mink coat, and caught the early-morning flight to New York. By noon, she had walked twenty blocks up and down Madison Avenue, in and out of the galleries, and spent $97,000 for a Utrillo. By three o'clock she had bought four Manzu bronzes. Then she took the six-o'clock flight home. She was getting rather chilly in her chiffon dress.

Now that she had decided to be a collector, she began building a gallery wing to her father's house.

"Well," the Old Man said, "this house is becoming quite a monument."

She shrugged. "It does begin to look like Grant's Tomb, Papa, but I like to build things."

"As long as you have fun."

She began to collect with enthusiasm, doing the selecting herself. She smuggled a trunk full of pre-Columbian artifacts from Mexico. In Vienna she bought half a dozen Chinese scrolls from a Polish Communist; in Hong Kong a dozen Tibetan altars. She flew them back, with faked bills of purchase. She went to London to pay three-quarters of a million dollars for a small collection of Egyptian hawks and Greek vases. "Papa," she said, "it's the way they look at you. Like they were saying: She's crazy but she's got money; look at the old bag."

"What do you do with the stuff now?"

"Well." She scratched her head and made her most comic face. "Sit and look at it, I guess, Papa."

But she rarely did that. She was too busy finding more.

S H E W A S , Margaret thought, completely happy. If Josh ever asks me—years from now when he has gray hairs— Mother, what were the happiest years of your life? I'll tell him these were. But Joshua of course would never ask. . . .

I F   I T hadn't been for Robert. If it just hadn't been for Robert. There were times when she craved him, the taste of his skin, the faint abrasions of his body hair. Strange random times when her body burned and throbbed and panted, half nauseated, half smothered, repelled and attracted. In the middle of the night, another man in her bed. Even then. The emptiness inside her body would vibrate and echo, her flesh crawl and quiver—a kind of singsong laughing of the skin.

H E   H A D no sense of balance, Margaret thought; that was the trouble. Like his women. He displayed them proudly, flaunted them publicly. Phyllis Lorimer, for instance. He'd park his helicopter on the beach in front of her house and saunter in to her bed. While the neighbors complained to the police and all the little kids and their nurses came to stare at the strange machine. (When he bought the helicopter, Margaret thought grimly: Maybe he'll kill himself. She'd thought the same thing years before when he learned to fly, but he was skillful even when drunk. No luck there.) And his little girls—who would have ever thought he'd be so successful with high school girls? At least Louisiana's age of consent was low, no statutory rape charges, Margaret thought: I am thankful for the Lord's small favors. . . .

He was a fool. The way he had of telephoning at odd hours. . . . Of letting himself into her house. Three or four times she'd waked to find him standing by her bed. Once there was another man with her. . . .

And that was enough, that was the end. Her annoyance changed to anger. He'd kept it up too long; she was tired of it.

He stopped by her office to whisper his afternoon plans in her ear.

"I'm busy here, Robert," she said. "I can't possibly get away this afternoon."

"It will all wait."

"No," she said, "something else will wait."

He flushed dark red across his cheeks. "I'll beat the bejesus out of you tonight."

She leaned back in her chair. "Robert, you are a nuisance. I've had enough."

"You're crazy about me."

"Don't come to the house tonight, Robert."

"You'll like it," he said, "you always do."

She was waiting for him in the living room, smiling and silent. When he took two steps beyond the door, Mike Bertucci tapped him gently over the right ear with a blackjack, and even managed to catch him before he fell.

H E   W A S , Margaret thought over and over again, just trouble. For everybody. Less than a week after Mike Bertucci took him home, put him to bed, and waited the rest of the night to be sure he hadn't hit too hard—the Old Man said to her: "Have nothing more to do with Robert."

A sound like breaking china in her ears, then a rustling like egg shells or dry grass. Margaret said slowly: "Papa, are you worried?"

The Old Man folded his hands in his lap, the arthritic knuckles pointing up like accusing fingers. "Anna is concerned."

Margaret's voice seemed far away, like somebody talking across the room; but it was, she noticed approvingly, quiet and level. Unconcerned. Unrevealing. "Papa, this is beginning to be a twenty-question game. Why is Anna concerned?"

"Because," the Old Man said, and his folded hands never

moved, "Robert had a bad bump and a terrible headache and told her about you."

"That son of a bitch."

"Anna had no idea." The Old Man could sit perfectly still. Not a shift of body, not a flicker of expression on his face.

"At this point I think I could kill him."

"Oh, no," the Old Man said.

Margaret yanked open the curtains and stared at the orderly patterns of her Japanese garden: swirls of gravel and occasional clumps of porous black rock. "Why the hell do you suppose I put in a Japanese garden with this house?" She let the surge of her blood subside, her pulse slow to normal, her breath move smoothly in and out.

"It doesn't make sense," she said to the gravel. A bird landed and, fluttering, began a sand bath, spoiling the carefully raked patterns. "Papa, you're playing some sort of game with me; this one doesn't make sense."

The Old Man said: "You've become a very shrewd woman."

"I can't see Anna complaining about me. If she did, she said it as part of something else."

The Old Man rubbed his nose with his crippled left hand. "Anna was asking me some questions. She was wondering about her husband, what sort of value I put on him."

"Why?"

"She was considering a divorce."

"For God's sake."

The Old Man rocked his wheelchair back and forth. The rubber tires squeaked softly. "This needs oil. I told her a divorce was impossible."

The bird was still flapping around in the gravel. "And that stopped her?"

"Yes."

"I don't believe that, Papa. She wouldn't stop so easily."

The Old Man leaned back in his chair and rubbed his paralyzed hand. "These things go on aching. . . . Anna is not getting a divorce."

"What did that cost you?"

The Old Man sighed. "Too bad you were not a man, you are very astute."

"Come on, tell me how you bought off Anna. How much?"

The Old Man stared at his hand as if he had never seen it before. "For me, nothing. Only a change in my will."

Margaret said: "What change did Anna insist on having?"

"Robert's share now goes into a trust managed by you and Anna."

Margaret turned around, leaving the darkening garden. "That's almost everything, Papa. Robert has very little in his own name."

The Old Man nodded. "The fund is to be dispensed completely at your discretion."

"Anna drove a hell of a bargain—and you sure sold him out."

"Yes," the Old Man said.

"And you kept him around here. . . ." Margaret stared into her father's pale face and wondered again how they could be related. "Robert know any of this?"

"No," the Old Man said. "But when he finds out I will be dead."

"So you won't care. . . . You know what Anna will do once she has control of the money?"

"You will be there. You can take care of him."

"Not me."

"Yes, you will." The Old Man smiled his crooked smile. "We both love him."

"Shit," Margaret said.

MARGARET CALLED her pilot. "We're going to Collinsville right now."

"Ma'am?" His resonant Texas voice rattled over the wires: "The lead-in lights aren't adequate for night approaches. If we found a pocket of fog, it could be very dangerous."

She clucked in annoyance. "Is there anywhere you can go?"

"Yes, ma'am, at Pensacola—"

"Okay," she interrupted, "let's go."

At Pensacola she rented a car for the rest of the trip.

Traffic was heavy; she swung around oil trucks and big semis, pounding her horn. She shaved across fenders, occasionally ran along the dusty shoulder, blinking into a steady line of headlights. Finally the traffic lessened; for the last two hours the roads were completely empty, with only the thin night shadows of pines flicking by on both sides of her.

As she unlocked the entrance gates, she heard the distant pack. Half a mile along the narrow winding road she saw them: a flood of brown-and-white bodies across her way. Robert's hounds were out again, the wind in their teeth. Before morning they would probably ruin Anna's new gardens. They loved the loose soil.

Wearily, she turned off the main estate road and drove along a smaller one, hardly more than a cut in the sandy ground. She would tell Osgood Watkins that the pack was loose again. Palmettos scratched the sides of her car; the high sandy middle ridge bumped against the undercarriage. A deer leaped directly in front of her headlights. She jammed on her brakes, skidded up a side slope, bounced and hopped, and landed back on the road again.

I'll hit the next deer, she thought, before I get stuck in the sand out here with the pine rattlers.

There were no more deer and the night-blackened pines

ended at the Watkins clearing. Her headlights pulled it from the empty night, fence and white-painted house, lightless and sleeping. She blew her horn and leaned out the window to listen. At first, silence, then the strangled hasty barking of Watkins's house dogs as they tumbled off the porch and raced toward the fence. They crowded the front gate, yelping and throwing themselves straight into the air.

Osgood Watkins stumbled out, barefooted, shotgun in his hand. The dogs ignored his shouted commands. He kicked at them, remembered he was bootless, put his shotgun on the ground, grabbed one dog, and threw it into the pack. He picked up a second and tossed it the same way. The dogs retreated, yelping, under the porch. Margaret could see them jumping about, snapping at each other.

Watkins bent to pick up his shotgun. Margaret walked to the fence, the sandy ground sifting into her shoes.

"Watkins," Margaret said, "the pack's out again."

He nodded. Against the white of his T-shirt, his skin was perfectly black. "Hard to keep 'em in sometimes."

"Watch the gardens, will you?"

"It's the moon," Watkins said. "I'll get 'em locked up again."

"Just so long as we save my sister's precious gardens."

THE MAIN house was gray and sprawling and silent. Inside its massed shape, only a few lamps burned—but the gardens were fully lighted. The Old Man liked to see in all directions at night, and even when he was in New Orleans, the lights here followed his wishes.

Margaret circled the house, following the flagstone path —her key was for the front door. As she climbed the steps,

something caught her eye. Not a movement. Not a sound. A
sense that someone was there. A sense of another presence.

"Who's there?"

A pause. She was just getting ready to repeat the question when Joshua said, "Well, Mother, you really spoiled
that one."

She squinted into the profusion of lights that only
seemed to create bottomless spots of darkness. "My night
vision is terrible, Joshua. You'll have to come out."

Even as she said that she saw him, sitting under the big
azalea bush. "Whatever are you doing under the bushes in
the middle of the night?"

"Meditating."

She heard just a little hesitation in his voice, a little
shame. He does know better, she thought.

"In the lotus position," he said as he came to the steps.
"I was perfecting it."

"I've seen the pictures," Margaret said, "and I seem to
remember Buddha sitting under some kind of tree, but I'm
sure it wasn't an azalea."

"Of course it wasn't, Mother, but the spirit is there."

"Oh, sure," Margaret said, "spirit is the big thing."

"Mother, I want to ask you something."

"Why I came walking in at midnight?"

"Huh? . . . No." His thin face looked puzzled; he'd
found nothing strange in that at all. "Mother, very seriously,
I want to talk to you."

"About your plans."

"Yes," he said. "Yes."

"You have a long-range plan."

"Mother, I think it is possible to apply the mysticism of
Dr. Schweitzer—removing the racism of course—to the practical problems of a lost society."

"Joshua"—she stared at the tall young man, thinking:

I gave him too many vitamins—"I haven't the god damnedest idea what you are talking about."

"Oh, Mother, you make everything sound so cheap and horrible." Joshua disappeared into the night.

When Margaret was quite sure he was not coming back, she unlocked the big oak door.

She went directly upstairs, thinking: The whole house smells of potpourri; Anna keeps it all around, all those funny dry petals. . . . For something dry and dead, it smells so fresh. . . .

She knocked on Anna's door, watched the light come on under the crack, pushed it open.

"Morning," she said.

"For heaven's sake." Anna was sitting upright in bed, her oval face misty with sleep, her long black hair hanging straight down her back, unruffled even in her sleep. Perfectly straight black hair with a single streak of gray over the left temple.

"Is that gray real or did you put it there?"

"What?"

"Is it real?"

"Of course it's real."

"I didn't know. . . . You look like something out of a movie right now." The ruffled white linens, the pale blue blanket, the white nightgown with its square neck and long sleeves. . . . Margaret thought: I bet if I looked closely I'd see that everything is covered with some sort of expensive lace or embroidery. Conservative elegance, that's Anna. Theatrical conservative. What's mine? Sort of scrubby. Like my hair. And my round dago face. I look like the balls on a sour-gum tree, round and prickly. . . .

"Did you come all the way out to tell me that?"

"No," Margaret said.

"I'm sorry if I'm dense." Anna smoothed down the unrumpled sheet automatically. "But when did you get here? I didn't know you were coming."

"I just walked in this minute. I stopped to tell Watkins that the damn hounds are loose again. And I found Joshua sitting cross-legged being Buddha."

Anna's fingers went right on smoothing the edge of the sheet. "I suppose Watkins will have sense enough to watch the gardens. . . . Joshua has some elaborate future plans. He's put in quite a lot of thought and he wants to talk to you. Do you mind?"

"Mind?" Margaret stared into the shadowy corners of the room. This house, she thought, was always dark. There were hundreds of lamps but nobody ever seemed to turn them all on, so that nights always hung around the edges and the corners. Anna liked it that way. "No, I don't mind. How can I?"

"He's quite serious." Anna's fingers finished with the sheet and moved to the ruffled edge. Her fingers pleated it steadily, crawling inch after inch, across the top of the bed.

"I didn't come all this way to talk about Joshua."

I'd feel better, Margaret thought, if the whole thing didn't look so unreal. I can almost hear the background music. Anna goes around building stage sets and then lives in them. . . .

"Papa said Robert decided to tell all."

Anna's fingers stopped moving. They lay on the ruffles, slim and smooth and delicate olive. "Papa ought not to have done that."

"And he told me about your bargain."

The hands folded, fingers lying on top of fingers. For comfort? For strength?

Anna said: "It wasn't really a surprise to me after I thought about it."

Margaret waited. Thinking: I'll drive back tonight. I can hardly wait to get to the car.

"You see, Robert has had so many women, I'm not really surprised if he has one more."

"Well, he's got one less." Ought to tell her about Bertucci standing at the door, ought to tell her. But I won't. "I drove all this way to apologize."

"That isn't necessary." Anna's voice was light and dry. Completely without emotion. "I know Robert. No matter how much he has, it isn't enough. Not ever enough."

"Well, for me it is. It's finished."

"Would it have been finished if Papa hadn't told you?"

Margaret hesitated, startled. Was there a hint of malice under that smooth skin?

"You answer that yourself," Margaret said.

"Papa is so very fond of him."

"I know, like a son. . . . Well, look, I apologize and I'm sorry, and I'm going home now."

Margaret had reached the door when Anna said: "Don't worry about it. It's all in the family."

All the way back Margaret drove as fast as she could, fleeing the following tide of that anger.

STANLEY, 1965

IT'S ME, STANLEY, your friendly guide, your humble servant, your loyal descendant of slaves. Only there seems to be some argument about that. My brother-in-law's nephew—seventeen with an Afro haircut—he says to me: "You are a white nigger." I expect he'd have put it stronger, but his mother was sitting right there. "A white nigger." I just looked at him—me with my blue-black skin—and just about the only Negro thing on him is that hairdo; his skin's no darker than any Italian. . . . I got to laugh at that: among whites I'm a nigger, among niggers I'm white. That's really something now. . . . Maybe he didn't approve of me, but he sure accepted the bond I posted for him on that car-stripping charge. And glad to see it. His family all came running to me because the boy was a repeater and the judge had set bail pretty high. Got me out of bed with bronchitis and 102 degrees to save their baby boy. . . . I'm the only one has any money, me and Vera. (She doesn't like this kid either, but she thinks she ought to.) And you know, when I was driving down to the station, I kept thinking that this was how the Old Man must feel—people looking to him to get them out of trouble, people demanding things because they're related.

Not that I'm like the Old Man. Don't get me wrong. I don't mean that. I was just surprised to find any resemblance at all. If you know what I mean.

382) THE CONDOR PASSES

NO MATTER how you look at it, this past year with the
Old Man has been hard. Six, seven times—which was it?—
we rushed him to the Collinsville hospital. Sirens screaming,
lights flashing. And six, seven times he came back. Slow,
sedate, no sirens, just silence.

All those times dying.

Each time, after a week or so in the hospital, he'd go back
to the big house on the coast at Port Bella. It wasn't a hard
trip for him—only a little more than an hour's slow drive.
He had his own ambulance—Miss Margaret bought it a
couple of years ago—it followed him from place to place, out
of sight, but waiting.

That was the way they did things. And in a way you had
to admit it was practical. Because the Old Man did a lot of
moving about.

After his last coronary, when the worst was over, they
flew him into the big University Hospital in New Orleans.
There was a lot of talk about calcified heart valves. (Vera and
I looked it up one night—funny diagrams like a child's printing, big lopsided Y's. Vera studied them for an hour or so,
but me, I quit. I just didn't like thinking what the Old Man's
heart looked like, all holes and rocks and scars. Vera always
did have a strong stomach. Like, she could kill a chicken, and
I never could do that, not even when I was a kid.) There was
some talk about operating, but nothing happened except the
Old Man's ambulance brought him slowly, carefully, to his
New Orleans house.

This time was different. This time he wanted to make a
couple of stops on the way home. I was driving—he liked me
to drive him everywhere—and I can tell you that he knew
just exactly where he wanted to go. He wasn't senile or wan-
dering. He had the addresses—numbers and streets—and he
had them right. From the way he told them to me, you could
see that he had thought them out and arranged them in order.
We went all over town, first way down to Music Street, then

he had to circle Gayarre Square, then out Canal Street—I guess we made a dozen stops. Not that he wanted to go in any of these places, or knew anyone there—he wanted to drive by, turning sidewise in his litter, to look at them.

The effort of all that riding knocked him out. By the time I turned in to the drive, he was fast asleep. Exhausted. He didn't even stir when they carried him upstairs to his own bed.

A month later, he decided he had to go back to Port Bella.

Now, I don't know why that mattered to him. After all, what does he do, either place, but sit in the warm wet air of a greenhouse, talk on the telephone, and watch his birds flap around and sing in the big cage? It's not like you could see out—you can't, not from either greenhouse. It's all green leaves and flower shapes, growing and hanging and sprouting in all directions. Wet leaves arching and dripping, moving slightly in their own current of air. Nothing to watch, nothing to see. Nothing to move for.

Except the Old Man thought so.

I'll tell you one thing about these people—they don't see things the way we do. Me, Stanley, when I stand on the front porch at Port Bella, I see a grass slope, then a little bluff that drops to the beach; I see a white edge of sand and then the water. Nothing else—oh, I see how the Gulf changes color with the clouds and the winds, and how the grass is a different green in different seasons. But that's *all*. . . . Them? I don't know what they see. . . . Like Miss Anna . . . she never even looks this way. She never comes to this porch; she never walks on the lawn here. She stays in the gardens on the other side, away from the salt spray. There's something here she doesn't want to see. . . . Mr. Robert now, he goes down to the beach occasionally. Just a couple of weeks ago, I saw him there, shouting at the empty water. He was drunk—he's pretty much always drunk these days—but he's not one for seeing things.

I thought he sounded angry, but Vera, who was with me, said he sounded scared. Anyway we left him there; neither of us wanted any part of their ghosts or their hauntings.

So I don't know. Maybe, when the Old Man sits in his greenhouse and looks at the shiny leaves hanging in the thick wet air, maybe he really can see something that makes one place mean more to him than another. I don't know.

And something else. I think this is his last time, and I think he knows it. I think maybe that long slow drive we had around New Orleans was his funeral procession. Ambulance looks something like a hearse.

THE CONDOR PASSES

I T W A S a good period for the Old Man, Stanley thought, all that bright summer and way into the fall. Until one Friday evening in late October. Then came the emergency signal on the intercom, the electronic shriek sounding in all rooms at once, sending everyone running to the Old Man's room. After that it was morphine and oxygen and down the elevator and into the ambulance.

Though there were two seats in the back, next to the litter (the Old Man had passed out and was snoring loudly), only the nurse sat there. Mr. Robert got in front with Stanley. Sweat poured down his face, in the cool night; his eyes were round and flat.

Stanley drove fast as he dared on dark roads streaked with autumn fogs. Not once during the entire half hour, Stanley noticed, did Mr. Robert turn to look at the Old Man. He only said, over and over: "Hurry, hurry."

His steady rasping voice went on until they turned down Collinsville's Main Street and in to Pine Tree Hospital.

Two white-jacketed attendants were waiting outside. They had the door open almost before the wheels stopped. The Old Man's doctor ran down the concrete ramp, hair fuzzy and greenish in the brilliant fluorescent lights.

As Stanley watched, they wheeled and rushed off in the other direction. *Look at that. First you see round faces rushing at you, then you see square backs running away.*

Lord, Lord, Stanley stared after them as they spun off like a flock of birds, curved, and disappeared inside the shadowed door. *Lord, Lord, nothing like money to make the feet move....*

Stanley selected a parking spot marked "Reserved for Superintendent" and pulled in there.

Walking across the concrete lot, he glanced up, beyond the two-storied windows of the hospital, to the night sky. No stars yet, he thought automatically. *I'll call Vera and tell her I'll be late.*

There was a phone just inside the entrance, you could see it through the window, a bright red lucite marker, but Stanley decided to use the one on the corner. After he'd finished talking to Vera, he stood in the shadowy chilly dark, thinking: The hospital is the only new building in town, that and the road the state paid for, the smooth concrete strip right along Main Street.

There was nothing at all to notice in Collinsville. Small white houses with gingerbread porches and people rocking on them in the evenings, seven or eight stores with glass fronts that nobody ever seemed to wash, one bar, one ABC store, one café, and two gas stations, one of them also the Greyhound bus station. There weren't any more regular trains. The only thing that happened at the railroad station was in summer when the sheds and platforms were piled high with watermelons waiting shipment.

It was a small ugly town, but it was lucky. Lucky that the Old Man lived nearby—lucky that his daughter had devoted her life to good works.

Stanley walked back slowly. Even this early in the evening the town was completely quiet, with only occasional house lights to show that anyone still lived along the empty streets. He passed a high hedge, snapped off a blooming twig. He was still holding it as he crossed the fluorescent-lit entrance, still sniffing it absent-mindedly as he approached the door. He stopped abruptly, looked at the flower-crusted twig. It was sweet olive, sometimes called dead-man's bush, and carried to wakes and funerals. He tossed it away, as far as he could; it fell in the grass, and disappeared in the dull green spread. He couldn't be the one to bring bad luck inside. He couldn't be the one to hurry the Old Man along.

He recognized the yellow Mercedes convertible parked directly across the entrance. The Old Man's daughters had arrived. Stanley took a deep breath and marched in military fashion, precisely, accurately bisecting the rectangle of the door, and down the exact center of the hall.

Dig me, man, me and my invisible uniform.

Pity he didn't have farther to walk, he was marching so smartly. But the Old Man's door was no more than ten feet from the entrance.

His suite was really a special wing of the hospital building. There was a large living room, and next to it, the bedroom. Right now the door was wide open and people were running in and out, with a loud rustle of starched cotton and a squeak of soft-soled shoes, pushing and pulling bulky equipment on rubber-tired wheels.

They had to look busy.

Deliberately Stanley stood in the center of the living room. People hurried back and forth around him, but nobody asked him to move. *I bet me a nickel nobody asks me to move. Me that's standing right in the way. . . .*

At his elbow Mr. Robert said: "Good old Stanley, I knew you'd be here."

Stanley thought: he's drunk, where did he get the liquor? Then: No, that's fear.

"Good old faithful Stanley, how long have you been with us?"

"Since '46."

"Long time. . . . Well, I suppose the cardiogram will show that he blew out something else. . . ." He stopped, rubbing his face briskly with both hands. His skin was mottled, the color of decaying walls. "I feel the god damn hell like I was going to pass out." He walked to the far corner of the room, stared through the polished window at the parking lot. "Is there anything to drink in the car?"

"We came in the ambulance, sir."

"Look, go to the liquor store and get me a bottle of Scotch."

"It's almost ten o'clock; they're closed."

"Sure, sure, sure." Mr. Robert made a pattern of fingerprints on the clear glass.

Miss Margaret came out the bedroom; instantly Mr. Robert spun on his heel; he must have recognized her step among all others.

"How is he?"

Her cool even brown glance ran over Stanley, who remembered immediately that he should have straightened his tie. Her eyes touched gently on Robert, then moved off down the hall, as if she found the sight distasteful.

"He is still with us, Robert."

"Thank God."

Wearily her brown eyes returned to him. "Don't come apart, Robert."

"Look, I'm worried."

"We all are."

Miss Anna came to stand beside her. Stanley thought: *They do look alike. Standing together like that, you can see the resemblance that you ordinarily miss.*

"How is he?" Robert asked.

"You just asked me that," Margaret said.

"It might be different."

"No, Robert," Anna said, "it's no different."

Her face was a little more set, a little smoother. In the glazed reflection of the shiny walls, that perfect oval looked harsher, its mouth firmer. The wide streak of gray hair rose sharply like a crest.

"Look," Robert said, "how about flying him to New Orleans?"

"There's no reason to move him, Robert."

"I want to see that idiot of a doctor."

"You're in no shape for that, Robert," Anna said.

"Come on now." Margaret took Robert's arm, coaxing him toward the door. She kept her arm in his, guiding him out the door. "There you are," she said, "hop an ambulance home."

The thin thread of her joke snapped against the dark.

"You don't seem upset." The fear in his voice was gone. He now sounded sulky.

She patted his arm, very gently. "Robert, go home."

"It's like there was you and Anna and not me at all."

"I've got enough to worry about," Margaret said shortly, turning away. To Stanley, she said, "Just drag him home, if you have to."

IN THE morning when he came to work, Stanley found the broken Scotch bottle in the hall near the stairs. It had rolled under the big bombé chest, leaving behind a wide trail of gummy varnish.

Miss Anna, Stanley thought automatically, would be furious. These floors were special; they had come from some famous house—was it Jefferson Davis or Alexander Hamilton or General Beauregard? He swept up the glass, ignored the rest of the sticky mess, and was drinking a cup of coffee in the kitchen when Vera walked in.

"Guess what I saw?"

"A four-headed cow or something like that?"

"You know where Mr. Robert is?"

"Passed out upstairs, I guess."

Vera looked at him, her pecan-colored eyes dancing with amusement. "Nope."

Beyond the wide kitchen windows the sky was filled with racing scud. Stanley squinted into it. "Vera, you remember what we called those clouds when we were kids?"

"Yes," she said, "bishops."

"Why?"

"Just a name."

"They don't look like bishops. . . . Where is he?"

"The tennis courts."

"Lord, how'd he get down there?"

"He's got a tennis racket in one hand and a bottle in the other."

"You remember, years ago, how I carried him up here after he passed out on the court?"

"Don't do it again," Vera said. "You're not that young any more."

"You know the Old Man's still alive."

"The Lord takes his time," Vera said.

And that struck Stanley as very peculiar, because Vera wasn't religious. He never remembered her saying anything so pious before.

They saw Mr. Robert coming up the slope. He walked quite steadily until he stumbled into the line of tree gardenias that edged the herb garden, fell through them, and regained his balance halfway into the neat intricate low maze of green. He paused, sighted carefully on the house, and then walked directly across the garden, flattening whatever plant stood in his way.

"There goes Mount Vernon," Stanley said. The garden was a perfect copy of the one in Virginia. "You suppose George Washington ever staggered home like that?"

Mr. Robert crossed the garden, skirted the last big

azalea bed, and, straight and perfectly proper, climbed the steps, not even using the railing. When he opened the door, the wind pulled it away, smashing it into the wall, rattling every hanging pot on its hook.

He did not even seem to hear the crash. "Ah, yes, good morning. Stanley and Vera, good morning."

He looked much worse than a night of drinking and a morning of sleeping on his own lawn. Bits of grasses, of yellow and pink flowers clung to his gray suit, like camouflage. His dark eyes were sunk way back under his cheeks. They seemed to peer over the blue-black smear of his beard, hanging on for dear life, harried by the unrelenting growth of hair.

Hair, Stanley thought suddenly, that grows after we are dead. . . .

Mr. Robert swayed very slightly in the wind. "You ever see crawfish hanging on to bait, when you pull them out the water—you ever see that? . . . That's what I feel like. Nothing more nor less than that."

He wandered through the kitchen, hesitated a moment at the edge of the dining room, then went into the hall. He stopped, hooking one arm over the balustrade. Stanley slid silently into the room behind him.

"I lost a bottle in here last night, Stanley, you find it?"

"Yes, sir."

"Ruin the varnish?"

"Yes, sir." Impatiently Stanley thought: Was he going to pass out or wasn't he? If he'd only do one or the other.

"Well, there goes General Beauregard's floor and to hell with it. Get the Old Man on the phone, will you?"

Stanley dialed the number. "It's Miss Margaret."

For a moment Stanley thought he would refuse the phone, but he finally took it. His hands, Stanley noticed suddenly, were filthy, the nails black-rimmed, the whirls and pores of the skin outlined with dirt. But he sounded usual. "How you, sweetie? How's Papa?"

Stanley went back to his coffee.

"You check the birds yet?" Vera asked.

"Without the Old Man there didn't seem any reason to."

"Why don't you look?"

"You curious? About the birds?" Stanley marched his measured butler's step across the entrance hall, past the elevator doors—closed so firmly, like lips—and up to the double glass doors of the greenhouse.

When he opened those doors, heavy thick air fell on him like a thing with mass and weight. He held his breath and dodged quickly through the trailing bits of green, avoiding the fleshy drooping orchid leaves.

The birds were singing, loudly. They were fluttering in the trees, knocking off the white gardenia blooms; they were swinging on their foolish toys, they were careening wildly around the open upper reaches of their cage.

Mr. Robert came in. "Stanley, you're a mind reader. Bring me breakfast in there."

"Here?"

"Over there, over where the Old Man sits." He pointed to the high white wicker chair, under a curling loop of flowering bougainvillaea.

"Yes, sir," Stanley said. "Will you be having coffee or tea?"

Mr. Robert didn't hear. "Old age, it gets you. And the whole world's changed when you weren't looking at it."

He absent-mindedly began rubbing the tips of the giant fern that brushed his shoulder. "You know what's the worst damn thing? The first gray pubic hair. That's hell. . . . She should have let me talk to the Old Man, you know."

"Coffee or tea, sir?"

"I wanted to talk to the Old Man. No, no, he's resting. . . . They're always there, one or the other. . . ."

He spun around and walked off, head hunched against the dripping vines.

Stanley brought both coffee and tea. It was easier than getting an answer.

He spent the whole day stretched out between two chairs, a blue-flowered pillow propped behind his head, sleeping. He did not change, or shave. Once Stanley found him urinating on a huge ficus. "That's what I think of the whole thing, Stanley," he said. "Look at that funny fiddle-leaf tree, and that one over there—it's got red veins running under the leaves. I've been sitting in the chair looking at it; damnedest thing. I never noticed it before. Take a leak, that's about what they're worth."

STANLEY DID not mind hospitals at all. They had always seemed to him places of rest and comfort, vaguely friendly in an impersonal way, places to relax, to be taken care of. He'd learned that twenty years ago, in the army, when a hospital was the loveliest place to go, safe and secure. Best place to be. . . . He could tell when there'd been a big strike called—the line at sick call would be out the door and clean around the building. All the scared bastards trying not to fly. . . . *And me,* Stanley thought, *I stand and watch and smile, on the inside of my face. Because it doesn't matter to me. I'm a black man, I don't get to play in your wars. I just get to pour drinks and swing trays for the ones that come back. . . .*

Stanley still liked the smell of oxygen coming out a tank. Little oily, little crisp. The way the Old Man's room smelled right now.

Miss Margaret said: "My father wants to give you something, Stanley. And I want you to understand exactly what it is."

Stanley nodded.

"Today my father gave you two hundred acres of marsh, a part of the Bonaventura tract."

"Yes, ma'am."

"It's nothing now, just marks on a surveyor's map, but if you wait five years. . . ."

"I can wait," Stanley said.

"My father has held that land for twenty years. He was right, as usual. The interstate is going to run directly through most of the tract, and you understand what that means?"

"Yes," Stanley said. "Yes, ma'am."

Miss Margaret smiled a half smile. "I'm sure you do. My father is putting together a shopping center. Your land is the northwest corner. You should also have a sizable piece outside the area suitable for general residential development."

Stanley thought slowly, carefully. "That will be worth quite a bit of money."

Margaret smiled, briefly. "At the very least three-quarters of a million. I would imagine something around a million and a half."

If you're giving me that, Stanley thought suddenly, how much are you making yourself? . . . Greedy, he thought, I am getting greedy. . . .

Stanley said: "I don't understand why."

Her smile flickered again briefly. "Because my father liked you." (He glanced at her quickly and decided she had really used the past tense.) "Because he wants you to be free to do anything you want."

Stanley thought: He is paying me off. Because he expects to die.

The Old Man said: "You know about a condor, Stanley?"

"Yes, sir," Stanley said. "You told me about the condor."

"Place for keeping gold dust." The Old Man chuckled, a flat smile-less sound. "You keep gold dust in his feathers."

"Yes, sir." Why, Stanley thought, is there a tickling at the nape of my neck, like a breeze blowing the little hairs there, when there's no breeze?

"And the Indians—they said he carried messages to the next world. They'd fill the quills with gold dust and bury them with the dead; that way the spirit would always have money."

He's looking at me, Stanley thought. Me, the big black bird. Where you going to put the gold, Mr. Oliver? Mr. Oliver, I ain't got no feathers to put gold dust in. I ain't your condor, so stop looking at me.

"I used to see condors all the time," the Old Man said; "forget where it was. They were always way up, way way up, riding air spirals over the mountains. Everybody would stop to watch, until they passed."

Then the Old Man's hooded eyes slipped down. The rate of his breathing changed. He was asleep.

They heard Mr. Robert come down the hall. "Hell of a fine day, isn't it? When do you suppose it'll stop blowing?" Loud, faintly alcoholic good cheer. Other voices answered him, a bubble of conversation and laughter.

"He does have charm," Margaret said. She picked up a bottle of cologne and sniffed it.

"He's doing better," Robert was talking to somebody outside the door. "After all that attack was only three days ago."

Margaret looked straight into Stanley's eyes and made a wry face.

"Hey," Robert said, "look who's here."

"Ten minutes earlier and you would have found Papa awake, Robert."

"Hell." Robert pushed back his hair from his forehead. "I knew I should have gotten an earlier start, but I was talking to the office."

Margaret opened the cologne again and sniffed it, as if she had never noticed it before. "You did? I wondered when you'd sober up enough to call in."

His dark skin flushed. "They said you'd taken care of everything."

She shrugged, closed the bottle, and put it down with a click on the glass top. Robert spun around, his heels squeaking on the vinyl floor, saying over his shoulder: "Stanley, I'll need you to drive me to the club."

Stanley looked quickly at Miss Margaret. "I suppose he means the yacht club," she said. "And maybe that's the best place for him." She glanced at the shadowy gray form, so thin it hardly lifted the sheets. "He'll sleep three or four hours. Stanley, do you get the feeling today he's keeping a secret, that he's hiding something?"

Outside, Mr. Robert shouted: "Stanley, come on."

"Go ahead," Miss Margaret said. "Be sure to bring him back at eight."

STANLEY DROVE him to the yacht club. "Let's see if I can line up a piece around here," Mr. Robert said as he got out.

Stanley parked the limousine and stood a moment, looking around—the terrace, the gardens with their white-painted furniture, umbrellas all taken down against the wind, the usual weekend crowd of young people, playing shuffleboard or tennis, or just chattering in the front entrance. Heavy tadpole-shaped drops of rain began to fall, then just as abruptly ceased. It would storm before too long.

Stanley went in the screen door marked "Employees." He looked first in the kitchen—too early; nobody there except the salad girls, thin young bodies and hair carefully bound up under white hairnets. "Hi, sweeties." They giggled at him, and waved black hands speckled with green parsley. He went down the concrete hall, faintly wet and sea-smelling. He pushed open the door to the employees' lunchroom. That door was kept closed, the air conditioner always running. Howard, who was in charge of the place, wanted it that way.

The door squeaked, but moved smoothly. And Howard called: "My friend, where you at!"

He was sitting in his usual chair, his extra flesh falling off the sides like frosting from a cake. For years he'd played trombone with the Eureka Brass Band in New Orleans. Until he got too heavy to march. "Man, the backs of my legs would be on fire, them muscles just on fire. And every breath killed me. . . ." And his last parade: "We was playing 'Just a Closer Walk' and the next thing I know I was looking up at a piece of sky and people was looking down at me and blood was running into my collar from where I hit my head. After that I figured there was nothing I could do but head for the pine trees."

Stanley sat down at the table opposite him. "Howard, I been thinking, why don't you go back to that trombone?"

Howard grinned his steady broad grin. "My friend, I play nothing but the accordion now. I don't want death wings that close to me again."

Stanley stared at the formica table top. "You reckon death wings got feathers?"

"How the hell would I know?"

"Maybe they'd be black feathers?"

"Oh, man, you are talking nonsense. Beer?"

Stanley nodded. Howard got up slowly, the chair creaking as he left it, and went behind the small bar. He got the can and glass, still dripping, and made a mark in his account book. "Charge like always?"

Stanley nodded. "One of the benefits of the job."

"Is he here?" Howard asked.

"Upstairs."

"Another blast?" About three weeks before, Mr. Robert had fallen down the stairs leading to the boat landings.

"He's got to be back at the hospital at eight."

"That old man going to die?"

Stanley felt a little catch in his stomach. "Why should he die this time when he didn't all those other times?"

"Death," Howard said solemnly, "is the final trial."

"You been going to church again."

"We are all in need of the Lord's help."

"Maybe I better be sure he really went upstairs."

There were three white-jacketed waiters at the service bar—Stanley nodded to them; he knew them all, the club staff never changed. "He out there?"

One of the men pointed. "This is his order." A very large tray, eight or ten glasses, and in the middle a plain heavy-footed goblet from the dining room, filled with colorless liquid, with two pieces of ice and two olives side by side at the bottom. "You ought to recognize that, Stanley."

"I sure do," Stanley said. His Martinis. A very bad sign.

"His party's on the terrace." The waiter lifted the tray.

Beyond the dim wood-paneled bar he could see the terrace, glittering in the yellow light of a stormy October afternoon. The brightest light of the whole year, Stanley thought, when you could see for miles. The sort of light that made hunting difficult, and distances hard to estimate.

Stanley couldn't actually see Mr. Robert, but could see a crowd of people around one of the tables—young people, all of them. Mr. Robert must be storytelling again, long Cajun dialect stories: the kids liked them. Mr. Robert said once, "The little broads think I'm so cute; I'm the fatherly type. And it's funny how many of them want to screw their father. . . ."

And that, Stanley thought, was pretty close to the truth. Mr. Robert never did exaggerate. The Collinsville Yacht Club was his happy hunting ground.

The waiter with Mr. Robert's tray of drinks approached the group, had trouble entering, circled around, and tried again from the other side. The group broke—Stanley thought of a plate shattering—then closed again. He recognized most of them: the Roussel boy; the two Clark girls; the Boissac girl, who was married and divorced while she was still in high school; the Robinson cousins, as alike as the brothers some people said they were. A few others he didn't recognize—on weekends there were always a lot of strangers around. A girl stood up, made her way laughing out of the tangle of chairs and people. I'd know that hair anywhere, Stanley thought; we found her and her Sailfish out in the bay. The same blue-black hair, same round untanned face.

She looked back, she waved. Mr. Robert stood up, returning her wave across the seated crowd. He sat down at once; she stood hesitating, her face open and eager, in the blazing-yellow light.

Well, there's his latest, Stanley thought. Love showing all over her—no wonder he was in such a hurry to get here.

A waiter, tray filled with glasses, said: "Hey, Stanley, Vera's here."

Vera was in the lunchroom, drinking a highball—she didn't like beer—talking to Howard.

"I didn't expect you."

"I was coming back from Rachel's when I saw the car."

You couldn't miss it, Stanley thought; only limousine for miles around.

"You look pretty," he said; "that dress makes you look young."

"Too young for me," she said.

Milo Thomas, the night watchman, came through the door, pale blue uniform freshly starched, Sam Browne belt shining with polish. "How you, Miss Vera? What you say, Stanley?" He sat down on one of the red stools at the counter.

It was exactly six o'clock; Milo had punched in and come for his first drink. He would be back and forth all evening, until the bar closed and Howard went home; on Sundays that was two o'clock. The club allowed him four drinks a night, the rest he had to buy himself.

Howard put a sheet of paper on the bar and he and Milo began whispering together. Weekday evenings, they worked on football games, with Howard calling the bookie every now and then to check prices. On Sundays they figured out how they had done.

"You bet this week?" Vera asked.

Stanley shook his head. Sometimes he gave Howard five dollars to bet for him. "I can't even remember who's playing this week."

"You saved five dollars," Vera said. Howard, for all his work, for all his telephoning around to beat the price, never came out a season ahead.

Stanley watched the two figures hunched together in the corner of the small bar. He liked Howard and he liked Milo and he liked sitting here, in this windowless room with the big color TV always out of focus from all the different hands that tuned it. (The Old Man had given that. "You're going to spend so much time waiting," he said to Stanley years ago, "you might as well have a good set to watch." The set was changed for a new one every year, regularly, on the first of March.)

"Vera." He reached across the table to touch her arm, to be sure of her attention. "The Old Man just gave me some money, real money."

She shifted her round wide eyes from the group at the bar.

"We are two rich niggers."

"That's not funny, Stanley."

"They're putting together a shopping center." Without intending, he repeated Miss Margaret's words. "Our share could be worth," he hesitated, afraid almost to put the numbers in the air, "something like a million dollars."

"Why?" Vera asked.

"Because he's senile," Stanley said with annoyance. "Why else? He thinks he's keeping me forever. I'm his messenger and my feathers are full of gold."

"It's too much." Her fingers patted her hair, gently; she

was checking her wig, Stanley knew, and she only did that when she was nervous and upset.

Stanley said, "We can go anywhere we want, anywhere. You always talked about going other places."

She had; she even dreamed about it sometimes. Let's go, she'd say, where all the faces are black. I get tired sometimes, seeing white faces. . . .

"We don't need much money," she said. "We don't have kids to worry about."

"It isn't only kids." With a start he discovered finally that having no children hurt her. "Wouldn't you like to be a real rich nigger? Just think how that would bother some of the damn woolhats around here. . . ."

Her eyes left the television and turned to him. "I don't want to do that, do you?"

The reason was buried back in his mind, with vague atavistic pictures of burning crosses and hanging black bodies. An anger he would do anything to vent. An anger that increased steadily as he grew more and more successful in the white world. He felt his whole body shake with it sometimes; he would then rehearse to himself his list of accomplishments: I got a new house better than any white man, a kitchen with every gadget any white man's wife could want, and I got a better salary than anybody in this little town, I got stocks in my bank box. . . . All that and I still got a black face . . . Jesus God.

"Yea," Stanley said. "I'd like to have a lot of money."

VERA HAD another drink and they played poker with Howard and Milo. After an hour, Stanley had won a dollar and a half.

Milo said: "I'll be right back." It was seven-thirty. Time

for his round. He would go out the service door, circle the building, walk down to the harbor master's office, have a word with him, and come back. It would take about ten minutes.

The evening supply of ice arrived and Howard began dumping the bags into his coolers.

"It's time for me to get him," Stanley said.

"All right," Vera said. "I'm going home."

Milo came back, raincoat dripping around his shoulders. "God damn rain and me without boots all night."

"Rain?" Vera's fingers went to her wig, automatically patting it, protecting it.

"Well," Stanley got to his feet slowly, "at least that means I don't have to hunt all over the terraces for him."

"Raining *and* blowing," Milo said. "You know, some damn fool just put out. I could see his lights. And me with wet feet all night long."

Stanley kissed Vera on the cheek. "See you in a little while, honey."

"You'll be late?"

"How can I be late? I'm sure Mr. Robert's got a date tonight. I just have to take him to see the Old Man and then turn him loose."

Vera smiled, her square teeth gleaming softly.

She was sad tonight, Stanley thought, and it was a shame about the children. Maybe they ought to look around for one to raise. They could afford it, they could sure afford it.

The windowless corridor already smelled of the rain outside, and there were muddy tracks down the center.

Vera pushed open the door and disappeared toward her car. He heard the rattle of rain on gravel, and the sighing swish of wind. He climbed the stairs slowly, feeling his beers in the weight of his legs. Two bus boys trundled carts of dirty dishes through the pantry—they had begun serving in the dining room. That would thin out the bar crowd, Stan-

ley thought, and make it easier to get to Mr. Robert. People
were annoyed when he had to elbow a way through them, but
Mr. Robert was never one to answer a discreet signal. Stanley
actually had to tap his shoulder to get him moving.

The bar was almost empty. There were only four drink-
ers, each one sitting in an island of empty stools. Mr. Robert
was not one of them. Automatically Stanley glanced out on
the terrace. It was rain-swept and empty, with only an occasional shred of paper napkin fluttering from cracks in the
flagging, and a few chairs blown over by the force of the
squall.

Stanley checked the dining room. No. Then all the men's
rooms; he'd sometimes found him asleep there. Not this time.
Maybe the billiards room; he sometimes played if the stakes
were high enough. Glancing at his watch, feeling a rising
impatience, Stanley hurried down the hall. He passed a young
couple, rain pouring off their slickers, umbrella blown inside out.

"Wet out there, Stanley," the boy said.

Stanley nodded politely. He had not recognized them,
though they knew him—sure, sure, he was as much a charac-
ter as Mr. Robert or the Old Man.

Me, the perfect old retainer, Stanley thought as his heels
clacked on the parquetry floors. Perfect. The Old Black Butler, the Old Friend of the Family Who Knows His Place. . . .
He changed his walk, shuffling just slightly, leaning a bit to
one side, neck bent a little, deferentially. . . . How about that?
Faithful Old What's-His-Name going about his duties. . . .

Stanley was so sure Mr. Robert would be in the billiard
room that for a moment he thought he *was* there. . . . Leaning
against the table, cue raised. . . .

He isn't here, Stanley thought slowly, so where is he? Is
he playing a trick?

Stanley called the hospital. "Miss Margaret, is Mr. Robert there?"

"Did you lose him?"

A vague flutter of annoyance. "He doesn't seem to be here anywhere."

"Wait a minute." Her voice moved away from the phone. "Anna, Stanley has lost Robert; you have any idea where he could be?"

"I did not lose him," Stanley said petulantly.

"Sorry," Miss Margaret said. "Do you have the car keys?"

"Yes, ma'am."

"Then he's around there somewhere. The damn fool. Papa is here, feeling fine and waiting for him." Stanley heard the hollow heartiness of her voice. "Ask around. See if somebody knows."

"Yes, ma'am."

"Papa wants to see him. Now wait just a minute—What did you say, Papa?" More murmuring and whistling of voices on the line. "Tell him Papa particularly wants to see him tonight."

As she was hanging up, Stanley heard her say, "Wouldn't you expect some—" And then the empty line buzzed.

He'd start asking around.

He walked quickly across the long hall, passing the entrance again. The big front doors were washed with a solid sheet of water, as if a fire hose were playing on them.

He did not notice the girl—Mr. Robert's dark-haired girl—until she called to him: "Stanley!"

"Yes, ma'am." Well, he thought, at least I know Mr. Robert isn't with her.

"Stanley, did you see him leave? I mean I almost died when he walked right out into the rain. You could see the water gush out his shoes before he'd gone six feet, it was coming down that hard."

Stanley looked at her, blinking. Be polite, he thought. You are a worthless nigger, be polite. . . . "Who?" . . . Now the afterthought. Always good, let the kid know you don't mean it; who the hell is she? "Ma'am."

"He didn't tell you?" She pushed her hair back with both hands, quickly, from her forehead, pulling it back behind her ears. To see better, Stanley thought, or to hear better? "He invited us, you know, all of us talking out there on the terrace, over to his house tonight."

"Yes, ma'am," Stanley said. "Who?"

"Mr. Caillet."

And there it was. "Mr. Robert invited you tonight?"

"He was telling us about his Party House; then he said come over tonight and we'll have a party. He wasn't joking, was he?"

"No," Stanley said. The Party House was in the pinewoods, not far from the entrance gates, a Swiss chalet on a small lake. "He often entertains friends there. It's his special place."

"When we told him we didn't have enough cars, he said you'd drive some of us over." The girl smiled, the gentle frightening slow smile of a child. "He even bet me a dollar he'd be there first."

"How was he going?" The words stuck on his tongue, hanging like burrs.

"Why, he said with this wind, his boat was the quickest way. . . ."

Stanley remembered Milo's words: Some damn fool just put out. . . .

"Well," Stanley said, "well . . ."

"Is that wrong? He said it was perfectly safe, just blowing a little."

"I don't know whether it's safe or not," Stanley said. He went to the phone in the manager's office. "Miss Anna," he said, "Mr. Robert is on his way home by boat."

"Tonight?"

"I suppose he forgot about the hospital. He invited some people to the Party House and he's racing them over."

Without moving from the phone, Miss Anna said, "Papa, it seems Robert has gone for a sail."

A pause; then, sound shrunken and hollowed by the distance from the receiver, Margaret said: "Son of a bitch."

And Anna said, "Stanley will you come back here, please?"

"Will he be all right?" The girl was waiting.

Look at all that love, Stanley thought. All that for Mr. Robert. "I don't know," he said.

He didn't have a raincoat; he'd have to run. His leather soles slipped on the wet pavement and the wind sucked at his breath. He felt cold almost at once, in a kind of flush, as if the rain had struck through his clothes.

He jumped inside the car, banging his thigh against the steering wheel. He sat for a couple of minutes rubbing at it, cursing without words, leaving the door open—the soft suède lining turned brown, then black, as the rain soaked into it.

The parking lot was blocked by two cars with hooked bumpers. The drivers argued in the rain for a few minutes, then staggered back inside.

For another drink, Stanley thought.

He swung the limousine sideways, across the curb, through the flower beds, into the street. Ten minutes later he parked at the emergency entrance.

In the Old Man's room, Miss Anna was smiling patiently; Miss Margaret was angry; the Old Man's doctor, whose name was Doyle, looked confused; the nurse (it was Miss Hollisher, she'd changed her shift, Stanley thought) was trying to make herself invisible against the corner wall.

The minute Stanley stepped in the door, the Old Man's eyes grabbed hold of him. He wants to say something to me, Stanley thought, and he's getting up his strength to do it.

"But sir," the doctor was saying, "you cannot keep your-self in this agitated state. In your delicate health, it's a form of suicide."

The Old Man's eyes stayed with Stanley. He's using me to pull himself up, Stanley thought. He's holding on to me, and pulling up. Slowly.

He'd never seen eyes so deep. Cones, wide open at the top. You could walk into those eyes, and keep walking until you reached, somewhere way down there, a blank wall, where everything ended. Those eyes shivered and threw off light, great exploding cartwheels of light. . . .

Miss Anna jiggled his shoulder. Stanley moved out of the range of the Old Man's glance. "Is something wrong, Stanley?"

"No, ma'am." There wasn't any use trying to explain.

She turned back to the Old Man. "Really, Papa, we've called the Coast Guard. Be reasonable about it. Watkins has turned on all the floodlights at the house. That's all you can do."

Margaret said, from the other side of the bed, "Papa, it's a good boat and he's a good sailor; if he just isn't so drunk that he passes out, he'll make it without trouble. He can pick up the light at Hatcher's Point, and then run di-rectly for the house. He's done it often enough before."

The Old Man shook his head.

Stanley thought: I didn't know he could move his head that way at all; the paralysis is less than we thought.

The Old Man said: "He didn't come here."

For a minute everything was absolutely quiet, just the rain on the east window and the wind around the corner of the building and the steady hiss of moving trees.

If he had any tears, Stanley thought, he'd be crying. . . . A quick sharp stinging and Stanley was crying for him.

The Old Man's eyes found him again, saw the tears. And the Old Man's eyes blinked them away.

My God, Stanley thought, is he inside me?

"Papa," Margaret said, very quietly, "Robert is like that. He forgets."

Across the bed, Anna said, "Papa, Robert has disappointed us all, one way or another."

The Old Man said: "I wanted him to come."

Christ on the Cross, Stanley thought. Woman on each side; I saw that in a church somewhere, maybe in England during the war; some famous church, only I forgot where. . . . The only places I ever saw, only places to matter, was in the army. Vera and I, now, we have to go. I'll ask Vera tonight where she wants to go.

Margaret said: "Wouldn't it be funny if that son of a bitch really did drown?"

Instantly Dr. Doyle became restless; he glanced toward the door.

He could just turn around and walk out, Stanley thought, and they'd never notice. They were too busy with themselves to care about him.

"No." Anna's voice was level and correctly modulated, neither affected nor coarse, the smooth voice of the perfect lady. Like that sleek shining head of hers, with its gray-dappled hair. Lady of wealth and dignity. The polish that only money gives.

As beautiful as money itself, Stanley thought.

"No," Anna repeated, "it wouldn't be funny. It would be ironic." Margaret tossed her head with impatience at the correction of a word. "It would be very ironic if he should die like Anthony."

Now the doctor really did turn to the door. Stanley watched him with amusement.

His frightened hazy blue eyes passed Stanley's, and he stopped.

Dr. Doyle, Dr. Doyle, Stanley thought, you are caught. And I caught you.

"You know," Margaret said, "I've often wondered about Anthony. I think he meant to die."

"No more than Robert does."

The Old Man moved. They stopped talking.

"No," the Old Man said.

Distinctly. Clearly. The word hung on the still air.

"No what, Papa?" Anna said quietly. "No about Anthony? Or about Robert?"

The Old Man's eyes slipped shut.

He's playing, Stanley thought. Behind those lids, he's waiting, he's ready to pounce out.

Anna settled back in her chair, picked up her petit point. "It *is* storming. I suppose I should be more worried about Robert, but I guess I don't really care."

"Margaret cares," the Old Man said slowly. His lids stayed closed. His lips hardly moved; for a moment they all wondered who'd spoken.

"Margaret cares . . . ," and the face relaxed, smiling almost.

"The hell I do," Margaret said, as all their eyes swung across to fix on her.

She does, Stanley found himself thinking over and over again. She does, she does. . . .

"And the little boy, what happened to the little boy? . . ."

Stanley thought: What's gotten into him?

"Papa, you know Anthony was sick; you know—" Anna hesitated, and Stanley saw the nerves beneath the skin, the pain that ran along the blood, that twitched beneath the unmoving surface— "you know he had leukemia."

"I should have brought him home." The Old Man sounded breathless now, as if he'd been running. "He asked me to and I didn't."

A long silence. The Old Man seemed really to have fallen asleep.

Margaret stood up, shaking herself all over like a dog.

"Anna, he's right. You should have brought Anthony into town instead of keeping him shut up all that summer."

Anna stood up too, her dress falling in perfect folds around her. She looked with real loathing at the piece of related flesh across her father's bed. "We all would have done things differently."

Margaret hesitated: "Ah, the hell with it, what's the use of fighting, I'm going to take a ride."

"I could do with some fresh air too," Anna said, "I'll come with you."

Margaret puffed out her cheeks and swung her finger in a mocking circle. "Whoopeedoo."

The sound of their heels hung briefly in the corridor, then vanished.

Miss Hollisher emerged from her corner, gaining size and stature, the way a balloon does. Dr. Doyle tinkered with his equipment, turning little hissing valves. He found something he didn't like; he tapped one gauge with his knuckle, impatiently. "I'll be back in a minute," he whispered to Miss Hollisher. "I want to change this."

She nodded serious agreement.

Stanley looked at his own hands. They had come to rest on the rail of the bed, the black fingers were curved around the iron, gripping like claws. He saw himself a bird, big black bird, perched on the Old Man's bed, waiting. . . .

He loosed his fingers. "Well," he said to Miss Hollisher, "I'll be getting along."

"No," the Old Man said.

Stanley jumped, actually hopped a couple of inches into the air.

"It's time for me to go home," he said lamely.

"No," the Old Man said and his eyes slipped open. "Not now."

"I'm wet."

"Change," the Old Man said.

Miss Hollisher got up from her chair: "Stanley is tired, sir. I'll be right here."

"Damn fool," the Old Man said softly. "Hurry."

Miss Anna, because she was such a careful housekeeper, kept a locker with extra clothes for him in the staff room. He stripped off his wet clothes, tearing his shirt in his hurry— What do I care, he thought, I'm rich, I can afford it.

He wiped the mud from his feet and legs and tossed the towels into the heap of his clothes. He put his undershorts on backward and had to take them off again before he put on the formal butler's black.

He's asleep, Miss Hollisher's lips said silently to him, just as the Old Man's eyes popped open.

Like hell he was, Stanley thought; he's been hiding in there, hurrying me on.

"Bring the car," the Old Man said.

"I left it at the entrance."

"Help me up," the Old Man said.

"No, no, no, no," Miss Hollisher said.

"I'll get the wheelchair," Stanley said.

"I'll walk," the Old Man said.

She grabbed for him and caught Stanley's arm instead.

He lifted her fingers. "Quit that, Miss Hollisher."

"What-what-what are you doing?" She was so excited she stuttered.

"He wants to get up," Stanley said patiently.

"I'm calling the doctor, that's what *I'm* going to do; you've lost your mind."

The Old Man's eyes reached out and touched her with their hatred, their loathing. "Woman, get away."

"You heard." Stanley took her shoulders and pushed her back gently into her chair. "Now don't have hysterics, but if you get up again, I'm going to slug you."

The Old Man's darkened eyes patted him for that.

Like a dog that's done something right, Stanley thought.

Miss Hollisher opened her mouth and closed it, with a little plop of saliva.

Stanley slipped his arm around the Old Man and lifted him to the floor. They began walking slowly, very slowly. Even so, after two steps the Old Man's strength gave out, and Stanley had to support him completely. Not that he's heavy, Stanley thought; it's just that having him on the side is awkward. If I could carry him in my arms, it would be easy—but he wants his feet touching the floor.

They were noisy, those soft leather feet dragging along the polished tile floor in the hospital silence.

Stanley began counting the seconds. Forty-five, forty-six. The corridor remained empty. Just the pale green walls, like a shiny aquarium, and the mirror-polished floor. And the Old Man's feet moving feebly, like fish fins.

At least they weren't going to have to explain to anyone where they were going.

Seventy-six, seventy-seven . . .

They were at the door; the car gleamed wet and shiny just outside. The Old Man twisted his head around. Something flickered in his eyes, amusement, laughter: Stanley was positive. Way down at the bottom of those depths, there was a small child sitting cross-legged on the ground. (Stanley almost could see him in there. Or was it himself he saw reflected?) Laughing.

The Old Man slowly lifted one arm and pointed.

"What?" Stanley said. "What?"

"The alarm." The Old Man's voice was perfectly clear. "Ring the alarm."

He was pointing directly to it: the red-painted fire alarm.

"Ring it, sir?" Stanley stared at the box. "I think you're supposed to break the glass or something."

"Go ahead," the Old Man said.

Holding the Old Man with his right arm, Stanley

pounded on the glass with his left fist. The glass shook—
I'm not going to smash my hand through it, he thought.
But . . . wait a minute—the glass *shook*—so maybe. . . . He
pushed it sidewise, no luck. He pushed it up, too hard; it
popped out and fell shattering to the floor.

We're making a hell of a lot of noise, Stanley thought.
And then: What does it matter how much noise we make
when we're about to ring the alarm?

The Old Man reached for the alarm, stretching, trying.
Not quite enough. Stanley slipped his left hand under the
quaking elbow, steadied the arm, and lifted it. The Old
Man's fingers touched and held the handle. And turned.

On the first wave of sound, Stanley lifted the Old Man
into the car, gentle, unhurried. There was an alarm bell
ringing outside, its sound strangled and broken in the wind
and rain.

The transmission shifted with barely a click. The noise
faded behind them; there was only the swish of wipers and
the muddled sound of rain on steel. Stanley drove steadily
and calmly, keeping within the speed limits, watching for
other cars. As if he were carrying something very precious.
Like the big black car was full of gold. Careful. Careful.

The Old Man said nothing—Stanley checked once in his
mirror—his head was tipped sideways and rested against the
soft tan wall, next to the little round light. And the light
was on. Had he deliberately put it on, or had his falling head
just touched the switch? The soft lamp glow separated the
back seat from the front, so that the Old Man rode in another
compartment, distinctly apart from Stanley's.

Stanley stopped under the porte-cochère on the west side
of the house. From its scalloped glass panels rain poured
steadily in even sheets. He braked the car so gently that it
was hard to tell when he actually stopped—except by the
silence of rain no longer drumming on the roof and windshield.

The Old Man's head was still tipped to one side, but his eyes were open. Stanley straightened his head and then carried him into the house. The wheelchair was waiting, as it always was, by the door. He put the Old Man in it and stood back waiting for orders.

The house smelled strange, he noticed. In cooler weather the air-conditioning unit did not work well, and air hung in pockets around the house, small quiet backwaters in the flow of ventilation. Here was one. The machine-oil smell, so faint in the rest of the house, was strong here.

The Old Man said something so softly that Stanley had to bend over. "Go on."

"Where?" The dulled eyes flashed anger at him and Stanley added hastily: "The garden room?"

The light faded. So that was it, Stanley thought.

The rubber-tired wheels squeaked across the wide boards, then bounced gently over the slate flooring of the greenhouse.

"Chair," the Old Man said, pointing with his eyes.

His big chair with its high fan back. His soft padded wicker cradle. The throne, Miss Margaret called it. The place where he sat day in and day out, watching the birds flutter in their bamboo cage.

Stanley picked him up, as he had thousands of times before. He seemed lighter, Stanley thought, almost buoyant in his arms.

The birds were silent in their cage. Not a sound, not a flutter. Stanley set the Old Man down, tucked the light wool blanket around his legs.

There now, Stanley thought, the Old Man was established in his cage. Maybe he'd nod off and sleep like the birds.

The eyes were watching him, shiny button eyes. "Stay," the Old Man said.

"Yes, sir." Stanley noticed that the cigar case was out of position on the table, about two inches from its regular spot; he moved it into line.

The Old Man breathed in and out, whistling a bit each time. Stanley waited, hands behind back, parade rest, trying to make out the huddled dark shapes of birds in their cage. The phone rang.

Automatically Stanley reached for it. "No," the Old Man said, very loudly. Stanley jumped back. The Old Man smiled slightly at his haste, a lopsided, contemptuous smile, ancient and supercilious.

Skull grinning, Stanley thought. He let the phone ring out.

The noise woke a few birds, they fluttered and squawked. From the other side of the greenhouse there was a soft plop— one of the heavy swollen flowers had dropped of its own weight.

"Shouldn't we call your daughters, sir?" Stanley realized he was whispering.

The birds fell silent. Farther away than the falling flower there was a sudden trickle of water: one of the sprinklers had leaked.

"I don't want them," the Old Man said. And then: "Now you can go."

He was silent after that, his head resting easily against the padded chair.

Stanley took a couple of steps backward, to a stretch of smooth slate under a heavy loop of bougainvillaea. In the entire room there was only a single small lamp burning, next to the Old Man's chair. Total black surrounded them, sightless and close with the feel of wet leaves and wet ground, its only sound the steady rattle of rain on the glass roof. Stanley stood perfectly still, muscles deliberately relaxed, mind deliberately empty. Occasionally his legs ached and he shifted his stance, but he did not move or sit down. He stood quiet guard in his dark shelter. He could see the Old Man, vague figure without color in the dim light, and he could see a little way into the bird cage. He watched first one and then the other. Nothing moved.

He was not quite sure how he knew. Except that his feet were in a way released from their ground. He felt the wet air around him change, felt the leaves shiver and fill with the triumphant evil. He did not go near, he simply turned his eyes away from the mocking arrogance of the shell presence.

The Old Man was dead.

STANLEY BACKED away, not daring to turn from that seated figure, so long dying and finally dead. He groped his way toward the door, leaves brushing the back of his neck, making him duck his head and hunch inside his collar. He felt for the knob, twisted it, stepped backward into the main house. After the glass door closed, he turned around.

The lighted house was no different. "Funny," he said aloud.

He felt very strange, as if a part of him were missing. Had the Old Man carried something away with him?

He saw the flickering headlights of cars in the drive as he walked through the pantry, into the kitchen. He filled a glass of water, then set it down untouched.

"Stanley," Miss Margaret called. He did not answer.

He took the limousine key from his pocket and dropped it on the counter.

"Stanley, where the hell are you!"

He opened the door; the east wind pulled it from his fingers and slammed it inward. He did not bother closing it. He walked across the porch and down the steps. The wind was very strong; walking into it was like pushing against a soft wall.

"Stanley!" Both sisters were on the porch now. "Where is he?"

He turned, the wind slamming the side of his face. "He

didn't want you," he said, but the wind twisted and mangled the sounds until they were nothing.

"Where is he?"

So they hadn't heard.

In the glare of the yard floodlight he saw Mr. Robert. Held up by Watkins, he was vomiting into the grass just beyond the corner of the house.

He had made it, Stanley thought, with nothing worse than a bad hangover. . . . Funny, he wasn't more than a hundred feet away, but it seemed he was miles off. Like looking through the wrong end of a telescope. . . .

Somebody pushed him aside; he almost slipped on the wet bricks. Miss Margaret was running across the grass, she was bending over Mr. Robert.

Miss Anna stood perfectly still on the dry porch, under the shelter. She was very straight and thin, a tall white candle.

Stanley walked on, away from the house. Behind him he could still hear shouting, voices strung out on the wind, flapping like clothes on a line. He didn't listen. Like the Old Man, he was finished here.

Rain poured into his eyes, blurring his vision. No matter. He knew every turn and pebble along these stretches. It would be strange not coming back, not coming this way again, a little bit like being dead.

Two floodlights from the house cast his shadow on the path ahead, a huge broken wavery shadow, black wings fluttering on each side.

A NOTE ON THE TYPE

The text of this book was set on the Linotype in Baskerville. Linotype Baskerville is a facsimile cutting from type cast from the original matrices of a face designed by John Baskerville. The original face was the forerunner of the "modern" group of type faces.

John Baskerville (1706–75), of Birmingham, England, a writing master with a special renown for cutting inscriptions in stone, began experimenting about 1750 with punch-cutting and making typographical material. It was not until 1757 that he published his first work, a Virgil in royal quarto, with great-primer letters. This was followed by his famous editions of Milton, the Bible, the Book of Common Prayer, and several Latin classical authors. His types, at first criticized as unnecessarily slender, delicate, and feminine, in time were recognized as both distinct and elegant, and his types as well as his printing were greatly admired. Four years after his death Baskerville's widow sold all his punches and matrices to the Société Philosophique, Littéraire et Typographique, which used some of the types for the sumptuous Kehl edition of Voltaire's works in seventy volumes.

The book was composed, printed and bound by The Haddon Craftsmen, Inc., Scranton, Pennsylvania. Typography and binding design by Cynthia Krupat.